ORPHANS OF THE ORIENT

To My Friend

Louisa

Jesse Bedwell

徐中言

CEDAR HILL PUBLISHING

Orphans of the Orient

Published in the United States by
Cedar Hill Publishing
P.O. Box 905
Snowflake, Arizona 85937
http://www.cedarhillpublishing.com

ISBN 1-932373-51-9

Library of Congress Control Number 2004090664

Message to China Marines

This book is written as historical fiction.
Some of the battles were told to me by
Officers and Nationalist Soldiers. I inserted
the characters of the book into some of the
battles, however the book contains more
truth than fiction.

It is not politically correct, nor is it word-
perfect. It is written from my diary and notes
of some fifty years ago.

~ Jesse Bedwell

THE T'IEN Lung Dragon
A GOOD DRAGON

ORPHANS OF THE ORIENT

The 3rd China Civil War
1945-1949

This is a fiction novel written about historical events that took place in China's 3rd Civil War. The author is a Marine who served in the Orient near the end of WW II.

PREFACE

Historians On The 3rd China Civil War

The writers of history are for the most part honest in their approach to the writing of history. However they did a damn poor job covering the 3rd China Civil War.

They always look for flaws in any administration, be it a President or congress. The writing of post WW II had a theme that may have been on target." Truman proved

5

anyone could become President and Ike proved we didn't need one". We all know how it works.

A famous war reporter of WWII by the name of Erie Powell was standing on a battlefield in WWII behind General Patton, Col. Ike and General Macarthur. A shell was coming in from their backside, and he could see it was going to miss. As it exploded he made the following comment on each of these men as they heard the loud explosion "Ike flinched, Mac remained expressionless, Patton cussed one of his favorites (BASTARDS)" That's the way he measured the three men. I feel the same way.

I would like to add a comment to an article I read knocking General Chiang Kai Shek.

"Some of the ole China Marines returned to China and they found that the present day Chinese have been told that Mao took the surrender of the Japanese in 1945? That's strange, as most of the Marines were standing at attention watching General Sheppard and the Japs sign the papers of surrender? I also found that Chinese students believed the same thing. I showed them pictures of our presence in China that got their attention. They now know they were "snowed" by the great wonderful dung carrier, Chairman Mao.

Tons of pictures and documents of China Marines that are still alive to prove this was all bullshit. Hell Mao didn't even control China at that time. General Chiang had full control. Of course his name never came up.

Recently an article appeared in a magazine stating that Chiang was corrupt and that President Truman was correct in pulling the Marines out of China. The article is incomplete and full of "holes". He talked of a battle, in which Mao's Communist cutthroats defeated the Nationals, yet that was only one of hundreds of battles taking place all over north China.

You take Mao, the communist, I will take General Chiang Kai Shek and given the same support and the same size army we will kick your communist friends asses. I was at Chingwangtao the same time they were and all over

6

North China, Manchuria and Mongolia, so don't try and blow that communist shit up my ass. Mao gave the Chinese wonderful things. One of which was breaking families up putting them into communes, next came the Red Guards. Wonderful things happened in those days of the Mao cut throats rule even the Chinese now look at Mao as "misguided*. Yes Truman pulled the plug pulling the Marines out, and yes it signaled the end for General Chiang. BUT what else happened to put the cement in this move? When President Truman cut the aid to Chiang those wonderful Russians tripled their aid to Ma. This is when the Chinese Communist took over and began raping and killing every person that had been friends with the Marines. They continued to loot and killing all over North China "?

Let us not forget Mao's wife and top Generals that help set up all the so-called reform. The new leaders in China called them the "Gang Of Four." You know what happened to them? Of course you do.

The people loved Chairman Mao so much that they killed off his wife and those that helped him win the Civil War. Such great love coming from the people that loved Chairman Mao- so very much.

Foreword

In 1945, four Marines were separated from their division during a battle near the port City of Darien, China. During the next six months, these Marines lived and fought with the Chinese Nationals. After a four-day battle at the Port of Darien, these Marines plus 500 Nationals, whom they had assigned to the American Trained twenty-eighth Nationalist Army under General Chiang Kai Shek, were separated from their units as the battle raged on. The Nationals were fighting on several other fronts from the shoreline in, and Mao's Reds were holding a sickle-type formation extending more than three hundred miles in Northern China.

Trapped between both forces these Marines had to fight their way out. At times it looked like they were home free, only to find the Red Circle surrounding them again. When the American government decided not to continue supplying The Nationals, and Russia was still supplying the Chinese Reds, it signaled the beginning of the end. Most Marines had left by 1947. The few who remained were in danger of never coming home. Would the transport coming to pick them up at Chin-Huang-Tao make it in time? The Marines decided to wait until the last possible moment, when it started to look hopeless, to devise a plan to bring themselves back home. It was one hell of a plan. The long struggle was to bring these Marines in touch with China's past and to help to form its future.

On Oct. 17, 1948, two Marines and four Nationals arrived by sea at the northern tip of Formosa, and then on to safety. A second rescue trip was formed to rescue one more Marine and several Nationals. They arrived on the Formosan Coast on Nov. 11, 1948.

DUTY . . . HONOR . . . COUNTRY.

The returning solders made it home with major battle scars. What happened to them through the years to come? Some could never return to a normal life. They were young and stuck in a nursing home. People came to see them for a time. But a couple of years later, the visits had stopped. Most laid there for years hoping someone would come by and see them, but as time went on, they were forgotten. The Red Cross would come from time to time, as would the Salvation Army, and old comrades.

Then you have these kids that go crazy over dope attacks, rock stars, and ball players who are treated like gods, while the young men, who went to war, lay in their beds dreaming of a life that could have been; a marriage, a family, and all the things everyone takes for granted.

The schools have a day for everything. They honor trees, land, water, and so on, but how many take the kids to see the real heroes? For that matter, who teaches the kids about the war and the veterans? How many adults take the time to visit their family members in a nursing home? I am also guilty of this. I hate to go to nursing homes, so I only go when I feel that I must. My friends and relatives might die before I can find the time to see them. I'm sure that I'm not the only one. There is NO excuse for any of us.

I was a teacher and basketball coach for more than thirty years. Before teaching, I found time to fight a war. (Actually two wars if you count the battle with my ex-wife.)

When I taught history, my students knew about the great WWII. They knew what took place on Dec.7, 1941. During the 1950's my school had six history teachers. On the morning of Dec. 7th, I looked into each room to check the boards. I was disturbed to find nothing on the boards about Dec. 7th 1941 anywhere in the school. As I remember, it was the start of National Education Week that was found on every board. I understand the importance, but let's not forget those who made it possible for us to live the

9

good life here in America. Bitter, yes, I'm bitter about how in the living hell can we forget so fast. How can we forget what made this country great?

The deadline for completing this book is the year 2004. It's now or never, as I am getting some miles on me. In our world of using the term "lifestyle" as a copout, you can piss on the flag or the Bible and people will say, "That's OK, it's a free country. He is just expressing himself." Let's face it; he is another lost soul, trying to get attention. Many have asked the question; how can a man get elected for our highest office that has the morals of an alley cat? It's simple, because more than half of the people in this country are just like him. We must do something before we end up, as the most perverted country the earth has known. In fact I think we are already.

The dumb talk shows have every lowlife the world has to offer, parading their sick lives in front of the world. Give me a break.

While I'm on a roll, when I was teaching, we had to watch a bleeding heart kids' program geared toward making our past leaders and our role in the world as something we should be sorry about.

Let me set a scene for you: it's a show about, when we dropped the bomb on Japan in 1945. An American girl and boy are sitting on a bench, overlooking the scene from the past, where the atomic bombing took place. She has a tear in her eye as the camera zooms in; her words are, "I am ashamed to be an American." Say what? I am thinking, let me tell her about us warning the Japs that the bomb was coming and what it would do." Over and over our planes dropped leaflets. On the other hand, the Japanese purchased our scrap metal for years and sent it back to us, with surprise attacks, long before we dropped the bomb. Or I could tell her about how the Japanese killed women and children on every mission, or about the Bataan death march. Interesting reading little girl.

The Orphan's of the Orient is much more than a story of four Marines. It's about honor, duty, and country.

It's also about poor people in the 1930's, coal miners W.P.A. workers people stuck in the big cities, out of work with little hope in the future. I am going to try to explain this to you, the reader, as seen from the eyes of a young man. It was tough growing up during the depression. The crash of 1929 had the whole country going downhill. However, we had pride in our president and our country.

Hitler was real. He had plans to take over the world, and you would have to have a blindfold on to not be able to see it coming. I read somewhere that a nut says it never happened. Hitler never killed all those Jews? Really? What about the fifty thousand men who marched by the death camps? What about the miles of film that was taken within hours of the German surrender? It shows me the number of nuts, we have running loose. Why do we give these people the time of day? Why print their lies?

This was a time of gold stars in the window, a star was put in the window when the family's son was missing or killed in action. The boys would come home from the war, and we were damn proud of them. That silver battle star on a ribbon on his chest was a clear message that you had a super star. He had paid the price of freedom. His buddies sometimes paid a bigger price with their lives.

I wonder, and I hope you also wonder, what happened to those thousands of boys who had their bodies blown apart and still lived?

Gung Ho, yes, that's right, that's me, I fought for it, and I still fight for it. I am (as they say today an old dude, well this OLD DUDE has never backed down from a punk yet, and as long as I can stand I will stand up. Period. I believe this phrase we used to say in China, "Here's to us. Those like us. Damn few left."

From my "Grapes of Wrath" beginning to my fiery end in 2004 (I was told by an ancient Chinese wizard that I would die in that year. It sounded pretty good in 1946).

This is the complex story of one man's chasing of life's game. His soul and his were being changed and reformed like the wind. It's about the losing and winning

11

everything that life has to offer. At times, love, honor, and duty are all cast to the winds in the never-ending quest to find his destiny. My buddies and I were what one would call today "free style". In today's bleeding heart world each of us would be in and out of trouble for stating our opinions and our actions. I have pulled off some of the greatest dumb ass capers that anyone could ever dream up. I look back and wonder how that could really have been me? Yet at times I stood above everyone else in positive actions.

To add to the Marine code "once a Marine Always a Marine".

Recently I joined another special club, which only 10% of us belong. It's the cancer club.

Going into the hospital for just a check up, I spend the next eight weeks fighting for my life. As an ole Marine we never do anything simple you know, its got to have a flare to it. So I got a heart operation coming and a colon operation coming.

After I beat the odds (so far) and I am in recovery from the colon caper I remember feeling someone patting my arm. Later the doctors relayed the conversation they were having at my bedside "Dr. Jacobs and I had our doubts about Jesse making it. Yes I feel the same way," says Dr. Paul. "He must be an ole Army Ranger".

They told me as I was coming out of recovery that I made a little comment (they were quite amused by it.) "Not Army Ranger assholes, Marine." However I do have great respect for all Special Forces. An Army cook (not by a Ranger) hit me so hard one night in Hong Kong that my head hurt

You see our Drill Instructor told us any Marine could whip three doggies any day of the week. I cocked off and learned a lesson. Never mind the uniform, check the size of the bastard before engaging.

THE WOMEN

Barbara, my young pretty wife, stayed as long as she could. In my final years I realized that she was my only true love. Yes, there were others, such as Mae Ling, of China, Marian of Hollywood, Marion of Dugger, Bobby Jo Of Indy and Bonnie Mae of Shelburn, but those were fleeting corridors of time.

GIVE ME THE POINT SARG

In combat actions I was near the cream of the crop, never any reflecting, you need me on point today Sarg, say the word I am the man. Hey, you got a dumb ass plan that might work-count me in (that was me). Along with Too Sack, my Chinese Nationalist friend, Sgt. Lally, Gordy, and Link, we faced Mao Tse Tung's armies from village to village in North China and into Manchuria.

My son, the all-American boy in every sense of the term, made his daddy's dreams come true. I wanted a son who would be a great basketball player, an outstanding student, and also a good caring person who loves Jesus and God. I got it all. No father ever loved his son more--no way--period. I would have loved him just as much if he had been much less, but God was good to him. I must somehow pay God back for being so kind to him.

I have seen the end of my dreams for almost 60 years yet won the life long struggle against the odds, as he got most of life's desires. Or did he? The reader must decide.

DUMB CLUCK

Before we get into my story, let the following be known:

I do not consider myself to be a hero. Hell a million military guys saw more combat than I ever did. I do not consider myself to damn smart. I had a few things going for me; I was brave, fearless, and loved my country. On the downside I was young and in many ways a dumb cluck. By the age of 18 years I had the following credits:

Me and another dumb cluck hiked to California and stole a train. Why? Because Frank wanted to. He figured my name was Jesse so it all made sense, we only stole it for about a mile, jumped off and ran like hell. Frank was a complicated guy. A world of athletic talent could have been a pro, but something was missing in his total make up. Basically he never gives a shit. He was greatest high school quarterback in Indiana, first team all state (no classification in those days). He had the size, the looks, yet you can sum it up in these words " he just never give a shit". A good-looking woman, a new car, nice wardrobe, that was just about it.

I knocked a famous movie star on his ass one night in L.A. when on leave while stationed at Oceanside. Sgt. Lally spilled his drink on this guy by accident, the guy says," you know who I am you stupid jarhead"? I decked him with one punch. Later we found out it was the actor that played "Howdy Doody " the most popular kids show on TV." Oh-well.

Fell madly in love with a little 14-year-old girl from my hometown. Pulled off some of the world's greatest dumb cluck acts to impress her that has ever been witnessed.

At fourteen years old, road a freight car from Indiana to Nashville Tenn. to get a personal look at a famous country singer by the name of Hank Snow.

This one is a real_classic. The Army was training near us at Camp Pendleton, another dumb cluck and I decided it would be one hell of a good stunt to sneak up on the guards at the army compound, disarm the two guards on the main gate and have them tied up in their birth day suits

14

with their right arms tied up in a salute, when the people started coming into the camp at daybreak. We dressed up as cowboys (I was the Lone Ranger, the other dumb cluck was Tonto) we got the stuff at a novelty store in L.A. It was the only rentals that fit us, so we took them. We made one mistake we used are own rifles, so they started looking for Marines. Many questions were asked but they never traced it to us. A few weeks later an army guy asked me at the train station if they ever found out who those guys really were? " I said sure, one was Clayton Moore and the other one was Jay Silverheels (another fight started). I am sure there is a dogface out there somewhere that will remember this caper.

CHINA & DRAGONS

The year of the "Dragon" comes every twelve years in China. The next period starts in 2012. Dragons are legendary, mythical, nasty, irritable, obnoxious beasts. They were the dreaded symbols of evil, however some were cherished.

The (T'ien lung "Dragon" represented happiness, immortality, and much more. Sort of a good Dragon as dragons go. Its got 5 claws, the others all have three or four claws. The T'ien lung is the one you see in this book.

Hey what kind of person are you without your personal dragon? Chinese Marines have a dragon somewhere around.

CHINA SITUATION 1945

Nearing the end of WW II, all the nations that had a presence in China and Manchuria were busy with post war ambitions.

The first order of business for the United States was to send occupation forces to occupy and set up the surrender of the Axes powers, mainly the Japanese. Russia and the Red Chinese (Mao Tse Tung) had designs on both countries.

The United States occupation force consisted of the 1st Marine Division to be located in the far North of China and the 6th Marine Division to be located in the central and southern part of North China.

The first order of business was two parts: first was to disarm the Japanese Empire, and secondly to free the Japanese prison camps located all over North China. Many small arms firefights developed during this process. Many Japanese solders had no idea the war was over and they continued to fight.

This occupation was resisted by both Russia and Red China, causing a major threat to our occupation forces. However this resistance was soon wiped out and the transition was very successful.

President Roosevelt and the United States government supported General Chiang Kai Shek and the Nationalist Government. The Russians continued to supply the Reds.

In 1947 after president Roosevelt died and Truman became President he pulled the plug on helping the nationalist government (whom at that time was winning on all fronts - it would seem our political leaders forgot that it was Chiang Kai Shek that gave us air bases to attack the Japanese. Within three weeks the Russians made a stronger commitment to the Reds. It signaled the beginning of the end of the nationalist government, forcing General Chiang and his Armies to retreat to Formosa. It also meant the end of the US occupation in China. By 1949 all Marines had left China.

It was not the first time that Marines occupied China, the 4th Marines were there back in the " boxer rebellion, fighting to keep the peace. Many gave their lives, as did the Marines in the 1940's.

The 15th Army was also present in China, in fact was there before the Marines and stayed a much longer time.

Prior to the end of world war two, in the 1930's the Japanese had control of most of China and Manchuria. Millions of the Chinese were made slaves of the Japanese. It has been estimated by historians that the invading Japanese killed more than thirty million Chinese.

Many historians fail to address these atrocities at the same level as Hitler killing six million Jews. It makes one wonder about their motives?

WHAT IS THE AVERAGE CHINAMAN LIKE

What is the average Chinaman like, his customs, his life style? We found many things were much alike, however many things were different, like his morals, his traditions, his day-by-day life.

One village may have strict moral codes yet another was very open. For example the village of burning rocks that was located deep into North China and within a hundred miles of the Manchurian border, had a valley that was rich and the rice crops were some of the best we ever saw. They had vendors that would travel to sell silk items as far as Peiping. The women still put a binding on their feet so they would have very small feet. It had been the custom for centuries.

Since very ancient times the Chinese have considered their country as the center of the geographic and cultural world, a land surround-ed by inferior barbarians.

Think what they may, when we arrived in China the country was torn by the Japanese Empire. People by the

17

dozens lay dead in the streets to be moved later to a hole in the ground. Finally each morning or the next morning 100's would be picked up and dumped into a hole outside of the village or town. At this period of time the Barbarians were Japanese.

The Confucianism factor

The Chinese seem to separate its many faiths into a great following of Confucian, however it can be summed up as follows:
If a man is in a position of authority he is a Confucianist. This doctrine supports the status quo.

If he is out of office he becomes a Taoist because this doctrine - Taoism deprecates both worldly authority and individual responsibility.

If death approaches he quickly takes up Buddhism, because that faith offers hope of salvation

So you can see why the China-Man is very complicated. By the way Mao Tse-Tung was a communist and a devout Buddhist (makes sense to me?)
General Chiang Kai-Shek was a Buddhist, later converted to Methodism.
Both General Chiang and Mao attended the military Academy at the same time. Mao was a dung carrier Chiang was in Charge of the Cadets. Tell you anything?

<u>WHAT IT MEANS TO BE A MARINE</u>

It goes much deeper than just being in the Military. From the first Marine I ever saw and talked to in person was Gil Thacker, fresh back from Guadalcanal. I watched the differences from other returning service men to compare. There was something special about the pride this man had in the Corps. I also noticed that most men returning home to pick up their lives, when asked about if they served, they would answer" yes I was in the service, where as a Marine would always say" I was a Marine and I always will be". To a kid of 14 it was really a profound statement. Boot Camp at Paris Island and my tour of duty in China for me to fully understood the motto "Gung-ho". Walter Winchell, a famous reporter of the times made this statement in his radio address as well as his newspaper account " If your son is overseas – write him, keep him in your thoughts, but if he is taking Marine boot camp at Paris Island- pray for him.

It seems that the Marines that made it home from "fighting the little Jap war machine" were in a nasty mood and those that decided to stay in the Marine Corps and become drill instructors must have really been pissed, because they tried to kill us every day. It was the worse time in Marine Corps history to be at Paris Island. The timeframe was Jan 1945.

By the way, any of you want to go head to head day and night for twelve weeks –write me. You will lose.

One of the attributes that play strong in Marine boot camp is PRIDE IN SELF & CORPS. Another thing to consider is- at least in this period of time is that you never see an officer. Your officer was the Drill Instructor. He was a tin god. Your very life depended on him. No PX, No Vending Machines, No passes, No reading material-except field manuals, No parent visits (god forbid if a girl showed up)

Total control of your life. No phone calls I could go on for hours on the entire No's that were in the Drill Instructor's head. Its my understanding that in today's military you are to call Mommy as soon as you arrive at basic training, to be sure you made it there. ARE YOU KIDDING ME? The DI'S got to us before we arrived, stopping on the train at Port Royal and ran us up and down the hillside for 30 minutes. No call to Mommy, the Drill Instructor is now your mommy and daddy.

19

What was all this for anyway? Well you see a time will come in combat when reaction without thinking about it comes up very often. The squad leader says move – you move no questions, no doubts you move simply because the Marine Corps has taught you to react in a split second. The killed in action list becomes much shorter.

Another thing that impressed me about what being a Marine is all about was, when you go to Boot Camp you are not a Marine, you cant even wear the Marine emblem. When you graduate and pass and review –then and only then are you a Marine. Tradition I loved every minute of it. Semper Fi

Marine boot camp methods are designed to break you down and build you back as a team player. One must remember here the purpose of training (its war and that means the possibility of killing a human being you don't even know. In view of the known facts of history – one knows we will face war again. It has been with us since the beginning of time .so someone has to be ready to defend the homeland.

Yes defend you bleeding heart liberals that call us baby killers. Are you listening {**JANE-BITCH**}.

Below are some reasons what it means to be a Marine.

You may see several servicemen at a train station where large numbers of troops are present. Some have their tie off or out of uniform in some form. <u>IT would be rare to see a Marine degrade his uniform</u> The pride to be able to earn that uniform means more to a Marine than any outsider could ever understand.

The training you receive will carry you though any thing you may ever face in a combative situation. Every Marine has it drilled into his brain. It's there forever.

A Marine trusts his fellow comrades in combat. For example: The Plt. Leader waves you to go forward. No questions enter your little brain.

QUOTE FROM THE WIZARD

"Life's work is done, when one can no longer help those one loves. When life's energy is focused to self and self alone, life should cease to exist."
Sgt. Li Chin (a.k.a.Too Sack), A Chinese Wizard, Manchuria 1945.

QUOTES FROM THE AUTHOR

Let it be known here and now that there is **no fiction** in any of my opinions and statements they come from my experiences and my study of history, I have lived through 70+ years of war and peace in our country's development, that's what I base my observations on. What do you politically correct bleeders base yours on? I been trying to find that out for years? Do I consider myself a hero? Hell no, the real heroes died for their country. I got shot at several times, mostly by bandits, Red solders and Russians. In China the enemy wore many different uniforms. The villages we passed would see us coming, check to see if we were Americans, Japanese, Red Chinese or Nationals THEN they would come running out to greet us, with the correct flag.

WAR CRIMES

"The war crimes of the JAPANESE against the American and British civilians in Shanghai seems to be all but forgotten by the historians, as well as the millions of Chinese that were degraded and killed by the invading Japanese Military.

All the bleeding hearts of America want to pay the Japanese-American civilians that were en turned during the war. Lets get something right here. They were well taken care of, well fed and housed in heated building. Granted they lost their freedom for three years, which I consider

21

over reacting on the US government. In fairness to the US Government, many attempts were made by Japanese-Americans to help the homeland by trying to bomb the defense plants making war materials to fight Japan. Counter this with the Japanese Americans that also had many young boys join the army and fight for Uncle Sam. It's a mixed bag people.

BUT trying to compare this to what the Japanese done is just stupid. What was the first thing the Japs did when they arrived in Shanghai? Went to the hospitals, raped and killed those with child then continued to kill the nurses.

You people that bitch about the USA, if its so damn bad why don't you take your sorry ass back to wherever you came from, you people don't have a clue. You make me sick. When I think of all the young men that gave their lives so that others could live in peace and have the freedoms that the forefathers created, I think they must be turning over in the graves.

O – yes I have a suggestion to our government. Since we cant seem to keep the people from Mexico coming across the border? LETS just make Mexico another state and solve the problem. Sam Houston would be proud of us . Hell we took Texas didn't we ? . History tells us that we did the right thing in doing that. Give each Mexican a SS card, food stamps etc. include them in all our give-away programs. Grease the Mexican politicians and it's a done thing. Just a thought.

You people keep on whining, knocking down all the standards, using all the loopholes, the race card, whatever gets you a free ticket. It's going down the wrong track. If in doubt it- check out the history of the Roman Empire.

The bleeders are still at it. You think it ended with the hippies of the Viet-Nam era? College professors are the greatest bleeders of all time. It has not stopped, in fact its accelerated. Timeframe is 2003. A college professor told a young Air Force Cadet in his class that he was a criminal and baby killer for wearing that uniform. You are out there killing black people. Did the guy get fired? (Are you kidding me) sure he got some heat (which is rare.) but fired? Liberals don't fire liberals.

Let me take you back to the Korean War time for a moment. I was taking a history class at our biggest university in southern Indiana the class was very large maybe 300 students in a gym area. Let me sit the scene for you: In walks the professor by the name of Dr. Snyder. He looks down from the stage and makes this statement:" I see we have a few veterans here today. You people will not like this class. You see I don't like solders, airmen, Marines or sailors, they are all baby killers. I have already spent time in jail for these statements and you can see I am still here".

I was out of my seat heading for the stage to take the SOB out. I looked behind me and all the veterans moved at the same time. The little prick ran off the stage. Needless to say we dropped the class. By the way this university promoted the same jerk department chairman later on.

Mark my words- When we get into another war with one of these country's, our so called friendly nations that make big money from the USA, they too will bite us in the ass, degrade our flag, raise a big fuss.

Look for France, Russia, Iran, Iraq, and La Canada (yes I said Canada) to degrade our country. A Canadian once told me they had better roads in Canada than we had in America. My answer was " Why not you have no military capable of defending your country, you depend us to cover your ass, so you save multi-millions on that one."

I got no comment on that one. We got enough whine-bags and liberals in the country to fill up the state of Texas and South America.

HOLLYWOOD, INDIANA
Grapes of wrath Beginning

Hollywood, Indiana is a real place. It's the place where it all started. The poorest of the poor lived there.

23

Comparing Hollywood, Indiana, to Hollywood, California, is about the greatest comparison that can be made. This story would not be complete without including my childhood buddy, Buster who died fighting Hitler in German, or of Johnny Keenan who went on to retire from the navy.

SEARCHING FOR THE SUCCESSFUL BY ACCIDENT AND DESIGN

He has met and talked with famous personalities. Some he even stayed with some of them for a time. Phil Harris, Phil Russo, Glenn Miller, Hunts Hall, Bill Nickerson, Bob Knight, Adolph Rupp, Tony Hinkle, Rick Mount, Billy Keller, Bobby (Slick) Leonard, Reggie Miller, Frank Sinatra, Billy Holiday, John Ritter, Oscar Robertson, Red Auerbach, John Wooden, General Chiang Kai Shek, General Lewis Fuller, U.S.M.C., Audie Murphy, Nat King Cole, and many more. He made it a mission to search these people out, some by accident and some by design. The purpose was that these people were highly successful, and he must learn from them their winning ways. Thus, he would make the final effort to become a winner in life's game.

THE THIRD CHINA CIVIL WAR THOSE THAT SERVED

The armies of Chiang Kai Shek were at battle all across China from Sian to Manchuria. A mad rush for the control of Manchuria, the China mainland was unfolding. There was a cold war between the USA and the USSR. Armies advanced on all fronts in the struggle against the Communist Armies. There were more than a hundred battlefronts. It happened just as Chiang Kai Shek and Mao Tse Tung squared off during the third Chinese Civil War from 1945 to 1949. That is the official timetable, but it had really started before the last shots were fired in WWII.

This is the story of four Marines caught up in this massive confrontation. There were many other Marines and Army personnel who played parts in this Civil War dating back to the old Chinese hands of the 1920's and 1930's. But, I can only relate what we saw and did. However, this book is dedicated to all military personnel who played a part the Chinese Civil War.

Somehow I knew that I was seeing history in the making. I took notes. I kept a diary. The highlights of this book include the following:

Four marines separated from their units after fire fights at Darien. A journey of 300 miles, that lasted more than six months traveling around Mao's perimeters trying to find an opening back through our lines.

HIGH LIGHTS OF THE JOURNEY

-- Searching out Prison Camps
-- Operation China Pearl - The Gold was not staying on the Mainland
-- Life as a train guard moving materials to the north.
-- The many battles fought from village to village.
-- The story of our Chinese friends, Too Sack, Sgt. York, the Lone Ranger, Col. Sing
-- Wu, Major Chin Lee, Major Wong, General Peng and so many more.
-- The village of the burning rocks, a village memorialized by Confucius centuries before.
-- The final days and Sgt. Bedwell's masterful plan, expanded with the help of Master Sgt. Lally
-- General Chiang's escape from Mainland China to Formosa.
-- It was a plan of survival and deception that defies all logic.

Nationalist Comrades

Plt. Sgt. (temp) Jesse (Shelburn) Bedwell-USMC, Rifleman, Demolitions, Hollywood, Indiana.

Pfc. Gordon (Gordy)- USMC, 705 Riflemen, Demolitions, Cleveland, Tennessee.

PFC. Robert (Bob o) Link - USMC, 705 Riflemen, Demo, Upper Darby, Pennsylvania.

M/Sgt. (Blue balls) Lally- USMC, 720, Demo, Upper Darby, Pennsylvania.

Mae Ling of Sian- a wonderful Chinese girl I will never forget.

Sgt. Li Chin, (Too Sack), of the Nationalist Army of China

Jack and Jill - two Chinese kids

Lt. Col. Sing Wu - Nationalist Army of China Commander

Major Chin Wong, part of operation Gung Ho

Chapter One

OFF TO WAR

We sailed from San Diego, Lally, Gordy, Link and I, fresh Marines being sent off to battle while the war in the Pacific was winding down yet still very much alive.

Lally from Upper Darby, Pennsylvania, was a tall young man with lots of humor. Oh he loved the ladies, with great passion, from California to China to the Island of Malloy.

Gordy was a strange little bird. He was an excellent Marine; a sure section-eight from Cleveland, Tennessee. He was a rebel by nature. But, when the call to battle came, he was the first to be heard from.

Hollywood was the name I was given. In fact, I was also called Shelburn. I was special for I had several nicknames. Back in Shelburn, they called me "Peehole" my middle name is Leo so you see how that came about (bunch of assholes). I was a tough kid from the wrong side of town. All of my family was coal miners, and we gleaned coal and corn to keep alive. Hard times were nothing new to me. The poor are always driven.

Link (Dink) was a quiet boy from Upper Darby, Pennsylvania, with cold, steel blue eyes. He was a smart and dangerous Marine.

Let's now go back to the beginning: to a place called "Hollywood" where it all began

CRASH Of '29--PEEHOLE-BUGGER-BUSTER
Summer 1939

As my mind goes back to the days of my youth and innocence, it seems that I even remember the bad times as good times. My earliest memory is but a flashing moment of time. I am sitting at the supper table in a high chair. We lived in a small house on Mill Street in Shelburn, Indiana.

27

My father had scolded me and I was afraid. It is one of the four fleeting memories I have of my father. The second memory is a visit to the county jail in Sullivan, as my uncle Wayne took me to see him. I learned later in life that my mother had put him there. The reason is unknown to me. I vividly remember that visit like it was yesterday. A huge door swung open and my uncle and I were in a smelly drab cell with my father. The only thing I remember was my dad showing Wayne how he and a prisoner in a room below, passed smokes on a wire, down a drain pipe. I remembered no hugs or goodbyes. Although there may have been, I think I would have remembered. I do remember he was a slim, pleasant-looking man, with a big smile. My third memory of my dad came when he visited my mother in Hollywood, a nickname for our poor area. I was about five years old. My mother would not let us see him. I tried to get around her to see, but I remember no more. The fourth and last time I ever saw my father was at his funeral. He had been killed while he was working in the mines. I remember the black hearse coming up the hill to my Grandfather Bedwell's farm, and my Aunt Gladys saying, "Jesse, your daddy Jesse has come home to rest in peace." At the funeral I was lifted up and told to kiss my daddy goodbye. I was afraid, but I remember his cheek was scratchy. That is the last memory I have of my dad. What he would have been to me, had he lived, no one knows? I only know that out of the dozens of kids who lived in Hollywood, I was the only one without a dad.

In today's world being without a dad happens more often. Kids would always say, "I'll tell my dad on you." or " My dad can whip your dad." My brother Jack and I never had that option. When these situations came up, I always said, "My cousin Jeannie or my Uncle Burlap will whip your butt, or he is taking me to Sullivan this week." It seems like a small thing now, but in the eyes of a little boy, it was big.

Our little community had about two hundred homes in it spread over about a two-mile area. To the north was the big city of Terre Haute, and to our east were small towns. Highway 41 was the only way to go south. We were west of a town named Shelburn, a town of about twelve hundred people. It had several stores and a movie house that cost a dime to get into; only nobody could find a dime. To the west of Shelburn was our little area call Oakland, but we called it Hollywood. Of course, we knew the real Hollywood was rich and famous, so since we were dirt poor, we thought it made sense. A lot of silly ass things we thought and did made sense (to us anyway).

Our people were all coal miners. They worked fourteen hours a day for fifty cents a day. It was hard times. The stock market crash of 1929 had left the nation crippled and looking for leadership. Two men stepped up to the task, our President Franklin Roosevelt and our mine President John L. Lewis.

THE HAUGERS – MY MOTHERS SIDE OF OUR FAMILY

My great grandfather arrived in southern Indiana in the late 1800.s with his family. They came from Kansas looking for work in the new deep coalmines. They lived in tents for 5 years. A creek and woods was their home.

Later they were able to buy the land they were on and starting farming to go along with fifty cents a day they made at the mine.

My grandfather Auza married my grandmother Ida Dale.

Today's people could never make it like they had to live. The industrial age was yet to come.

In our home lived my mother, my brother Jack, my uncles Lloyd and Wayne, and my grandfather and grandmother Hauger. It was a three-room house that was painted white. We had an outhouse, a cistern, and no electricity. We heated the house in the winter by gleaning the coalfields. (There was no money to buy the coal). In the summer we gleaned cornfields. We picked berries with the gypsies during the summer. My family was the poorest of the poor, in this place called "Hollywood". It was named Hollywood as a joke by the townies; they were better off than we were.

Somehow we carved out a living. At 7 years old I worked alongside the adults. Most of the time picking fruit ten hours a day. We were paid two cents a basket for picking strawberries One week I averaged 50 baskets a day. I wanted to buy a basketball goal so I worked extra hard. Kids got the weekends off. Hollywood had one store and nothing else, so everything revolved around the store. We lived next to the store, so we had it made. There were plenty of kids to play with since more than seventy families lived in Hollywood. We learned to share, we learned to fight, and we learned about God.

As I look back on those days, Hollywood helped in many ways to shape my life. More often than not, I was learning what not to do. They taught us to honor the family and not to lie or cheat. (However, a goodly share of Hollywood people never got that one down right). It was in the true sense "hard times." As I look back, I wouldn't have had it any other way.

My grandmother was the power base in our house; my gramp thought he was, but when it came to push and shove, ole Granny Ida had the last word. Ole Gramp Ozzy cussed as good as any human I have even seen, but when the cussing died off, ole granny was still in gear. Hollywood townsfolk called her the "Mayor of Hollywood."

We walked along the dusty road leading to Truman's Creek. It was about a two or three-mile walk. "We could have ridden our bikes, if we had any," chirped Buster.

"Yeah," I said, "those assholes that live in Shelburn all got bikes."

"Not all of them," added Buster. Buster was a year older and a hell of a lot tougher.

"Well, I know one damn thing, we don't have any."

Buster said, "Look at that ole Guernsey laying on her ass, while all the other cows are up moving around."

"Yeah," said Bugger, "fire a rock at her, Buster, and see if she gets up. Ole Buster fired a Bob Feller strike in the middle of her big ass; she jumped up and ran right at us.

"You dumbass," I said, "that is Clyde Mills' prize bull. We ran like a son of a bitch, and that damn bull jumped the fence and chased our Asses up two walnut trees off the side of the road. He bumped Bugger's tree real hard. He had a small tree anyway, and it damn near dumped ole Bugger on the ground.

Buster yelled at the bull, "Hey, you silly fucker, are you half goat?" We all started making goat sounds.

Finally ole man Mills came up from his barn. He looked us over and said, "You know, boys, that's one smart bull, 'cause he knows already whose ass to kick. Damn strange thing about that bull. Other than the son of a bitch is mean."

"What else you know ole farmer, John Mills?" said Buster.

"I know for one thing, he has been in this pasture for four days, and never bolted the fence. Wonder how that come about boys?" He looked at me.

"Hell, I don't know, maybe he saw a female cow across the road and just decided to take us out on his way to get some nookie." Bugger and Buster laughed their Asses off, but ole Mills was still pissed.

Then it was time for ole John to have his say. "Tell you what I am going to do. I am going to let you off with a warning, but the next time, you come down here, I'll turn the bull loose, and you can run up these walnut trees. Then, I'll saw the sons-a-bitches down. What you think about that?"

He was waiting for an answer, but we knew better than to say shit, because the damn bull was still standing guard. Finally, the ole fart got his bull back in the pasture, but that damn Bugger had to have the last word. He yelled,

"Hey, Ole Mills, your wife's been screwing Charley Mason. He shook his fist at us, as we went on down the road.

Bugger got his name from me. He was a little younger and was always bugging us, so I named him "Bugger" his real name was Billy Scott). Bugger took up the conversation "I didn't know Mills' wife was screwing ole Charley Mason."

Buster looked at Bugger, and said to me, "You know, Peehole, Bugger will believe anything you tell him."

"Oh, he is as dumb as owl shit, Buster, and he still thinks babies come from the stork."

We laughed, "Hell, we know better, don't we, Peehole?"

"Yeah, I know Dipstick."

"Who else?" I asked.

"I know," said Bugger, "but I hate that sawed off runt." Dipstick was well known for getting into a good share of all the bedrooms in Shelburn. Every time a baby came along, we said his middle name was "Red" and we pissed off a lot of women, but we didn't give a shit, who we made mad, it was as close to truth as one could get in ole Shelburn. My Uncle Sig said that when Red died they had to break ole Red's dick to get the lid down on the casket.

The fish decided not to give us the time of day, so by noon we were back in front of ole Slobber Davidson's "Got Em Down Store", trying to find somebody coming out of the store with an apple in hand or a pop. We always asked for seconds, thirds, or the core on the apple, and seconds or thirds for swigs on a 5-cent Pepsi or Coke.

After twenty minutes of threats, begging, and lying, it was time to go down to Tubs Field and get a game going. The older boys seemed to have something else to do, so we had a shot at getting some time in with the round ball (basketball).

"Let's go over to Bad Eye's, and see what he is up to," said Bugger.

"It sounds good to us," we both answer.

Bad Eye had a real name, but I figured Bad Eye was good, because he was almost blind in one eye. If you had a name like Clivus Leon, hell, Bad Eye was a step up.

Bad Eye's ole mom was a frail little thing, but she had a sharp tongue, and cussed like a pirate, she could. His Pop worked at Decker's Junk Yard. He looked like a weasel; a puff of wind would blow him away. Bad Eye was about the same way. The reason we liked to go over there was we liked to hear ole Lizzy cuss. She was the only woman we knew that could cuss as good as us.

Lizzy greeted us at the yard. "I know why you peckerheads are here today."

"Now, how is that, ole Miss Lizzy?" asked Buster.

"You know I bake pies on Monday. You never miss a Monday, now do you, Buster?"

"She's got us cold," said Buster, "smart woman, that Lizzy.

"Damn right," said Lizzy.

Buster looked around and said, "Where is ole Bad Eye?"

"Oh, he went down to the junkyard to help Lovie. (She called her man Lovie.) Buster always said that one look at ole Lovie would puke a buzzard.

Lizzy didn't like Vera Dean, so Buster always got her pissed off on ole Vera Dean. Well, when ole Vera Dean was about fourteen, she taught me how to screw. (I was nine, but we all started early in Hollywood.) Vera Dean had no age limits or looks limits, and to her, screwing was screwing. Her motto was if it felt good, do it. Damn, did she ever do it! Wow!

Buster said, "I hear Vera Dean was walking in front of your house the other day, Lizzy." He winked at Bugger and me.

Lizzy, busy with the pies, still had time to react. "Yes, the little tramp was here last Saturday evening, probably wantin' to get next to my Lovie. I took a broom to her, and beat the livin' shit out of her." We all laughed, and she continued on. "That girl should be sent to

33

Evansville to the nut house, that girl's not right in the head, carrying on like that all the time. She keeps that up and ole Hayfield gets to her, why you boys will have to get your tail someplace else."

We all looked at each other, grinning. I said, "Well, Miss Lizzy, how you think it would make any difference if ole Red got to her?"

"Well," said Lizzy, "they say he's built like a mule, and after he gets to one of the men's wives, she don't want to bed with her man any more."

Bugger said, "Is that why you don't give ole Lovie much anymore?"

It was time to run, but Bugger was close to ole Lizzy and she nailed Bugger across the head. It sounded like a school bell going off. She chased us out into the yard.

I said, "Lizzy, we didn't say anything, let's us come back in. We need some of that cherry pie."

"Well, come on back, but no pie for that wise ass Bugger. Bugger hung his head and started home. Lizzy continued on, "Boys, I never had anything to do with ole Dipstick. Oh, I had a few dreams about him, but that's all, and that's all it will ever be. I don't like his Red Hair and beady eyes. He gives me the heeby jeebies."

"You're a good woman," said Buster, "and your pies are the best in Hollywood."

"Well, thank you, Buster," she replied. After we had two pieces of pie, we got up to leave. Lizzy said, "Boys could you carry that tub in for me? It's out back on the fire. I got to take a bath today, 'cause Lovie is getting in the mood again." She laughed a silly laugh, and we laughed a silly laugh. It was time to move on.

Buster said, "Boy, ole Lovie's in for a big ride tonight, right, Peehole?"

"Well now, Buster, if you remember, tonight is the Odd Fellows meeting and ole Lovie always goes to his lodge meetings.

Buster said, "You got to admit, ole Lizzy makes one hell of a cherry pie."

34

"Wait a minute," I said, "I remember this is the night Bad Eye goes and stays over to his grandmother's. Well now, seems like we may be on to something eh' Buster?"

"Yep, that's damn odd, Peehole. Damn odd."

Basketball and the Store
I could smoke anyone- Except -Mentheny
I loved the game so much it obsessed my every thought.

Kids from Hollywood never went out for the school team. We were looked down upon, poor white trash. I played against the townies every time I got a chance. The better players always let me play with them (of course when I did I had to fight the kids in Hollywood for kissing up to the townies. Every time I came home they were waiting for me. One time ole Beryl Hyatt and Bill Davidson were waiting for me. They worked me over good and started to leave. I got up off the ground and remembered what Gil the Marine told me " he up from that inter-energy you have trapped, get up run them down and fight like a mad man. I got up ran them down I got hold of Bill first, he was older, meaner I knocked him on his ass, he got up and I give him an upper cut and he dropped like a sack of shit .Ole Beryl ran off like a little sissy boy .It was that fight that turned the corner for me. No one messed with "Peehole" again if they tried they lost. You see Gil taught me how the Marines fought in battle, even how to kill a man with little effort (No I never took him up on those).

So I finally tried out for the basketball team when I was a 9th graded. The coach who had a good coaching record, but didn't want a poor boy with a built in attitude and a chip on each shoulder.

The first game the reserve coach put me in with 7 minutes left to play, we were down by 11 points. To make a long story short I scored 19 points in 7 minutes had three steals and two rebounds.

In the next practice our varsity "star" the principals son got a lesson from me on how to play the game. I smoked him on every play. The coach said I was fouling him, some of the players yelled at the coach saying" Hey coach Bedwell is tough

He can play." Later I stole the ball from our star, coach yelled at me saying I fouled him again. I said ok –ok lets let our hero score when he wants

As I walked away he gave me a blind shot hitting me in the head, said take a seat. When my head cleared I returned the favor. I gave the coach a blind shot sailing a ball knocking him on his ass.

Practice was over and so was my basketball career at PO-Dunk high school. Later in a semi-pro game I was playing for another town. The coach and the town fathers were sitting upstairs behind the hoop, the game was almost over, it was against my old team we were winning by 18 with seconds left. I scored 38 points.

It was nothing to play from three P.M. until dark, and then come back and play four more hours. Basketball and boys went hand in hand in Indiana. It was our way of life.

Dick McHugh came by on his new bike. He was peddling papers for the Indianapolis Times. He, Don Tincher and Dick Sweet were the few townees we put up with. We were roaming the streets of Hollywood again that night.

Slobber Davidson's store was a little shotgun building. We lived next door to it, which was great because all the action started at the store. Life was simple back then; simple folks doing simple things. Most were coal miners; my gramp and my uncles all worked the mines fourteen-hour days, six days a week. Forty-five to fifty cents an hour was the starting wage, but back then a Pepsi cost 5 cents. It was still almost impossible to raise a family. Back in those days of the great depression (1929), people had big families. Hell, Crosscut Turner had seventeen kids. Ole Maude popped one out every ten months, and yet she was strong as an ox and mean as one, too. But if you had to bear seventeen jug heads, you would be mean, and you'd have to be

It was a hot July day in southern Indiana. We went out early because it was show night. We had bottles we could sell to raise the ten cents admission price, meaning we would need to come up with a little more. As we passed Ole Maude Zurhide's house Buster yelled out, "Hey, Peehole, that looks like a piece of iron in the alley."

I said, "It looks more like Ole Maude's clothesline to me."

"Well let's give it a look," said Buster. As we approached the alley, we were surprised to see ole Tom getting his morning smokes in so early in the morning. "How do, ole Tom," Buster said.

"Morning, Buster," answered Tom, proving he was awake. "You too, Peehole. What are you two birdbrains doing today?"

"We are looking for some iron so as we can hit the show tonight."

"Well, keep your eyes off Ole Maude's clothesline pole, or you may not live past your tenth birthday."

"How do you know how old I is I ask?"

"I live less than five hundred yards from your house, Peehole. Even a pea-brain like yours can add that up."

"Besides, that pole has not been used in years, and you know it, Tom."

"That's true," said Tom, "but Maude would have a shit fit. By the way, Peehole, that Pearl Wilson kid was over sitting on my favorite chair the other day. He said your little brother, Jackson, made his little sister eat a mud pie, and said she was sick all day, couldn't eat her supper."

I thought about it a minute and answered ole Tom, "Well now, ole Tom, Pearl's little sister is two years older than Jack and twice as big. I reckon she can take care of herself. Anyway, I'll have a little talk with ole dumb cluck Pearlie."

37

Buster added, "Remember the last time you come up against ole Pearl? He put a knot on your head."

"Yeah, but I told ole cousin Jeanie about it, and he gave ole Pearl a black eye, a skinned up arm, and a bent finger, his pointing one, too. He will think about it before he attacks me again. The son of a bitch is as big as a horse.

"Say," adds Bugger, "did your cousin Bobby get over his broken arm?" Yeah, he learned to use two hands while climbing.

"That's how he broke his arm in the first place," added Buster. Some tree climber that boy

"Oh, he is as dumb as owl shit, Buster." (Later Bob was to become an engineer and my lifelong buddy. He also quit climbing trees, and as best we could tell he kept both hands on the limbs.)

We moved on down the block passing Bud Rhompson and Bill Crooks on the way back to Slobber Davidson's 'Jot Em Down' store. Slobber had big lips, thus the name.

"Hey, Buster, we're in for a treat. See Ole Mert She's going to do a little shopping and maybe a little stealing." Buster and I watched in fascination as Mert went about her morning shopping.

"Elmer, give me some of that hogjaw (bacon), some of that loney (bologna), a can of grinds (coffee), a gallon of coal-oil (kerosene), and a box of sparkles (matches)." After she was done, we would go outside to take fun with her. She would smile and cuss us out. We were satisfied and moved on to other important things, as Buster said.

Little did we know we were as big of a dumb cluck as Mert. We had a language all our own, sort of a "Hollywood dictionary". Like who ever heard of something being "tumped over"?

We were the poorest of the poor. We would wait sometimes for hours to find some kid with an apple so we could ask for seconds or the core. A swig of Pepsi cost a nickel, but we couldn't even come up with that much. No electricity in the house, any running water, and damn little heat in the winter, and hotter than owl shit in the summer. We didn't even have a fan. Our family all gleaned corn in the summer and coal the year around to get what heat we had. We lived on cornbread and beans, sugar syrup, greens and potatoes.

It was a world of hard times. Hitler was taking over Europe with talk of ruling the world. My folks were coal miners, when they could get work. Gramp and Granny Hauger, after they came to Hollywood in a covered wagon, they lived in tents the first few years.

My grandfather Ozzy worked in the coalmines. He got up at four A.M. every morning and got home about six P.M. every evening. He would eat, cuss everybody out, and go to bed. It was the same every day, except sometimes he would have the weekend off.

We had a three-room house with no indoor plumbing, no electricity, and no water. My two uncles, my mother, my grandmother and grandfather, my little brother Jack, and I all lived in our house. My uncles worked in the mines part time.

My ole Gramp Hauger left at dark and came home at dark. He came home to eat something, cuss for an hour, and go to sleep, and start the same thing over again the next day. Granny Hauger was the real power base in our family. She would stand like a rock listening to ole Gramp cuss her out for an hour, and as soon as he went to bed she would start singing softly and go about her business.

Back to ole Buster and me. As we were just getting ready to leave Slobber's, up came trouble. Bill and Bud are eyeball to eyeball with us. It was to late too run. They were four years older than us and picked on us almost daily. They thought they were tough, and in fact they were tough. Last Halloween they captured us and took us out to the Fairbanks graveyard about four miles out of town. They tied us to some stones and left us there for the night. We cried and cussed, and then cussed some more, and kind have gone to sleep, but we got wide-awake, when someone was coming. I said, "It's that's Ole Melvin Poven drunk as a skunk. Let's scare the hell out of him."

As he got near, we started by saying in a slow weak voice, "Are-r-r-r-r you-u-u-u-u-u out-t-t-t-t yet-t-t-t-t?" That's all it took. Ole Melvin run like Jim Thorpe, and we laughed our Asses off. Finally about four A.M., here came the smart ass Bud and his yes man to see if we are crying.

I said, "Buster, we better cry like a son of a bitch or they might pull this shit again." Buster agreed and we put on a show for them. When they took us back to town, we set up a plan to pay them back.

"Peehole, I know what we need to do. We got to wait a week because if we do something now they will know it's us." So we waited for about ten days before we struck.

Bud had this ole goat he was always bragging about. It could do this and it could do that. So Buster and I fingered, if it was so damn smart we'd see how it could handle this plan. Bud liked military tanks, in fact, he liked them so well he later joined the army and was a tank driver for ole blood and guts George S. Patten.

So anyway, we knew George Banfield was taking his hogs to sale the next day, so we captured Sherman later that night and put him in with ole Squire's hogs. Since Squire is hard of hearing and turned his earpiece off at night, we knew those hogs and ole Sherman would have a great time. Anyway, the next morning, Squire went and turned up his hearing aid, and heard the damnedest racket he had ever heard. It seemed like, somehow a goat got in with his hogs. He said the hogs had bumps all over them and the goat had some skin missing and one horn looked a little kattywompus. Buster and I listened to this story down at the White Hut, an eating-place. We sat there in pure amazement. Ole Bud looked for someone to blame, but he never traced it back to us. He put first aid stuff on ole Sherman, but he still looked like shit months later. Bud got kind of mean after that. Hell, the dumb ass was mean enough before Sherman took a trip on the wild side.

It was getting warmed up in ole Hollywood. It was July and in the summers, Indiana gets real hot. Of course we never had electricity, so a fan wouldn't have helped us if we could have afforded one. We did have hand fans and old newspapers. We also had the latest catalog from Monkey Ward's in our outhouse.

It was nice to look in the girls' underwear section. We saw the older boys doing it, but at that time, we were really more interested in cowboy outfits.

My uncle Wayne, nicknamed Zeke, was about eighteen years old. He had been picked to ride a flatbed truck all papered up for a democrat rally down at the Sullivan Fairgrounds. I remember he was so excited, and so was I. Wayne was going to be a part of things that only the townees·got to be in. Well, it didn't work out too good. They all got so excited about getting down to the fairgrounds that ole "Buttcut" McKinny rounded the Banfield curve too fast and wrecked the flatbed. No one was hurt real bad, but ole Zeke would never forget it. Town Marshall "Bing" Crosby was the first on the scene, and the first thing he saw moving was ole Zeke trying to get unstuck. It seemed his head went through the big brass drum. Bing said it was the damnedest thing he ever saw, Wayne's little head looking up at him saying, "Can we still go, can we still go?" Bing had to cut and tear ole Zeke's head loose from the drum.

Squire Banfield was very upset, when he arrived, because he had sent all the way to Indianapolis to get that big drum, now it had a dumb ass from Hollywood with his head hanging out of it. "Zeke, couldn't you find another place for your damn head? You got a little head, it don't need a big drum to fit into."

Vergy Sanford who was the driver said, "Now, Squire, Zeke didn't have much time to make up his mind."

"Well," countered Squire, "that drum cost us twenty dollars, and we will never raise enough money to replace it." With that Squire shook his head and wandered off.

41

Zeke came home very upset, not really about the drum but more that he didn't get to the rally. However, ole Zeke was not done. He came up with another plan later on that made him famous in Hollywood. For a time, we called him 'Big Drum' and then ran like hell.

Uncle Lloyd (Burlap) had a mess of kids, a mean mess of kids. I remember the day I got up one Sunday morning and saw a young blonde looking at me not more than ten feet away laying in ole Burlap's bed. I said, "Who in the hell are you?"

She giggled and said, "I am Burlap"s new wife."

I looked her over and said, "The hell you say?" I'd heard the big boys talk that way. "You're not much older than I am, Burlap must have got drunk."

"She interrupted and said, "Yep, he was drunk all right, but we still got married."

"How old are you I questioned?"

She said, "I am fourteen, soon be fifteen." That damn Burlap was for sure a cradle robber. She laughed, and about then, in came Burlap.

"You meet my new wife, Peehole?" That gave her another chance to giggle. "She's kind of young, but she is a good cook, kind of good looking, and she really loves ole Burlap."

I was thinking this is going to be one hell of a mess. Burlap was about twenty-six then, but to me he was older than owl shit. Her name was Kit; she came from a large family.

Kit's parents had thirteen kids, but Kit and Burlap passed that mark with fifteen. Each and every one of them was mean as hell, and most of them got in trouble as soon as they were old enough to throw a rock. The only way I remember Kit was with a big belly, popping them out every nine months. Ole John Keenan and I passed their house a couple of years after they set up house keeping. We were sitting on his back porch talking about the day's activities, the lights were out, and everyone was asleep. All of a sudden we heard a lot of cussing coming from the coalhouse. Bugger says," it sounds like ole Burlap". Yeah I say those damn kids locked him in the coalhouse again. Bugger yells at Burlap" its us Peehole and me will come back later and bail your ass out". Burlap tells us to go to hell.

"Well," says Bugger, "I am going home. I don't need this shit."

I answered, "Me either." We didn't care about that crap. Hell, we were only twelve years old. We thought it was stupid but funny as shit.

We laughed a good one. I waved at Bugger, and home we went.

Waking up to ole Granny Hauger singing her favorite song "Little Boy Shit Up the Wall". That was it all right; can't remember the rest of the words, but those stand out. The laundry was an every day chore. With my uncles and ole Gramp working in the mines, coal dust was everywhere. Mom and Granny would get up at first light, heat the water outside in a number three tub, and dip the clothes in and out. Then, they would move them to another tub with a washboard hanging on the side. After that, they would hang them on the line. I always tried to get up early and escape, but most of the time I had to help.

Wayne (Zeke) was in high school and was in charge his class activities. This was a big deal to Wayne. He was a small little guy, kind of frail. In today's world, he would be sort of a "geek". But he was a great guy. I miss him so much. He died when I was forty-four years old and he was fifty-two.

I will always remember the day we got a radio. We were the last family in Hollywood to get one. I remember like it was yesterday. Wayne started in front of it, telling us how to work it, because he had used one at the high school. He said grinning to no one in particular, "That's Lula Bell and Scotty." It was the first sounds of music we had ever heard in our little three-room home. We thought we were big stuff.

43

The next day after we heard Burlap, in the heat of the night, so to speak, Buster and I noticed ole Zeke gathering bits of wood here and there." What the hell is Zeke up to?" says Buster.

"I don't seem to know," I answer, "but he has been like a ground squirrel here lately. Look at that stuff, Buster, he must have gathered every damn nail in Hollywood."

"Yeah," adds Buster, "try and find out, Peehole. He's your uncle."

Today it would be called a theme park. Buster and I were witness to the first homemade one ever dreamed up.

Nails were hard to come by, so Wayne had us looking everywhere for

Nails. One day the Johnson girls came up to Wayne and said, "If you will show us your peters we will give you the nails we have." Without a look or a word Wayne,

John, my little brother Jack, and I whipped out our peckers. They laughed and

Gave us the nails. Rosie was eleven, and Marie was about thirteen. Both ended up with babies before they were fifteen.

As the days rolled by the theme park started to take shape. Wayne had set it up in a lot next to our house. Behind that was a large field, so ole Zeke had plenty of room to work. First, he built a gate, followed by a fence around an area fifty feet or so. (We knew where he got the fencing, because the school had put up a new fence.) Zeke had dragged it all home on his wagon.

Every damn kid in Hollywood was hanging around. So Zeke got cousin Bud and his idiot followers to keep them out of the way. The first thing he built was a teeter-totter, and next came a sort of monkey bar. Day by day something was added. Within two weeks of starting, his little park was ready to open. He already had ten different things to do. It was very good. He had four wooden cars set on homemade tracks in a circle that the little kids could ride in. It was really good. People from Shelburn came down to give a "look see". It was ole Zeke's first business venture. He would have many more during his lifetime.

The fee to get into Zeke's park was five nails and a penny, or some wood he could use to build more things. He would have over a dozen 'rides' to do in his park before it was over.

The park lasted until the wintertime came. It was a hard winter in 1939. People needed wood to start their fires. They came in the night and hauled it off piece by piece. It liked to killed Zeke. He didn't even get a picture of it to save. We managed to catch one ole woman about eighty years old. (She left a note on our door that said, "I am so sorry, Wayne, but we are very cold, and we have no wood today." Three years later an ole lady died in Hollywood. No one knew her much; she lived alone with her cats.

In her will she had around one hundred dollars. She left it to her cats except for twenty-five dollars she left to Wayne.

Uncle Wayne went on to another project at school. He was to get a country singer lined up for a big doings at the school. Wayne was able to line up Paul Groves, a picker out of South Chicago. Actually this was a big deal for the school and the town. He had a radio program from WXLW in Chicago. The place was packed and everything went off well. (Zeke's place in our little town picked up a might.) Big drum had his big moment.

I asked Wayne, "How did you get him to come to a jerkwater town like Shelburn?"

"Well," says Wayne, "I told Paul the whole town just loved his music and listened to his show all the time. Then, he told me he had a gig. (Wayne said that was radio talk for another date.) It seems since ole "41" South leads to Evansville, it was right on his way. "Any more questions, Peehole?"

"No," I answered, "ole Buster and I got to go find some iron or something to sell. We need to see the show

45

this weekend; the serial starts all new tonight. Bob Steele is in this one.

The movie house wasn't all that great, but it was all we had. My cousin Shorty Hauger and Melvin Povin ran the projectors. Boob McCracken's tavern was two doors down, and ole Shorty and Melvin would slip over for a snort or two. Sometimes the film would run out or burn a hole, and we had to run like hell to go get them out of Boobs. I asked Oat Sebring, owner of the show house, "Why in the hell don't you fire them both, Oat?"

He answered, "Well, Peehole, in this town it's hard enough to find two people with enough sense to find their ass with both hands on a clear day, let alone run two 38 mm projectors."

"What your saying, Oat, is that they are both boozers, but when sober, they got some sense?"

Oat looked me over with his evil eye (a glass eye) and said,

"Go home, Peehole."

Our Home in Hollywood

When I was eight years old, I started to notice things about my surroundings and just how poor we really were. When I visited my relatives on the Bedwell side, it seemed they were rich. In reality, they were just poor dirt farmers. But, they had plenty of food on hand, and the table was always loaded with things I never got to eat at home.

Our daily meals went something like this. We had sugar and water mixed to put on pancakes for breakfast. Dinner was almost always navy beans and some cornbread. For supper sometimes, we had some fried lunchmeat with some greens, canned corn, or potatoes. It never changed too much.

In the winter, we picked the coalfields every day to keep the house heated. In the summer, we picked fruit with the Gypsies.

46

We had to walk to school over a mile away no matter what the weather. We also came home for lunch. We could not afford sandwiches; that's how damn poor we were.

All of Hollywood was poor, however, none were as poor as we were. When Gramp got sick and could no longer work, Mom and Granny took in washings to try and help. They lived a hell of a life. I hope they have some rewards the next time around. We all tried to help. Later, Burlap and Wayne got married and moved away. It was still very hard. There was no pension; just what we could all bring in.

The Bedwell Farm

Part of each summer I spent time at my grandfather Bedwell's farm. It was a welcome change to my life in Hollywood.

Hard work, but plenty to eat. My gramp farmed 300 acres and worked at night in the underground mines, as did all his 9 kids. Bill was the oldest, my dad Jesse was next, then came Gladys, then Lex, Goldie and pearl, Cecil and Delbert and the youngest Gene.

Bill never worked much on the farm; he spent all his daylight hours working in the mine. His job was as the safetyman, checking all the rooms for gas. I can see him as if was yesterday with his bird "Jim Beam" telling the bird what a great bird he was then he would always tell the bird what a great life he had as a bird. Bill always added at the end of his little talk " You know you will die before I do (if gas was found the bird kicked up his heels and fell over dead, and Bill ran like hell. Bill spent his free time playing pool, gambling chasing wild women and drinking ole Jim Beam.

Later on when I was back from China I got a letter from aunt Goldie saying that Bill got on a toot and was stopped by the police at 4am driving drunk as a monk on ole highway 41 clocked equal to his age 87. With a sweet young thing (38 years old) at his side.

The cop told Goldie when she went to bail him out that Bill (told the cop (all 6'8 of him} he was going to kick his ass right there and now) Bill was 5.7 138 pounds Bill also told him why. Bill told him he was just getting ready to get some tail.

Goldie said the whole family was very upset with Bill bringing down the family name.

My reaction was somewhat different. I had the shop teacher make Bill an award. It went something like this: " Bill you are my hero. Any son of a bitch that drives his age (Bill always said he liked to drive equal to his age) 87 years old driving 87 miles an hour at 4am in the morning and getting pissed for missing a peace of tail should be honored. There fore I present you with this award for your outstanding performance. JESSE LEO".

My dad **Jesse** they called him "Red" was another of Gramp Bedwell's pain in the ass sons. He was wild and run with a gang through out the county riding their horses like a bat out of hell.

Gramp told me one time he and ole Fat McCalla had a model T they purchased together. It was always breaking down, gramp said mostly they cranked and cussed for hours trying to get the damn thing running. They got so mad they kicked the tires and pushed it over a big hill and watch it hit a big tree. The "T" fell apart in small pieces. They just jumped up and down slapping hands. Gramp said they were high-spirited young men, but hard workers. Maybe a little nuts. He was to later join the Army and went overseas served three years and came home and worked in the mines. Gramp said when he came home he came sit down and lit up his cigar with a five dollar bill, Goldie said Lex and Pearl were trying to stomp out the fire, my dad It seemed was a character to be sure.

Gladys was the first girl in the family; she was the one that tied the family together. She insisted that each Sunday the entire family of Carl Bedwell would climb the big hill and arrive (in time to fix the Sunday Dinner). As the years went by and as long as granny Alice and ole gramp was still kicking, the gathering grew to more than fifty people. I remember ole gramp saying" he would rather feed 5 men that said they were hungry that one that said he was not too hungry"

Aunt Goldie, my favorite of them all. A little thing with a wonderful sense of humor, a nice smile and extra good to my brother Jackson and I. Always leaving us a little bit of change when she visited us. No one else ever did that. I am sure some just didn't have any money to give away. Hell a Pepsi cost only a nickel- but in those days a nickel was had to come by.

Aunt Pearl left the home early and got married moved a few miles away. She married a coal miner and part time farmer, just like her dad.

What I remember most about Pearl was that woman was tight as hell. When we came to her farm to bail hay she would feed us a peanut butter sandwich. It almost turned brown. If you were at the farm for dinner (coming in from the field) you got left over cold egg and bacon. Yes I said (1) egg; yes I said (1) bacon.

Uncle Lex He was a small man he too farmed a little bit and drove a gas truck for most of his life.

When the Peabody mine company came in to tear up the land (strip mining) promising the area that they would put the land back better than before, most people sold their farms to the mine company. Those that would not sell the mine company had that one figured out to. They just moved in the biggest digging machines in the world, rocked the foundations of your buildings, and then if that didn't work they broke your water tables with their explosives. If you really got a hard core farmer that said – go to hell I am not selling, they had yet another little trick, they would check out all the ole boys relatives, give one of them a job as a foreman and let him work on the ole man.

Wonderful people the mine bosses.

Delbert and Cecil

Brothers that went off to war and might you know it they ended up in the 3rd

Army under the worlds greatest field general George S. Patton. Old "blood & Guts". They were in the Battle of the Bulge; they were in Operation Overlord invasion of Germany. Between them they earned: 11 battle Stars in combat. Both received battlefield promotions to Sgt. They both came home.

Delbert worked in a factory and while standing on a ladder he fell and the fall killed him.

Ceil also worked in the same factory. He lived until he was near 90 years old.

BILLY HOLIDAY

Buster, John Keenan (Bugger), and I were watching the cars go by at our usual station, the Blue Goose, when a big bus full of niggers stopped in town. We didn't know back then, that we shouldn't call them niggers. It was the only name we knew. They scared the hell out of Buster, Bugger, and I. We went and hid behind Aunt May's house. In fact, John Keenan ran all the way home. Even Buster bailed out on me. So I watched and waited. It seemed they were not allowed to go inside, so they sat at the tables out back. That I didn't, understand then or even now. One young girl saw me, and I froze stiffer than a cold fart. "Hey, young man, would you bring us a pail of water?"

I finally got enough courage to come close, since she seemed harmless enough. I got up enough nerve to say, "You can sit at my Aunt May's tables here in the back yard." She had a bucket in her hand, and I took the gallon bucket from her hand. I remember she smelled good. Most people in Hollywood took a bath once a week whether they needed it or not. Of course, some people stunk so bad you had to stay out of range and down wind. I returned with the water. By then several of the group had gathered and were eating at the tables.

She thanked me and asked me to join them. She said she would sing me a song. She told me she was a singer. I told her Vaughn Monroe came here last week, so she says, "Oh, yes, I know Vaughn." I looked up about then, and a white man came out of the bus. She saw my surprise and said, "That's our lead trumpet player, I never asked who he was at times I wonder about that. This man next to you is Cozy Cole, our drummer. My name is Billy."

I said, "That's a boy's name."

She laughed and said, "Well that's my name, what's yours?" As sure as shit stinks, I told her Peehole. They laughed their Asses off. She said, "No, your real name."

I said, "Jesse."

"That's a nice name, Jesse it's a bible name." She then told me they had a date down south, and gave me a small card, and like a dumbass, I lost it. It said Billy Holiday and Her Band, and it gave her address. I will never forget that day, because it was not the last time I saw Billy Holiday.

A few years later while on leave in L.A., I saw a billboard in front of a nightclub. It said, "Billy Holiday and Her Band, featuring Cozy Cole on drums." That night I heard Billy sing "My Man", the same song she sang for me so long ago. I waited until the show was over and went out back where they would leave the building. There were several fans, mostly black, and I was wondering what the hell I was doing there. As they came out, I yelled, "Hey little boy, could you get me a pail of water!" People looked at me like I was nuts. She stopped for a moment, and then got in the car. As I turned to go, disappointed of course, suddenly the car stopped. She looked out the window and said, "Oh my God, it's you!" She jumped out of the car gave me a hug and kiss. All those black and white folks didn't know what to think. Anyway, I had one night left before going overseas. She invited me to come back the next night. She visited with my date Marian and me in between sets. She sang for me and only me that night. Try topping that act! I never saw Billy again. No contact was ever made. I read in the paper that she died of drugs. I still play her records every night before I go to sleep. She and Patsy Cline were my two top ladies of the music world. Sleep well, ladies.

Buster Joins the Army

The years passed on, and the country was at war. It was 1943. Buster hitched a ride to Indy and joined the army. Wouldn't you know it, he was assigned to ole blood and guts Patten's third army in France and Germany. I received one letter from Buster after he got to Germany, telling me about the war and how rotten it was. Still, I could feel an excitement abound within his letter. He was a part of the biggest event in the history of mankind, next to the coming of Jesus.

About a month later, early one Saturday morning, I looked up at Buster's window. As I always did, I would say, "Buster, you dumbass. If you hadn't joined the army we could be down at Truman's Creek skipping school." Yet, as I got closer, I could see something new in the window. It was a gold star. This meant that either Buster was killed in action or missing in action. I rushed in to ask Mrs. Wiggins what was going on? She told me she'd gotten a telegram from the war department saying that Buster was missing in action.

For the next week, I went out to Truman's Creek. I sat by myself most of the time, and sometimes Ole John Keenan would show up. We talked of things we had done together with Buster. Ole Bugger also moved away, his family moved to Kansas. I never heard from him or his family to this day. Winter was coming. I was back to school, playing basketball twelve hours a day, and I mean twelve hours per day. I could outshoot and outplay everyone in town except Metheny. He was one tough athlete. But it didn't matter; Buster was gone. Even my buddy John Keenan moved back to West Virginia when his dad got a job in the mines there.

In my first year of high school, I started my first basketball game and was the team's leading scorer in the junior varsity game. During a practice session, I guarded our senior star too good. The coach said I was fouling him. Well, the other players told the coach Peehole can smoke him any day of the week. Well sir, the coach didn't like having the principal's son closely guarded like that. Later, he screamed at me and bounced a ball off my head. That was a blind cheap shot. You just don't do that to kids that come from Hollywood. The only cheap shot I ever gave back was a few moments later. I drilled him in the back of the head. They carried him out like a sack of shit. Needless to say, my basketball career was over at Shelburn, however, it was a long way from over.

I went on to become an outstanding player on an all-star Marine team. Later, as a coach myself, my team won the state championship. I had a great son who led my teams to state titles and college championships. He was named small college All American. He was a super kid, tall, good looking, and an excellent student. You name it; he is everything that is good.

It all started with my days at Shelburn and the early years with Buster, Bugger, and John Keenan. I will treasure that time in Hollywood for the rest of the days of my life. We all had it so hard back there, why would one want to go back? I guess because for so long it was all we knew; it was all we had.

I had several relatives in Hollywood. I had all kinds of kids to play with. We didn't have anything, and yet we had everything.

The call to the military was too strong. It was a time of HONOR, DUTY, and COUNTRY, something that is lost on the present generation. I am glad I lived in this period of time. As a people, we won the greatest battle history has ever had to face, World War II.

53

I remember the cowards who ran off to get married or started college. Most of them never finished, they just stayed in long enough to get out of the war. Cowards can justify anything.

As the battle cry of the Marine Corps "Semper Fi" and "Gung Ho" were heard throughout the land, the calling was too great. I wasn't afraid of anything then or now, only God and his son Jesus. I do hope He understands the bad words and bad things in this book. As I have said before, we were young, stupid, and just plain crazies. But, we were not cowards. We served our country in its time of need. I am very proud to have been a Marine, the greatest fighting force on the face of the earth, serving in the greatest war the world ever faced.

Chapter 2

Symbol-USMC

USMC "SEMPER FI, MAC"
PARIS ISLAND, SOUTH CAROLINA
BOOT CAMP
JAN 1945

It was really easy, just like Buster had said, "Find some wino to sign the papers with you, give him a Jefferson and you're on your way." I was sixteen years old when I enlisted. I had seen too many war movies, and I was sure the war would be over before I got there. I wanted to be a part of the world's greatest war. You would have to have lived in that period of time to understand, so don't even try. In those days, you had two types of people, one type was afraid of their own shadow, and the other type was ready to defend their country.

Walter Winchell was the top broadcaster of the times. He stated on national air in one of his broadcasts, "If your son is overseas, write him often, but if he is going through boot camp at Paris Island, pray for him." You see, we had all the psychos from WWII as drill instructors who were making sure we went through as much hell as possible.

The heat was on even before we got off the train. They stopped the train just outside the base. At that point two Marines got on board, yelling and giving us a barrel of crap. They called us faggots, fairies, low lives, assholes, and some other things I had never heard before. They got us out on a steep grade and had us run up and down the hillside until we either passed out or turned blue. They didn't give a shit which. One guy mouthed off, and they hit him so hard I saw one tooth come flying out.

Don Baker was sitting next to me, and he said, "JL, what has we got ourselves in for?"

I said, "They can pull all the shit they want, I'm from Hollywood, Indiana. I can take the best they got." There were times I had to eat my words! Too many incidents took place in boot camp. As all Marines have gone through boot camp, I am sure some of these things they put us through will bring back memories for many jarheads. "Semper Fi, Mac." We said those words a lot back then.

Port Royal

We looked out the train car windows and saw large flat bed trucks backing up to the doorways. Recruits were being prodded with swagger sticks and pushed forward like cattle. All the time, they were screaming at us to move forward. "You had better move fast or you get a little help on the way," was heard. We were packed in like cattle.

Finally our truck was loaded, and we arrived a few minutes later at the quartermaster's buildings. We were herded off and pushed into another line, with constant screaming of course. I saw a long line of barber chairs with recruits getting their heads shaved. Some were bleeding! The clippers were so dull it hurt BAD. As soon as that ordeal was over, we were herded to another long line to gather in our clothing. They actually threw everything at us.

"Name, Skinhead?"

"Private Bedwell, sir."

"Shoe size, maggot?"

"Ten, sir." A pair of size twelve boots came my way. I soon learned this was the way you got everything; fit didn't mean shit. Later, in the barracks we traded for something that would hopefully fit. Pushed, shoved, and screamed at, we got to what was to be our new home. We were sixty recruits in an upstairs barracks. We knew what that meant--climb, climb, and climb some more.

The moment of truth had come. We waited like lambs waiting for the knife to come. In walked the head DI,

Ramrod, with straight killer eyes and five rows of ribbons on his chest, including six battle stars. Gunnery Sgt. T.S. Steel was about to lead us into a valley of the dead.

"GOOD EVENING, SKINHEADS!" and we all just stood at attention. We knew enough to do that already. "WHAT A POOR EXCUSE FOR BOOTS WE HAVE HERE, CPL. KELLER! THEY LOOK MORE LIKE AFTERBIRTH TO ME! SKINHEADS, WHEN I MAKE A STATEMENT OF ANY KIND IN YOUR DIRECTION, I WANT your answer SCREAMED AT ME LOUD AND CLEAR! DO YOU UNDERSTAND, FEATHER MERCHANTS?"

This type of thing was to be every few moments for the next one hundred days. I was lucky though, Paul Thacker, from Hollywood (Shelburn), Indiana, was back from the war in the Pacific. He told me how to handle myself when I got to boot camp. He also taught me how to march.

Everyone got their turn as the drill instructor made his way through the ranks. He finally got to me. "Private Shithead, why did you join my marine corps?"

"Sir, it has always been my plan to join the greatest fighting machine known to man!"

"You hear that, Sgt. Keller, this s.o.b. Wants to die for the corps!" He walked a few steps away from then came running and me. "WHERE IN THE HELL ARE YOU FROM SHIT FACE?"

(NOW I COULD USE MY TRAINING FROM GIL THACKER THE EX-MARINE.) "I AM FROM THE ARMPIT OF THE WORLD, SIR! I COME FROM A LONG LINE OF ASSHOLES!"

"OH SHIT, Sgt.! WHERE DID YOU GET THIS GUY? WHO PLANTED THIS GUY IN MY PLATOON, GUNNY? IS HE A SPY?"

"NO, SIR, TOP, HE IS A REAL RECRUIT!"

"WELL, I'LL BE DAMNED! YOU KNOW WHAT YOU ARE GOING TO BE? THE RECRUIT

LEADER OF THESE FUCK-FACED FAIRIES!" screams the head drill instructor. "YOUR NAME, BOY?"

"Private JESSE L. BEDWELL, SIR."

"NO, NO, NO COMING FROM A LONG LINE OF ASSHOLES, YOU MUST HAVE A NICK-NAME! WHAT'S THE L. STAND FOR? LEONARD, OR LAP DOG, OR LESTER, OR FESTER?"

"NO, SIR, IT STANDS for Leo. They call me Leo the lion."

"No shit!" yells the top as he gets right in my face, "you wouldn't shit me would you, Leo?"

"No, sir. Lions don't shit marines, sir."

"He doesn't shit marines, Gunny Keller, just doggies, swabbies, and airmen! This skin-headed asshole from Indiana has made me feel good, Gunny! I feel so damn good I am going home and pump my wife! And if I still got a bone on, I may pump the family dog!" He finally moved on to harass someone else.

Gil told me, if they put me in charge, I would have to fight some of the other boots who would give me a hard time. But, I would have it made with the drill instructor, which was the better of two evils.

"The top moves onto the next man," said Private Clarence P. Kelson.

"Tell me, Sergeant Keller, is this the guy?"

"Yes, sir, top, that's him."

"Tell our shit faces what you told me about this hillbilly from shit gut Kentucky."

"Well, top, when we had our 'short arm' inspection (the corpsmen check for sores, etc.), Private Kelson measured out at ten and one quarter inches. That's at parade rest, sir!" added Sergeant Keller.

Top looked at Private Kelson in pure amazement. "Private Longdong, being a hillbilly and isolated from women most of your life, I bet the only thing you ever stuck that in was mules, donkeys, and bears. Isn't that right, Private Longdong?"

Getting on a roll, master gunnery Sergeant Steel continued his badgering. "You know, you should have a license to carry that thing boy! Make sure, Sergeant Keller, that Private Dong gets extra rations to help feed that monster! Damn, corpsmen Baker, are you sure about that measurement?"

"Yes, sir, top!"

"Damn, boy, you can never be sent overseas . . . that damn thing would kill a well-used Jap whore. This boy needs to be near farm animals. Get back in ranks, Private Dong, and keep that damn thing under CONTROL!"

There were many scenes like those mentioned; too many or the book would be a thousand pages. Boot camp finally ended, and new adventures awaited us at advanced combat training at Camp Pendleton, Oceanside, California. I was to finally see the real Hollywood, in its golden age.

Boot Camp Ends

After what seemed like a lifetime, boot camp came to a close. It was a proud moment, graduating from Paris Island. It was the first major task I had ever completed in my young life, yet it proved to be a guiding force throughout my life. It gave me purpose and direction; just knowing I had been trained by the best in the world--DI's from PARIS ISLAND. The harassment was unequaled. In no other training, outside of Special Forces, do you get that kind of training. That level of harassment came only from Paris Island's boot camp during the late 1940's and early 1950's. If anyone wants to take it day by day with me, you can write me in care of the book. YOU WILL LOSE.

Troop Train

We were told that we would get a ten-day leave after boot camp. Wrong. We were boarded a troop train heading for Oceanside, California. For a under age Marine (15) crossing the country, seeing things I had only seen in a book was really something. One must remember that we had no television. What we saw in the movies was it.

Our first stop was somewhere in the South. It was somewhere in Georgia. We marched to the center of town, which was about four blocks from the train station. We stacked our rifles in the center of an old confederate square, posted a guard, and had four hours to walk around.

As Lally and I passed a tavern, I said, "Well, look what we have here." A sign out front said "No Dogs or Soldiers Allowed."

We went in and Lally, six feet five and two hundred forty pounds, ordered a beer. The bartender and two customers were the only people in the bar, as it was only round noon. The bartender, a big fellow, leaned across the bar and said, "Didn't you read the sign?"

"Yea, I read it, and I want to see the guy that put it up. And just why he would do that since we are fighting a war?" said Lally.

"Well, you see, jarhead, my pardoner and I don't like the war, or jarheads, or… He never got the rest of the words out, because Lally pulled him across the bar and crashed a bottle over his head. He went down like a sack of shit, and the others in the bar ran out the door.

I said, "Let's go, Lally, before we get in real trouble". On the way out I took the sign down, laid it on his chest, and lit it up with a zippo. He was moaning and rubbing his chest, as it was pretty much on fire. I figured we were headed for the brig, but nothing came of it.

Lally went into a restroom to clean up, and I waited outside. The first thing I noticed was two public drinking fountains; one marked "colored" and the other marked "white only". My thoughts at that time, as best I can remember, were, "Hell, they are only drinking water. What is this shit?" I went over to the colored fountain and got a drink, taking my pisscutter off and wiping the sweat off my forehead since it was a hot July day. I looked up and never saw so many white and black mouths locked open in my life. Two young girls about fifteen walked by and winked at me. One of them said, "You're crazy, boy, and you're about the best looking thing I have ever seen. How old are you"?

I said, "Eighteen."

She said, "I think not."

"Ok, so I am seventeen," I answered. It would take some explaining if I told her I was only sixteen.

"My name is Maybelle, what is yours?"

"Jesse," I answered and continued to say, "and, Maybelle, you're about the prettiest thing I ever saw or ever will see." She laughed and wrote her name on a card with her address.

She was there waving as we boarded the troop train. I wrote Maybelle, and for two years, she answered every letter. We talked of our chance meeting and of our instant attraction to each other.

Then I received a letter while I was in North China. Her girlfriend Heather wrote telling me that Maybelle and three of her classmates were killed in a car wreck. The car bringing the cheerleaders home from a football game hit a bridge on a fog-filled highway. Heather told me that Maybelle had made up her mind it was love at first sight and was going to marry me when I got back from overseas. She also told me that Maybelle had never had a serious boyfriend. She lived a few days after the wreck and was in and out of it. Heather also said that Maybelle whispered to her in her last moments, "Tell Jesse."

I wonder what might have been? When I think of Maybelle, I see her shining blonde hair and her great smile with just a hint of flirtation.

I was told a few times I was a good-looking guy, but never the "prettiest thing anyone ever saw." Well, I was a Marine, and it was a time of war and quick romances. I was five feet ten inches tall and I weighed one hundred sixty pounds. I had coal black hair, and plenty of it, except most of it was gone because of boot camp. Anyway, thanks, Maybelle, I'll see you in my dreams, sweet girl.

Soon we were on the tracks again. I relaxed and was looking out the window as the conductor yelled we were entering Tennessee. Then, he started pulling the shades down. I said, "Why are you doing that?"

"It's the law. No northern black folks can look out the windows in this state, so if you want to see out, go up to another car."

I said, "Hell, I don't see no black folks except you."

He said, "You got it right, Marine."

I said, "That's a crock of shit." He just smiled and sat down.

Can't look out the window? (I was talking to myself.) I felt sorry for the South when the North won the Civil War, but this crap was inhuman. I had a lot to learn.

The next morning we were in the mountains bordering Route 66, as we moved through New Mexico. I remembered the Painted Desert was out there somewhere. So much land to see, yet I was too young and too stupid to grasp it all. The pure beauty of it all escaped me at this time.

We hit the hot desert entering California. I wondered how the wagon trains ever got through this kind of heat. The train was hotter than Vera Dean on a Saturday night.

After five nights and six days, we finally stopped in Los Angeles. I noticed the train yard was bigger than Terre Haute. I'd never seen so many people in my life. I thought, "This is too many people, it's not for me."

SYMBOL FOR USMC
ADVANCED COMBAT TRAINING,
FEB / APRIL 1945

Oceanside, California

As an extension of P.I., twenty-mile hikes with full gear to Mt. Baldy were a daily experience. The lecturing about the "little Jap fighting machine" got to be boring, but the training was really strong on weapons. Some of us were selected for demolition training, along with our navy friends. All of this training was for the invasion into Japan to knock old Tojo off his white horse. This is where I was to meet my fellow Marines that were to be with me for an extended romp across Manchuria and North China. It was my new Marine buddies that made it all possible and worthwhile. They were Sgt. Lally, Gordon Anderson, Robert Link, and later the Chinese Nationalist, Li Chin, better known as" too sack".

It didn't take long for us become fast friends. It seemed like we matched all the same areas of interest: girls and good times. We were meaning, nasty, and as I look back, just plain dumb Asses who were put together to make a set.

Into our third week of advanced combat training, we took our usual stroll up Mt. Baldy, 17.4 miles up and 17.4 miles back down, carrying full packs of basic combat readiness gear. I was lucky enough to be a carbine man. That meant I no longer had to carry the BAR, Browning automatic weapon, around. It was a very heavy piece of equipment.

Our Platoon Leader was Staff Sergeant H.A. Crowder. We figured the HA stood for hard ass. He was about five feet, ten inches, and one hundred seventy pounds with a mean streak up his tail.

He had a thing about keeping close together, and not letting the platoon get scattered out too much. He was always on Gordy's butt, because ole Gordy didn't care much for these little field trips. On this day, Gordy overloaded his ass and told Sergeant Crowder that he saw no need to keep up front because he had seen the damn mountain yesterday. Sergeant Crowder called a halt, walked up in front of Gordy, punched him in the gut, and asked Gordy to repeat what he just said. Gordy recovered from the punch, and as quick as lightning, he decked Staff Sergeant HA with one across the chin. The fight continued until we broke it up. It was pretty much a draw.

We all figured Gordy would go to the Brig when we got back, but nothing was ever said about that fight, from the Sergeant or Gordy. However, the day we were leaving, packing up in the barracks, Sergeant Crowder came in. He stopped at Gordy's bunk and said, "You are one hell of a tough Marine. I hope it will serve you well in combat, and to make sure you understand me; I want to give you something from me to take with you.

Gordy said, "Well, thank you, Sarg, no hard feelings, and held his hand out. At that very moment, Sergeant Hard Ass decked ole Gordy and knocked him upside down.

He stood over Gordy and said, "Yeah, Gordy, no hard feelings. Semper Fi, Mac."

It was early morning in March 1945, and all the troops headed for overseas were standing in formation on the parade grounds of Camp Pendleton. We were more than two thousand strong. Lieutenant Colonel John Walton was addressing the troops. He informed us that our overseas assignments would be handed out that very morning. We had our sea bags and were ready to roll.

When he came to our company, it was all we could do to see what fate awaited us. Not all of us were going to Okinawa; some would be in different parts of the world. It didn't take long for the assignments came fast.

Our outfit got its call. "Company C. Third Engineering Regiment will be deployed to the Navy Transport ship, the USS Breckenridge. You will disembark at 1400 hours. Somewhere in the Pacific, you will join forces with other transport ships," yelled the Troop Sergeant.

We knew what that meant. We were headed for Okinawa and then on to attack the mainland of Japan. We welcomed the assignment. It was a chance to take out the enemy. I saw two things in my mind as I was standing there listening to the words of the colonel. My first thought was of a battle star on my chest, and I was standing proud. My next thought was that of a body bag.

Both thoughts were pushed to the back of my mind as the Colonel yelled, Godspeed, and good luck, Marines, you're the best damned fighting force the world has ever known!"

Sergeant Lally broke up the mood by saying, "Yeah, that includes you too, Bob-O-Link." Link just grinned and said nothing, as usual.

On my first weekend in California, I set up my invasion of Hollywood on the famous corner of Sunset and Vine. It was here I got to talk to many of the stars I had seen in the movies. It was also the place I ran into my first true love, Miss Marion Ford of North Hollywood Park. She was just like the song. She was five feet two inches, eyes of blue, and one hundred twelve pounds of pure woman, but I was too young and stupid. Damn, I've missed that girl. After I returned from China, we started up where we left off. Marion and her sister traveled over seventy miles to visit me in a Navy Hospital. She wrote my mother for years, but I was too busy to write back like a dumbass. One good thing about being in L.A., we got a seventy-two hour pass every other weekend, which gave me a chance to look over the real Hollywood.

Marion was from North Hollywood and was a senior at North Hollywood High. I was her escort to the prom, and it was at the Hollywood Palladium, a famous club. I was in my dress blues, and she had on a formal pale blue gown.

Ted Bennicky and the Glen Miller Band played. Talk about history; what a night!

As I look back through the years, she was only one of two girls that I went with and never had sex with. Am I sorry about that? Hell no! I like the idea of having two girls that would never go all the way. It now seems refreshing, but back then I was upset that it was taking so long.

I returned after the China Civil War, and we spent another year together. I should have married that girl. No, we never had sex. She was a very strong Catholic girl who

65

believed in no sex before marriage, and I respected her for that. (Pretty good for a young dumbass, right?)

SYMBOL FOR USMC
USS BRECKENRIDGE
August 1945

33 Days at Sea

We boarded the buses at Camp Pendleton in the afternoon headed for San Diego to board a troop ship called the USS Breckenridge. By the time we arrived at our point of departure, it was dark, very dark. The ship with steam coming off it, looked like a monster of the night.

Lally could see my concern, as he said, "It's only a tub, remember, sailors are already aboard. It can't be too scary, right, Shelburn." Well, it turned the trick, because it silenced my fears for the moment.

We were marched up the plank, so to speak. Everywhere you go in the Corps, you march. We carried full packs, knapsacks, haversacks, rifle, and sea bag weighing about seventy pounds going uphill. With piss pots on our head and piss cutters in the sea bag, it seemed like we were going down to the bottom of the ocean. Four levels down under, our group arrived at our new home. A home that was supposed to be for twenty days became thirty-three days.

Platoon Sergeant Maxwell was yelled and gave us direction as to where we stored our gear and assigned our bunks. If you had claustrophobia, you were shit out of luck. The iron top of the fourth level was only eighteen inches above our bodies, and as far as you could see there were bodies. Once in your bunk, it was hell to get out. You had to climb over at least seven people to get to the head. After a few days at sea, the smell of stale bodies was something else. Ole Uncle Burlap back in Hollywood said that a person could wear shit in his hat if he had to. Of course, Burlap was certifiable.

The first thing we heard the following morning was that damn ship's whistle and heard, "Heave Up and Trice Out Carry all Trash to the fantail!" We understood about carrying trash to the fantail, and the heave up, but the term, a trice out? Damn scabby talk.

Sergeant Maxwell gave us the daily procedures. At O600 hours, we formed a line in the midsection of that level. Upon command we filed out to the walkway leading to the first level. We were on the port side of the ship. After reaching the top level, we were directed to the starboard side of the ship to return to our quarters. That was to be our only exercise of the day. After returning to the mid-section we waited until our squad was called for our turn in the head for a shit, shower, and shave. Upon returning from the head, our squad was called to line up for the morning breakfast. It would take about two hours in the line, so be ready to deal with it. They had over a thousand Marines and three hundred Sailors to feed. We ate two meals each day and only two meals. Refreshments were served in the midsection, a large area in the middle of the tub, between the hours of eight and ten P.M. Lights went out at eleven P.M. By the time we got back from our first meal, it was time to get in line for our second meal. The supper meal took much longer to get everyone through. At approximately 1800 hours, we lined up again to see a movie on the top deck.

Finally, our platoon was rotated to sleep on the deck every sixth night. They wanted to make sure we got some fresh air. We were to save our questions for the squad leaders. We were dismissed.

To Lally, the squad leader, I said, "Lally, did you get all that shit down?" Yeah he says," remember I have been to sea already."

"Oh, yeah, that's good, Lally," said Gordy, "at least somebody knows what the hell is coming next."

Link had been very quiet, which was nothing new. Gordy said, "Ole, Bob-O- Link, what do you think? Are we going to make it?"

"Sure," answered Link in his slow laid-back voice. "I think it will be real interesting."

Lally said, "It can get interesting, just don't get in any high powered poker games and fights. They throw your ass in the ship's brig if they catch you fighting. After a few days everyone gets on edge, so remember how it is here on level 4. Believe me, they got the Brig down near the engine rooms, and its hot as hell and the noise is out of this world."

"How do you know about the Brig so much, Lally?" I asked.

Gordy answered for him, "He knows, Shelburn, because on the way to Guadacanal, he got into a card game. It resulted in a major fight which landed thirty Jar Heads in the Brig for ten days."

"Who told you that, Gordy?" asked Lally.

"Corporal Larson back at Oceanside."

"It's true," said Lally, "but remind me when we get back, to look my dear friend Corporal Larson up, so I can kick his ass again."

"I know that guy," added Link, "he is an ex-boxer, tough as THEY come."

"I got news for you, Link, Lally was also a boxer, and I guess a better one than Larson," I grinned and said, "Welcome to our club, Sergeant Lally, I am glad you're on our side."

Lally just grinned and walked to his bunk. Gordy continued on about Lally. "You know, that Lally can really get the women. He is a good man to have around, a mean bastard, but good to have around. (We were to find that was the truth many times over.)

Going to the movies, I have never seen anything like it. You get top side and you see all the sailors, in chairs (up front) of course, and then you see the Marines, hanging from gun mounts, cable boxes, or anything that was tied down to the ship's decks. All the movies were cowboy movies or musicals. No sex stuff; just plain clean movies. It was just what a Marine with a seven-day hard on needed. (They were right of course, but it gave us something else besides sailors and saltwater showers to bitch about.)

Gordy was talking to one of the swabs and asked him, "How come you guys get all the good seats at the movies?"

He answered, "Because it's our ship."

"I hate a smart-ass sailor," said Gordy.

A few days out to sea, and past Pearl, we heard the call to battle stations over the loudspeakers. "What the hell now?" said Lally?

"I hope it's not a sub attack," said Gordy. We were on the main deck when it all came down.

"Look over to the left, off the port bow."

"Yeah, I see it, Lally, but what the hell is it? There's a whole damn sea full of them."

"We are in the middle of a floating mine field." They were black or gray, about six feet in diameter with several prongs sticking out of them. Lally said, "If we hit one of those, our ass is grass." We watched helplessly as this was a Navy situation that had to be solved by the Navy.

Soon several boats were launched. They were trying to tie on to the mines closest to the ship, on both the Port and Starboard sides. As bad luck would have it, the wind picked up and the waves were as high as twelve feet. Then, the boats were trying to get back on board, before the storm picked up. One boat was drifting away and didn't seem to be making any headway back to the ship. To our horror, we saw one of the mines slap against the boat. The men jumped overboard, but it didn't detonate. However, another mine hit it from the other side, and lit it up, causing a big puff of water and a big hole with parts flying everywhere.

We finally got clear of the mines and sat about one thousand yards away waiting to see if there were any survivors. After several hours of searching, the Navy came back with three bodies.

It was the first burial at sea funeral we had ever seen. It was very impressive and also very sad.

How can you write a mother or father and tell them the war is almost over, but the enemy killed your son anyway?

We were within sight of Guam when we hit a minefield. We thought we were in the middle of nowhere. You would think our guys would have a few minesweepers out looking around. Link said, "They are all counting their medals and thinking about going home. Hell, they don't care! Let those Marines coming over clean up this Pacific mess." (I am sure he was close to right, hell if I had gone through all the stuff they had been through, I would feel the same.) In a few days the war would be over, but we didn't know that at the time. Actually we thought we were going to Okinawa, and then on to Japan. The atomic bombs changed all that.

The ships loud speakers were barking out a message we will never forget…Attention all personal .The United States has dropped an Atomic Bomb on Japan…. Peace talks are getting under way.

As soon as the message was over we heard a roar from the sky. We looked up and the sky was filled with B-29's on their way to attack Japan. Lally says the Japs better sign fast there must be a hundred of them, and they carry a big payload. Gordy answers " I hope they drop there bombs before the assholes give up". All agree on that statement.

We knew that if the bomb caused the Japs to give up, we might all make it back home. Many questions? Will they surrender? What will be our role if they do? If the don't surrender we know the answer to that one, on to Japan to fight a final battle that experts say will cost 1000,s of lives.

We sailed right on by Guam. "Damn," said Gordy, "I thought we would get a little action at Guam." Gordy you better hope we don't, anyway the scuttlebutt is Guam is secure, adds Lally.

"I still think living in this whore's nest for a week is good enough for a couple of nights on the town," replied Gordy. It was to be much longer than a week on board the old troop carrier. In fact, it was to be three or four more weeks at sea.

SYMBOL FOR PORT DARIEN (Map)
LANDING AT PORT DARIEN, MANCHURIA
MAY/JUNE 1945

After thirty-three days at sea, none of us will ever forget waking up that morning and looking at the strange landscape. We saw the odd, shaped structures and most of the entirely deserted port city. During the night we had come together with more than a dozen ships. Lally said, "What do you make of that Shelburn?"

"Man, I don't know, but we must be going to attack! This is not Japan or any of the islands."

"It looks like we are in China to me," said Link.

"Yeah, you're right Link Dink."

"Oh shit!" said Gordy. "Look at those tanks and those L.S.T's being unloaded!"

About then the announcement came over the ship's speakers. "This is not a drill. Go to full departure combat readiness immediately. Prepare to board landing crafts. We all ran for our gear and stood at the ready in the hold for loading into the landing crafts. Within twenty minutes we were loaded onto the landing crafts waiting for the signal to disembark.

Then, the speakers started to belt out a series of orders. "All field grade officers to the bridge."

Lally said, "So, we must be saving the top brass for another day, huh Gordy?"

"Sure," said Gordy.

We all agreed--candy assed officers! It was a time of waiting, but we had no idea how long. As time started to pass up to two hours of silent speakers, we began to relax some. "Hell, I know what happened, Mao Tse Tung got out

71

of bed, saw all this invasion force, and shit his pants. So now we're going to be told we have to wait to attack until Mao's gooks can clean him up so he will be a respectable POW."

"Oh bullshit, Shelburn, they didn't put this together to turn and leave."

Finally the speakers were crackling again. "Now hear this. You are in the port city of Darien. You are to stay on ready alert, and in your battle stations. Our mission here is to secure the rail center and to secure the port city. The Russians and Red Chinese have refused our entrance to the port. We are waiting for orders from the joint chiefs and General Chiang. As soon as we get our orders, you will be informed."

So we bitched and we waited. Finally, after twenty-six hours, all landing craft commanders were called to the upper deck. Twenty minutes later the word came down to us.

We received the word from China Operations Command (FMF) and the General to go ashore. We are told to expect heavy resistance. We had over two thousand Chinese Nationals fully equipped for any combat situation. The objective is to secure the port city and the rail center west of the port city. Orders came down that {US} military personnel will not land until the situation is clear and under Nationalist control, with the one exception. The four demolition teams will go in with the fourth wave.

Platoon Sergeant Maxwell, our demolition team commander of the 3rd Engineering battalion, gave us our attack plan. We were to land and move away from the frontal action working our way to the rail city, which was about two miles west of Darien. By avoiding as much of the fire as possible, two bridges needed to be blown so that no mass attack could be launched by the Reds. The elite twenty-eighth division, a Special Forces group, belonging to Chiang Kai Shek, would secure bridge number three. The estimated enemy forces were set at about two thousand--mostly Red Chinese.

72

With us were forty Chinese Nationals and four Marines. Our Chinese National, American-speaking soldier was Sgt. Li Chin. Later, we were to nickname him 'Too Sack'. The American Marines were Private First Class Bedwell, Sergeant Lally, Corporal Link, and Private Anderson. The Navy UDT Team 32 aboard ship gave us all special training on plastic explosives, if four days aboard ships training with explosives makes you well trained. Our Chinese Commander was Lieutenant Colonel Sing Wu, a veteran Nationalist with many combat missions behind him.

As the LST, No. 485, hit shore, we charged out to the rattle of small arms fire. Mass confusion took place. Nothing worked the way it was planned. The Reds were attacking on three fronts, including coming from the west. Between our objective and us was a battalion of Red Chinese coming in our direction

And about ten clicks away. Two tanks were moving with them. They looked like Russian T-34's; if so, they really had some big time firepower. With us moved two companies of Nationals. The firing opened up within a range of two hundred yards. We were ripped up the middle by waves of Reds separating our troops. The troops with us and another three hundred or so Nationals were completely separated from the main force. We were retreating to the rail yard where we could get some cover. Over a hundred men didn't make it. Bodies were everywhere!

Finding cover under a railroad car, Lally, Link, Gordy, and I managed to stay together. Gordy was firing away with his Thompson machine gun near the front of the car along with several Nationals. Link and I were near the rear of the car trying to hold back a rush of some twenty Reds. All of a sudden, Sergeant LI Chin dived under the car with a hail of shots following him. He had been hit with some shrapnel and was bleeding in a lot of places, but it didn't seem life threatening. His pants were blown off. Link looking up said, "Look at ole Two-Hung-Low, his bag almost drags the ground."

"Let's call him Too Sack from now on," I added.

"Right on, that's it, Too Sack." He was one of our American speaking Chinese. We were damn lucky he was with us, but at that time we didn't know how lucky.

LI Chin, Too Sack, was at one time in the Red Army and had come over to the Nationals' side. He had been with the Nationals only a short time, but was a very bright young man who was maybe nineteen years old. He could speak American, some Japanese, and of course excellent Mandarin.

The Reds finally gave up on taking us out and moved in another direction. We spent the rest of the evening and that night waiting for the worst, but nothing happened. All action seemed to be near the beaches. Lally said, "Let's get up on that hill over there and see what the hell is going on." It sounded like a good idea, so we asked Too Sack to run it by Col. Sing. Too Sack came back with the 'skinny'. The colonel already had that idea in action with our troops that we had left.

"Looks like we are down to less than a battalion," said Lally. "We better get some fire power. I see a couple jeeps and several trucks. But, I don't see anything heavy that we can take with us". We moved up the side of a large hill. As we neared the top ridge Colonel Sing called a halt. We were ordered to approach the top with caution, to stay low, and to be ready for anything. Several of us hit the top at the same time. We looked in silence at what we could see. A sinking feeling crossed us because all the ships had loaded up and were withdrawing.

They had left us behind!

We had over one thousand men unloaded. We were fighting against probably two battalions that were well covered, firing from cover, and picking us off like ducks in a pond.

I wondered if they were going to reset the attack and move up the coast. "It doesn't matter we can't get back," exclaimed Lally. He was right! Our future looked dim. Piss on the chicken shits! At that moment I hated the

Corps and all the bull shit about never losing a battle. What the hell did they think this was… a British Tea? I later found out that it was not a Nationalist decision, but it came from the American JCS. The one lone vote was our Marine JCS. That helped, however, it was two years before we found this out.

"You got to remember, Hollywood, this is not a Marine operation. We are just helping train the Nationals. We got to roll with the cards that are laid out," said Lally.

"Well, somebody is a candy ass. I know that from now on, for as long as I am alive, I am keeping a record of all this shit, and someday I will write a book about it!" (Of course I can't spell or write, but it's my damn book, and I'll write it anyway.)

Colonel Sing Wu called his remaining troops to order. It looked like we had about two hundred men that were left behind. We were lucky because we knew most but not all of the Nationals liked us Marines being around. However, these Nationals were trained by American forces and were used to having us around. We seemed to have only seven officers left, and the highest-ranking one was a Captain named Chow. Lally said he was a good officer. Too Sack said Lally liked Chow because he shared his women with him.

The first order of business was to find out what we had for food and equipment, so the Colonel gave orders for us to scout the area around the port city and get what we needed. The Reds had moved out, as had the Russian troops. It was easy because the Reds were really hated in this town. It seems they raped their women and looted the shops. The Colonel left us with very stern orders to lay off that crap and stick to strictly business.

We managed to get enough of a food supply for two hundred men that would last for four days. Plus, we picked up medical supplies and firepower. Most of the weapons were our own. All of us Marines managed to get hold of machine guns and rifles; plus several Chinese rifles and hand grenades.

75

Lally also picked up a flamethrower ready to fire. Gordy came back dragging his ass with a Bar (Browning Automatic Rifle), one heavy sucker for sure. We moved outside the city and regrouped. After my first taste of combat, I was still alive.

Again my thoughts go back to Hollywood, Los Angeles, and Marian Ford. I will always remember her senior prom, with me in my dress blues, and she looked like a doll. We danced to Glen Miller's band lead by Tex Bennicky at the Paledium. We won the queen and king contest, and we were runner-up on the dance floor. What a night! She wrote me after I returned home, but I let it all slip away; proving no matter how far I traveled or how many things I overcame, I was still a basic dumbass. I have always said, one part of my brain is outstanding, and the other half is filled with space. Marian came to see me when I returned from China. I was in a Navy hospital about seventy miles north of L.A. Marian loved me, and that's more than I can say for most of the other women in my life. Mostly they loved themselves too much to share their love.

The Golden Years Of Hollywood, hey, man, I was there. I walked the streets, and I saw it all. I saw the stars, the places, and everything.

It seems like all you do in life is say goodbye. When you have lived all over the USA and have been overseas, you meet a lot of people. Of course, in the Corps you meet many lifetime friends. What that amounts to, is saying goodbye so many, many times. It hurts because in most of the cases, there is someone you might be with on a daily basis. Then, all of a sudden, it's over like a puff of wind. Oh, there is talk of getting together again, the famous words, "I'll see you," are spoken, and then it's over just like turning off a light. It hurts, and it damn sure hurt me. A hundred times I have been in this position. I always knew that ninety percent of the time, you were looking into a face you would never see again.

Sometimes I go back to Shelburn and just drive around, just for the memories. Bill Mentheny still lives there, and so does Dick McHugh, two old running buddies from my childhood. They have never left the yard so to speak. To them everything is the same, and has been the same for fifty years. In some ways I am sure that is good, however, I would have died of boredom before I reached the age of twenty-one, let alone a lifetime there. No, I wouldn't trade all my experiences or even all the pain in my life. I wouldn't trade all my great friends and comrades, no way.

SYMBOL FOR LIAOTUNG PENINSULA
(Mandarin Language)
HULUTAO BEACH
1945

After a day of marching into nowhere, we were back on the beach area in this coastal town called Hulutao Beach. We moved into this town without any problems, for we were Nationals, and this was Nationalist territory. The Reds had no interest in this town. The coolies told us the Reds came through on their way to DARIEN, shot a few people on the street, and moved on through. The coolies said that more than ten thousand troops had moved by, and they didn't know what to think.

Where was the Great General? How could he let the Reds take over? We told them it was a one shot deal, and he was trying to take over Upper Manchuria.

Colonel Sing found us pretty good quarters in an old compound that was once used by the Japanese. The big problem for us was learning which way the Reds would turn their troops after the attack at Darien. If they moved north, they would soon run us over.

It was strange, for at this point in time, the main objective seemed to be to make sure they controlled the Port City. By not having any information about the locations of Red support in the north, we really didn't know which way to turn. We ended up guessing right, because they turned back to the northeast, and toward Mao's stronghold.

This gave us time to regroup. It gave us time for Colonel Sing and his officers to plan a way for us to make it safely around Mao's troops.

We learned a lot about the Chinese in this area. I said this area, because every section of China was like entering a different model of what makes up the standard China man. We found there is no such thing. They are very much alike, and yet the customs of one area will not hold true for a group one hundred miles down the road. This area was thought of as "San Pa Tao", or Three Blades. It was known for fishing, cooking, and tailoring. Anyway, that's what Too Sack told us.

For the first few days, it was all work. We had to clean everything in sight, as old Sing was a neat freak. He also gave us a speech about how things were really going to get bad at times, and that we had to be careful when we entered each new area. He said that what was Nationalist Territory today, could lean toward Mao the next day. He explained it was a time of taking sides. He said that the Reds and Nationals had stopped their civil war and banded together to fight the Japanese, but now that the war was almost over, it was a time for sorting out the territorial claims of the victors. He went on to explain that the Russians were supporting the Reds, and there was a big rush for control of Manchuria and Mongolia as well as for China itself.

"You know," said Link, "this is the first time since I have been in the Corps that we actually got the real skinny."

"You're right," said Bobby "O", "the Corps said move, shit face, and off you go."

"Yeah," I countered, "you're right, this is the first officer who ever told the troops the whole truth. We got to like this guy." We all agreed that Colonel Sing was an ok officer and a great leader, but that didn't keep old Blue Balls from banging Sing's girl friend when he wasn't looking. But one must understand, this Lally creature was different. He was blessed with a twenty-four hour hard on. He just looked at things like that in a different way. Ok, so he was nuts.

We spent two days of squaring away. As I look back, I can see the reason that Sing made us act and look military. Even though we were out of direct control of the Nationals or the Marines, he had to maintain discipline. A lazy, 'I don't give a damn attitude' had to be suppressed. What better way to suppress it than by maintaining a military posture?

Colonel Sing sent out scouting parties to find out the best route to take us to the Nationalist lines. We were split in two groups on this. Too Sack and I were assigned to go up to Yang Kor, about ninety miles to the northeast. We took eight Nationals with us, and Too Sack was in charge. Sing was hoping that we had some kind of outpost or some Nationals at Yang Kor. Also, he wanted to gain more information about Mao's newly controlled area. Colonel Sing was pretty sure that the only dangers would be bandits. We took two Jeeps with mounted 30 caliber machine guns, plus a half-track, some extra gas, and other supplies.

We pulled out at daybreak. Lally yelled out, "Be careful, watch your ass and bring back some women."

Too Sack said, "Old maggot, Lally's always thinking of women. He crazy marine, right, Shelburn?"

"Yeah crazy, but not as crazy as Gordy."

It was a bright sunny day, and rolling along the old roads was a battle of its own. You had to watch, or you would hit a rut that would send the Jeep upside down. The fields were clean, and we saw no one on the road for the first thirty miles. Then, as we came down a small grade, we came upon a couple of carts pulled by coolies. We stopped, and Too Sack talked with them. After twenty minutes of arm waving, grinning, and fast talking Mandarin, Too Sack came back to the Jeeps. "Well, I asked, "What the hell is going on?"

Too Sack said, "Well, old Shelburn, these coolies haven't had any meat for long time, and they like white meat. They would like you for dinner, grinned the little bastard.

"OK, OK, what's the dope?"

"They say no Reds on this road. They know of merchants traveling up north and coming back. No talk of Reds; they not near here. All Nationalist Chiang Kai Shek territory."

"Well, that's good news, let's hall ass." We started our journey again to Yang Kor. After another hour of bad roads, bad backs, and piss calls, we finally arrived. The town was a town with plenty of action. Lots of Chinese were doing business. This town had a lot of little shops on each of the downtown streets.

"Too Sack, what makes this town so busy?"

"Only town around, no place else to go, trade. All Road Traders stop here." As we drove through the main area, several Chinese came out to take a look. Too Sack said, "Shelburn, pull up here. It's the local police station." We stopped, and Too Sack went in taking two Nationals and me with him. Too Sack said, "This is high class Police Station."

A grinning fat Chinaman came out to meet us. I think he is the only fat Chinese I had ever seen. Too Sack said to me in American, "He like a goat; have two bellies!" while grinning back at the local official. "We are part of General's twenty-eighth Division. I am Sgt. Li Chin, and this is Corporal Bedwell, a member of the American Occupation Forces."

He saluted us and bowed, "I am Police Captain Yi Cha. Welcome to our little village. How may I help you?"

"We need maps of the area and a radio. We are separated from our units and must return. With Mao's troops in the area, we need to find good communications."

"I can help you, Sergeant. Several months ago, we had a battle here between the Japanese and the Nationals.

80

Two radios were found and several maps. I am sorry, but the maps are in JAP language.

"Ding how," said Too Sack, "let's look at those radios."

"They are no good to us, we no understand stations."

"Well, Too Sack," I questioned as he looked them over, "what do you think?"

"They are in need of batteries," said the wizard, "but we have plenty of these back at our base camp."

I said, "Now, maybe we can contact somebody on our side."

Too Sack cautioned, "Lally is right about these weak-assed batteries, Shelburn, unless we get within forty miles, these are useless, but just maybe, in time we will hear something.

Sgt. Lin took us out to eat. We had more rice and some fish heads. He and Too Sack talked for some time.

The girl who served us stood in the doorway and waved for me to come back to the kitchen. I told Too Sack I had to go to the head. He was busy talking so he never even missed me.

As soon as I went through the door, three girls grabbed my hands and put them on their breasts; they were all over me. I lay down on a cot, as they undressed me. I have never had three girls before or since, and IT WAS WONDERFUL!! They had never had a "Mig WA bing" before. It was like hitting the last shot in regulation time. (That's basketball talk.) She screamed a whole mess of Mandarin, and pulled me back down. In came Too Sack and the Sergeant. I figured my ass was grass. But the Sergeant grinned and said, "It will cost you for good time. No problem for you, he told Too Sack, or you, Sergeant, my guest. My friend no cost, but Corporal pay $3.00 American.

Too Sack said, "He no got three dollars American anyway, right?"

81

"So have a good time on me, one time only," said the Police Captain.

So, Too Sack went three for three, and I went three for three. At least the old wizard had to settle for seconds.

As we left our Police friend and the girls we promised to return. I knew damn well I would, if I got a chance. Too Sack said, "You know, ole Shelburn, these girls are whores?"

"No shit, Dick Tracy. Mig WA swell up.

"You betcha," said Too Sack.

"Maybe, maybe not. You don't get the clap every time, don't you know anything?"

"Ole blue balls Lally, be very unhappy pervert when I tell him of great wampum party. Right, Ole Shelburn?"

"Yeah, you're right. Let's pour it on ole Blue Balls when we get back."

If all went well, we could be back before dark, but we had orders to check out another road leading west, about half way back.

"Too Sack, do you remember where to turn off?"

"Yes," answered Too Sack, "it's just after we pass the ole man standing by the road."

"You are a piece of work, you know that? You think that ole man is still standing beside the road, after five hours?"

"He be standing by road, you see, you see."

"That's nuts, Too Sack. Do you have any other way of remembering?"

"Yeah, me remember creek nearby. Ole man is there anyway." How in the hell can you figure the Chinese out?

An hour later Too Sack said, "Road up ahead, see ole man standing by road." As sure as shit stinks, the old buzzard was standing by the road. I have never gotten over that. Too Sack never explained it to me. He just knew.

"Ask him if he has been at the road all day." Too Sack talked to him.

"OK, so what's the deal?"

"He say you no need to know."

"Up yours, you little dipstick."

"What in the hell does Sing want us to go this way for?" I questioned.

Too Sack responded, "Ole Sing, wise coolie, want to know everything. He no worries if he know everything. Maybe some Reds still near by. This is way the Reds went home. This road, maybe we get more information." Damn, I hate it when he is right.

Too Sack said we were to drive at least twenty miles to gather information. It was about time to turn back, when we came across a little village. We came to a halt in front of a mud hut where several coolies started waving at us. Too Sack had his usual long conversation, while all I could do was pick up a word here and there. Two young boys came over and got a closer look at us. One said in pretty good American, "You American Marine, yes?"

"I about fainted, but managed to say, "Yes, but how come you know how to talk American?"

"Mission people from USA, they have a school here, nearby. "I was really excited. Never in my wildest dreams did I believe that mission people were still here. I figured the JAPS shot them all!

I asked the boy where this school was. He said, "Let me ride, and I show you the way."

"It's a deal, boy. What is your name?"

"HSU CHU, but mission teachers call me Teddy."

"Well, Teddy, I am very happy to have found you." Teddy says to me "You too young to be a Marine looking at me.

Too Sack heard us talking and told Teddy that I was only 15 years old, " but when they find out he be only 15 year old in Brig". Too Sack continues on " How you do that ole baby Shelburn- Lally say to be a Marine your must be 17 ? In China no matter how old you were as long as you can hold a rifle up". For your information I am now 16 dip shit. Too Sack grins and changes the subject, Ole Shelburn some whites faces still in China like you be home

83

again, go to store get candy with mommy and daddy Ha Ha. I let this shot go.

We moved our convoy using Teddy's directions and we soon arrived at a large hut, much larger than the others. As we arrived, out of the building came three Chinese women and two white women. They had on the long skirts and were dressed in black. One of the white women was about thirty-five years old and kind of pretty. The other was much older, maybe fifty.

"My name is Helen Travis," said the older woman, "and this is Sister Carol. We are missionaries from Canton, Ohio. Welcome to our village. It's been so long since we have seen another American."

I went on to try and explain our situation. I also explained that we had to return to our base, but we were only sixty miles away, and I would return and we could talk then.

Too Sack explained that we needed to report to our command as soon as possible. I managed to ask one question before we left, "How did you survive the JAPS?"

She looked at me with the saddest eyes I have ever seen and stated, "We were treated as whores, and many of us were killed. They came this way several times in the past four years, but we would hide. One time they found us. They raped and degraded us all. We had twelve nuns, and now we have two. All the rest are with God in heaven."

"Sister, I will be back. I will be back."

We headed back to the compound. "Too Sack, they went through hell."

"Yeah, I know, Ole Shelburn, life in China is so cruel and so hard. It's always been this way. We will come back again. I got good news, too. They say that Reds are long gone. They heard that they all up near east Manchuria, and others going back to Mao's main lines, to the East. They many miles, over two hundred miles away."

"Well, that's good news anyway."

Just after sunset we arrived at the compound. Lally greeted us at the barracks and gave us an update on what had happened during the day. If anything, it seemed that Colonel Sing was ready to stay put for a while. He felt that in time, we could make contact with other units. I told Lally our report confirmed that there were no Mao troops within three hundred miles of our location. Lally said, "Good, because all the other scouting parties say the same thing. We have no problem here as long as we behave. Why the hell is everyone looking at me for?"

"O shit, Lally," said Link, "you know you're always the first out of the box."

"Yeah, but I got to cool it. When we get back, I want to make sure ole Sing gets the rest of my stripes back."

"Yeah," said Shelburn, "how many times have you gone from Sergeant to Private and back to Sergeant again?"

"I believe it's been three times. You feel better, Shelburn," countered Lally. "And, Shelburn, it seems I remember you made the same trip as I did, at least once."

"True, ole Lally," answered Shelburn, "but I never got past buck Sergeant. You were a Master Sergeant one time. Damn, how does it feel to be a tin god one day and a beetle stomper the next?"

"It's a real bitch, but rank here don't mean shit, but my back pay,

If we ever get out of this mess alive, would be much greater.

We told Lally about our encounter with the nuns and about getting laid, not by the nuns. We told him about the gook girls at the village, and we told him about the radios. He wanted to hear more about the girls. Lally asked, "Now, is it a whorehouse? Or a stop at a hut pump?"

"Both," said Too Sack. "Shelburn, you say ole Lally be excited and piss pants. He be on road before morning."

"True, Too Sack, I am sorry you missed out," added Shelburn. I had to tell ole Blue Balls. Look at him, Gordy, his eyes are clouded over."

"Yeah," said Link, "that's the way he gets. When the lust builds up, this happens."

"He big time Lust builder, right, Shelburn?"

"He is the best going, Too Sack, he's a 4.0."

For the next several days we continued to build up information, however, the radios were useless so far.

It seemed ole Lally was busy doing laundry several times a week. So he never headed towards the North to check out our "Village." After a couple of weeks at the compound, we decided to see if we could go on another scouting trip. We still were getting nowhere on leaving the area. I was sure the longer we stayed, the harder it would be to find our way back to General Chiang's lines.

Colonel Sing thought it was a good idea, so we got our convoy together.

Only this time we took ole Boss Man Lally along. Lally wanted to take a flatbed holding an Anti-Air Craft 88 with us so he could practice along the way. He used to be an artilleryman. I never did get that ten clicks away shit. Lally told me one time to fire when the enemy got within forty clicks. He told me that was about eight hundred yards. The lying sack of shit! That little lie cost some chink his mud hut. Thank God no one was in it! Lally shot at a truck coming up the road and blew the hell out of the chief's main hut, which was way on past where the truck was. Finally, ole Too Sack took it out with a 4.2 mortar shell. It was owned by a group of bandits who had a Red Truck they'd found or captured.

We were about fifteen miles out when we heard a plane overhead. We stopped and Lally said, "I'll be damned, that's a Zero." We looked up and you could see the markings. He came in low, and we thought he was going to strafe us. Lally headed for the 88, but didn't get a shot off, because Too Sack was supposed to be his gunner, in case we ever had reason to use it. Ole Too Sack was still watching the plane.

Gordy yelled, "That son of a bitch waved at us. What do you make of that, Lally."

Lally said, "He probably gave us the finger, dumb-ass, so keep undercover, while I get the other dumb-ass over here to help me."

Too Sack answered, "Number one coolie on way, o-master."

Then, here came the Zero again. Only this time he was much higher. About that time we heard the sound of Lally's 88. The next thing we saw was the pilot bailing out of the plane. We all cheered.

"I can't believe it, ole Blue Balls got a Zero!" yelled Link.

We got over to the pilot before he could get off the ground. Too Sack could talk some Japanese, but it wasn't needed. He stood up, and in perfect English stated his name and rank and asked to be taken prisoner.

Lally, after looking like he lost his marbles, finally said, "How come you can speak American?"

He answered, "I went to school, flight training at Scott Air Force Base, in Illinois. After I got home to Tokyo, I was drafted into the Japanese Air Force. I just arrived in China three months ago. I have been hiding out and also hiding my plane. I had planned to fly it back to Japan, since I heard the war was over last week."

"Your telling us that you never had any combat kills?"

"That's right, I was an instructor. No kills. I never killed anyone. Looking at Too Sack he said, "Including Chinese."

"Well, said Lally, "Let's go look and see if anything is left of your plane, because I know the JAP pilots paint their kills on the side of the plane. Let's hope we can prove you have no kills, or your ass is grass for lying to us." We had heard the plane crash about 20 clicks away. We drove a jeep over to the plane, which was spread out over a pretty big area. However, luckily for the Pilot, we found enough of the markings to show that he was "just a trainer", and the cockpit area showed no markings for kills.

"See," said the pilot whose name was Lt. Trea Kanoka, or something like that. I decided he needed a much simpler name. Lieutenant, you will now answer all questions as Smiling Jack. (In the WWII days, one of the comic books had a pilot named Smiling Jack.)

Jack answered, Oh, after the comic book hero?"

"Lally said, "What the hell is there that you don't know about the US of A?"

"Me know not to start sentence with word "me", but me use it anyway," and he laughed really big.

"So," asked Lally, "why did you stop to look us over?"

"My gas was not enough to take me over the sea, so I took a good look and saw American Marines. So I think maybe they not kill me, but you shoot at me anyway."

"Yeah, and he knocked your ass out of the sky, too, didn't he?"

"No," answered Smiling Jack, "he missed me. I bailed out and almost got into the flack of the shell, it was real close. Look, you can see. The plane was not blown out of the sky.

Lally looked so sad, I thought he was going to shoot ole Jack on the spot.

Seeing his mistake in not confirming a hit for Lally, he continued, "but I really had no choice, because the flack did cause the engine to lose power."

"So, Lally, it's still a confirmed hit."

"Yes," continued Smiling Jack, "a confirmed hit." Lally felt better now.

Link was looking over the cockpit and said, "What in the hell stinks here? Don't you guys ever talk a bath?"

Jack smiled and said, "Very sorry for stink, not very professional, but when I hear shot, I shit myself." I thought Gordy and Too Sack were going to die laughing, and even Lally loosened up after that one. "Me need pair of pants. Anyone got a pair?" Everyone shook their heads no.

Shelburn said, "I'll bet you got that skirt you took off Miss Titty at that Village packed away."

"It was on your bunk, Lally. I saw it," added Gordy.

"OK, so I like to keep memories. Yes, Smiling Jack, you can wear the skirt."

"OK, Sgt Lally, "I no care. It will keep the family jewels from freezing up." Again we got a big laugh. This guy might be a JAP, but he was quite a funny guy.

Link said, "How in the hell are we going to explain bringing back a JAP pilot in a damn skirt? You tell me that."

"And old Sing might have him shot anyway," I added. "Too Sack, what do you think?"

"Well," the great wizard said, "Lally, he is not like any JAP I have ever known. He looks JAP, but he talks American. He is very funny, and I believe him. He no kill anyone. Eyes tell story."

"You got to remember," I added, "he did shit all over Tojo's Zero."

"Damn it, Shelburn, we got to get serious."

"OK, OK, OK, let's get serious. Let's take Lt. Smiling Jack to the mission. They can keep him there until we can figure what to do."

"Good idea," agreed Lally.

I added, "He will be safe there."

Meanwhile, ole Jack was changing clothes. I noticed something around his neck. It looked like a picture. "Is that your wife or girlfriend?"

"No," said Jack proudly.

I took a close up look, "Well, I'll be damn! Look at this, Lally, this Jack is full of surprises." Lally looked and saw a picture of movie star Betty Grable. Again, he left us all shaking our heads, as we continued on this unusual journey. It had to be the only time in history that something like this ever happened. To get the picture, we have sitting in our Jeep's front seat one Chinese wizard and one Japanese pilot dressed in a skirt. In the back seat we have one hayseed from Shelburn, Indiana, and next to him is ex-Master Sergeant "Blue Balls" Lally. We had a hell of a crew. We were on a road in North China, and we were

89

headed toward a missionary village and a Chinese Boy named Teddy. Mercy...Mercy...

Soon we were pulled into the missionary village. Again, the sisters came out to greet us. They drew back when they saw Smiling Jack, "the evil enemy." Too Sack said to the sisters, "He raised in America; he no like others." The sisters were not sure, but they trusted us enough not to run and hide.

We unloaded some medical supplies and other items they were in need of. I asked, "Where is Teddy?"

Sister Carol lowered her head and said, "The police took him away to Yang Wao."

"What for, sister?"

"They say he steal money from whores at eating place."

"Well, did he?" asked Lally.

"No, he never goes to that place. He have girl here. He would not steal."

"Don't worry, sister, we will get Teddy back. We know the Sergeant in charge of the Yang Wao Police."

"Please bring Teddy home; he is like our son. Please bring him home. We had no hope for this, until you come."

"Well, fellows, it looks like we are going to be a little late getting back to the compound. We'll have to make up a big ass story- sorry, sister, a big story to cover this one," said Lally.

"Good show, ole Lally," I added. "Let's not waste any time. If we leave now, we can get there before dark."

"Right," said Lally, "let's load up. But, first we have to ask you, sisters, if Lt. Smiling Jack can stay with you for a while? We will leave Sergeant Gordy here to make sure everything is OK." It took some time, but we convinced Sister Helen that our Jap was indeed a good Jap. They weren't happy about it, but when we told her one of us would stay, then it was OK. Of course, Gordy raised a barrel of hell about staying, so Lally got some sticks out and the one who drew the short stick was the one to stay.

He closed his hand and asked Gordy to pick first. His stick was very short. Lally put the others in his pocket. Of course Gordy wanted to see the other sticks, but Lally told him, "Trust me on this one, Gordy. Would I cheat you?"

"Damn right," said Too Sack.

Lally said, "Just for that I should make you stay."

"Can't do that, ole Lally, me only one can speak American and Chinese."

"Too Sack, one of these days, I am going to pull your arms off and beat you to death with them."

Too Sack held his arms close to his sides and said, "Oh, Master Lally, no take Too Sack's arms off."

"Just get in the damn Jeep," said Lally.

Finally, we were off to find Teddy, and my mind went back to the three girls for some reason. After spending the night at the mission and talking with the sisters, we were on our way by mid-morning. It was pretty good day weather wise, so we were feeling pretty good. It seemed the weather had a lot to do with our well-being. Smiling Jack and the sisters were a real mismatch, but it was the best fit we could make.

Soon, we again arrived at Yang Kou, and as before Sgt. Lin was waiting with his big toothless grin. As we got out of the Jeep, Lally said, "He thinks we want push-push, and he is right."

"Ding How, my friends, you like our Village? You come to see girls, or you have other business?"

Too Sack responded, "Yes, Sergeant, we are looking for a young man from the missionary village. He is a friend of ours."

"Oh, yes, he in big trouble. He steals from storekeepers and from whores."

Then Lally said, "Too Sack, and ask him what it would take to get him out of jail." Too Sack asked.

The Sergeant rubbed his chin and said, "Well now, he in big trouble." In Mandarin he asked Too Sack, "Why you want him, how is he your friend?"

Too Sack replied, "He helps the nuns and is good to them. He only takes things they need. There was no sense trying to say he didn't steal anything, for it would be useless. The only thing this guy wanted was to trade the coolie for something he needed. Then Too Sack said, "Let's talk trade here."

The Sergeant said, "What you got I need? One thing I can use is American dollars."

"How many American dollars?"

"How many you got?" laughed Lin.

Too Sack said, "We give you much boo kou, $20.00 American, plus you throw in push, push for the seven of us, OK?"

Sgt. Lin rubbed his chin again, "Seven orders of push-push wear girls out. Me only got two girls today. OK, Too Sack, me make you deal. Seven push-push and one coolie for $ 25.00, good deal, very good deal."

Too Sack said, "Have we got the money, Lally?"

"Yeah, we got the money, Too Sack, but everybody has to pay me back."

"No problem, no problem." Lally had plenty of money. He was always loaded, because he always gambled, and he always won.

We made the girls happy, they made us happy, and we picked up Teddy, which made him happy. We were all happy sons-of-bitches; that's what we were. Lally had to pay more because Lin found out Lally was going for seconds.

Lin said, "He built like horse, ruin girl for regular trade, should charge much more. He come back, he pay double."

On the way back, Too Sack got in a shot at Lally. "You know, Lally, ole Lin right, you should pay double."

"No, triple," said Gordy.

"You're damn lucky I had some money, gook faces."

It was late as we pulled back into the village, but Smiling Jack and the sisters all came running out as we unloaded Teddy. Too Sack asked Smiling Jack how everything went. "Good, good," said Jack, "the sisters and I are good friends now. Me understand their pain and dislike for Tojo Japs."

I asked, "What in the hell are we going to do with Jack, Lally?"

"Hell, I don't know, Shelburn, why don't you figure it out? This whole thing was your making. I'll think about it. What would you fairies do without me?"

We stayed the night and headed back to the compound. "I'll bet ole Sing thinks the Reds got us. What's going to be the story, Lally?"

"Oh, I'll just tell ole Sing we got in a little firefight and were hiding out for a couple of days. Now, Too Sack, you make sure the mouths on those Marines that were with us keep their traps shut, or no more pussy for them."

"No problem, ole wise one, me tell Gook soldiers shut traps." (Too Sack would call the Nationalist soldiers "Gooks", but didn't like us to.) He really got pissed when we called him "Yellow Man". He reminded us that Japs were yellow and Chinese were just Chinese.

Things around the compound were changing. It seemed Colonel Sing was about ready to move us out. We were looking for orders any day now. That meant we had to solve the Smiling Jack problem. "I have an idea, Lally, let's just tell Sing the whole story, he can tell the troops, and maybe since he has not fired on the Chinese, they will let him live.

"Yeah," said Gordy.

"Link said, "Hell, we got Red deserters and all kinds of misfits already."

Too Sack added, "Yeah, look at Blue Balls, he's a 4.0 misfit, right, Ole Lally?"

"Too Sack," added Lally, "you are a silly little bastard, but it's worth a try. Since you're Chinese, why don't you break the news?"

"Oh, no," said Too Sack, "you top rank, you tell ole Sing."

Lally finally backed off and agreed to tell Sing first thing in the morning.

About 10:00 Lally returned to the barracks with lots of scuttlebutt. "First of all," he said, "Ole Sing about shit himself, and then he finally agreed to approach the troops about Smiling Jack. I also found out we are moving northeast in a couple of days. Sing feels it's time to hit the road.

That afternoon Sing called his battalion together and told them of the plans for moving. He also told them about Smiling Jack. Some of the Nationals screamed Chinese profanity, which meant "Kill the Bastard", but Sing finally got them under control when he told them that Smiling Jack would go with us. Sing told Lally we would have to watch Sergeant Ping and some of his followers, because he might plot to get rid of Jack. Sergeant Ping was a poor excuse for a human. He treated everyone like shit, so we would have to be on guard. He was afraid of Lally, and we hoped that would hold him off. The next firefight would tell the story. Lally would waste him in a heartbeat, and he knew it.

A few days later, we were on the road again .We now had four hundred thirty-one troops and plenty of firepower including an anti-aircraft gun, 4.2 mortars, explosives, fifty caliber machine guns, and many Thompsons. We had trucks loaded with rice and other foodstuffs. We had medical supplies, and everything we needed to handle anything up to a regiment of Reds, and that regiment had better be well armed. We were ready to kick ass, if needed. It was a good feeling. Morale was high. Nobody was sick, except Gordy, as Too Sack said, "Sick in Head, ole Gordy."

As we neared the road to the mission, Colonel Sing ordered a halt. Too Sack and Lally were ordered to pick up Smiling Jack and say goodbye to the sisters. I wanted to go and so did Gordy and Link, but Colonel Sing was the man in charge, so that was that.

94

About thirty minutes later, they were back, and we continued on up the road. We were bypassing our playpen, which were only a few miles ahead. I think Sing had heard our stories about push push and didn't want any complications. He was right of course, but we were sad anyway. I asked Lally how the sisters and Teddy were. Then he said, "I hope you told them we couldn't come by."

"Yeah, they said they would always remember you guys, and for our kindness, and they hoped Jack made it back to his homeland."

Link said, "I wonder if they will ever make it back to their homeland?"

We would continue to make friendships and move on, saying goodbye a hundred times over. It was never easy. We were rolling again, a powerful fighting force, and the sun was shining. All was good. (The adventure we were witnessing was something most only dream about. It was exhilarating! I have never felt more alive! I was proud of all of us, because we had the ability to organize into a mean machine. I credit Colonel Sing Wu; it was his leadership that made it work. We had killers, bandits, deserters, and some pretty tough guys with us, and to make us all work together, it was truly "Gung Ho".

It was time to move on now. We were told that with the coming of first light, we would be moving out.

The night before we moved out we came across two Nationals that had a young Chinese coolie girl tied in the air as they degraded her in every perverted way possible, She was only about 11 years old. Just as we were about to take them out here comes a bunch of other Nationals. They ran the two perverts off and cut the girl down. It took three more weeks, but we finally got them both. We found them alone one night, but we decided killing was to good for them, so we just shot their feet and hands off. That way the assholes would spend their lives as beggars. It was only fitting

We moved on the next day, to who knows what? We found out pretty quickly that someone was following

95

us. Too Sack said, "It's not those kids because they didn't follow."

I added, "I think you are wrong, oh wise one. I see two coolies with my field glasses." After traveling many more miles and seeing no action of any kind, it was time to settle in and rest our tired bodies.

Lally got up to take a leak and heard a sound, "What was that?"

Link said, "Let's take a look."

For the past two hours we had noticed a couple of kids tagging along behind us. That night, we stopped to rest alongside an old burned out village. Lally heard something during the night, and we went to take a look-see.

It was the two kids who had been following us. I grabbed them and told them to be quiet. They were too scared to scream or run. I got them food and took them to our tent. It was a young boy and a young girl. The boy was about ten years old, and the girl was about nine years old. We decided to try to take them to the next village because if and when the Nationals found out she was a girl; they would make her their whore. I had Too Sack, our Chinese wizard, cut off her hair and dress her like a boy. Too Sack found out by talking to them that they had come from a well-off, high-ranking government family. The Japanese had killed their parents, and for the past year, they had lived off the land.

JACK AND JILL

Jack and Jill became my kids and our buddies. However, we knew we had to leave them at a village. There were opportunities to drop them off, but I just couldn't do it. Things were about to happen that would force me to make a decision.

We were near the China Wall when Jack got sick. He had a really high fever. During the night he died, while he lay in my arms. I told him stories that he never understood. We buried Jack the next morning a few yards

96

north of the China Wall. It was so hard leaving him, but it was a time when death was everywhere in China. People lay in the streets everywhere. We took one final look and moved on toward our own destiny. A simple cross with the words "Jack, age 10, was a good Marine" marked his burial spot.

A few weeks later, we found a village that we felt would be OK for Jill. Too Sack found a doctor and his nurse wife who wanted to take her in. I will never forget our departure that morning. She laid her head against mine, since this was the Chinese custom for parting. I had given her a Marine Corps emblem, and she had it pinned to her shirt. It was tough. We were the only family she had known for a long time.

The Chinese have many customs. Jill hugged us and kissed us goodbye. She followed us for a long time. I almost ran back to get her. As we approached a turn in the road, I looked back one last time. A sudden wind came up pushing dust in my face, and just like that, she faded from my view and into the past. I will never forget. Nor will my memory dim as the years roll by. Someday I will come face to face with this little Chinese girl. I know it as well as I know my own name.

It was at this time, a change came over me. I was no longer passive and defensive about war, I became very aggressive.

JAP PRISON CAMP

Too Sack and I looked down more than one thousand feet at Hugh Lake.
It was nighttime. We could rest now. There was no fighting, we were well fed, and it was a good moment in time.
Too Sack said, "You know, ole Shelburn, my Grandfather Wa one time told me that when you find a moment in time that is good to remember, put it somewhere in your mind, so that someday you can draw it back. Ole Shelburn, for

97

me, this is one of those times. Someday this time will pass. We will live on, or we will die, but at this very moment, time has stopped. No one but you and I will capture and keep these moments. This is a time when two comrades can take a moment away from the war and share our hopes and dreams."

That night, we shared our hopes and dreams. We were a United States marine and a former communist soldier, now a national soldier, on a mountaintop near the end of the world, and we were sharing a moment in time. That time will always belong to us. I will never forget April 9th, 1946. (Nineteen years later, my son was born on April 9th.) It was also the date we returned to Mainland China for the gold during Operation China Pearl. That's when Too Sack decided to stay on the mainland. Too Sack told me he had a little brother named Lu who was four years old whom he might never see again.

Too Sack told me about the War Lords, like the Manchu, who still exist. "My grandfather, the ancient one, told me of kingdoms laid out with silver and gold. The warlords were very bad. When they rode through the villages, they would chop off the heads of anyone who looked up at them. They would do it right on the spot. They would rape and kill. After getting done with a rape, the warlords would push a blade up into the girl and rip her guts out. They were bastards one and all."

Murkden

After we had moved another twenty miles up a pretty beat-up road, we came to the town of Chinchow. As we entered the southern part of the town, we were met by the usual small gathering of the town's leaders. They were standing at the edge of the road as a welcoming or not welcoming committee. Since we carried the National Flag on the fenders of each jeep and were accompanied by a Lieutenant Colonel sitting up front, everything was, as it seemed. They were friendly.

Colonel Sing had given us orders prior to our entry. "Number one, leave the women alone, and don't take anything. I will do all the bartering. Number two, don't shoot anyone unless you are shot at first."

At this time we had no need to barter for anything, and after talking with the locals, Colonel Sing had us move on through. It pissed off several of us, because we could have used the rest, and Lally could have used some push push.

Another fifteen miles down the road, we ran across one of the worst atrocities the world has ever seen. The area we were approaching was deserted, but it hadn't been deserted very long. "Maybe four days," said Lally. The ground was still warm where the Japanese had been burning something. Later, we found out that it was a pit in which to throw body parts. The damn Jap doctors were doing experiments on Chinese coolies. We found all kinds of bones, from adults as well as little kids. The smell of death was all around us. We could almost hear the voices crying out: full of outrage and wanting revenge.

Lally said, "You know, Shelburn, they said Hitler was doing this to the Jews in Germany, and these little yellow-bellied bastards are just as bad."

We also found parts of several British uniforms. They were all burned, but one name appeared on the remains of a field jacket. There could be no mistaking this identification. It read: Sgt. T.A. Collins, BRAF (British Royal Air Force). This gave us the thought that this might have also been an Allied prison camp. We had been told that several were in this area.

Lally said real excitedly, "Look over to my right." I saw a young man standing at the edge of the building. He was about twenty-five years old, and he looked Mongolian because of his higher forehead and wide jaw.

"Too Sack, go over and talk to him. Maybe he can tell us about this place."

Too Sack went over and talked with the Mongolian. So did Colonel Sing. What we found out confirmed our thinking. This is the story as translated by Too Sack:

"My name is Wao, and I'm from Outer Mongolia. I came here with my father looking for work and a better life." He went on to tell about this place of shame as he called it. He had been made a slave by the Japanese, as had many other coolies in the area. He had worked to bury the dead and clean up after the doctors. He explained to Too Sack that when he came here in 1944, the camp had already been there for many months. Allied prisoners were shipped there from the Pacific fighting area as well as Burma. Americans, Britains, Canadians, Aussies, and many others had stayed here. As many as eight hundred prisoners had been there, but not all at the same time. The number stayed in the hundred plus area. It seems that as soon as a prisoner arrived, he was given an exam, and if he passed with nothing whatsoever wrong with him, not even a cold, he was sent to the hospital where tests would be run on the prisoners. Sometimes the doctors would take out parts, while a prisoner was alive and screaming. Their only purpose concerning the prisoners was to experiment on their bodies and to kill them. They killed them all; no one ever escaped. They killed Wao's father like he was nothing. No one ever escaped. Wao, repeated again, "NO ONE EVER ESCAPED, EVER."

He estimated that in the fourteen months he had worked here as a slave, the Jap doctors had butchered more than five hundred allied soldiers. He named several of the doctors, but only by their numbers. None had a nametag, only a number. Even the Japanese commander had only a number on his uniform. Wao told us he had found a notepad one time that had the Commander's name as a Heading. It was Captain Otca TaJama, Commanding Officer: Code 7.

He went on to explain that, when the Allies started winning the war in the Pacific, they closed the camp. That had been a few days ago, but the day they left, they came

100

out early in the morning and shot and killed everybody in the camp, including the Jap doctors. The only way he survived was that he was very lucky. That night he had awakened early and listened to the Japanese talking. He was locked down for the night and couldn't leave, yet he heard them saying everyone would die in the morning.

As he was let out earlier than usual, he was told there was much work to do today so we must eat at an earlier time. Of course he knew what this was all about. After doing his part of feeding the soldiers, he lowered himself down into one of the water wells. It was his only hope, and it worked.

He heard the last screams and then the silence. For many hours, he sat in the water bucket, waiting and praying they were really gone. Finally, he was getting very cold, so he decided he must take a chance. He climbed up and out of the water well and looked at the worst that man can do against man. He cried for the dead for many hours.

He spent four days by himself digging a mass grave. He used an old wheelbarrow to cart the remains. He buried over a hundred bodies in four days.

After this I said, "I have come across many true Chinese heroes during my time in China. This Mongolian, I would go to hell and back with him."

Too Sack asked him, "What will you do now?" He asked to go with us, so Too Sack asked Colonel Sing, and he agreed. Wao became "Mongo". I named him the minute I laid eyes on him.

Symbol of Mongolian Flag
The Mongolian Woman

At Kalgon as we geared up to move on, something strange was happening. Too Sack told us that Col. Sing Wu was meeting with officials concerning a mission they wanted him to undertake.

It seemed they had an important person they wanted Too Sack to escort into Mongolia, which was about two hundred miles away. Also this included getting into part of the Gobi Desert.

After an hour or so of talks, Col. Sing came back and called in fifteen of his most trusted Nationals. The deal was this: We were to take a woman of about thirty years of age to the Mongolian border and turn her over to the Mongolian ruler's troops. She was the sister of the ruler of all Mongolia, the feared Chiu Tse from the family of the Yuan Dynasty which went back as far as the thirteenth century.

Colonel Sing's first question had been, "Why don't they come and get her? They have an Army."

The Mongols figured that if they crossed the border, Mao might send troops to overpower them. Sing reasoned this was true, since the Mongolians had been careful not to get in either Chang Kai Shek's way or Mao Tse Tung's way, at least at this time.

The price for her safe return would be more than one hundred thousand American payable in silver, gold, and jade. Half was to be paid now, and the balance on safe delivery. The exchange rate was five thousand to one. Too Sack said, "It won't make us rich, but we should be well off."

'Yeah, said Lally, "it depends if we can pull it off and how many of us are left to share it."

There was one catch though; we could only send fifteen soldiers. Colonel Sing picked Too Sack and I to go on this one. Lally, Link, and Gordy stayed behind.

The Plan

Colonel Sing, the old taskmaster was at his best. Each piece of equipment was directed and laid out by the Colonel himself. We took the following:

The Demolitions team with Too Sack in charge, two well-trained Nationals, and myself. Our explosives included the usual C-1, C-2, and TNT.

102

The Guards were hand picked and the best we had. They were all experts with machine guns, rifles, and 4.2 M's. All of them had been with the Colonel for years.

Operation Mongolia
(We called it "Operation Royal Pussy")

The first order of business was to bribe the train master at Kalgon. The Colonel took care of that one. When we arrived at the station, everything was set. The train people, a total of six, were all in on the operation.

At 1600 hours on a cold day, we were on our way. Lally and four Nationals were to drive the jeeps and trucks back. The trip was uneventful. There was just barren land and a few coolies about.

We arrived on time three hours later. We said our goodbyes to Lally and boarded a seven-car train and loaded our supplies in the rear three cars. The caboose was set up with four guards. On top we had two guards. The rest of the guards were in the first car behind the engine. Too Sack, the girl, and I were in the second car. It had some mats on the floor to sit or lay on plus food and water. It had all the comforts of home. There was a makeshift outhouse with a screen around it and a hole in the bottom. It reminded me of home.

Very few people knew about this mission. We knew it would not be a simple two hundred mile train ride. Along the way we faced many pitfalls. One, of course, was the ever-present "bandits". At three different points in our journey we had to stop for water. We had enough coal to make it to the border of Mongolia, and the Mongolians would supply us with coal at the border for our return trip.

The people of Mongolia were tribe-like and were one the most undeveloped nations on earth. They still used horsepower, those with hoofs. They had come across some cars and Japanese jeeps, but only the officers had these. Their armies were equipped with old long barrel Chinese rifles and were pretty much a Calvary type army. Their numbers were like the Chinese (you never run out).

Too Sack and I were looking out the window of the old dining car as we moved away. Too Sack said, "Shelburn, we see nothing out window but rolling hills, a mountain pass, and two tall bridges as train go over rivers. There's not much farming here."

"What do the people do to make a living?" I asked.

"They very poor. They raise some wheat here, also some corn, just enough to live. Nearer the mountains they have goats, which they sell or trade and eat. Make ding how supper."

I looked at Too Sack and thought, "…And I thought Hollywood was bad."

It was a two days trip give or take whatever trouble we ran into. As I looked out the window at the drab countryside, I settled back in the seat, turned my head to the side so I could see the rolling countryside. The rhythmic clack-clack-clack of the train wheels passing over the rail joints was hypnotic.

My thoughts went to Too Sack. We had found him in a village next to the China Wall North of Peiping. He was sitting on a box with part of Red Chinese uniform on, looking like he had lost his last friend. Pointing in Too Sack's direction, Lally had said, "Look at that little bastard over there. He looks like shit warmed over."

I looked over, as we got closer. About that time the little fart said in broken English, " Hey, guys, me go with you, OK?" We looked at each other, and I pulled the jeep over.

Lally said, "Where did you learn to speak English, China Boy?"

Too Sack said, "Me learn from mission school in Canton; me Christian China Boy."

"What would you say if I said we should shoot you?" asked Gordy.

"China Boy not like that. Already shot one time by Mao Tse Tung. Get uniform from dead Red soldier."

104

"Are you a Nationalist soldier?" asked Lally.

China Boy said, "No way, me bullshit artist."

We all laughed our Asses off at that one. "OK, China Boy, you can ride with us," added Lally.

Then Gordy said, "If you're lying to us, we will cut your dick off and feed it to the dogs."

China Boy answered, "Me not worried, only rich Chinaman have dog. We eat rest of them; very good to eat."

"What kind of country are we in?" asked Gordy. "Hell, that's worse than those shit-kickers in southern Kentucky eating greasy-ass opossum."

"Yeah," I said, "my old Uncle Burlap says that if you go without eating for a couple of days you could eat shit with the chickens."

"Me, already heard your Uncle Burlap stories, Shelburn," said Too Sack, "He's one of the certified nuts in your family."

It took us a long time to trust him. Finally, in combat he proved he was one of us. When you find a twenty-one year old kid in China who could speak American, Japanese, and Russian, it made us wonder if there was more than we knew about this China Boy we found.

As the train slowed to make a steep grade, I looked at the Mongolian woman, and she spoke to me in a dialect that I could not understand. When she realized I didn't understand, she spoke to me in Chinese Mandarin and asked, "What is your name?" I answered and gave my name. She responded, "My name is Cha Kang. My brother is the ruler of our country; his name is Chiu Tse. He will reward you greatly for my return."

"Why were you in China?" I asked.

"My brother sent me there on a trade mission. My guards were over-powered by bandits, and all except two of them were killed. They took me to Kalgon. It was several days before contact was made for my return. I have been living in great fear for all this time."

(I could only understand some of the words, but with her expressions, this is what I made of the conversation.)

I also found out she was not married and was still virgin. She was a rare female in China. She was really pretty and was very small. Her hair was long and tied at the back of her neck. She looked younger than her twenty-five years.

Darkness fell upon the land, and she had fallen asleep. I woke up with her head on my lap. I realized I had a hard on, and it was lying under the cheek of her face. I was uncertain about what in the hell to do. Her two Mongolian guards were asleep at the other end of the car. There was a curtain between us, and Too Sack was up front. If I didn't get control soon, I could be a dead man very soon.

I stroked her face, and she started waking up. She said something I didn't understand, but I had no trouble with her movements. Later, she sat on my lap and we did the nasty thing. After playtime was over, she moved really close to me, and her words were very clear. "I am no longer a virgin; I am a woman," she told me. "Darling, you're the best."

Later Too Sack said to me, "I peep, and I see you kissing woman. What you think of that?"

"I think you're a nosy little bastard is what I think."

"I think you get us shot. You pull ole Lally trick," said Too Sack.

"Never mind," I said, "We are getting ready to stop at the first water hole. We'd better get sharp, oh wise one." There was no sign of trouble as the engineer slowed the train. The guards jumped off the train and maintained positions near the train.

Thirty minutes later we were on the way again. We started to relax. Then Too Sack said, "If the word gets out, about what we are doing, there will be trouble. There will be a big reward for the safe return of the ruler's sister."

I answered, "Too Sack, you have a great way of lifting me up and bringing me right back down."

The rails had a soothing effect on us. We were put off guard as we rolled along the barren countryside. There was nothing much to look at. I did notice a small village now and then, but few people could be seen. I wondered what kind of life they must have. They knew nothing of the outside world. Maybe it was just as well.

The trip went well; soon we would be at the border. The first sign of activity was about 15 miles from the border. Too Sack said, "Look over there, Shelburn." I saw around twenty solders on horseback about five hundred yards away. They were moving north just the same as we were. When I asked Too Sack what he thought, he told me that they probably had riders set up along the way to report our progress.

As we neared the border, the woman came to my side. Her eyes told me she would always remember me; they also said we would never meet again. She hugged me one last time, kissed me long and hard on the lips, and retreated to the other end of the car.

Finally, the journey ended as the train came to a small station a few yards from the border. I asked Too Sack to tell the leader to let me go across the border for just a moment. I wanted to say I had been in Mongolia.

He said, "They make keep your Marine ass, ole Shelburn, but I will ask."

The guards from both sides went together. They were riding magnificent huge horses, and the riders were well armed. I knew I was looking into one of the oldest cultures on earth.

Too Sack and some of the Nationals were talking with the leader, and since I couldn't understand a damn thing, I just had to wait. Three big trunks were given to our guards and were put on the train. Too Sack examined them, shook his head, and said, "Very ding how."

The woman walked toward a waiting horse that would take her to her people. Too Sack gave me a signal, and I went to his side, "Shelburn, you may walk to where the leader is standing on Mongolian soil." It was about fifty yards away. As I walked the longest fifty yards of my life, the woman pulled her mount alongside. Then, a strange thing happened. In perfect English, she passed me an emblem, pressed my hand into it, and said, "I will always love you, Shelburn. I will never forget." She turned her mount away and rode into the past. She looked back one last time. As I neared the train, I blew her a kiss and never looked back again. In my dreams she comes to me. Fifty years later, I still see her face so very clearly. Time has erased nothing.

Later Too Sack said she came to him to teach her the words she said to me.

Trouble came without warning. Two shots rang out, and the two guards riding on top of our car were dead. The train slowed. Too Sack looked out a window and said, "They have the rails blocked. I see many bandits and traitors. We hurried to get to the front of the car. Others ran to the back of the car and looked out. Shots rang out and two more Nationals were dead.

There were too many, and we had to retreat to the rear of the train. The bandits got the gold and retreated. "All for nothing," said Too Sack, "ole Sing not be too happy."

"I am not so damn happy myself," I replied. We counted the living and got started again. Nothing else took place. "Too Sack, what are you going to tell Colonel Sing?"

Two Sacks answered, "The truth, just the truth."

The whole experience had been worth it to me. I had been on Mongolian soil, and I had made love to a pretty girl, the sister of the ruler of all Mongolia. Later, Colonel Sing gave us about five hundred dollars American. I lost all of it. I gave some of it to the kids in the villages we came through. I also lost some of it to poker and pussy.

Thinking of the Mongolian woman, I started adding up my personal scorecard. One could not keep score in

108

China, so I will relate the score in terms of conquest by state and by country. From Maine to California, from Canada to Florida, from Portland to Mexico, Okinawa, Guam, Pearl Harbor, and Manchuria, I slept with…Well, to go on would be considered bragging.

We took a lot of crap from everyone when we got back. Lally was upset after hearing about the Mongolian woman and me. However, we had little time to discuss it since Sing had us on the move again.

JAPS STILL FIGHTING THREE MONTHS AFTER BOMB
Nov 15th 1945

Col. Sing Wu received word from a former village mayor near Liaoyuan that the Japs were at a compound near by, who stated that they were killing and stealing everything and taking their women. The former mayor was unaware that the war was over.

Col. Sing had been to this place many years ago, at that time it had been training compound for Chiang's Commanders. He even had some old maps of the compound. Sing sent out a scouting party to confirm this information. Upon the return of his intelligence people he was told that a Japanese Garrison of more than 600 men had been there for some time and was unaware that the bomb was dropped and Japan had surrendered – every coolie that they talked to had no idea the war was over. - Hell this was three months after the war ended? One has to remember that communications in the part of the world amounted to little or none. Anyhow: Col Sing knew this location was within 170 miles of North Korea (under the French at that time –the Koreans must have felt very secure). Col. Sing was sure he could contact General Chiang from there.

The location was about 70 miles northwest of Murkden The mission was to find it and take the Japanese prisoners.

109

OPERATION END ZONE
We called it game over Nips

This was to be our 2rd encounter with the Japs and as we found another allied prison camp. For the next several days' preparations were made for our journey. At 0900 hours on a bright September morning we
On our way taking everything we had. Up front did the rest of our commanders follow Col. Sing's jeep? All 7 Jeeps had mounted 30c Machine Guns. The rest of our troops were following in trucks, some were loaded with are food, medical supply's and ammo.

Link was taking with Too Sack about the bad road we were on, stating that" it was the pits" Too Sack countered with his usual " you candy ass Marine ole Link".

We didn't know then but we were to have more battles with great loss of lives before we left

Major Zin spelled out the operation in detail. The demolition teams were to play a major part in this operation, he made this clear from the git-go . He also made it clear as to why the American Marines were chosen for this operation.

Very simply put he stated " because those four crazy bastards and ole Too Sack have blown up half of the Orient already".

Since the Japs were still fighting for ole Tojo, thinking the war is still on, they would fight to the last man.

The Jap compound was walled in by Hugh stonewalls, with the guard towers reaching as high as twelve feet. There were four guard towers that could see across open terrain with good visibility up to 800 yards in all directions.

RE-CON TEAM

Col. Sing Wu sent his scouting team forward to see, in fact there were Japs at the compound, secondly to check their fire power capabilities and the number of Japs on hand.

The scouts returned in four days with a pretty good read on what we were up against. No firefights were encountered on their trip, as Mao and his cutthroats were far to the east trying to get ready for a continuing civil war with General Chiang's Nationals.

Lally said if they hadn't stopped off for "Some pussy" they could have made in two days. Then again Lally had a one-track mind.

Operations tent Briefing

Col. Sing Wu

"Comrades this is what we are up against. Yes the Japs are there, and yes they think the war is still going on. Our scouts have many reports from coolies as they traveled to the compound. All confirmed the following:

They think the war is still on

They estimate a force of 600 solders

Several tanks (maybe 10)

A dozen 50-caliber machine guns

Several large troop trucks + many smaller trucks-jeeps.

All the near-by villages reported that they rob them for food and other supplies.

Col. Sing presented us with a map of the compound and a diagram of the operational plan for our attack. SEE Diagram 1-C

We were well armed with automatic weapons and 4.2 's, flamethrowers and grenades. Plus T.N.T. C1, C2 explosives and tons of ammo. But nothing to fight their tanks with. We had 321 solders all of which had seen much combat.

111

The next day Col. Sing Wu was ready with his battle plan, it was presented to his commanders that day and now it was for the unit commanders to take over.

BATTLE PLAN FOR OPERATION

Our part in the operation was to blow up the guard towers, retreat past the open areas. Set up on the top of a large hill overlooking the compound from the west side.

To do this A-Company would open fire from the North side and we would take out the two guard towers on the east side. B- Company and C- Company would start a frontal attack.

After this was underway A-Company would be relieved or supported by D- Company and move back to our troops in reserve. See Diagram A-1 & A2.

To counter the tanks, Col. Sing had few options; he knew if they all got loose on us we would lose this battle. His reasoning for blowing all towers was the massive degree of Hugh chucks of concrete created would slow the tanks making it possible for his Assault Plt's to get in close and disable as many as possible.

Major Zin a career solder had be with the 28th Nationalist Division for several years and was in the enter circle of General Chiang's most trusted officers along with Col. Sing Wu. The major told us that many would never live past this battle. With odds against us I was sure he was correct.

However this was always the case when outnumbered 3-1. Didn't bother Audie Murphy much, nor did it bother General Patton; in fact he loved those kind of odds. So did Marine General Chesty Puller.

Our thinking (being dumb-ass young guys) was hell if they want to die for ole "Tojo" let the bastards die" "ole Gordy our certified nut stated the odds should be 5-1 get more Japs that way".

This operation was going to be night mission. Col. Sing figured we could get pretty close maybe within a mile

112

or two or perhaps on top of them before His scouts were sure the coolies were never give us up to the Japs because of the extreme treatment they had for the past two years, and history shows us that the Japs have always degraded the Chinese since time has been recorded.

FINAL BRIEFING

We were told that if we within two miles before a shot was fired, the seven Jeeps with the mounted 30's would fan out

And be approaching from the east bank as soon as the demolition team got all the explosives set up, hopefully all four towers. After that it was going to be full-scale shootout.

The basic plan was if we failed to blow all the towers, and the tanks got out are ass was grass. Fall back head for the mountains.

FILL THE NIGHT WITH FLYING CONCRETE

Lally and Private Cheng were to blow the main gate (South tower), Gordy and Sgt. Jung had the North tower, and Too Sack and Private Chu Yang had the East tower.

Link and I had the west Tower.

Every tower was to blow at the same time. For this operation we had do our job, there was no back up, no one else knew shit from apple butter about setting explosives.

If they had built 5 towers we would have fall back and head for the hills.

The operation went well in regards to getting there without detection. Sing called a halt and told us it was time for the demolition teams to fall out. Major Zin gave us a pep talk, and off we went. Now we faced a long walk. Each team had a map directing us to the compound. We had no idea what we faced however we were sure the Japs had no workable radios or they wouldn't still are fighting a war that was over.

The only communication went like this- the first team to reach a tower and have the explosive set would be Too Sack, his position was the closer so he should be the first one to get set.

Once we hear the big blow, the rest of the teams hit the plunger. We were using TNT only on this one.

If any of the towers failed to blow, it was to head for the hills. Get the hell away from those tanks.

Our troops would attack as soon as the first blow took place. Sing also had a designated area some 4miles to the east to regroup. In case we failed to blow any of the towers.

Link and I started hour-long walk to the compound the estimated time we would get near the tower was set at 0300 hours. The first order of business was wait until Sing set off a stick of TNT   out of range and at the edge of the woods leading into the compound.

As we approached we found that they only had a couple generators and had no security lights on our tower, however we could see the guard had a flashlight.

We carried our explosives and a 30cMachine gun on a slider dragging it along behind us. I said Link this damn slider is one heavy son of a bitch. Yeah I know Shelburn but remember we only have to drag it one way. O that helps a lot asshole.

We finally just at the edge of guard tower, so far so good. We got busy setting and waiting for the big boom. It was 0433 and things should start at any moment. The wait was pure hell. Anything could happen like getting spotted by the guard. Link asked if I had any water left in my canteen

We got up to the edge of the tower, the guard was 18' above us- he was not walking around so we were not sure if he was sitting or leaning over the edge, the tower was made so that looking straight down would be difficult. I placed the TNT as close as I could, hooked up the wires and Link starting rolling the spool. We had about seventy yards of line to unroll before we got to our cover. We

114

settled down and waited. Link said we sure wont have to wait long. I agreed. Not much time for idle talk with had to been a sharp lookout to make sure no surprises came up.

We never said a word for the next 15 minutes .I broke the silence " Link in 45minutes it will be I never got the last words out the signal came and I pushed the plunger BAMB

I never saw so much concrete flying in the air in my life. Japs were running in every direction. At the mail gate our assault Plt's were on them before all the concrete came down.

At our gate it was the same thing – we never even saw our assault team and we were within 40 yards of them. Damn I was thinking they must be good and I mean good.

Two tanks were lined up to try and get through flowed by a company of solders. We could do nothing at this point but watch. The Major told us to stay put unless a tank got through or we were attacked in our position. It was hard to lie there as some of our comrades went down, but we saw a lot more Japs being taken out.

The Jeeps were doing the most damage with those mounted 30's. Link yelled Grenade and we ran and dived for cover, the rifle grenade landed some 20' from our position, and we both got a few fragments from it. Link got a big cut on his face and my arm was covered with blood. But it was nothing to what we were seeing (guys would get a purple heart for much less in today's military. How could you ask for one when looking across at another bed and see guys with arms? Hands, and legs missing and you with a few cuts? Don't brother today's military. Different breed of men back then.

We could not tell how the guys were doing it was such as mess. Bodies everywhere, 50 or better weapons firing at the same time.

I said look at that National coming up to the side of the lead tank (the tank was almost clear of the debris) the National lobbed a grenade against the tread and blew it off – now it was blocking the way of the tanks behind him.

We watched as the soldier ran back to his squad. He never made it; he was cut down before he had moved ten yards.

It was at this point that Link and I lost are cool and ran to the assault squad and joined the ranks, under the command of Lt. Tein. Link and I both had Thompsons and 45's for weapons.

Lt. Tein told us 10 Nationals to try and get around to the North gate as less action was going on there. However he told us that the Japs were up to something because he had seen more than 30 Japs run over there and enter a building, a building that was thought to be where the prisoners were held and they maybe killing them off.

We got around to the back and got past the open gate that had bodies and three tanks blocking the entry. TNT really did a job on this one.

The solders in the open areas were easy targets, but unless they noticed us we were not going to open fire – that was not part of our orders.

One National found an open hall way and Lt. Tein (who could speak some American) about then we heard shots going off at the other end of the building.

The Jap bastards were executing the prisoners cell by cell.

We tried everyway we could to get to the cell area and could not find a way. Lt. Wein realizing that we would not be able to save them decided the next best thing was to try and get into an area where the bastards would be coming out.

We rounded a corner and found what we were looking for. Japs had two ways out. The way we came in and where we were now. The Lt. Split the squad, Link and I went out the way we came in and waited. It was a living hell waiting for the bastards to kill the last prisoners.

Finally the shooting in the prison cells ended. Link and I could hear them coming, laughing and having a good ole time. Until the little squint eyed pricks saw us.

Link and I plus a few Nationals set up on the ground and waited and it wasn't long because some of the Japs were getting shot full of holes and decided to try the back door.

We let several out before we fired (get as many as we could). When the smoke cleared we had taken 32 of those bastards to meet – their Japanese God (whom ever that might be – probably the Devil himself).

Our assault squad lost three men we killed 38 laughing devils.

Fighting now centered at the main tower. However we had one more job to do – see if any of the prisoners will still alive. All 71 were executed.

As for as we could tell – only one tank got through. It did a lot of damage and was responsible for half our losses.

As many as 200 Japs ran off into the woods, and a team was sent out to find them and execute them, just like they did the allied prisoners. However none were located.

Other than those that ran off not one Japanese was taken prisoner. They all died in battle.

SUMMARY

What a waste of human life. They could have gone back to Japan and joined the families. And lived a full life.

To me it had to be their commander's fault. Its like Col. Sing said, " They could have traveled to Korea and find out the war was over. They would have been taken captive but they would have lived."

No that was not in the plan. Ole Tojo and his cruel policies was the way it had to be.

Symbol Japanese and Red Chinese Flag
The Brotherhood of Hell

Moving away from the Mukden area, we continued our journey. It was very cold, and the trails were very hard. Many days we had to find cover from the wind and just wait it out. We were headed in the direction of Chihfeng, about one hundred forty miles away. The damn cold weather forced us to leave some of our heavy equipment by the roadside. We were now down to two jeeps and two half tracks. We also had a ten-wheeler we'd taken from the Japanese. We put all of our ammunition, food, and what medical supplies we had in the ten-wheeler. At times, we ran across enough Japanese equipment to supply a battalion.

We were about forty miles northeast of Mukden when our scouts came back and told us that we were about to meet a company of Japanese soldiers and some Red Chinese holed up in the next village. We always had scouts at least two miles ahead of us. They got a pretty good look at them, and they were armed with rifles and machine guns, but no heavy stuff or no motorized transportation. What really shocked us was the fact that the Japanese were fighting on the same side with the Chinese. Colonel Sing shook his head wondering what in the hell was going on. The Chinese Reds and Nationals had fought side by side against the Japanese during the war. Also the Japanese had always killed off the Chinese, since the beginning of time. Strange as it seemed, it was real. In time I came to realize the frailties of the human being. Some people would sell their soul for a cup of java.

Colonel Sing left no doubts about this situation. I have never seen him so mad. He called us together and made the following statement, "Comrades, my heart is heavy from what has taken place on Chinese soil. The Japs are fighting beside the Chinese. What I am about to command has to become an option for you. From this moment on, those of you who want to separate from my

118

command may do so and go your own way. If we all make it back to our lines, I will not turn you over as traitors or deserters. I plan to make war on this company of half-breeds. Those who follow me are expected to kill every single one of them. I want each Chinese soldier tied to a fence and beheaded. Tie a Jap next to him, but the Jap will not be decapitated. A sign will be posted as follows:

"The Brotherhood Of Hell." Not a sound was made as we listened in fascination to sing as he laid out his plan of attack. "It is time now for those who want to leave to do so. I know some of us are going to die this day; I also know that this attack could be avoided."

Everyone was looking around, but nobody moved for a few moments. Then a few of the Nationals finally started to move away from the group. One private asked if they could have some food to take with them. Sing looked at them and said, "You take only yourself, and for those that have decided to go, you must now go. You may not change your mind."

Twenty-one Nationals left the area headed south in the direction from which we had just come. As in all things in China, they having a saying to cover this situation, "They now walk into the past; they must now face their fears."

Link said, "Let's get it on."

Lally looked at Link and said, "You know, old Blue Steel Eyes is getting as mean as Gordy, do you know that, Too Sack?"

"Yeah," answered Too Sack, "he ole mean-ass maggot."

"Shelburn, are you up to this?" questioned Lally.

"Yeah, Lally, let's get it on, but Gordy can help with cutting the heads off, I want no part of that. I have enough bad dreams now."

"Oh, Shelburn maggot, ole Too Sack good head chopper. Red Chinese, no have spirit, no bother me, and anyway ole Gordy will chop off your share. (I knew that was the truth.)

119

As we approached the village, Sing moved us into a four-prong attack. He wanted no one to escape. We found no way to get them grouped; they were sleeping all over the place, so it was going to be a hut-to-hut combat.

Lally gave the assault signal, and as Gordy and I approached the first series of huts, I set my flame-thrower to long range and pulled the slide. Death was spouting from its barrel. I fired point blank at a doorway. Screams and shots rang out in the night. A blaze of machine gun fire from a window, kept us on the ground seeking shelter. I saw Too Sack run up to the window and drop a grenade. A few seconds later, the firing stopped, as the grenade did its job. At that moment one of the Nationals was shot in the chest while he started to make a charge. The same thing was taking place all over the village. Colonel Sing was on the radio with Too Sack. He gave the order to fall back to the edge of the village and regroup. It seemed we were taking a lot of hits on the East side of the village where most of the half-breeds were. A few minutes after that we got further word to wait until daybreak. We were to go back, hold our positions, and complete the job in the morning. If anyone came out to escape or surrender, they were to be shot.

We had lost twelve Nationals during the night, and that put us down to less than a hundred men. At this point, we had no idea how many half-breeds we had killed, but we did know it was much higher than twelve.

At first light we started the assault again, running and firing, hiding and running some more. After twenty minutes it was over. Those remaining came out with their hands up. There were about thirty Japanese and twenty Chinese. Sing had the Nationals line them up with one Jap and one Chinese, side by side all down the line. The ten or so that were left, he had moved to the front right in from of Gordy and me. I just knew he was going to tell us to kill them. I was praying that I was wrong.

Then Colonel Sing did a strange thing. These were his orders. Speaking to the ten who were moved to the front, he said, "You are the lucky ones; you might live. Perhaps you will live if you let me tell you the reason you may live. You are to tell the people you witnessed Colonel Sing Wu of the Nationalist Army do what is about to take place. The people must know that Chinese must never take up with the Japs. Let this day be a lesson to all."

He then ordered the Nationals to shoot the prisoners. It was bad, very bad. I had never seen it this bad. It was terrible, but we could do nothing. This was a Chinese thing.

After they were all dead, the medieval job of cutting off Chinese heads followed. I couldn't watch; I turned away. I noticed Colonel Sing watching me. I didn't give a damn that watched. To me this was bullshit. Link followed me around a corner away from the death scene. I said to Link, "The Colonel is a great warrior, and I know how deeply he feels about the Red traitors, but this is dead wrong, and Link."

"I agree, Shelburn, but as you know these guys don't think like us: those of us who only kill when someone is trying to kill us."

"Link, did you see Gordy use his weapon when Sing gave the order?"

"No, Shelburn, he didn't fire, and Lally didn't fire either."

"There may be hope for Gordy after all," I said.

We waited for a long time until Lally came and got us. "It's done, guys. There's one hell of a mess, and there's blood everywhere."

All of the villagers had run off. "Who could blame them," said Link. "Well did you take part in any of this shit?"

"No," said Lally and neither did Gordy or Too Sack. He fired his weapon to impress Sing, but he was aiming high. He never hit anyone."

"Good for Too Sack," said Link, "I know it was harder on him than us."

121

The fence was lined just as Sing had ordered. The sign was made, and the assault was over. We counted thirty-six Japs and over twenty Red Chinese dead. We lost sixteen Nationals.

Colonel Sing called the four of us Marines together. He stated, "What you have just seen is the hardest thing I have ever done. I felt it had to be done. When you have seen this type of thing done over and over to you, your friends and your family, maybe then and only then, will you come close to understanding what you have just seen? May none of us ever see this thing again."?

We moved on from this place: a place that will live in our memory forever. It will be in our dreams forever.

We were on the move again. Walking beside Mongo I said, "Did you help with the fence, Mongo?"

"Yes," he answered, "it was an honor."

As darkness came my thoughts returned to the early days of "Hollywood" and my boyhood. Looking at a quarter moon ten thousand miles away from home in a strange land, I found myself thinking of some of the people who had crossed my path. Those who are in your life for a fleeting moment and then gone. Those who are gone forever, except in your mind. Sadness came over me. I was thinking if Lally, Too Sack, and the others would just be a memory of the time that would pass into the inner chambers of your mind?

FLASHBACK TO HOLLYWOOD

When I was about nine years old a kid older than I, maybe sixteen or so, always came over and played his guitar and sang songs for Buster and me. He would sing of hard times and of life, as he knew it. I called him Red Guitar. I guess I never knew his last name. He was good, and he could sing and play for hours in front of ole Slobber Davidson's "Jot-'em-Down Store". As I remember, he never cussed or acted better than Buster and me. He was kind and caring toward everyone who passed his way.

The last time I saw Red, my Grandfather Bedwell and I were driving south on highway 41, and I saw him hitch hiking. I asked Gramp to stop, but he said he never picked anyone up. I looked out the back window of the 1941 Pontiac and waved to him. He waved back real big and raised his guitar over his head, as I'd seen him do so many times before. I was never to see Red Guitar again, but I will never forget him.

Another memory is of My Uncle Wayne he had one of his wife's relatives come by for two or three weeks every summer. I guess he never held a job; he just stayed with his relatives a few weeks and then moved on. However, he was not a freeloader. He worked hard doing house painting and things like that to earn his keep. He taught me how to swim and how to play basketball and baseball. Wayne called him "Traveling Sam". He came until my twelfth summer and was never heard from again. Wayne said no one ever heard from him again.

My little friend- folks called him "Little Billy"; he lived across the street from me. From the time I was four until I was nine years old, we used to have a code. We used coal oil lamps after everyone was asleep. We each put one in the window facing each other's houses. I remember one of the signs. It was three waves across the light meant I'll meet you outside as soon as I can. Two waves meant I couldn't get out tonight.

One night my mom told me that I was going to go over and stay for a few days with my cousin Peach; Lavern was his real name.

After I got home from staying with Peach, I went over to Little Billy's house. When I asked where he was, his sister told me he'd gone to stay with relatives in Ohio for a while. I kept asking about him, until one of the older boys told me he had died, and they just didn't want to tell me.

I think it hurt me worse than if they had told me right off. I still go see Little Billy from time to time at the graveyard in Shelburn called "Little Flock".

As I started to get tired and sleepy, my last thoughts were of Mom, Granny, Wayne, my little brother Jackson, Buster, Bugger and little Billy.

So many places and so many people have crossed my life. It seems that most of the time, it's the same kind of ending.

ZIN-TE VALLEY
Ambushed and Out Numbered

"Never have I seen the Nationals fight braver and harder than at Zin-Te". Sergeant J.L. Bedwell (Hollywood)

North of Linya
North China, 1946

We were up at daybreak and on the move. After traveling about seven miles, we passed through the Zen-Te Valley. We had no idea of the great battle that was about to take place. We were traveling along an old road full of rockslides and washouts. A bridge loomed up ahead, and Colonel Sing Wu called a halt. He sent his scouts to check it out, because he knew this would be a good place for a trap. Once past the bridge, the road snaked through a thick forest. There was one way in and one way out.

The first indication of a trap came from the small arms fire from our scout patrol. Colonel Sing received a short message from his lead scout Lt. Yen Li, "We are under fire! It's a trap!" Then the radio went dead.

The order was given to take cover to the right of the Bailey bridge we had just crossed. We pulled our trucks into the woods as far as we could go and started setting our cover. Lally yelled, "Keep close together; we are in for hell on earth! We are sitting ducks!" We set up a rectangular perimeter protecting an area about the size of a football field. Already we were receiving fire from the south side of the bridge and from the north where the scouts were.

Too Sack said any attack from the west would not come until darkness, since they had to come across a large open area to get to us. The colonel knew his stuff. About seventeen miles to our east was the China Sea, a possible way out.

The Nationals began to build steps up trees and set up sniper stations around our perimeters. I never saw such precision, of Gung Ho (working together) in my life. Within twenty minutes we had ten snipers in the air. The northern perimeter was already taking form. We had about a half-mile of heavy woods the enemy would have to come through to get to us. The most dangerous area, or so we thought, was from the south. However, they would still have to come through a half mile of woods to get to us.

At this time we weren't sure whether they were Reds or Bandits. As far as we could tell, they hadn't sent troops into the woods to the east of the road and bridge. Colonel Sing thought this was a major mistake by the enemy.

From the road to our perimeter was about a half mile. That area had some open spots they would have to cross before they could break through our defenses.

Heavy rifle fire was coming from the south where Captain Wu Tao's troops were. The captain had about fifty Nationals defending us to the south. They already had a thirty-caliber machine gun in place and several sharpshooters in the trees. Sing had already gotten one report from the Captain stating they were holding and they had at least ten kills with the loss of two Nationals on the ground.

Another attack was forming near the Northeastern side of the road. Several enemies were now approaching this area. Lieutenant Ou-Yang was commanding this area. He had platoons 4 and 5 with about 80 men. This was where the main attack would start, according to Too Sack, and he was right. He also said the main force would come at night from the open area to the west.

It was warm; there was no problem with the weather. There was about three hours before darkness would fall, and we had plenty of time to get ready for the main assault.

Sing would try to send a scouting party out at night to see what we were up against. Also, the colonel had sent a scouting party out toward the sea. This scouting party had radios and could keep in contact. The first thing they reported was finding a road to the northeast of our location. They reasoned it must have connected to the main road north of our position. It could lead all the way to the ocean.

As darkness came the firing stopped. It was just like some dogs barking, and then suddenly they stop. At 10:00 P.M., Sing got a report from the scouting party he had sent out to the west. It was not good. The first reports indicated a force of approximately five hundred Chinese red troops. With information we already knew, we would be facing a force of more than eight hundred. They would be coming from three sides.

Too Sack said, "Two hundred Nationals against eight hundred Reds… sounds about right to me." We all knew it was just a Too Sack reaction to everything. We were in deep trouble.

The scouting party returned to within our perimeters at about 0300 hours. Their report began to shed some light on the situation. After conversing with his scouts, Colonel Sing called his officers together and gave us the 'skinny' (Marine Corps talk). His scouts had come across a prison camp. It was not more than twelve miles from us and three miles from the ocean.

The camp held about fifteen hundred prisoners: a mix of Chinese, Japanese, and Koreans. Approximately forty guards were in the process of bringing prisoners out and shooting them. They also added that the prisoners being shot looked like the sick and dying.

It was Colonel Sing's opinion that we had walked into a troop movement heading toward this camp. They were probably supposed to relieve the guards and move them closer toward areas under the Red control.

Now what were we to do? Whatever we were going to do would have to wait, because at that very moment the attack from the west was started. Lally ran up and said that more than a hundred Reds were moving up across the open terrain. They were on foot and almost within firing range. We had managed to set up some explosives and land mines just outside our holding area, and they would soon be approaching them.

The first land mine went off within one hundred fifty yards of Gordy's position. It was black out. There was no moon, just darkness. Gordy and I were hiding behind some huge trees. Lally was overhead in a tree acting as a sniper. Too Sack was also in a tree about thirty yards to our right. We had about thirty Nationals on the ground near us. Reports from the radio confirmed it was an attack from the north, the south, and from the west. However, the big numbers were right in front of us.

For the next three hours, the battle raged on. We were able to hold our positions, but the question was would we be able to hold them much longer?

As daylight came, they backed off, at least for the time being. Colonel Sing got a body count; it was not good. During the night raid we had twenty-one dead and fourteen who were wounded so badly they would not be able to fight again, even if they lived. Our medical supplies were limited. We had four trained medics and no doctors. The wounded were at the mercy of God. All that could be done was ease the pain.

The estimated body counts for the enemy showed some sixty-plus were dead. Our head count was two hundred twenty-nine men. With the scouts missing and probably dead, we came up with a count of two hundred nine men.

Colonel Sing was a great thinker and a great leader. He came up with a plan for us to defeat the enemy. His plan was daring and dangerous. Basically, the plan was to immediately attack the guards at the prison camp, take them out, and tell the prisoners they would be released to fight their enemy, the Red Army. Colonel Sing knew they hated the Reds, because they were the ones responsible for letting them starve to death. It was a plan that could make us or break us. He would promise to take them to safety and a ship back to Japan or Korea.

We had plenty of firepower to give them. We had more than seven hundred rifles and plenty of ammunition. Most of the rifles were Japanese-made anyway. Using them would be no problem, as long as they didn't use them on us.

Within an hour half of our total force was on its way to the coast. If we were attacked during the daylight hours, we would be facing superior odds that were nearly superhuman. Our only hope was they were planning another night attack to finish us off.

"There are too many. It's here," said Lally. "It will take a good eight to ten hours for Sing's troops to return with the reinforcements, if in fact it works at all."

Too Sack was assigned to the group that left. Lally, Gordy, and I were on our own; it was a sick feeling. Too Sack was always with us, side by side. At this moment we all felt the same thing. We felt that Too Sack, our wizard, was our good luck charm.

At 010:00am an attack was formed from the north and the south. So far no attack came from across the open terrain to the west.

Lieutenant Shu Wen was the Nationalist Commander to our north perimeter, and Lieutenant Mi Teng was in charge of the south perimeter. The two commanders had about thirty-five men each. The remaining troops were with Lally, Gordy, and me defending any attack coming from the west.

Gordy said, "Let's move some of our people to the north. Lieutenant Shen is losing ground. He's outnumbered twenty to one. I just talked with him on the radio."

Lally said, "Give me the radio, Gordy. Lieutenant, what is the situation at your end?"

"Very Bo-how, Lally, me already lose five men. We have fifteen kills, yet they keep attacking."

"Lieutenant, try and hold as long as you can. If you lose another ten men, you must retreat to the woods. We'll send a few men your way. Keep me posted every five minutes."

"Semper fi, Lally, me hold as long as me can!" answered the lieutenant in broken English.

Meanwhile, the attack from the south had slowed. Lieutenant Mi Teng reported he had driven back the attackers, losing two men and killing twelve of the enemy.

"Damn it," said Lally, "at this rate we can't last the rest of the day. They don't give a damn how many they lose. Hell, they can always find more China men. I think that must be their plan, keep hitting us, a little during the day. Come tonight, they'll charge across the open terrain from the west and clean us out."

"I think you're right," said Hollywood. "It's 0100 hours now. Colonel Sing will never make it in time to save us."

"Now, Shelburn, since Too Sack is holding Sing's hand, I, the Marine wizard might have figured out a way to buy us some time. What time was that attack last night?" Pointing the question to me.

"About 0200 hours, Lally," I answered.

"Well, said Gordy, "the Chinese always attack at the same time, right Sergeant Ni?" He was assigned to the west sector.

"Ding How, Lally. Reds always use same times for attacks."

"That's kind of dumb," I said.

"Yeah, but I like it, I like it," countered Lally. "Listen up, assholes, if we are still around by dark. I want to use every one of us on the western front to go to the trucks at first dark. Gordy, how many five gallon cans do we have?"

129

"About thirty-five."

"Good, now, how many dumb Asses will it take to pull and push two of our `gas trucks' up from the woods?"

"Oh shit," I answered. "It will take twenty guys over an hour."

"Ding-how, guys, we are going to fry the bastards. That grass out there will go up like a Chinese fire drill! The wind has picked up today, and it's blowing from east to west."

"Perfect," said Gordy.

"Yeah," I answered, "if the winds don't shift."

"Shut up, Shelburn! Let's think positively, unless you got a better idea?"

"No, Lally, I stand corrected, you are a damn Marine wizard!"

As darkness came we strained our guts out moving into the open area. We were lucky because for the second night in a row, we had no moon. We carried gas from the half-tracks holding about eight hundred pounds of gas each. We loaded up our five-gallon gas cans. We were so high from the gas fumes we got sick as buzzards. However, by 0100 hours, it was all set. The enemy was none the wiser; we had pulled it off.

Lally set some explosives up in several locations, ran a line, and set the plunger. We had covered the open area ten yards deep and more than five hundred yards across. That left two openings. Each was about fifty yards across. We loaded this area with land mines.

We returned to our positions and prayed for a 'divine wind' as the Japanese say. Lally tried to get Sing on the radio, but got no answer. This didn't bother us much because these radios were useless further than a distance of ten miles.

The waiting was a nightmare. At 0330 hours, Gordy said, "So much for the Chinese time table."

Lally shouted, "Look...here come the bastards! I've got to wait until they get within fifty yards, because that's when they started firing before. Let's hope they don't

130

smell the gas and then turn back. Oh, fuck it, let's rock and roll! With that, he pushed down the plunger setting off the sky and turning it into a blood red instrument of death by fire. The grass burned so fast we could not believe it. The torching had begun.

We would never forget the screams and the outlines of men burning to the death. At the same time this was taking place, they attacked from both north and south.

A frantic call came from Lt. Shen's radio by one of the Nationals. The sergeant picked it up. He stated they had been overrun and that Lt. Shen was dead. The rest of the troops they had left had run into the woods for cover. He also informed us that more than a hundred Reds would be upon us within a few minutes.

We also received another report from Lieutenant Mi Tang, and his troops were holding so far.

Lally moved us into position so we could take on the northern invasion, since the western side was well in hand at this point in time. It was now 0400 hours. Right on schedule, the Reds from the north arrived at our position. It was so dark that everyone was shooting anything that moved. The best place to be was in a tall tree, but it was too late for that. Lally said, "Let's stay close together. If we get separated now we are done. Let's move back into the woods another five hundred yards." It was now every man for himself. We ran as fast as we could. We found an area we liked. We decided it was the place to make a stand. We climbed some trees and waited. It was now 0500 hours.

The battle raged on nearing the daylight hours; we could only guess what was going on. We tied ourselves in the trees and waited.

Lally said, "I think we are winning. I hear Jap rifles firing. Old Sing has made it back!"

We waited another two hours until the firing died down. Finally, there was no sound of gunfire as daylight came.

On Lally's order we came out of the trees and started back to the scene of the killing ground. Lally got on his radio, and I'll never forget what he said. "Colonel, Sir, I would like to inform you that Shelburn, Gordy, and I are alive. Also Sergeant Ni Tran is alive. If you're alive, please confirm."

We were very happy to hear the voice of our great leader on the other end. Sing answered, "I knew somehow you guys would make it. You have made quite a mess here, ole Lally."

"Thank you, sir," said Lally. "Sir, we will be with you in about fifteen minutes."

When we cleared the woods, what we saw was unbelievable! The dead were everywhere. According to the colonel's final count:

300 Reds were burned to death in the fire.
The Nationals and Japanese killed 270 Reds.
157 Nationals were killed in action.
32 Nationals were wounded and lived.
16 Japanese prisoners were killed fighting alongside Colonel Sing's troops.

The smells of death were too much, and Sing ordered us out of the area. We marched to the sea. The Japanese had done well. I wondered if the Colonel would have acted the way he did at the brotherhood of hell, if he had seen how well the Japanese had fought with the Nationals? The Colonel was good as always to his word. Plans were made to give them a choice. We would give them food and water and head them for Korea, or they could stay with us. Over two hundred decided to stay with us. The balance headed for Korea, but most of them were Koreans.

Too Sack, walking beside us on the way to the sea, said, "Good thing ole Too Sack had Lin Tzy looking after you, or you be fried Bing, fried Marines."

"Who in the hell is Lin Tzy, Too Sack?" asked Lally.

"He over all Chinese Wizards, ole Lally," said Too Sack.

Lally looked at Link, Gordy, and I and shook his head.

"You start big ass fire, ole Lally?" questioned Too Sack.

"Who else but a Wizard would dream that one up, oh smart one?" replied Gordy.

Too Sack looked at Lally and said, "Another year or so, and you be first class wizard like ole Too Sack." It was a good moment, the first in a long time.

We would never forget this battle. It would be in our dreams forever. We lost so many good warriors. The China Marines, Colonel Sing Wu, and the Japanese--we were comrades now. How strange? The hated enemy was now our comrades, overriding ToJo, the Marine Corps, and everything else. We were comrades forever.

We moved away from this area and headed northeast. Again we were a walking army of over three hundred men strong. We were a combination never before formed anywhere in the world: American Marines, Japanese, Mongolians, Chinese, Koreans and a few Manchurians.

As we moved toward the hills ahead, my thoughts went back to Shelburn and the days of Buster, Bugger, and Peehole. We had gotten up one June morning and decided to spend some time down at the Gob Pile, an ole deserted mine area. We could throw rocks, cuss, look for snakes, and knock them out with our slingshots. Buster could take out a copperhead ten feet away. Bugger shot at one behind me that was sitting on a tree limb. He shot at it, hit the limb instead, and the son of a bitch landed on my pecker and took a snap at me, before Buster took him out. "Did he nail your pecker, Peehole?" asked Buster.

"No, but he sure as hell tried."

"He must be a damn pervert," added Bugger.

"Hell, Peehole, its no big deal. The only thing you use that for is to take a leak with," said Buster. "We can take you up to Claude Hall's garage, and have him drill a hole in your belly button and you can piss out of that."

133

"Vera Dean wouldn't be happy about that," added Bugger.

Yeah, I forgot about her," said Buster.

We all laughed and moved on down the mine. Buster said, "Look, here comes ole Beryl Hiatt, and he has his rifle, so don't piss him off, Peehole. Remember the last time?"

"Yeah," said Bugger, "you called him a skinny morfidity, and he fired a round at you before you got all the way around the coal shed."

"Oh, piss on ole Beryl," I said.

Cue Ball, his Hollywood name, had a pale white, round head, and I named him the only human Cue ball.

Ole Cue ball got the first word in. "I don't want any shit out of you, Peehole, or I'll put a round up your ass.

I had to be careful, because ole Cue ball wasn't zipped all the way up). "Don't need to worry about that, Cue-ball. I am no match for your twenty-two."

"Damn right," added ole Cue ball, thinking he was in control.

"But as soon as I could get close enough, I was going to shove that rifle up his yang yang. I moved closer. He didn't notice because Buster had him busy telling him about the snake. I jumped him and took his rifle away; he was mad as hell.

"So now, Cue-ball. As you were saying?"

"I weren't going to shoot you, just shoot at you," Cue ball said.

"Oh, give him the damn rifle back, Peehole. He isn't going to shoot you."

"OK, but, Cue-ball, watch where you point that thing."

"Yeah," added Buster, "if you shoot Peehole, I'll kill you off, and then Bugger is the only one left to shag Vera Dean." We all laughed, and things were fine for the moment.

Many years later Cue ball did shoot and kill somebody and spent his life in prison.

134

An order to halt brought me back to China. It was time for Colonel Sing to get his troops lined out. "Get the sharpshooters assigned, and see what skills these Japs can add. We will camp here for the night. In the morning, we will move out toward new adventures and new places. Maybe we'll get closer to the Nationalist lines.

It seemed so strange to me that at the "brotherhood of hell" battle, Sing had wasted everyone. Yet now, he used the Japs to help us. I asked Too Sack about that one.

He said, "The colonel so upset by what he had done, he had to make up for his actions in some way. This is his way."

"It still seems crazy to me, Too Sack."

You think we crazy? You Americans crazy, to. You have dogs for pets, crazy ole Sheburn."

"Yeah," I thought, "we pet them; you assholes eat them."

SWEET MAE

Sergeant Li Chen and I came upon a village which had been looted only hours before and laid to waste. Too Sack found a young girl with a note still in her hand as death looked out of her eyes. I closed her eyes as Too Sack read the note. "My name is Mae. Time is short as the Machos are upon us. My father worries about the rice, my mother worries about our future, and my little sister worries about silly things. So why do I worry about so many things? Like who will I become? Will I be a good person, or will I be much less? Will the God in the sky love me, or will I become like the Godless souls of the Red Army who live by the hand of death? Will the Red Army come and rape me and kill us all? Will I have a husband and a child? What will I be?"

We buried a pretty young girl of no more that fourteen years that day that never lived to find out what she would be. I think in death she left this world having committed little, if any sin, and from that moment she was in the

135

loving arms of the God in the Sky. Our marker for Mae simply stated: Worry no more, sweet Mae, you are now in the arms of the God in the Sky... October 12, 1946. We signed the marker : Red Army Killed this young girl . Sgt. Bedwell USMC and Sgt. Li Chin Nationalist Army buried sweet Mae.

SYMBOL FOR CONFUCIUS
VILLAGE OF THE BURNING ROCKS

We continued our journey through the North China countryside. The air was cool, the wind was strong, and we were tired. The troops were restless. Needless to say, tempers were short. Our supplies were rationed. We had two meals a day, one at daybreak and at evening light we had a bowl of rice before bedding down. Our numbers stayed around one hundred as we picked up a few as we moved from village to village and lost a few during various battles.

We approached a very prosperous village. We looked down at the lowlands coming in from the mountainside. It was a beehive of activity. Never had I seen such prosperous people in China, but something was wrong. Too Sack told us it was the spiritual village Confucius wrote about it. It was a forbidden city. Legend said that even the Japanese stayed clear of this village after countless adverse tribulations. In 1937, the Japanese had attacked the village. Then, one of the worst windstorms in history, including fierce rains and flooding, wiped out the entire Japanese force.

Even the warlord Fung Chu tried to attack in the 30's; he, too, was repelled by nature. The area outside of the village was surrounded by ground that was laden with sulfur-filled rocks. I gave it the name "Village of the Burning Rocks". The eruption of a volcano nearby helped to create the legend. So, through time the village had prospered. The rules were, if you were born there you were welcome. Harm seemed to come to anyone else who

136

entered without permission. Since those early times, no army had ever tried to take over this village. Colonel Sing was in a pickle. We needed supplies, but we had nothing to trade. He debated moving past this village. His troops were close to mutiny at this stage.

Our resident wizard, Too Sack, had decided upon a brilliant plan. He told Sing that part of the legend talked about foreigners of a different race who would come and offer guidance to the village explaining the creation. Too Sack may have been referring to the missionaries. But history didn't show missionaries ever ventured this far. Too Sack's plan was to put the four of us back in our Marine uniforms. Too Sack would come with us, since he was not afraid to enter the village. He was one crazy gook who was not afraid of anything. As we entered by the road leading into the village, we looked for disaster to take place. At the entrance gate, we met the village chieftain and four elderly gentlemen sporting white beards.

Lally said, "Shit, they're Mennonites!"

Too Sack reminded Lally again of the legend about the different colors of people who would some day come. His proposition was to tell the villagers that we were searching for the village to fulfill the village's destiny. Too Sack said we would be treated like gods and no harm would come to us. Colonel Sing and the high-ranking Nationals still with us said Too Sack was nuts and they would not go near the village. Much discussion took place. Finally, two of the elders came up and looked us over while hundreds of village warriors were on top of the mud huts ready to take us out.

We were escorted into the main area about half a mile long. The whole area was lined six feet deep with curious faces looking upon four white men for the first time ever. It was unreal. This was a little town with stores and farmland like any town you would see on any river basin. They had it all. The women still had bindings on their feet. Out in the center of the road, a long table had been set up. Too Sack listened for over an hour before he was allowed

137

to speak. They were asking about us. He had to make up stuff as he went along. He told them a mission sent us from Shanghai. He said that we would tell them about the great oceans and the peoples of the world.

"Too Sack sure got us into a mess this time," said Link. What it really amounted to was that we would actually be teaching them about the rest of the world through Too Sack's translations. In exchange for this, we would be granted supplies of food. We could pass around the village, but we could not go into the village since no one was allowed to enter. Finally, a schedule was made, and for about three hours a day, each one of us would pick a subject area.

Each of us had different lectures. Lally talked about the cities of the world, of course Too Sack was busy translating for each of us. It got kind of screwed up but they did learn about the outside world. I talked about the industrial revolution. Gordy's area of expertise was to be the advancement of modern weapons. Link discussed the lifestyles of the Europeans at that time. The rest of the time we were free to visit around the stores and stuff. However, even the four of us were asked to leave at dark.

After about three days, they quit coming up and touching our skin. I don't know if they thought of us as gods, but they certainly approached us with caution. Lally was the first to get us into hot water with girls. Sex was so open that it was scary. The men and women had the same toilets. Breasts were bare. When anyone needed to take a leak, they did it anywhere. They'd just stop and squat. Of course, Lally was the first to show off and take a public leak. He was built like a mule so he drew a crowd of women. The very next morning all the women would point at our privates and utter the Chinese words for "big peckered man". This had to come from Too Sack since he was the only one who understood them. Colonel Sing could talk some English, but Too Sack was the best.

The women came out of the village and took care of the troops as soon as it got dark each night. Lally had a sign, written in Chinese, placed in front of his tent that said, "Too Big For Chinese Girl". Well, they still came every night. You could hear all kind of noise coming from Lally's tent. The first sound you heard was Oooh, then followed by a scream, and then followed by a Chinese word Too Sack said meant Yes, Yes, followed by another scream. It wasn't too long before the villagers knew what was going on.

The chiefs had a big meeting, and our stay was much shorter than we had planned. Too Sack blamed Lally, because the chief's daughter was the first one lined up in front of Lally's tent every night.

I enjoyed teaching the Chinese about America, even if I had to wait on Too Sack to explain everything I said. I think we all did. I guess I had to agree with Too Sack. It was Lally and his abnormality that pushed us out of a very nice village. Too Sack told me the chief in his words " Chief really liked us telling them about the outside , but just too much "push-push".

Head them up and move them out. As Too Sack said, "We push, forever forward, looking for our destiny."

Walking alongside Too Sack, I looked down and noticed he had new boots. "Girls give me boots to get in ole Lally's line first."

"Damn, you know what you are, Too Sack?' you're a pimp.

He answered, "Yes, Too Sack one smart coolie. , a damn pimp is what you are ." Too Sack in no mood for Shelburn bullshit."

"Well, Too Sack, in the States we got a name for those who take gifts

For lining the girls up. That makes you a big time pimp."

Too Sack grinned, "Ok, Too Sack pimp. Damn good pimp, too. Get boots and plenty push push from the mountain girls.

"Say, Shelburn, maybe we find our way home today, yes, maybe today..." It was wishful thinking.

Chinese symbol for the old ones
Ancient One
June, July, August 1946

As we approached any village, it was a usual move for us to regroup. Colonel Sing and his officers, four lieutenants and one captain, laid out the plans for what lay ahead. It seemed we had one hundred fifty-three men total, plenty of ammo, two jeeps that would run, a couple of half tracks, thirty and sixty caliber machine guns, damn little food, and damn little medical supplies.

"Wonderful," said Link, " we need to find food. Everyone is starving to death." Colonel Sing knew what he had to do. On his map, there was a village. It was within thirty miles, and it was away from the Reds' line. We were to march to this village and barter or take what we needed.

"Let's hope this village has a good supply of pussy, too!" added Too Sack. "You know how Lally gets!"

"Yeah," added Gordy, "I hate to see him start climbing trees and hunching."

"Up yours, frog face," countered Lally.

Everything looked peaceful as we approached the village area. The people were working in the rice fields. They were dressed in their drab clothing, the usual dull gray, and the wide rimmed hats to protect themselves against the sun. They looked unconcerned as we neared. However, in the middle of the village, about one hundred armed men were taking defensive positions.

Colonel Sing put the glasses on them and reported that he saw no tanks or Japanese equipment. He saw only small arms. We pulled up about seventy-five yards from the main entryway. Colonel Sing sent Lieutenant Ki to speak about our interests and demands. Too Sack, our wizard, told us we were asking for food supplies in exchange for ammunition and some weapons. We could see their chief waving his arms and shaking his head no. Lieutenant Ki returned and reported to Colonel Sing. It seemed they wanted more than we wanted to give.

Lieutenant Ki was getting another plan from Colonel Sing. Finally, after more than an hour of negotiations, it was agreed we could have a supply of food that would last us ten days. In exchange, we would give them one of our thirty caliber machine guns and five hundred rounds of ammunition. That was Sing's final offer. If that was not acceptable, Colonel Sing told Lieutenant Ki to tell them we would take what we needed and kill any who protested.

Lally said, "That might have done it, wouldn't you say, Oh Watson?"

"Certainly, Ollie," I countered. We were always quoting the sayings of radio and movie stars

Little did we know of the adventures awaiting us? We were four Marines and a battalion of Nationals right in the middle of China's third and final civil war, the war that shaped China for the future. Lally was the oldest at twenty-one, and I was the youngest at sixteen. Yet even then, I knew we were making history.

As we walked along this ancient road leading to the unknown, my thoughts went back to Hollywood, my mom, my old granny, and my little brother. Would I ever see them again? I was almost ten thousand miles away from home in a strange land. Later, I found out that my own government had written us off and left us behind. Pulling the plug on us is what it amounted to.

I was jarred from my thoughts by a rifle shot from the side of a hill.

"Hit the ground!" yelled one of the Nationals. After we took cover beside the road, sing sent a patrol into the woods to see what we were up against. Lally said we needed to get off this road and into that wooded area away from the shot. About then, all hell broke loose! We were being cut down by a cross fire of rifle fire. It was a trap set by the village we had just left. They must have sent a runner ahead, because we were being attacked by soldiers, and not by village people. We regrouped our forces and held them off until dark. They hit us again about one o'clock in the morning with everything they had. Link and

Gordy were to the north of Lally, and I was about five hundred yards away, and I was taking the hardest hits. I looked up and saw half a dozen Reds coming right at us blasting away. I opened up with my bar and made a hole; Too Sack took out the rest. Two more times they attacked, and two more times we held them off. Then, as suddenly as it started, the firing stopped. We waited and watched until daybreak. At that time we started to check out our dead and wounded. Colonel Sing had two hundred fifty men when we started, and we found one hundred twenty-seven Nationals still alive. We counted over two hundred bandits and Reds who were no longer with us. We also lost a comrade that day; Mongo was found slumped over his machine gun.

"What a waste of human life! People are stupid Asses," complained Link.

I agreed we all must be nuts. "What the hell are they fighting for anyway? The Reds want to run things, and the Nationals want to run things. The winner gets to be the 'big shit', and the losers eat shit. That's what it's all about."

"Yeah, but only the top generals get the good life; everyone else eats shit, commented Link.

"Anyway, do you see any generals around?" asked Gordy. "Hell no," Gordy answered himself.

The conversation ended as Colonel Sing gave orders to move out.

No one in his wildest dreams could have come up with what we were about to run into.

After seven hard days of climbing up into the mountains, we stopped to rest for a complete night and day. It was here that Too Sack went off looking for something to kill and eat. Instead, he came back with an old man. Gordy looked up and said, "You expect us to eat that old bastard?"

"No eat old man," Too Sack said. "This old man over one hundred years old." He looked it, too, but his mind was clear and he could walk fast. Really, he was quite remarkable. He told Too Sack of a village far off in the mountain range, which had never been found by the Japanese or the warlords; it had been there since the beginning of time. He had been banned from this village for many years. But since his banishment was over, he would like to go home for the end of his time. Too Sack said he seemed sure of the time he had left. The old man wanted us to take him home. He said it would bring us great fortune. He told of a wonderful way of life, and it sounded so good that if we went there, we would never want to leave.

Since we didn't have too many options, Colonel Sing decided we would try to find it. Too Sack said he had heard stories of such a wonderland in fables, but never believed it. Many of the Nationals knew stories about it. Gordy asked Too Sack about the gook women. So, Too Sack pumped the old man about that subject, and it got us all excited. The old man said that each man had at least three wives because there were many more women. Well, that was all ole blue balls needed to hear.

We had gone without food for three days. Some of the Nationals had given up and deserted; we were now down to less than one hundred fifty men. Prospects for a good meal looked slim. After our third day of walking over the difficult trails, the weak, sick troops of Colonel Sing Wu looked into the sun shining down on a beautiful village. There were mountains on each side with a large lake and several waterfalls coming off the mountains. Colonel Sing called the old man forward and asked, "Is this your home, old man?"

"Yes," he cried, "this is my home. I have been away for more than twenty years. My time of exile is up, and I will be welcomed home. I have served my time away."

As we moved down the mountainside, we were not alone. Several villagers lined the other peaks, moving down as we moved down. They were not armed as far as we could see. But we soon found that without the old one's

143

directions, we could never have found this mountain pass. We could see why no one could ever find it. We came to many dead ends, as we looked downward toward seven thousand feet of space. It was a very hard trip full of detours. After we traveled three hours, Sing asked the old one if he knew where we were going. We had heard that story from more than one gook. "No problem. You see, ding how, you see." It was like going into one of those houses with all the mirrors or worse.

We could tell the deeper we moved down the mountain, the more concerned Colonel Sing became. He repeated his questions to the old one several times, which was not like Sing.

Link said, "Well, old Sing knows if the old man is wrong about us getting back out of here, that we are supposed to be protected by the ancient folklore.

We found three more of these special villages before we finished our tour of duty in Manchuria, Mongolia, and North China.

As we moved into the village, it seemed no different than any other village, except this village was very clean, and everyone seemed to be busy. However, many had stopped to look us over. When they saw us, the Marines with the fair complexion, they were in a tizzy. Some even got down and bowed.

We brought the old man to the front. Too Sack related the conversation back to us later. This is his translation of this event:

Honorable leader, this old man has asked us to bring him home. As you can see, he is too feeble to return on his own.

The leader looked at the old man. "What is your name, oh ancient one?"

"Wu Cha," answered the old man.

"How long have you been gone, and why were you banished?"

144

"More than twenty years I have been gone. I was banished by the great Fu Wing for being lazy. I had sickness and could not carry my load."

The leader conferred with the elders and came back to the old man. "Wu Cha, the old one, Ding Yu says he remembers that time, and that you are to be welcomed back after such a long time. Fu Wing was sometimes a very cruel leader, and you will find your remaining years will be in great comfort."

"Thank you, great leader, but can I ask one great favor?"

"What is it, Wu Cha?"

"That my soldier friends be helped on their journey to find their home."

The leader Wo San answered that they would help us.

When Too Sack gave us the information, we started to relax some. As Colonel Sing and Too Sack continued to talk, the village leader directed his soldiers to give us food and to arrange for our shelter.

Soon, we were in a barracks type of building where we ate well for the first time in a long time. Then, we were shown our sleeping quarters. Shortly after that, Too Sack came back with both good news and bad news.

The good news was that they were not going to eat us. The bad news was that we needed to stay away from their women. Too Sack added, "We may have to tie ole maggot Lally up. He's too horny to run loose."

"Up yours," answered Lally.

"Hey, Lally, he's not kidding. We better be careful. They got their own army here. I saw several soldiers in uniform. It's not a soldier uniform, ole Lally, it's the village police uniform."

"I don't give a shit what kind of uniform it is. The assholes got weapons, and there are more of them than us."

"Good point," said Link. "Let's just take it easy for a few days."

145

"Too Sack, did you get any idea about how long we may be here?"

"Maybe several weeks, or maybe some less," replied Too Sack.

"Well, I'll tell you one thing, I'm not going without pussy for weeks when the place is full of it. Do you see those girls giving us the 'I want you' sign?"

"Oh, hell," said Link, "what's the use? We will end us shooting our way out of this place, sure as hell."

"Some of these people think we are gods, and some think the white ones are evil spirits. Boy, Too Sack, you are a piece of work," stated Gordy.

We had never been in such a rich village. They had their own homemade equipment, which was all made out of wood. They had rice fields full of grain. They even had storage houses in which to store the grain. They had little shops where they made things to sell. I asked Too Sack, "Who in the hell do they sell to? Nobody even comes here."

"They don't come here, ole Shelburn, they make trips out of here and sell along the main road leading to the ocean about two hundred miles from here."

I thought, "That's one hell of a trip with oxen pulling the carts. But then again, everything in China is done the hard way." Within two weeks, we made the same journey again. It was such a mess of turns, hills, climbing, hiding, and walking. We all would rather have been shot than make this trip. Finally after several days, we came upon an old road, and this is where they left us.

A few words to Colonel Sing Wu, and it all became part of our past. Too Sack said, "Ole Lally, you set a record back in the village."

"How is that?" asked Lally.

"No Push-Push."

"I wouldn't bet on that," added Gordy.

Lally just grinned. He never told us, but given the time element, I am sure he found a way.

P.F.C. Jesse Bedwell USMC
Peiping China (age)17 - 1946

BRIDGE 26 (Bailey type) Near Tsingtao China
3rd Eng.Batt. 6th Marine Division 1947

Pfc. Bedwell - Cpl. Link - Sgt. Lally

One Of the Transport Ships
We were on

USS J. C. BRECKENRIDGE
(Courtesy Col (Ret) Tom Stevens, USMC)

Contact is made

After leaving the Village of the Ancient One, we were going over some pretty high mountains. It was here that Colonel Sing heard some talk of the Sea. According to the talk, there was a submarine off the coast, more than a hundred miles away. He tried to make contact and was finally successful. He reported our adventures, and it was from this radio contact that Operation Snow-White was set in motion. It seemed that an operation was already set in motion to take over some factories in Manchuria, but something had gone wrong. It was just our luck to be in the right place at the right time. Colonel Sing was told to go higher up into the mountains and wait for further directions. These directions would come by way of radio contact from an American submarine in the China Sea.

Symbol Mongolian Flag
Operation Snow-White
Manchuria

Too Sack came up with some very interesting news. We knew it was interesting, because he was in a big hurry. He forgot to talk American, and he was talking Chinese again. It was a little difficult for us to follow, but Too Sack had great news. We finally had a mission. At first, we couldn't figure out what he was talking about. We eventually got him calmed down, and Lally said, "Too Sack, start talking in American and stay in American, or I'm going to drill you." Too Sack settled down.

Colonel Sing had finally made contact with the Nationalist forces. We had been three hundred miles up the coast. We were in Manchuria, but we were close to Mongolia. Somehow, a radio transmission had gotten through. From the messages that were sent back, we were nearing an area where they wanted a mission to take place. Since we were there, we were possibly capable of carrying

149

out this mission. We could be the answer. It was all we knew at that point in time.

At the very least, they knew our location, and they could help us find a hole back through the massive lines of scout patrols. They could possibly get us back through the lines to Nationalist controlled land. This was big news. We had a purpose. It was starting to get cold, and we were running low on supplies as usual. We were particularly low on medical supplies. None of the four of us had really had any serious sicknesses. The Chinese had a way of taking care of themselves. They used a lot of things to keep going. They could live on brown rice and sometimes on green rice forever.

Too Sack was the bearer of great news. It took us a little bit of time to digest that. The Nationalist troops were really excited; we all were. We didn't know what was going to happen, so we just had to wait. We camped for the night after that news. We could see up the side of the mountain to where Colonel Sing had positioned himself so he could pick up signals. We weren't sure if the signals were coming from the China Sea or from on the land.

Finally, after three hours, Colonel Sing Wu and his advance party came down off the side of the mountain and called all the officers and non-coms together. Too Sack gave us the final scoop about what was going down. It seemed that whenever Too Sack came back with some more news, we would abruptly change our course. We were going to go northeast. We had been going northwest.

The reason for this change in direction was because this Operation Snow-White was off to the west of our position. We had another one hundred sixty or so miles left to travel, and we were on our own. However, a supply drop was supposed to take place about twenty miles out, since they knew we were down to almost nothing.

Speculation on our part ran rampant. It had to do with our new mission. Was it to liberate another Japanese prison camp? Or maybe we were to free General Wainwright who was reportedly being held in this area?

He had been General MacArthur's second in command in the Philippines. Our numbers were now less than two hundred, so we figured it had to be a small operation. Then again, could we be only a part of a major attack?

We did find out that Colonel Sing was to be contacted by a sub off the coast of northern China. In order to get a good signal, we had to move up the mountain to a higher level. So the next day we climbed. We had to remain there for a couple days.

Lally said, "Damn it, my rags are running thin. Pretty soon I'll be walking on bones."

Gordy replied, "Yeah, this is a major crock of shit. Let ole Sing and his fish-eyed, asshole officers do the climbing."

I added, "My feet are so sore I can't touch them. Hey, Too Sack, ask your foot god to send me down a pair of shoes."

Too Sack, always ready with a smart-ass remark said, "Oh, honorable feet god say to kiss his ass by the numbers. He no got time for sad sack Marines with big feet. He only help poor coolie with little feet. He say big feet show little brain in big head."

"OK, OK, dipstick, sorry I asked," I countered. The Chinese taught us a few tricks about getting by. Some of their ideas were good; some were dumber than owl shit.

Lally said, "Too Sack, what the hell are we climbing this mountain for?"

Too Sack replied, "Lally maggot, me not know. Me only little coolie. Just wait, and you see."

"You're a wise ass, little gook. You know more than you are telling us. He only tells us what he wants us to know, Shelburn."

"I don't know, Lally," I answered, "I think he tells us everything he knows." That night we climbed and then we cussed; then we cussed and then we climbed. We finally got to the position where Colonel Sing wanted us to be. He started getting signals, and before the night was over, everything was set, and Colonel Sing called us

151

together and gave us our final orders concerning Operation Snow-White.

It seems this operation had been planned by the JCS and was to take place from L.S.D.'s landing at a location above the North Chinese border. Since we were on location and had a demolitions team with us, everything was changed and diverted to us. The JCS knew the war was coming to an end, and they wanted this area in Manchuria to be under Nationalist Chinese rule and not the Russians. Of course, we knew nothing about any of this at the time.

It was Too Sack's understanding that we would be dropped medical supplies, ammunition, weapons, and food plus some kind of gear. It wasn't too long coming. Only a few days later in the early hours of morning before daybreak, we heard the roar of engines in the sky. This was something we seldom, if ever heard. The sounds seemed to fill up the sky. It was the goony birds, air transports, coming in to make their deliveries. We all ran out to watch, and we were told to stay away from the landing spot because we would get something dropped on our head. We tried to stay out of the way.

This airdrop was best described as a cluster-fuck. I don't know any other way to describe it. First, one of the drops landed on top of some Nationals killing four of them. Next, the commander Colonel Briggs, the officer who was to direct the Snow-White attack, was killed when his chute landed in a tree and he broke his neck. Also, two of the sleds were wiped out. Since all this took place, we figured that the operation might be scrapped. Only one of the three made it down safely. He was Lieutenant Williams. The orders from upper staff were recovered. Contact with the submarine offshore was made.

After many hours, the communication was completed. Word came down that we would still complete the mission on schedule. Lieutenant Williams would assist Colonel Sing with the operational plans.

Training for Operation Snow-White
Day 1, Aug 1946

Lieutenant Williams was a six feet two inch, one hundred ninety pound mean son of a bitch. He knew his stuff. Lally said, "At least we are taking orders from a Marine." Lieutenant Williams was at Guam when the war started, and he had faced combat already.

Link said that he had killer eyes. We always said Link had killer eyes.

The first people Lieutenant Williams, nicknamed Lieutenant Tightass, wanted to see was the four marines. Standing in front of us, Lieutenant Tightass was reading information about us from our G-4 files. "You know, fellows, it's almost impossible that four tightassed jar..." He never got the jarheads out of his mouth, because we all broke up, since we had just named him tightass. "OK, what's the damn joke?"

We couldn't explain it. But then Lally said, "Let's tell him. He will find out anyway. Well sir, said Lally we just named you tightass."

The Lieutenant fixed his cold eyes on us and said nothing for a full thirty seconds. Then he said, "I like it."

We all about shit.

He continued, "but don't let me hear you, or the price will be high. I want Iron Mike to be proud of me."

Too Sack questioned, "Who this Iron Mike?"

"A metal statue at Paris Island that we called our metal master."

"Watch your mouth, Shelburn," Gordy said. "Old Iron Mike knows all."

Having heard enough small talk, Lieutenant Williams was ready to get down to the business at hand.

"Your role in this mission is as follows. First, you will be trained to operate the snow machines, the new weapons, and how to survive in frigid weather. Second, you will be trained in the new plastic explosives, called c-3 and c-4. Third, I will teach you enough Russian to get by.

Then, when you hear some of their commands, you'll know what is going to happen. This is very important in combat." He gave us a lot more directions, but these were the highlights of our new training.

Training started the next morning. Lieutenant Tightass asked us how smart we were, "I mean, tell me how you did in high school grade wise? Bedwell?"

"Sir, I completed one full year of high school. I averaged a C-."

"Lally?"

"Sir, I completed high school and had one year of college."

"Link?"

"Sir, I finished high school with a B- average."

"Sergeant Li Chin, Too Sack?"

"Sir, me no go to school. I am a wizard!"

Lieutenant Tightass replied, "What the hell do you mean, you are a wizard?"

We had to explain how Too Sack was smarter than us, and more than likely smarter than him. After we told him some Too Sack stories, he was a firm believer. After a few more remarks, the lieutenant decided to follow up later.

He took us over to a supply truck to look over some clothing. It was all new stuff. Lally tried on one of those snow parkas and a pair of pants that went with it. Too Sack looked him over and said, "Lally Maggot, you look like a big white Lally Maggot. A big ghost."

Lally laughed about that, and Gordy said, "Yeah, he does, don't he?" We looked kind of goofy, but we blended in with the terrain. After this operation, there was an escape plan for those of us who survived. We had hope, but that hope was short-lived.

We had seventeen snow sleds. That was about half of what we were supposed to have for this mission. With two soldiers per sled, that meant that we would only have thirty-four soldiers going on this mission. It was supposed to be an operation of sixty soldiers. We figured that since we were the demolitions team, we were going. The rest of the men who were not chosen for this mission had gathered near the shoreline to be picked up by either a submarine or a transport ship. They would be re-assigned at Tsingtao, which was still controlled by the Nationals. Their mission was to return to the nest.

Day 1—

Our first order of business was to learn how to operate the snow machine. Actually, it was pretty simple. The biggest problem was how to handle the machine in deep snow. It was rather simple. When we were in or near the woods, we could tell how deep the snow was by watching the trees. If it was a fresh snow of a foot of a foot or more, we could bury the machine pretty easily. The snow machines seemed to go the best after a freezing rain had settled the snow in and made it harder.

After a couple of hours practice, Too Sack had the first mishap. He hit a rock just under the surface of the snow. It sent his ass flying through the air. It broke one of the runners, but we had a welder who repaired the damage. Too Sack had never seen anything like a snow machine, and had been running it like a bat out of hell. He thought it was just wonderful. Lieutenant Tightass had a shit fit. He told Too Sack not to travel so fast.

After about four more hours of practice, we were about as good as we were going to get. It was still hard to hold Too Sack down. The little gook was like a demon possessed. Lieutenant Tightass said. "It's a good thing he is our resident wizard, and also the house mouse for Colonel Sing. Otherwise, we would detonate the little bastard."

Operation Snow-White
Day 2

The session was on new weapons. We had a new version of the Thompson machine gun. It used a higher

155

caliber bullet, and the magazine was longer. Other than that, we didn't see any changes to worry about. We found out that after three or four bursts, it would still jam up on us, so we had to make all our bursts short. We set up some silhouettes. We were supposed to spray towards the middle of the target. Too Sack always shot the head off. Finally, Lieutenant Tightass went over to Too Sack and asked him why he shot at the head when he should be shooting at the body.

Too Sack said, "Me shoot at head because man like chicken. No head, head gone, body die."

Lieutenant Tightass looked at me and said, "So, Shelburn, this is our wizard?"

I answered, "Yes, sir, he is our fucking wizard."

Lally started laughing. Then we all started laughing and everything lightened up.

Day 3—

Lieutenant Williams showed us the new plastic explosives. They were called c-3 and c-4. The threes had a longer fuse and less explosive power. The fours were much more dangerous. We had to really be careful setting the fuse. Most of these were pre-set. Once we activated the fuse, we had less than ninety seconds to get seventy yards away. We didn't set any off; we just went through a dry rehearsal. We didn't want to attract that much attention. We messed with the explosives and equipment all day.

Colonel Sing was about ready to start this mission. We really couldn't stay here in the open too long. We were sure to be spotted. Mao didn't have air power, but the Russians had a few. They had no warplanes; they had the scouting type planes. Then again, the weather was getting too bad for much flying. If anyone tried to get around those mountain peaks in a storm, it would be all over.

156

However, we never knew how close a scouting party of Mao's might be. This area was a no man's land so we were safe from any type of attack.

A moment to think about my ole buddy's

That night I was back in Hollywood in my dreams. Ole John Keenan and I were up early, as usual. John had a new Red Ryder BB gun we wanted to try out. John's Hollywood name was Bugger, and he sometimes had snot hanging off his nose. That made me sicker than hell. If he did, he got a punch in the nose. Ole John figured it was less painful to wipe his nose.

We went out in the alley and shot a few cans behind ole Lonzo Bailey's house. A few minutes later, grouchy ole Perry Miller's wife Carol came out and gave us a raff of shit about being careful.

Ole Bugger said, "She's one to talk about being careful. 'Member last week over at the "Jot em Down", she knocked over a stack of cans. She had ole Elmer working his ass off getting them stacked again."

"Look, ole Carol's big fat girl is watering the flowers. She is as dumb as owl shit. Everyday all day," added Bugger.

"I got an idea, Bugger says Buster, as soon as she gives us a target, we send a BB up her ass."

"Damn, that's one hell of an idea right, Peehole, right up the shit shoot," laughed Bugger.

We got our chance real quick, because she was bending over the flowers. "OK, Bugger, any time now." Bugger took careful aim, and bang, Hazel grabbed her ass, screamed like a stuck pig and ran for the house. Around from the back of the house came Lonzo cussing like a preacher, "You sons of bitches, I'll kick the living shit out of both of you." We ran like Jim Thorpe and didn't stop until we got to the " Gob Pile", an old coalmine called steel tipple.

About that time, I broke up laughing, and Lally asked, "What in the hell is wrong with you?"

I said, "Someday, I'll tell you."

157

I was wide-awake, but my thoughts were still in Shelburn, trying to remember if the dream was the way it happened. Satisfied that things were in order, I was back again in Hollywood.

We were pretty safe from Lonzo and the ape woman at least for the moment. Bugger said, "You know, Peehole, they will get our ass."

"So I said, "We will just shoot ole hazel in the ass again and again."

Bugger chimed in, "Yeah, we can even have Buster nail her one. We might as well have him in trouble, too. There's no sense of us going it alone. That's why we are buddies, right." One for all and all for one; that's the way it is, Peehole."

As luck would have it, Bugger's shot was the shot of a lifetime. He shot that BB between the cheeks of her ass. It stuck just inside and hit a hemorrhoid. She bled, and they had to take her to ole Dr. Clark.

As soon as we saw Buster, he commented, "Boy, Bugger, hitting ole Hazel in the ass could be done by a blind man with such a big target." I was watching you pricks.

"She must go about three axe handles across," I added.

"That means by my calculating, her asshole measures about two inches around. Still not a bad shot," explained Buster.

Later that day we had to take congratulations from the boys down at Slobber's Jot Em Down Store. Bud Rhompson said, "Hell of a shot, Bugger."

Bud's yes man, Bill Crooks, added "Hell of a shot."

Big Rig Baker, an older guy, sitting on a pickle barrel added his thoughts on the subject. "I'll tell you boys one thing, I don't think it's a damn bit funny. If it was a girl of mine, I'd shoot your Asses off with a twenty-two."

"Wait a minute, Big Rig, you got it all wrong. You couldn't hit a bear in the ass with a bass drum," replied Bud. "Number two, since you were born without a dick, you couldn't have had a girl, and number three, you would never have time, since you spend all day running up to the wino store getting stoned."

"Oh, the hell with you guys. "You'll get yours someday. I hope someone shoots ole Bugger's balls right off his body,"

"Hey, that would take a hell of a shot, too. Wouldn't it, Bud?"

"You're right for once in your life, Peehole. Since Bugger's balls are about as big as a set of BBs, that would be one hell of a shot." (Years later when I had more sense, I felt bad about Buggers big time shot).

The next morning it was time to rock and roll. By 1100 hours Operation Snow-White was ready to begin. There were seventeen sleds three abreast with Colonel Sing and Lieutenant Williams out front. Too Sack, Lally, and I were in the second row. Link and Gordy were in the back. Each sled had a slider that carried the sleds, ammunition, weapons, food and clothing, mess gear, and other miscellaneous items for each two men.

Final instructions were given by Colonel Sing, "Gentlemen, this is the real thing; this is not a drill. During the night, I am sure you noticed that the rest of our troops started their journey to the sea. May the gods be with them."

Lally said to me, "Let's keep our God right here. They can have their gods." Colonel Sing didn't hear Lally, but Too Sack did. He gave Lally a shot about it later.

Colonel Sing continued his briefing, "Each driver will stay in formation just like we practiced." He gave Too Sack a strong look. "The first night we should reach our first resting point. It's about twenty miles ahead. We can make sure the sleds are in good working order. At this point, we'll be approximately thirty miles from our objective. We will wait there for the proper weather conditions. Any questions?" No one said anything, so Sing gave the signal to move out.

159

We fired up our engines, and I said, "Just like the Indy 500, eh Too Sack?"

"Too Sack no understand 500; what is that?"

"It's hopeless, Shelburn. Remember, this little bastard never saw an American, let alone the 500, until six months ago."

"Oh, yeah, I keep forgetting his lack of world communication." There was small talk for the first ten or so miles. All of a sudden, Colonel Sing gave the stop and shut off the engines sign, making a wave across his neck.

"What the hell is going on?" said Lally.

"Look up to the left on that ridge," I answered.

"So, we have company, do we?"

We were told to lock and load. "Our company appears to be bandits," said Lieutenant Williams. He was looking about eight hundred yards out.

"Yes," remarked Colonel Sing, "there are about seventy of them showing."

"This we don't need," said Lieutenant Tightass.

"No shit," said Lally.

"Listen up," stated Colonel Sing, "we are going to move forward until we get to the woods. That will give us some cover up ahead. Everyone with glasses keep an eye on them. Also, look for movement from all directions; it could be a massive attack."

We started moving again. As soon as we moved, they moved. Some of them had horses, and some were afoot. A few miles further, and we made it to the woods. They were still within six to eight hundred yards of us, and they were keeping just out of range, or so they thought. We had rifle grenades that could nail a dog's ass at six hundred yards.

We set up camp, and moved the sleds into hiding places around and behind the trees. Colonel Sing said, "If they get our sleds, we are all dead." Then we set up guards, and waited for whatever was coming. Colonel Sing told us we could have run away from them, but we would have

160

used up too much gas. The best way was to stand and fight, if need be.

Colonel Sing sent two scouts moving toward the bandits. They would signal us of any coming attack. About 2:00 P.M., one of the Nationals signaled that a troop movement was coming in from our south and our east. They were walking in, and about two hundred yards behind them were some bandits on horses. "Give me numbers," yelled Colonel Sing to his scout.

"Sir, about one fifty have been sighted," yelled the scout. Just about then, the first shot was fired. Lally and I were under good cover for the moment. Too Sack was with Gordy, but Link was out of sight. From the firefight, we detected firepower coming from Japanese rifles, Russian rifles, and Chinese rifles. No machine gun fire was detected yet. Lally and I were armed with M-I's. Too Sack had a carbine, and Gordy was armed with a Thompson machine gun. Off approximately twenty yards to our left, four of the enemy troops came forward blasting away. Gordy cut down the first two with a burst from his Thompson. Lally took out the third one, and before I could get a round off, the enemy was on top of me driving me to the ground. I took my K-bar in hand and tried to fight off a Chinese long knife. As soon as Too Sack saw him, he shot him with his 30-caliber carbine.

"Thanks, Too Sack, that was close! But, there was no time to talk; everyone was busy staying alive and trying to fight off another assault. It came from our right flank. About ten of the enemy fired as they were on the move. Walking straight up, several Nationals fired from the opposite direction catching them in crossfire. As quickly as it started, it ended. Like dogs barking all over town, then with a signal, it stopped.

We stayed in our positions for about twenty minutes. Then, Colonel Sing had us slowly advance in all directions to check for any remaining bandits. We knew when we heard all the different weapon sounds, that we were facing bandits, and not the Reds or the Russians.

Finally, the all-clear signal came, and we started the body count. Two Nationals and eight bandits were killed in combat. This left our numbers at thirty-two. We couldn't chance another firefight. Colonel Sing had told us the attack would be called off if we ever got below thirty men, because it would take at least that many to storm the compound.

Six Nationals and four bandits were wounded and in bad shape. The Nationals put them out of their misery. That sounds bad, but they were dying and wished to have it that way.

Gordy asked, "Where in the hell is Bob o' Link?"

"He is over to the left," I answered.

"Good, I was afraid he got his ass shot off."

"No such luck," yelled Too Sack. "Link ass still hooked up, ole Lally Maggot. Shelburn got his finger cut! I make him a 'dung medal'."

"Now, how are you going to give old Shelburn a medal for standing with his finger up his ass while we are killing bandits?" questioned Link. (Too Sack called a phony medal a dung medal.)

"Yeah," added Link, "he had the other finger, the one that got shot in the air, yelling help me, help me!"

"Sounds about right to me," suggested Sergeant Tu. He was another National who could speak some American. "Poor old maggot, Too Sack, had to save Shelburn's ass."

"Screw you guys," I said, finally getting a shot in. (If I didn't counter, they would rag my ass forever.)

H Hour

When night came, so did the snow. It came down really heavy, and shortly, Colonel Sing gave the order to mount up. We were expected to arrive at our target one hour before daybreak.

Our job, as the demolition team, was to go across the Bailey bridge, which had a span of a hundred yards; blow it; and move on to the south guard tower, which was about fifty yards to the northwest of us. We had an eight-member team, and half of the team would be working on the other side of the compound doing the same thing we were doing. The plan was to park the sleds about a mile from the compound and snowshoe in. This meant we would have nothing stronger in fire power than four submachine guns, rifles and pistols, and, of course, our explosives.

Finally, the engines were cut, and we left everything behind. I wondered if I would ever walk this way again, mount my sled, and drive off to safety. I'm sure we all had the same thoughts. The mile walk through the driving snowstorm was a real bear; it was a soft snow, which made it hard walking with the snowshoes.

I started thinking about some of Too Sack's stories of Ancient China and its early religion. They had looked for answers to questions like what controlled the darkness and the light. They based all their thinking on examples. So, if a tribal chief died on a river, this river was a bad river. If bad things happened on a mountain, it was a bad mountain. Then, if good things happened on another mountain, it was a good mountain. I asked Too Sack if he believed this crap.

He replied, "No, Shelburn, missionaries told me about God." He went on, "When the Tang dynasty came along about four thousand years ago, they started believing in a sky god called T'IEN, who was the source of energy. They also had a river god called 'SIRE OF THE HO', which meant the yellow river. They also believed in ghosts and greatly feared them.

We knew about the medicine man of the old west, but the Tang dynasty had one they called SHAMAN. Today, we would call it a medium, since it was a female, whose powers included bringing rain. If the rain didn't come on time, they burned the Shaman. It seemed that by 600 BC, most of this stuff was history in China.

Too Sack used to say a poem every once in a while, about CONFUCIAN TIMES about lazy know it all assholes. It was: "He eats without tilling, dresses without weaving, wagging his lips and cracking his tongue. He says he is the source of right and wrong in order to please those in power."

MY THOUGHTS AGAIN RETURNED TO HOLLYWOOD

Buster, Bugger, and I were on the move. It was a clear, sunny, and hot day in southern Indiana. We always sat out in front of Slobbers Store to make our morning plans. In those days there was no work to be had. It was in the thirties. There was no money and no jobs, so kids had to make do. We made our own plans, and we were damn good at that. We were called the best of the best. Sometimes we were called "a pain in the ass', and at other times we were called poor white trash. Sometimes, we were called young boys, but not too often.

Buster said, "You know, Peehole, we haven't given John Trimmer, the big cat nipper any shit lately." John Trimmer lived next to the store. His big fat wife named Sally worked at the telephone office, and she had about fifty cats. Bugger called it Little John's Cat House. Because John was a little sawed off runt, Sally ran the show. "I don't think Little John ever worked in his life."

"That's right," added Buster, "he is as lazy as Shade Nickerson. Remember when we stole ole Bud's goat Sherman?"

"Yeah, only don't say it too loud. Bud's got ears in his ass and all over town," said Bugger.

Peehole planned aloud, "Well, I was thinking... what if we was to take down old John's flag and tie cats all the way up the pole? Remember, John goes to Terre Haute today so he will be gone."

"Yeah, I like that idea, Peehole."

"Sounds good to me," chimed in Buster.

"We have to capture some cats in his barn first."

"What if someone sees us?" asked Buster.

164

"So what? They know if they tell, we will nail their Asses with something just as good."

"OK, let's do it," agreed Buster.

We took the flag down, trapped five cats, and tied their tails to the rope. They scratched the hell out of us as we raised the flag and took off down the alley. We lay in a ditch waiting for people to come and see what the hell was going on.

First, came old Whip Zerhide running up to take a look with Charlie Mason, "It's that damn Buster and his gang; I saw Bugger running toward the alley just a minute ago. By then we had gathered half of Hollywood, and they were laughing their Asses off. We had also made a sign and put it at the end of the pole. It said:

"SALLY'S CATS CLIMBED A POLE
TRYING TO REACH THE SKY
TO GET AWAY FROM SALLY'S EYE
LITTLE JOHN MAY WONDER WHY
5 CAT'S ASSES ARE IN THE SKY. "
SIGNED- BUD THOMPSON

It wasn't a good sign but it worked. It wasn't a good thing to do, but you have to remember that back in those days evolution came slow. We were meaner than shit on a stick.

A sudden yell from Gordy, our resident nut, rushed me back to China, "Let's blow their ass to kingdom come."

Lally and I were given the south bridge to blow. Then we were to move on and take out one of the guard towers. Link and Gordy were to do the same thing on the other end. Too Sack and Sergeant Tu were to take out the barracks center. As Colonel Sing gave his final orders, we filed off into the early hours of dawn. Lally and I reached our objective with no sounds of warfare. We started laying a line. We had twenty minutes to get under the bridge, climb up into the metal rails, and set this charge. Then we had another ten minutes to set the charge at the guard tower. It was hard work, and twice we dropped the line and had to climb down and start over. Finally, after twelve minutes we had set enough of a charge to take the bridge down, at least I hoped so. I said to Lally, "Shouldn't we have set two more charges?"

"Don't worry, this will do it." Lally seemed to be sure so I let it pass. But, Sing had said five charges not three. We got back to our detonator, set the fuse and timer, and headed for the guard tower.

Only one guard was on duty. "I'll take the line in and set the C-2. "You watch the guard."

"OK," said Lally. He took a position about thirty yards from the tower as I crawled in the snow dragging my line and my explosives. I had to cover twenty more yards before I had it made. Somehow, the guard spotted Lally and opened fire. Lally was hit, but he got the guard before he went down. While this was going down, I ran up to the tower and set the charge. Then I ran like hell toward Lally's position. Once any gunfire was heard, we were to push the handlebar and let it blow.

I reached Lally, and he was hit pretty bad. His leg and arm were both hit. His leg had a big hole in it; I took my k-bar and cut my thermal shirt. I filled the wound with the thermal material and had him press on it. I put another rag around his arm. It was a clean shot through his arm. I managed to stop the bleeding on his arm, but the leg really had me worried. About then one of our medics came and took over.

The shit had really hit the fan. I said to myself, "You dumb ass, you never blew the charges!" I raced back and blew the charges. It seemed that everything in sight blew all to hell. I covered my head and waited. As I looked up, several Nationals were attacking the barracks area, so I joined them. We came upon some Russians as they tried to get out of the barracks. Bang... Boom... Rip...Tear. The barracks went sky high taking many head choppers to the their motherland. By 10:00 A.M., all firing had stopped.

We rounded up all remaining Red Chinese and Russians, stripped them of weapons, and sent them down the snow-covered trail leading them to Korea. We gave them a three-day supply of food and water. Usually the Nationals just shot them, but Colonel Sing said they were brave soldiers and had to be given a chance to live.

Gordy said it was a damn little chance since they had to go one hundred fifty miles in the middle of the winter. I agreed, but I damn sure would like that option if I were in their shoes.

LINK IS KILLED IN ACTION

We counted the dead and wounded. We had twenty-one Nationals still alive and four of those had bad wounds. This included Lally, who would recover from his wounds. We had killed over one hundred sixty Red Chinese and sixty Russians. The bad news for us was that one Marine gave his life in Operation Snow-White. We set up a simple cross near the site" One of the Orphans Of The Orient PFC Robert Link USMC was killed in action in Manchuria 1947". Robert Link from Upper Darby, Pennsylvania he was shot setting a charge at one of the gun towers. We couldn't even find his dog tags. His comrades lost a great warrior this day. We will never forget you and this moment Link. Never.

Now we were only three Marines, Too Sack, and Sergeant Tu. Colonel Sing gave us the news that Lieutenant Williams had also been killed in the same explosion that took out Link. I'll never forget Link, and I'll never forget that day. He was only eighteen years old, to die so young? . I wondered even back then, "What in the hell is so important in an old factory to take the life of an eighteen-year-old Marine ten thousand miles from home?" I decided that if I ever got back that I would someday write a book about that day. Someday.

As for now, we had to clean up the mess and see what kind of a place we had here. We soon found out that

167

other than the diamond mine there were four main buildings. Each building had heavy machinery, and each of the buildings looked as if it could start operating any day. One building was a mineral-cutting building. Another was a final assembly set up. The third building held several small machines, such as a belt sander. The fourth building was set up for shipping and receiving. We had an idea several things going on there, but then found out we had just taken control of the richest diamond mine in the world.

Lally said, "Shelburn, we are going to be the richest sons of bitches the world has ever seen."

Gordy said, "Yeah, if we live long enough to get back home. Even if we get out of here, we have to get it home."

"Oh, we'll find a way... right, Shelburn?"

I saw so much Russian equipment it was unbelievable. Tanks, trucks, heavy equipment, and everything needed to equip a division.

"The Russians are coming back," stated Lally.

"Oh, yeah," said Gordy, "we better plan on it."

Colonel Sing set up assignments for us, and the demolition team was to take control of security at the main gate. Our assignment was twelve hours on and twelve hours off. Since Sing had communications with headquarters in China for the operations, based off the USS Monrovia, General Patton's former flagship, we received all kinds of congratulations and orders. An airdrop was expected as soon as the weather cleared. It would bring in food and other supplies.

One of the orders was for us to get the coolies back in the mine and get it working. We needed to hunt out the former mine's bosses and community leaders. We also had to search for the former Russian China Operation Commanders' names and rank for the FMF.

The headquarters of the Marine Corps also let Colonel Sing know two hundred miles north of our position, a battalion of Russians was moving our way. If they continued our way, they told us to be ready for a major

168

firefight. If necessary a battalion of Nationals would be air dropped out of the sky to help take care of the problem. So in a nutshell, we were to get the damn mine running again. We didn't know shit about diamond mining, but we were about to learn.

Lally was the top sergeant as far as our crew was concerned. That was OK, since he was now an old man of twenty-five, and the rest of us were all under twenty with me being the youngest at seventeen. Too Sack was about twenty-five, but he was a wizard and wizards could make themselves any age, according to Too Sack.

We had some pretty good quarters during this time. We took over a line shack back near the mines. Sharing the quarters with us Marines were Too Sack, Sgt. Tu, and two Nationals we called Sgt. York and Chesty. Sgt. York was a great hero from WWI and an excellent shot. Chesty was named after a tough Marine we all knew.

We had a coal stove heater and enough room to set up a little game room. It was actually a card table and a deck of cards. The rest of the troops were scattered around in different buildings. No one wanted to be in the barracks area; it was too big and too hard to heat. We had windows in the front and on both sides. From where we had been sleeping the past few months, according to Too Sack, it was a 4.0 with 4.0 being the highest rating for performance in the Marine Corps.

The guard duty was boring, and we would rather have been working with the coolies. That way the days would have gone by more quickly.

Sgt. York was, shall we say, different? He was a skinny little guy who always stood on his toes when he talked. He was also short, and he followed Too Sack around like a puppy. One day Too Sack said to Lally, "Too Sack you number one coolie, right?"

"Yeah," answered Lally, knowing he would probably be sorry.

"You keep Private Qui, Sgt. York, from following me around. He driving me nuts."

"Well, Too Sack, Qui is now a sergeant. We named him Sergeant York."

"Piss, Blue Balls, I don't care what you make him, make him a General, me no care, he drive me nuts!" countered Too Sack.

"Well, Too Sack, since you're so upset about this, why don't you tell him one of your stories about old China. For example, say it was written long ago that one who follows in footsteps of a wizard must pay all his bills forever when that wizard dies. If he fails to pay the bills, the wizard god will suck all the blood out of his body."

"Lally, you crazy son of a bitch. Even old Chinese men won't buy that shit," I added.

"Now, now, Shelburn, you know Private Qui is dumber than owl shit, it might just work, " Too Sack added. "He knows I am a wizard." Too Sack ran that over in his mind. "OK, OK, Ni migwa bing (big pecker headed Marine) me give it a try."

That night Too Sack made his pitch, telling a story to us all about the days of old China. Sergeant York listened to every word and when Too Sack got to the part about following in someone footsteps, including a wizard, the bait was set. Old Qui never got behind Too Sack again.

It was only a few days later when Sergeant York came up missing. We never knew what happened to him. Lally said the grand wizard got him.

From the day we arrived, the snow came down every single day for the next nine days. The ground was so deep in snow, that any kind of movement was a major struggle. The small huts that the coolies lived in were two thirds under, and some you could only see the rooftops. Colonel Sing had us out shoveling snow every day. Everyone shoveled snow from the number one coolie to Colonel Sing. The mountains in the background were very pretty, but enough was enough.

For weeks we stood guard duty, did a little work at the diamond mine, and attend some of Sing's meetings. The situation stayed in that mode for sometime. Finally, we got the poop from Too Sack that a Battalion was coming in to beef us up for an upcoming expected visit by the Russians and the Red Chinese. It seemed they were unhappy that we had control of the Diamond Mining.

On a cold Sunday morning in December, part of Chiang's American-trained Chinese twenty-seventh division came up the main road. They came with big snowplows leading the way; we could hear them for two days before they arrived. They had been on the road for two weeks. They had no trouble from Mao's cutthroats, but they had to keep opening up the road.

It was a big day for us, because we thought would get to see some Americans again. However, that proved to be wrong, because they were all Chinese Nationals, and none of them could speak American.

From all of the reports, we could be facing at least a regiment.

"They must think that we are super human," said Gordy. "How in the hell can three hundred Nationals hold off that many?"

Lally took up the problem, "Well, Gordy, we do have a few advantages. It's our terrain. We can see them coming for fifteen miles in all directions. Also, we have plenty of firepower."

I added, "Best of all, we have enough T.N.T. and C-3 to blow half of them up before they get to the compound, right, Too Sack?"

"I think it will be one hell of fight," Too Sack reasoned. Then he said that we should set traps as far out as five miles.

Lally hated head choppers. "All coolie 'Sloop heads'," said Too Sack.

"Hell, we call you sloop head, too."

"That OK, old Lally, but head choppers no call Too Sack Sloop-head. Me also call you pale face, beady eyes. Big time shots, right, Lally?"

"Yeah, Too Sack, big time shots."

171

"I wonder how much time we have?" added Corporal Wong-Ki. He was a National who could speak some American and had started hanging out with us. He continued, "I was in Sing's office when the call came in. It looks like we have two or three weeks to get ready."

"Hell that's more time than we usually get," added Gordy.

Diamonds and More Diamonds

The question is, how do we get some of them back to the States?" asked Gordy.

Lally said, "It's going to be a son of a bitch, I know how to get enough to set us all up for life, but they check all our gear."

"What happens? Where do they check it?" I questioned.

"Well," Lally continued, "when I came back from the Canal, I had to pick my footlocker up at the quartermaster. I had a couple pistols in it. They opened it up and took them from me. If I hadn't known the gunny in charge, they would have sent my ass up the river.

I know we can't keep them on ourselves. Coming from a diamond mine, they will shake us down. I'll work on it."

Colonel Sing Wu called an assembly at 01000 hours. This was very unusual, so we knew something big was in the making. Standing before us was a very serious looking colonel. "Comrades, our first major test in defending this area is about to take place. I have a report from Headquarters in Canton, from the Generalissimo himself, that the Russians have been reported moving our way. We expect contact within three or four days.

"General Chiang, will send us two hundred paratroopers, plus an airdrop of some thirty and fifty caliber machine guns. We'll also get some other weapons and ammunition. It is my understanding that this equipment is coming by way of the US Navy.

172

"All our energy must now be spent setting up a defensive perimeter around the compound and the mines. Plus, we must defend the village.

"Sergeant Lally, you will meet with me tonight at 1200 hours to lay plans for setting explosives. Bring Too Sack. I want all my officers in my office by 1300 hours. At ease comrades."

On the way out Lally said, "No sleep tonight, Too Sack."

"Yeah, as you pale faces and round-eyed maggots say 'Shit hit fan'."

It was a sleepless night for us all, as we waited up on Lally and Too Sack to get the skinny. We played poker until about 1400 hours. Finally, in came Lally and Too Sack.

"OK, Lally, what do you know?" I questioned.

"Well, I know our job. First of all, the flyboys are bringing in some bouncing Betty's, a German explosive that you put just under the ground. When the pressure of someone walking on it takes place, it releases a spring that shoots the explosive upward and then it blows. It's not pretty."

"Where in the hell did they get those?" I asked.

"I don't know, Shelburn, but they got 'em, and they have over five hundred of them. So in the morning, or I should say at daybreak, about three hours from now, we are going to be digging holes in the ground."

Too Sack said, "Let's get a ta-yi."

Gordy asked me, "What the hell does that mean?"

"It means get some rest, I think," I answered. "Hell, I don't know the whole damn language, Gordy. It may mean beat your meat."

At daybreak mass activity was taking place. We spent half a day marking off the areas where we would bury the Betty's.

At 1300 hours, we heard planes overhead: C-47's, and then we saw the white chutes opening. They just about filled the sky.

173

We spent most of the day gathering paratroopers and supplies. There were no major problems this time. Too Sack said, "I think they got it down this time." I agreed it went off well.

Colonel Sing held another meeting that night concerning our progress of sealing off our perimeters. Lally stated that we had planted three hundred of the five hundred Betty's. All that was left was to plant some around the village. The Nationals had set up barbed wire fences in all of the open areas complete with pillboxes, machine gun nests, and a few 4.2 mortars. It was estimated that we would be ready and waiting by noon the next day. The colonel was sure that we could handle what was coming our way.

The next morning it was cold, but there was no snow. It was a good time for an attack. We didn't know how much the Russians knew. They knew we were here, but hopefully, they didn't know we were loaded for combat and expecting an attack.

Colonel Sing got word from his scouts that we were going to have company within a couple hours. The estimate was somewhat more than we expected. It was more like a regiment. They had a column of tanks numbering at least a half dozen. They looked like T-34's. Plus, they had several trucks loaded with troops. The balance of the attack force was foot solders.

Colonel Sing ordered the two Japanese tanks and the two Chinese tanks to be moved into position. They were no match for the T-34's, but teamed up they could take one or two of them out.

We expected a head on attack, but that was not what the Russians had in mind. They stopped all forward movement within two miles of our compound and started shelling us. Colonel Sing had told us they would not shell the factory. They'd only shell the barracks area. The Russians wanted those mines to stay intact.

After three hours of shelling, it finally stopped. The Russians were on the move. They set their attack up in a cycle type formation. They placed all the tanks up front, firing and moving ahead. Each tank had about forty men behind it. The balance of the attack was set another five hundred yards behind. As far as our scouts could see, this was a two-wave attack, but we had no way of knowing what else might be coming our way.

Three Russian tanks rounded a bend and came within our vision. They zeroed in on our barracks, and blew a big hole in the side. At that very moment, we released our two Japanese tanks. They came at the Russian tank firing from two sides. At the same time the Betty's were taking a toll. A number of the Russians behind the tank were getting into the line of fire. The scene was getting larger as two of the enemy tanks were now in the battle. Our two Japanese tanks were finally able to shoot a tread off the T-34, and that made it a sitting duck. Then they teamed up on the other Russian tank. Before it could get into position, one of the other Russian tanks managed to disable one of the Japanese tanks.

Lally, Gordy, and I were defending the south end of the compound. The battle had not reached them as yet. Too Sack and several Nationals were further on down toward the front and were already taking fire.

After two hours of heavy fighting, the firing stopped, and the Russians moved back to regroup. It was a good time because we needed the same time to do some regrouping of our own. All was quiet during the night. No shots were fired; everyone held their positions.

At day break the attack was renewed. They hit us with everything they had. We would not bend or break. Finally, about noon, they retreated. Gordy and some Nationals who were scouting the right bank were the first to report that it looked like the Russians` were leaving. It looked like we had won this round. It took another two hours before we could be sure of their withdrawal.

Colonel Sing finally called in the troops, leaving a guard unit around the perimeter. He told us we were to stay on Red 1 Ready. It was over.

Too Sack relayed to us the next morning that Sing had communications with FMF from a transport, the USS Monrovia. His information concerned a Russian reference sent in the form of a meeting of the United Nations concerning the "Manchuria Situation". He said, "Yeah, I wonder if they reported that they got their ass kicked?"

"No," said Lally, "you can bet your ass on that one."

Colonel Sing told us later that he was told by FMF that we were not about to give up our control in Manchuria. That we planned on expanding our control to all of South and West Manchuria to keep the Russians and Red Chinese from taking over. It was now time for the politicians to take over. They pay Generals big money to fight the wars, but have little or nothing to say about the outcomes.

Our life at the compound and the diamond mines returned to normal. The mines were running fourteen hours per day and seven days a week. It seemed someone wanted some diamonds to bargain with.

The Sea Bees were sent in to open up the rails from Wenchaun, Manchuria, to Dairen, and from the ocean to our compound. This meant new duty for us. Each day more Nationalist troops were being sent up to guard the area and work on the rails. Most of the rails were in place, but guards had to be set up to keep them open. The Reds, the Russians, and the bandits were all trying to blow the rails up and take over the trains.

The tracks covered about five hundred miles total, so it took some manpower to keep the trains running. They had a different rail system in Manchuria than they had in China, something to do with sizing of the tracks and wheels, so lots of conversion work had to be done.

We had now come under control of the US Navy Sea Bees. They were the construction engineers. We were assigned to patrol areas bordering the tracks looking for trouble. We found plenty as the weeks passed by.

Near the Taverh River, the tracks passed over a Bailey bridge. Colonel Sing had word from the See Bees

176

that several coolies had been seen on the bridge. A reconnaissance photograph, showed them looking under the bridge. Our first job was to get down there and have a look. Before we headed out, however, we were to meet with the Third Engineering Company's headman, who was also a Marine. We now had two commanders. Our second was a Captain named Cotton Riley, a hardheaded Irishman.

Colonel Sing said we were to be used together as a four-man patrol. Another four-man patrol was set up on the East side of the track. We found out later that more than one hundred men were assigned as guards.

Captain Riley looked us over. He was a large man about the size of Lally. He let us know pretty quickly that he was in charge. "Sergeant Lally, I have heard about you guys, a remarkable story I must say." He stood there with a silly grin on his face as he continued, "I haven't had the honor of combat as of this moment, but I look forward to joining that brotherhood."

Gordy started to say something, but Lally waved him off.

"Oh, let him speak, Sergeant. I am sure Sergeant Gordon will have something to offer this moment."

Lally interrupted, "May I speak?"

"Oh, please do," said the Captain.

"Well, sir, it's been a long time since we have been under the direct command of a Marine Corps officer. We have pretty much had to call our own shots, but we are Marines, sir, and we can adapt, adjust, and overcome, sir."

"Very good," said the captain. "The paperwork says you're Marines, but you look more Chinese than American. For the time being, we'll leave you as you are, out of uniform, with hair down to your ass and looking like you fell out of a tree, but any of you cross me, and I'll have your asses up on charges. Do your understand that?"

He looked at Lally, and I thought, "It's time for Lally to make his move."

"Sir," said Lally, "you're right, we are out of uniform. But you must remember, Captain, for the last two years, we have been through hell. We've fought a hundred battles, and we are not in any mood to listen to the pile of dog shit you been giving us. Colonel Sing is still in charge of us and we are only on loan to you. Captain, your commanding officer is a China man named Colonel Sing Wu, and if you doubt that, call FMF headquarters and ask them. Furthermore, Captain, if you bring our names up, you will not be a Captain very long. The commanding general of FMF, General Casey, USMC, has told Colonel Sing as soon as we return to Tsingtao we all got some medals and promotions coming. So pull off your attitude and your dogs, and things will be just fine. One damn word, Captain, to HQ, and you will never leave China."

"Do you realize, Sergeant, that you have threatened an officer in front of witnesses?"

"What witnesses? You see any witnesses, Shelburn?"

"No, Sergeant Lally, I only see one chicken shit stateside commando."

"I will have all your Asses before I leave China. You can bet on it," said a very mad Irish Captain.

He turned and left, as I said, "Madder than owl shit."

All the time ole Too Sack was standing off a few yards. "Why didn't you jump in?" said Gordy.

"Well, oh crazy one, I may have to feed him cookies to keep your white asses out of the brig. Me try to get on his good side, and then me use the big Wei Ji on him."

"You're a classic, Too Sack."

After a few weeks with the third Marines and Sea Bees, we were ready to get the hell out of the area. Finally, the patrols ended, and our job here was over. We never had any more problems with the Captain. The rails were now secured, and it was time to head for Tsingtao.

TRAIN GUARDS

Life in Tsingtao was outstanding. During our two weeks off duty, we got to roam the city. Many people were in the market center, bickering, yelling, and pushing. The confusion was kind of fun to watch.

We saw a funeral moving down the main street. Those funerals are like nothing you would ever see any place else. Beating on pans and yelling, the Tsingtao police walked right through with the people. The Chinese have paid mourners, as well as family. That made it more like a parade.

Gordy said, "Shelburn, these people are crazy."

Lally said, "Look who's talking."

Finally, it was time to go to a new duty station, and we waited outside the headquarters building to report to the duty sergeant. After what seemed like hours, we were standing in front of Sergeant Major Keeler to receive our orders. A colonel stood near by. He must have talked to Colonel Sing, because he was smiling. He must have been told of our journey. Anytime you can get a Colonel in the Marine Corps smiling, you are in good shape. The colonel walked over in front of Lally and told us, "You have made the Marine Corps proud. You all have." We thanked him and he walked away.

The Sergeant Major addressed us and gave us our new duty station, "Sergeant Lally, it is my duty and pleasure to congratulate you and your fellow Marines on a job well done. I know that Captain Shin made presentations to you all aboard ship."

Lally said, "Sir, I have a request to make."

"Go right ahead, Gunney."

"Well, we had some Nationals who were with us from day one, and we would like them to be assigned to what ever we are going to be assigned to, Sir."

"I think we can take care of that, Gunney, but first you will all be given two weeks off. After duty leave, then we will see about reassignment. I will add one thing," said the Sergeant Major, "if any of you Marines wants state side duty, you will get it. That's after you can pass for Marines again, though."

He grinned and looked at Lally's ponytail and said, "Sergeant, all of you have been assigned together as requested. You're orders are sending you to Tsingtao. You're going to organize a unit to guard the trains from Tsingtao to Peiping, and then on up north to Chiang Kai-Sheik's troops. You will be guarding an area of some two hundred miles. These trains hold coal, ammo, and food& medical supplies. Bandits will attack them on each and every trip. We found out later that this was a fact of life.

The detachment was set up with a chain of command at various locations. The commanding officer in charge was a Captain Jerry V. Conners from Bakersfield, California. He was a career officer with fourteen years in the corps. He was a combat veteran. He was six feet tall and one hundred ninety pounds of tough Marine.

The top noncommissioned officer was Master Sergeant Gerald D. Lally. Blue Balls had finally got his stripes back. I had moved up in rank to Gunnery Sergeant, so I was now Gunny Peehole. In charge of outpost number one was Gunnery Sergeant Jesse Bedwell, alias Shelburn/Peehole. I was now eighteen years old, making me the youngest and dumbest Gunny in the Corps (temporary rank of course). In charge of outpost number two was Staff Sergeant Gordon C. Anderson. (C was for crazy.)

In charge of outpost number three was Sergeant Li Chin, alias Too Sack, our wizard.

As far as every day command, Top Lally was the man in charge. This was OK, because we all knew he would take care of us and wouldn't take any crap from higher ups. Sometimes we would get a ninety-day wonder from stateside and he could make our life a real pain. Lally was our painkiller. After all, he handled the Engineering Captain quite well.

My outpost was closer to Tsingtao than the other two, but there was a catch to it all. We did three weeks at our assigned location, and then we moved up the line. We were forever rotating. Lally said it was to give the whores fresh cock every three weeks. It made sense to us.

At Outpost Number One, I arrived at 0400 hours in a cold rain. We had escorted engine number eight with forty-two cars of coal from Tientsin. No attacks. Nothing. Well, we did have to shoot at some beggars as we passed through some villages. Kids would try and climb on the cars and throw some coal off. We had orders to shoot anyone older than ten. Lally told us not to pay much attention to that. People were freezing to death; let them have some of the coal, but not to the point of losing control. We never had to shoot anyone, however, some of the Nationals would shoot to kill sometimes. We had this one bad ass National who would shoot anything that came near the train. One day when we were going really pokey through a village, which was often, the National shot a kid that was maybe twelve years old who was climbing up the side of a car with a sack. Too Sack saw him, and in less than a second, the National was dead from Too Sack's special knife. We think the kid made it. One of the Nationals at the back of the cars, later told Too Sack that he lived.

The outpost was one long barracks, with two gun towers that had fifty caliber machine guns on deck. The outpost was for sleeping only, and we had to wait for a rotating crew to relieve us. The non-com in charge did not move; only the train crew itself rotated. The non-coms moved to Tsingtao every six weeks. So Gordy, Too Sack, and I were stuck in the same place for six weeks at a time. Too Sack lamented, "Ole Lally maggot, he got best job, yes, Shelburn?"

"Yes, Too Sack, ole Blue Balls wins again."

Each train had from ten to twenty-five guards. There was a limited air support in force that mostly checked troop movements up at the front. Outpost Number

181

Three was within a few miles of the ever-changing front lines. That is where the real problems were. Too Sack said, "If it can be cluster fucked, the Chinese can do it." I had heard of a Chinese fire drill, but after this I understood.

I would rather have been stationed in Tsingtao all the time, because it was a spot for good times and parties. But, this duty was better than anything we'd had so far. It's really hard to explain the procedure of this rotation. When I got settled in and was waiting for the next supply train, I was informed, that a special train was coming through in four days. Lally said to send a couple handcars out to make sure the tracks were OK.

I asked Lally, "What if the bad guys shoot at our guys' Asses? Four Nationals in open terrain are easy pickings."

He replied, "I know that, Shelburn, the Colonel knows that, but General Peng don't give a shit. He is doing the same thing in front of the train. In fact, yesterday he sent two handcars out. So when you send four, we got eight dumb-asses running up and down the tracks, yelling shoot me, shoot me, I want to die for ole Chiang Kai Shek. Anyway, that's the plan. Get your candy-ass tail out there and get those damn gooks on the tracks!"

"Yes, sir, ole Maggot Lally, Sergeant, sir,"

"Cut the crap, and I'll see you later Peehole." At first I didn't remember telling anyone that they called me Peehole back home. Then I remembered that I told that damn wizard. I hated that name, and I hated Bud Thompson for making the name stick and I give my little brother a kick in the ass for sticking that one on me.

I got ole Too Sack on the horn and told him the plan. He had to do the same procedure as we did, plus he was to call Gordy. He cussed in Chinese for a while and after he got done, I asked him to cuss in American for a while so I would not have to miss anything.

"Bullshit, ole Shelburn, you been out getting much push push?" Too Sack questioned.

"I haven't had time for pussy, Too Sack, I've been trying to keep these gooks happy while waiting to go back to Tsingtao. It is a real pain in the ass. You got any ideas, Too Sack?"

"Well, you could send them on a snipe hunt." The little asshole never forgot anything. "Remember the great mission you and ole Lally sent me and Ti on? Me never forget, Shelburn."

"By the way, Too Sack, how come you told Lally about me being called Peehole at home?"

"O that..." said Too Sack, "slip of Chinese tongue, it old Chinese custom."

"Fuck you, Too Sack. Well anyway, got to go now. Keep your ass covered."

Too Sack finished with, "Ole Shelburn, you watch for bandits. I watch for bandits. Gordy, he want bandits to come. He crazy Marine right, Shelburn?"

"You got it, real crazy," I replied.

From Tsingtao to the first outpost was forty-four miles by rail. From Outpost Number One to Outpost Number Two was about 15 miles, and Outpost Number Three was another 20 miles. So we had about 70 miles of no Man's Land to cover and protect by rail. It was a hell of a job on paper, and we found this assignment was just as hairy as some of our marches across Manchuria. The difference being if we made it back, we got four days off. The run itself was a ten-day run. We couldn't give the handcar guys a radio, because if they got taken out, our radios would be in the wrong hands. That meant we had no idea if they were alive until it was time for the train

Guards to change. After getting the Nationals on their way, I went back in my office. It was a makeshift corner of the barracks. I had it walled off so I could get away from the troops. Plus, it was where I could get my nooky without twenty other dumb-asses taking notes.

As I entered the room, the radio was yelling at me with sort of a buzzing sound. It was Sergeant Lally again.

I answered, "Gunny Bedwell."

183

"Shelburn, this is Lally again. I just got some good news, I think. Well anyway, that supply train has Marines on it. All your Nationals are being called to the front, and the Marines have the whole show now."

"Well now, Lally, that's interesting, but what about Too Sack? We can't afford to have his ass shot off?"

"Shelburn, I got that covered. He stays with you, and Gordy will be called back to be with you. They have changed the whole show. We got the damn thing set, and the Generalissimo didn't like it. So now it goes like this. The only outpost is number three, right behind the front lines. It looks like your ass is in high gear again. As soon as this train arrives, you are to climb aboard and head for Number Three. Since this is now a Marine operation, you are in charge. How does that grab your ass?"

"Bunch of shit, Lally. I have never been in charge of anything; you were always in charge."

"Yes, but Shelburn, you have the wizard. You will be just fine, unless you'd like me to put the crazy one in charge?"

"No, no, no. He would get our asses shot the first day!"

"Right, but whom would you rather have by your side in a firefight?"

"You got it, of course, it's the crazy one."

As the train moved into our sight, we all lined up to see the new crew. The first Marine off was a corporal. I thought, "Pretty low rank... taking these boots across no mans land." The corporal looked to be about twenty years old and about six feet and one hundred seventy-five pounds.

He approached Too Sack and me and said, "Good morning, you must be Gunny Bedwell."

"Hi, Corporal, did you have a good trip?"

"Yes, sir. My name is Corporal Gilbert Watkins. I am the escort for this train. My men need to hit a chow line and get cleaned up."

"How many Marines do you have, Corporal?"

"Well, we have twelve, Gunny. They're all fresh out of boot camp and arrived at Tsingtao, about ten days ago. They were given a couple days training for guarding these supply trains. In other words, they don't know shit. You are right there Gunny. One asshole fired his weapon at a gook walking near the tracks, so I got to write him up and take him back on the next train coming down from Outpost Number Three. I understand you guys will all be moving up the line, Gunny."

"That's what we hear. I should be getting a message from Sergeant Lally soon.'

"Well, Gunny, I have it right here." He handed me a sealed letter from Headquarters. TSINGTAO, as a letterhead, and M/Sgt. Lally were written on the front.

"Hey, Too Sack, ole Lally's big shit now."

Too Sack looked at the letter and added, "Yes, ole faggot Lally, he big shot now."

The corporal looked at me like who is this gook and why is he talking like that about Sergeant Lally? To make the corporal understand about Master Sergeant Lally and us, I said, "You see Corporal, ole Too Sack and I were with Lally at Operation Snow-White."

"Wow, that was you guys? Hell, you're famous at HQ in Tsingtao!"

"I don't know about that, but let's see what we got and move this outfit up the line." I read the orders confirming my talk with Lally. I put everything in gear to make the move. We had only been in operation two weeks when the change came down.

By the next morning, we had Nationals moving to the front and marine train guards moving to the west. Three hours later we could see the outpost. The trip was uneventful, and we were soon to move into our new home.

Too Sack said, "This is going to make a long trip each week."

"Yes, you got it. It's a long ride with too many dangers.

The barracks was pretty much the same. We ended up with Marines on rotation. Ten would always stay at the outpost, and the eleven would take the empty train back, go on their pass, and send back another crew. We knew one thing for sure. The danger was in making the trip up the line, because we would be loaded with food and fuel. All of us were together now except for Link who had died in Operation Snow-White.

It was now September of 1947.The new recruits were a pain in the ass. They had never seen hard times and bitched about everything. I put the hammer on them from day one; I played hardball all the way. They were so damn glad when it was time for me to rotate back, and they let me know it. But, as a gunny in the Marines he does as he damn well pleases, and it pleased me to kick their pussy cake asses at every turn. Hell, they were "Hollywood Marines anyway".

Too Sack said, "Ole Shelburn, you pissed off on twenty-four hour clock."

"Yeah, you're right," I answered, "until these pecker heads understand how to handle themselves out here, I'll be pissed and running in high gear."

Too Sack gave Corporal Gilbert Watkins his new name. He called him Chi Wie Ta, which translated in American; I think it meant Leader of Fuck-Ups. We later cut it down to Ta. He already had heard his new name and was happy with it. Gordy said, "He might as well be."

"You're right about that," I added.

I called Corporal Ta in to talk about his train guard troops, "Ta, where in the hell did you get these guys? That fucking Murdoch couldn't find his ass with both hands on a clear day, and furthermore, that Private Teapot…"

"It's Private Pisspot, Gunny."

"Well, Ta, thank you, I like that much better," I continued. "I never in my time in the Corps ever seen a walking, talking, useless asshole in my life. He can't sweep, he can't clean, and he can't even eat his supper

186

without spilling something. I can't figure out why or how he is still alive."

Ta responded, "Well Gunny, I agree with you. He is a mess."

"Where did Lally find these people? Hell, I know they have to be Hollywood Marines! (That means trained in California, which was also known as rest camp.)

"Yes, sir, you are right. They are Hollywood Marines."

"Does that go for you, too, Corporal Ta?"

"I am afraid so, Gunny."

"Holy shit," said Gordy, "Shelburn, he must be the pick of the litter!"

"Bring in Private Cumdumb, Ta."

"Sir, you mean Private Wattle?"

"Yes, of course, that's the same guy. He is the one jacking off behind the barracks every night isn't he?"

"Yes, sir, that's him."

"Well, send Private Cumdumb in." A few minutes later, he was standing in front of me. "Let's start off with a problem of yours, Private. Since your arrival last week, I have had sixteen reports of you jacking off behind barrels, buildings, wagons, huts, and who knows where else! What have you so say for yourself, Private?"

"Sir, that report is a little high in numbers, Gunny."

"Listen to that shit, Ta, the report is a little high. Well, Private Cumdumb, you will stop beating your meat in public or I'll send your ass packing with a court marshal. Do you understand that Private?"

"Yes sir, Gunny."

"Another thing, Private. It's hard to understand you beating your meat when we have fifty girls around here that can't wait for migwa Bing, big peckered Marine. Explain that Private." I whispered to Gordy, "I can't wait for this answer."

"Well, sir," continued the private, "they showed us films back at Tsingtao on the VD percentages. According

187

to the movie, it was up to eighty-five percent likely the Chinese girls are unclean."

At this point it was all I could do to hold Too Sack back. Too Sack responded, "Chinese girls very good, very clean. They washy-washy before push-push and after push-push. Lally Maggot push-push an all China record. Maybe he push-push over a thousand times. He no get VD. Films all fake."

I replied, "Too Sack, he gets the message." Addressing Corporal Ta, I said, "This is an order. Take Private Cumdumb out, and get him laid tonight. I want a report on my desk in writing in the morning at 0800 hours. If I like the report and we don't ever catch Ole Cumdumb pounding his tom tom again, we will give him a new name. Dismissed."

We finally got this crew on its way, and I told Lally never to send them back. I had never seen so many screw-ups in the Corps. We always got a dumbass or two, but twenty? Gordy asked, "What happened. Did the Army, Navy, and Air Force team up and we got the California Marines? Recruiters must have been on a three day drunk, and the assholes signed up anybody."

We had about five days before the supply train was expected in, so I decided to give myself some time off. Things were quiet, and we hadn't heard any boom-boom from the east for a few days, so what the hell?

I had heard about some tombs. These tombs of the old warlords and some of their gods were about forty miles to the north of our January 1948 location in the Chains Province area. This area was too far west for Mao to have any scouting parties nearby, so it seemed like the right time.

I left Gordy in charge, and I also phoned Lally to cover my ass. We packed my jeep up with plenty of gas, food, and a couple extra wheels since the Chinese roads were such that we sometimes made our own. Too Sack followed by in a half-track with two coolies. Hell, we had enough stuff to stay a month, but Old Too Sack and I knew

188

the rules of the road. We covered as much ground as old Mao and his cutthroats in north China and Manchuria and Mongolia.

As we traveled, I moved Too Sack up to my jeep and let one of the coolies drive the half-track. Too Sack said he had taught him how to drive it. He started out fairly bad; he looked like a drunk on the way home from the pub, but he got better.

Too Sack said, "He used to be a rickshaw driver."

I said, "Oh, good, Too Sack, I feel much better." I had wanted Too Sack with me, because he could give me some insight about the terrain and what we might see.

Too Sack called this area the beginning or the cradle of civilization, it was part of the yellow river valley. It was mostly plagued with misery. Millions of people still lived in caves in this area. The loess, wind and silt, had been hitting this area for a thousand years. So to go with that we had a few huts and too many caves surrounded by ancestral graves and fields of grain and cotton. At certain times of the year, Too Sack said the whole area would be under water. He had seen the river look like a sea filled with bloated bodies and rotting grain. Then there were periods of no rain, and it all dried up creating the other end of the weather problem.

Too Sack said that when the crops died, the people sold their children as servants, and others turned to cannibalism just to stay alive. Yet this area held more people than Russia.

I said, "Tell me, Too Sack, is this one of the good periods? I don't want to end up being someone's supper?"

He answered, "You no worry, ole Shelburn, this year was good year, much grain, no flood, and people OK."

I looked over at Too Sack and noticed he had his fingers crossed…the little prick.

We looked for an old imperial academy that was set up during the Han Dynasty, under Confucianism state doctrine.

As Too Sack explained to me about the Han dynasty, we came upon a small village. I stopped the jeep and used the glasses to look over the general terrain. About five hundred yards up were some mud huts. To our right was a stream. What looked like a young boy and man were fishing in the stream? The road curved, so whatever was ahead near the stream, we couldn't see. Too Sack took the glasses when I said, "Look at the stream Too Sack." He looked at the stream and the two people fishing. I said, "Look, don't stare for an hour."

He said, "Wait, Shelburn, it's a trap, something is wrong."

"What is wrong?" I demanded.

"Look again, you will see those fishermen are not moving. They're dead, tied up, and made to look like they are fishing so that we would maybe come down there to ask questions. It's a trap, Shelburn."

"I think you hit on it, Too Sack. Let's mount those two thirties we got in the half-track and show these assholes some real firepower. Do you think it could be Mao?"

"No way, no way, too far east. They're probably bandits. Chiang control this whole area."

"Well then, let's do it! We never let bandits bother us before. Let's do some cooking, too."

Tin Wa, one of the coolies with us, got his flamethrower ready. "Too Sack, can he rig it and shoot it?"

"Yes sir, he builds good fire balls up plenty good."

"OK, here's the attack plan. First, cover the thirties with this tarp. Too Sack, you take this side. Dong can take the other side, and Tin Wa can sit up front in the jeep with me.

We started moving and picked up speed and as we neared the curve. I saw movement on my left, and then movement to the right. I slowed enough to put the jeep in a spin, at the same time sliding the half-track in backwards. I dived for cover near the front of the half-track as the tarp came off. That began one hell of a firefight as the two

190

thirties got it on. Bandits were falling all over the place; the dumb-asses had never seen such fire power. Those who escaped the thirties were flamed or shot with a Thompson sub-machine gun. It was over in less than sixty seconds. The few bandits who were left ran off over a hill out of sight.

We counted the dead. "Wow," said Too Sack, - seven dead bandits in very short time, ole Shelburn."

"Yeah, we're good, Too Sack. We're the best fucking bandit killers west of the Pecos. Let's see what we got here."

"Looks like they in pretty bad shape, long time no food."

"I think you're right. Let's go and cut those bodies down." It was a man and a boy from the village. Later, villagers told us the bandits heard us coming and set a trap. They killed the man and the boy who were fishing. When I heard that, I told Too Sack, I don't feel so bad about wiping those assholes out now."

Too Sack said, "Me never feel bad in the first place."

I wondered how many times we were going to survive these battles? Too Sack added, "Shelburn, we like Lally."

"You mean we never seem to get bent out of shape."

"Well, me now talk about old China man," Too Sack lamented. "If China man out of power, he becomes a Taoist because Taoist don't worry about authority or power. Taoists believe it just supposed to be. Now, if I be in a good position and have some important job, I would be a good Confucian because this doctrine supports the status quo. However, if death approaches, a man turns to Buddhism, because that faith offers hope of salvation."

"OK, Too Sack, which one are you in?" I asked.

"Me think me Buddhist. This trip shows signs of belly up." Another term he learned from us; he learned so much from us. Important things like cussing like a pirate, plus many other low life activities.

I am not into abnormal sex. Even as a young dumb ass I considered those people sick. We sure saw plenty of it in China. Some of the villages we went through treated sex like dogs in the street. Yet, at other places, sex with women had better be after marriage, or your head may get lopped off. Strange place this China.

Too Sack went on to tell us more about Taoism. He said it had a symbolic emblem, a circle with two small circles inside, one purple and one is black. The black is the female, the ying or passive one; and the purple one is the yang or the active one, the male.

"Is that more bull shit, Too Sack?"

"No, no, me tell truth, ole Shelburn." With Too Sack who could be sure?

We moved on. Within two hours we neared where the old Han's remains were still in place. I looked at the odd buildings as we approached. All along one front were stone statues, as many as forty. They were all standing about five feet seven inches high, a normal Chinese size. All were alike on this first building. We moved on to the next building. It had an archway entry. Too Sack said this was the high courtyard where people were given punishments, which ranged from a slap in the face to off with the head. It was an odd, funny feeling, looking at something possibly thousands of years old. We walked around for about an hour. Too Sack gave me his usual history lesson. At eighteen years old, I had an interest, but not like an older person would. I did take a chunk of the old building with me, which I still have. I also took some pictures with my Japanese camera, and I still have those, too.

Finally, it was time to go. We wanted to get back before dark, and we sure didn't need another firefight on the way back. "No need to worry," said Too Sack, "we kill off all bandits. They hide out; take many days for them to regroup." Well, he was right again. Maybe the little bastard was a wizard!

I had a surprise message when I got back. Lally was coming to visit our little shack of dreams. That was good news; I was looking forward to seeing ole Blue Balls. Too Sack, Gordy, and I decided we would arrange a little party for old Lally. It was a masterful job. It almost cost us a stripe, but it was well worth it.

Let Too Sack set the scene for you, in his own perfect American talk, "Big chop chop train is coming round bend. Lally Maggot is waving at his buddies.

"He no see push-push coolie girls yet." We had three girls lined up beside the track. Each of them was in their birthday suit, and each one held a sign. The Number one girl's sign said, "Lally ni mig wa bing," the Number two girl's sign read, "Blue Balls welcome," and the Number three girl's sign was a masterful edition. It was printed and designed by Gordy and it read, "Pussy be sore when old Lally leave."

It was a very, very good plan. However as they got closer, I looked into the glasses of an American officer. He was looking into my glasses.

"Oh, shit," Too Sack.

"What's the matter?" questioned Gordy, beating Too Sack to the punch.

"Look," I said as I handed the glasses to Gordy.

"Holy horse shit!"

By then, Too Sack had grabbed the glasses and he said, "Me see ole Lally holding his head with both hands. Oh, Chinese shit, me see why. Big faggot officer is on board. He major, oh my, oh my, oh my!"

They were quickly within talking distance. "Explain this one to me, ex-Sergeant Bedwell."

"Old Shelburn Maggot, I said to myself," as Major Carl Gareth stepped off first with Lally right behind.

"Good morning, Sergeant Bedwell. By the way, please explain to me this little show you have put on for us. "Oh, I am sure it was for Lally and the troops to get a kick out of. I am not that damn far out of it, or at least he tells me."

"Well, sir, it's like this. Sergeant Lally is a hero to these Chinese girls. It was their way of saying Hi." I thought Lally was going to lose it, and Gordy was grinning like a dog eating shit.

"Did they make up the signs, too, Gunny, soon to be Sergeant?"

"No, sir, that was Too Sack's idea," Gordy added.

"No add Too Sack, me no write American. Gunny Peehole did it."

"Who in the hell is Gunny Peehole?"

"Sir, I think he means me, sir." I answered, while glaring at Too Sack.

"I'll say one thing. You assholes have been in China too long, and out at the front too long It's time to haul all your asses back to Tsingtao."

"Very good," said Too Sack, "Major good officer, a four point zero."

"Cut the crap, Too Sack, I have heard about you all over China." He looked at Lally and asked, "Is he really a wizard?"

"Major sir, he is a real wizard; he had seen the future many times," answered Lally.

"Well, Too Sack," said the major, "can you tell me what I am thinking right now?"

Too Sack waited and then said, "You no hurt Too Sack if Too Sack tell?"

"No, I wont hurt you. Let's hear it," said the Major.

"You were thinking of Number one sign girl, one with big titties. Yes, Major Sir?"

The major looked at Too Sack for a full minute before answering. We thought Too Sack was a goner. The major moved right up in Too Sack's face and said, "You're not bad. This son of a bitch is really a wizard! Why do you call him Too Sack?"

Lally answered, "He has big balls."

194

"So he has, so he has," said the major. Lally told us later that he had told the Major to expect anything and everything. The major was a Marine's Marine. He understood humor, and humor had to be around us at all times. Without it we would have been falling apart after all we had been through.

For the next few hours the major looked our little operation over. The very next morning he was getting ready to take the next supply train back, when news came from the front by way of a Nationalist runner from Colonel Wei, a relative of James Wei. He later became the China News Service Director on Formosa. He told us the front lines in this area were about to change, because Mao had sent another division into the area trying to get through Chiang's 177th regiment. The order was to get the train headed back as soon as possible with all aboard. It would take about four hours to do all of this. The question was how much time did we have? The major called Tsingtao; they didn't even know about it. Headquarters told the major to go with the colonel's orders and take no chances.

In less than four hours, we were on the road. At least we were five miles east of Outpost Number three heading toward Tsingtao.

Lally was the first to see a big roll of smoke rising over a hillside. It was a bridge that was part metal, part wood that the train must go over. It was burning. Too Sack yelled at the major, "Trap…trap!"

The major agreed and gave orders to stop the train. We were told to take off all the heavy equipment, all firepower, and get ready to battle. In the distance, we could hear the unmistakable sound of tanks; Too Sack had his ear to the ground and said they were two hundred clicks away.

We were equipped with four half-tracks with thirties mounted, plenty of TNT and sub-machine guns, and three 4.2 mortars. We were thirty-five troops strong including the major.

"There!" yelled Gordy, "Look! Man, oh man, I think it's over, Shelburn!"

"Never count us out, Gordy, we have been up against these kind of odds before. Even bad as this looks," I added.

Over two hundred Red Chinese rushed us from two sides. We put the thirties back-to-back and fired at will. We took cover behind the engine and the front two cars, which had a lot of metal in them. I saw at least seven Reds fall in front of the thirties. The Reds had Russian-made rifles plus sub-machine guns. We could tell the machine guns were Russian, because the ammo clips had a big curve to them.

Gordy yelled, "We got a Marine down!" I looked over and saw this kid holding his belly and I knew he was a goner. We couldn't get to him since they were overrunning our position at that time. The Major was trying to get the area in front of the tracks cleared.

I said, "Lally, what good will that do?"

He yelled back, "They won't blow the tracks; they need to keep the tracks open as bad as we do. By using the firepower from the half-tracks, we were able to get the train moving. The fire had been set near the tracks to make it look like the bridge was burning so we would slow down and get picked off. By now more than thirty Reds were laying on the ground as far as I could tell. We finally rounded the bend out of the sight of the Reds, and the firing stopped. After moving about ten miles, we stopped to take a head count and make plans for our trip back to Tsingtao. We were only eighteen miles from Outpost Number two, if it was still there. We had Chinese Nationals manning it, about five men, if they hadn't deserted it yet. We had supplies there--more ammunition and food, plus some medical supplies. I never said much about the wounded or medics. It's quite simple; we had none. In fact in all our battles, we rarely had any. So, if we got hurt bad, we died.

We started to relax a bit. The major had contact with Headquarters at Tsingtao, and all was well up ahead. We got a card game started on the tail car between Gordy, Lally, Too Sack and Ti. Lally, like in everything else was usually the big winner. We played for about anything: like seconds on Lally's whores, Chinese rot gut, bullets, guns, clothing, anything that was of value.

Too Sack stopped playing and said, "The engine is slowing down." We all jumped up, grabbed our weapons, and got ready for whatever was coming.

We saw the major walking back to our car and yelling, "Sergeant Lally!"

"Sir," Lally answered.

"We are in deep shit again. This damn train is deader than shit. The engine just quit, and the half-assed engineer doesn't have a clue. All he could do was point."

"Right...now what?" I said.

"Well, Gunny Peehole, it looks like we walk about fifteen miles. I'll radio ahead and see what they want us to do." In a few minutes the Major gave us our orders. He wanted Lally, Gordy, and I to stay with the train to protect it, until they could bring someone back to get it going. In fact, they were on the way from Tsingtao now. The crew, including the Major, would be picked on up down the tracks.

After they had started marching off, I said, "Lally, this doesn't make much sense."

"What...us staying here or them marching off? Well, it's like this, Shelburn. The major thinks it's better to lose three crazy bastards. He knows bandits have been working this area. He already has to account for one dead Marine, and three more dead Marines sitting beside a dead train won't look good in his G-2 file, but I guess he figures we are lucky s-o-b's, and we will find a way to protect the train." Then he said, "Hell, I don't know. Who can ever figure out officers?

"Oh well, Shelburn," said Gordy, "what the hell does it matter? We will never get back to our lines again. There's always something that happens to pull us back in one of the Reds' traps. Face it, we may as well start planting rice, find a coolie girl or two, fuck them night and day, and live a happy gook life."

Too Sack said, "Lally, honorable maggot, can you turn Gordy off? He make me sad."

"Yeah, Gordy, can that shit. We'll make it back; we just have a few things to do yet."

"But," Gordy said, "It seems like we are the only guys fighting this damn war. All our buddies are back in Tsingtao having a hell of a time. We never even hit that so called rotation plan, no days off, no nothing. It's a bunch of shit, Lally."

"Oh, things will start looking up, Gordy," I said. "The day will come, and we leave this place."

"Sure, and drill instructors are wonderful people."

"I am not even sure drill instructors are people," commented Lally. "It's never been proven."

Gordy just looked at Lally and shook his head.

"Lally, I don't think it's a good idea sitting out here in the open on top of a railroad car. Shouldn't we be taking cover while we wait?" I asked.

"Hey, that's what this radio is for," he said waving it at me.

"Oh, yeah, that will scare the living hell out of them."

"OK, OK, so we move to some cover."

I still couldn't understand why the Major sent troops on down the line. If we had a train coming to pick us up, it didn't make sense. There was no logic. It was nuts.

I took center stage and gave my two cents worth. I had been thinking about what was going to happen during the next few months and what might happen to us. "You know, this thing is going to come to a head. Old Mao and General Chiang will never come to terms. Old General Stilwell will try to cut out a peace agreement, but it won't hold. So, just maybe, let's take things into our own hands" Interested, Lally?"

"In what way?" he asked with a lot of suspicion in his voice.

Gordy was spellbound, and Too Sack was all eyes and ears. I had their attention. I continued with my

198

thoughts. "First of all, as I said, it's going to come to a head sometime during the next few months. Now, we have already laid our lives on the line many times over for Nationalist China and the USA. I think if things stay as they are, our numbers are going to be coming up. We can't always come out smelling like a rose. We have been damn lucky."

"What are you getting at, Shelburn?"

"Well, Lally, when we get back to Tsingtao, let's really try and get a feel for this civil war situation. If the war goes the way I think it's going, the Reds will overrun us within four months. Those supplies keep decreasing, and America is no longer supporting General Chiang, at least not like Russia is supporting the Chinese Reds. We are going to be here for the final battle. Winner takes all. Losers die."

"Go on." said Lally.

"If we see this war is lost, and I think very soon we will, then we need a plan. We have to outsmart both the Nationals and the Reds. I am telling you history has shown that we leave troops all over the world. When the shit hits the fan, the head honchos don't give a damn about us. Some big shot from Washington will pull us out ...too late as usual."

Lally interrupted, "Where do you get these ideas, Shelburn? It's not that I don't believe you."

"Well, Lally, I am a history buff. Notice I read a lot?"

"Yeah, Shelburn a real bookworm," Too Sack stated.

"So this is it. When that moment comes and we are still moving materials to the front, let's take out one of the supply trains. We can get on the spur that heads for Chengchow, then cuts over to Pen to Nanking to Nanking to Shanghai. But, I only suggest this if they don't try to get us out."

"So you're saying, if the situation is right, and we are going to die like probably a million Nationals will, if they lose. At that point in time we have to have an escape plan?"

"That's it, Lally."

"Damn, Shelburn, I like it."

"So do I," said Gordy.

Too Sack said, "Me stay with you guys. Since I be with you, I have been on great times, wonderful buddies, and me go with you guys."

"Ass hole buddies," Lally said. "Here's to us, and those like us. There's damn few left. And here's to Link, a warrior, one of our very own. We will miss him forever in our minds."

All went well. They soon returned with some half-assed mechanics and got Old Number fifteen going. Life then changed for us; we were taken off the train guard duty. It was all turned over to the Nationals.

It was starting to get cold again in China. We spent the next six months raising hell in Peiping, Tsingtao, and other cities along the coast.

It was a time during which we had to watch our backs, because the Chinese people had learned through history to bail out when a new force was about to take over. They played the middle line until they could get a pulse on things. The streets were unsafe. We had orders to never leave the compound with fewer than six. Several fights took place with the Tsingtao police and with just plain thugs. Times were changing, and even old Chinese friends could not be trusted in the Tsingtao area.

One night we all went to the Camay Club, and some Nationalist soldiers came by. We didn't know them; they had a division patch unknown to even Too Sack. They made a comment to Too Sack; he responded in a tone that we knew as some smart-ass remark. Gordy asked Too Sack what they had said.

He said, "They said it's time to quit hanging out with Marines, if I want to live."

"What did you say, Too Sack?"

"Me tell them me be outside in a minute, and then me send them to meet honorable ancestors. They wait for us now." I asked if they were Reds wearing National uniforms. "Me not know, but they very mad. Boo How."

"Well, fellow warriors, let's go see these traitors and have some fun," replied Lally. As we stepped outside, we could see eight Nationals standing by an alley. Too Sack and the Nationals started yelling at each other. Then, all hell broke loose, shots were fired, two Nationals lay dead in the street, and we went on our way. Gordy was reloading his forty-five.

At 0800 hours we were in deep shit. The Provost Marshall hauled us in. We stood in front of the Tsingtao police chief as well. Too Sack explained the situation. He told them the Nationals fired first, and explained how it all went down. Finally, after several hours, the Provost Marshall, a Captain Regular Marine Corps gave us the skinny. "Sergeant Lally, you are the highest ranking Marine involved in this mess. Believe me, I understand, but we are dancing to a new tune here in Tsingtao and even in China. We can't afford any thing else like this to happen. We are going to keep this out of Washington's ears, but let me make it clear, any more Chinese Nationals get killed by Marine personnel, a court marshal will be in order."

THE BIG 1947 CONFERENCE
Mao and Chiang standing side by side

This meeting was set up by the United States between the two civil war factions, to try and bring the "3rd China Civil War to a close".

What made me wonder the logic of our attendance. Here we are- field packs, weapons everything on the ground off the side of a large hillside.

Well here we are, plus 400 Nationalist solders at inspection for the big show. Bandits or anyone with firepower could have taken us out, just another dumb and dumber act by the top brass. This war was stopped only at this airfield for the meeting. Dumb and Dumber must have planned this show.

About half way into the meeting, a plane dived down took a close look at us, we grabbed our weapons and fired at it. All of us were given a barrel of shit, but nothing come of it. This ball of shit can only be summed up as a cluster-fuck.

End result General Marshall returned to his desk in Washington, next thing the funds for Chiang were taken away, the rest is history. Must have been a very rewarding trip.

After this cluster fuck we had some time off, before we started our journey back to the Tsingtao area so Too Sack and I went to a local bar to check the women out. We would have taken Lally with us but he was already roaming the general area.

We found a couple of ex- Pilots who before the war were flying the Flying Tigers and were now working for the Nationals. They had no idea that Marines were in North China. (No CNN to give our positions away).

Most of the veterans of the China-Burma-India Operations had no idea there were any Marines in North China. Very few people knew of operations taking place in Manchuria and Mongolia. The Marines have been a presence in the Orient since the early 1900's In fact one or two of the "Old China Hands" from pre-world war two are still around.

Few people would know anything about convert operations going on between Formosa and main land China. Covert means just that Covert.

China duty was great duty for most Marines after the Japs were returned to Japan. Marines still got shot at and killed by bandits. Red Chinese, and yes Russians. No one likes to talk about that. Not politically correct, you see. Why we think we have to kiss up to the Russians beats the hell out of me, after them working us over for all these years and finally the commie system falls on its ass, here we come; we will help you comrade, let us help-help-help? Hell they are still Russians? Believe me they will hit us again. Read about General George S. Patton and what he thought about them. For all you bleeders- after we get another shaft, drag this book and ole blood and guts off the shelf and read. I hate to admit that I hold a dogface as my greatest hero of WWII, even above Audie Murphy (doggie), and Chesty Puller (jarhead).

Symbol Picture of Bridge
BRIDGE 28-- TSINGTAO

Our next assignment was with the same unit, the Third Engineering Battalion. However, we were blowing up old bridges and making way for the new "Bailey type bridges".

Things went pretty good for a few weeks. Then on a patrol just south of bridge 28, we were attacked by a band of Mao's cutthroats, or bandits--at that time we didn't know which. There were four of us, all Marines except for Too Sack.

The area was filled with Red Chinese and Nationalist Chinese, but it was neither group who attacked us. It was the last hold out of the Fung Chu dynasty, a herd of left over bandits. We had heard the Japanese had rooted them out and destroyed them. We learned the hard way. This was NOT the truth.

We knew that earlier Bridge 26 was attacked and some Marines were never accounted for.

For the next few weeks we lived a life unknown to the outside world. Our lives would never be the same. Young men, fresh from the Pacific, could not in their wildest dreams, known what lay ahead.

We were overrun at the bridge many were shot and some were taken prisoner.

We took a two-day march though the mountain passes. We knew they were not going to shoot us, or they already would have by now. But, what was our reason for living?

After the march, we arrived at our location. We saw a strange looking village, armed and ready for any major attack. For the past three days we had seen troops from the mountainsides. We concluded it would take a regiment to take over this compound.

Too Sack took in everything during the forced march. He said we must remember these things when we escaped. (That boy never lacked for confidence.)

The bandits pushed us around for a while; then upon command from one of the leaders, we were put into small cells. The cells were made of a combination of mud, mortar, and concrete. There was one small window, which was more like a slit with a limited vision of the outside.

One by one we were taken to another building for questioning. This didn't work too well, because none of them could speak American.

First, they took Lally in and screamed at and punched him for a couple of hours. We could hear Lally taking the beating. Finally, they put him back in his cell. Next, it was Too Sack's turn. He was mistreated worse than the rest of us. He took some pretty good shots. We later found he had a few broken ribs. By the time they got to me, they had given up on getting any information, so I only had to take a few shots.

No one bothered us for the next few days. We were fed once a day, usually around midday, just rice plus some water.

Since Too Sack could listen to the guards and pick up bits of information, it was important for us to communicate as quickly as possible. It was the twenty-sixth day of captivity when a strange thing happened. I was looking out the little slit of a window, and a young coolie girl was looking in at me. She grinned and handed me a note. It was from Too Sack. In the note it said, "I have made a friend. At 1400 hours our doors will be unlocked." At 1400 hours right on the money, the cell doors were unlocked, and we were on our way. It seemed Too Sack had talked to the coolie girl Le-Wan and promised her she could go with us as far as Chi-Cho, a small village near the ocean. The guards were all sleeping. (You can get shot for a hell of a lot less in China.)

We walked down an old road leading to the village of Chi-Cho and encountered no problems. Everything went well, and we saw no one until we moved into the village. After a four-mile walk, Le Wan rejoined her family and told the villagers we were A-OK.

As promised, we dropped the girl off before we got to Tsingtao. After getting food from the villagers and taking a two-hour rest, we headed for Tsingtao. We entered the city and walked to the nearest police station. We told about our experience. Soon the Military Police arrived, and we were taken to the Provost Marshall's office.

They checked with the Third Engineering Battalion Commander who confirmed our story. One of our patrols had seen the Red Bandits overrun our group, but they were too far away to help. After our story checked out, we were sent back to our unit.

"No medals, we're just glad you're back," said the Provost Marshall.

I asked, "Don't we get a P.O.W. rating or something?"

The Marshall answered, "P.O.W. my ass, you were only gone for about a month. Look at all the rest you got."

"Rest, your ass, sir! They beat the living hell out of us!" countered Too Sack.

"OK, so I'll put it in my report," said the Captain. "Good luck, and get out of my face!"

Colonel Sing had one more operation in mind, and since we were a pain in the ass to everyone, he realized that we were only worth a damn while on a mission. I guess we had lived this way for so long that we needed action to keep us going.

The Colonel did put in his report that we were POW's, but the Marine brass said, "Let it go. We have enough explaining to do to Washington now."

Too Sack said that the POW meant, "piss on Washington".

I remember when Marines were told it was a dishonor to be captured. Now things are different. Don't get me wrong; I know a little bit how that act goes. We went through hell; it's funny how things change. For example, a few years ago a pilot was shot down and hid out for four days. We found him and took him home that's great. The orphans of Chiang Kai Shek spent twenty six days in a hellhole and escaped. We returned to a few words from Master Sergeant Tyler Briggs who said, "Glad you're back. By the way, you guys have four days off before you have guard duty again. What a deal!" We had a thirty day "war" a few years back, and the whole damn country went ape shit over our "returning veterans".

OPERATION CHI WAN

In 1947, as the Third China Civil War was in full swing, an elite force was formed by General Chang, including only his most trusted men. The operation needed a demolitions team, so we were invited along. Since we were the only ones trained in nitro, it would be our job.

206

Within this group were a team of Chinese Nationals, plus Too Sack, and the four of us. General Peng set up the details of the operation. We were located near Tientsin at what used to be a German girls' school. We were to spend the next four days gathering information about the mission. Most of the time, we had to wait for the translation from old Two Bagger. He got mad because we asked 'forty times per minute', so he told us to kiss off and he would tell us later.

The basic operation was for us to get behind Mao's lines and interrupt their supply lines. This gave General Chiang time to seal off the central China perimeter. The team had twenty-seven members, and all members were highly trained and had seen much combat. We were to attack on two fronts with two demolition teams. Lally and I were split up because we were the only ones trained in Nitro. This operation had several assaults planned. The first one was for us, and we had to do it alone.

Li Wing Bridge

Mao had been using this as a staging area for a future attack on Tientsin. Chiang's spies reported much action in this area. It was located next to a river. The land near it would flood every time the monsoons came.

General Peng's plan of attack was to mine the nearby dam, which was holding back the floodwaters. The General estimated we would need four hours to wire the dam and get out. A diversionary attack was to take place at the same time about two miles up the river. All the coolies working the rice fields were going to be told to run off and hide. They were also to be told that anyone still in sight would be shot. The General wanted a clear shot at the target. The dam was about five miles north of the staging area, so no counter attack was expected. The only way a firefight could develop was if a Red patrol happened to come by.

207

We were briefed and ready to go. The weather was abnormally cool for that time of year. We finally departed at 0500 hours, boarding two trucks with Nationalist flags flying from both front fenders. Their flag was a white sun with twelve points around it and a blue sky over red land.

The dam was about one seventy yards long and about thirty feet high. To blow it we had to hide the nitro in holes in the concrete. All the explosives were set on timers. Any massive movement creating pressure would set them off.

Lally said, "You know, old Shelburn, we have to climb like mountain goats to set this shit."

"Yeah," I answered, "and Old Too Sack hates high places!"

"You no worry about ole Too Sack; no wizard ever drown in river. Me got two sets of balls, plenty big."

"Oh, shut up you guys," said Gordy. "It's time to get to this shit." He was right; it was time to get serious about this mission.

As we approached the North end of the dam, the climbing began. It would have been better if Too Sack had quit making those damn goat sounds. Lally said in Chinese it sounded like a whining sissy with Saint Vitas dance.

It was dark before we got the explosives set and covered up. At two A.M., Too Sack shook me awake and said something was moving. I got my Thompson at port, cleared the trigger guard, and watched as three forms came closer. Lally said, "They are fucking goats, mountain goats--big bastards at that." He threw a rock at one and all three charged us. I fired a burst in their direction, and then everyone was up cussing and firing.

We soon found out we were dealing with more than just three goats. They had brought all their relation. It was morning before we could assess the damage. Too Sack came back with the causality report. He said, "Big ass goats cause much pain in ass. One dead goat; five Nationals asses hit hard, much damage; one Captain, with two holes in ass; five sticks of TNT missing; one Marine with big hole in back, name is Blue Balls."

"I don't see anything funny about this shit, Too Sack!" yelled Lally.

Too Sack said, "You tell me, ole maggot Lally, that Marines never turn and run? How come you got horn sticking out your back?"

"You want a purple heart, Lally?" I questioned.

"Screw you, Shelburn," screamed back Lally.

"It's OK, Lally, we'll fix you up when we get to base. We'll make you an award. It's called the Running Away from Goat Award. We had to laugh, but I know the guys who got nailed were in a lot of pain, mostly in the ass.

As we started on our return to Tientsin, we heard the sound of TNT going off, but we could see the dam was not a part of that explosion. Too Sack came up with a good answer, "Missing TNT now accounted for, big ass goat blow up."

It's a wonder we didn't have company. We must have awakened half of China that night. We returned to Tientsin without any more sideshows or conflicts with Reds or Bandits.

We never knew if any of those explosives were ever blown, because we were transferred back to our regular outfits. We did hear explosives going off in the distance during our last days in Tsingtao, but were they the ones we planted?

We had talked many times about a plan to get out of China, if we missed the last ship out. Since we were on train guard duty far from the coast most of the time, we figured we needed a plan. Even though we were now off train guard duty, we still needed a plan. The Old Master Planner Lally came up with a beauty. He sure as hell needed to have it operational soon, because things were heating up in North China.

There were many rumors about the Marines being sent back home. Lally named our plan Operation Gung Ho. Transports had already picked up Marines from further up north. At the time we thought they were just moving them to Peiping, but Lally knew what was going on. We found out that Mao's Army was on the outskirts of Peiping, as well as one hundred fifty miles from our location. The troop carriers were one hundred miles north of us, so Lally figured we needed to haul ass pretty damn quick. Truman had pulled the plug and America was no longer supplying Chiang Kai Sheik's Army. When the Russians heard this, they doubled their support to Red China's Army.

History has written about Chiang's misuse of American money to fight the war against Red China. I was up front for more than two years; the Nationals were winning on all fronts until Truman pulled the plug. Then of course, Russia sent all kinds of help into Chiang's former dung carrier, Mao Tse Tung. The Chinese Nationals were the ones who gave us bases from which to fight the Japanese, not the present Red government on the mainland.

A couple of generals landed in China on a fact-finding mission. They wrote a couple books about what was going on in China. Hell, none of them were ever near the front, except for Stilwell, and I am not sure he ever was actually near the front, but he may have been. Some of these people were only there for a few days. None of them ever was up front as far as I had seen or heard of.

History records that Chiang left for Formosa on a certain date. That information is wrong, and I can prove it. Why bother? Columbus discovered America--wrong. George Washington was our first president--wrong. If it is written, so it must be true. How dare Gunny Peehole question his peers!

Symbol for Operation Gung Ho
OPERATION GUNG HO
SEPTEMBER 1948

It seemed old Lally had been a busy boy since we were gone. He figured we would show up, and he knew if we were dead, the plan was also dead. But he had to go on as if we were there. Being a Master Sergeant at Headquarters Tsingtao, he could set Operation Gung Ho in action.

It was a Sunday morning. Lally had taken Too Sack, Gordy, and I out to the rail center to see our train. As we drove up, a guard stopped us, saw Lally and then said, "Yes, sir, go ahead, sir." Lally had assigned the guards and had changed them many times over the past two months. He didn't want anyone to know what was in these cars. As we drove up to the engine, we could see at least four guards posted, one at each direction. At night there was also one in a tower. Lally didn't want anyone getting that good of a "look see" in the daytime.

Lally said, "The first three cars behind the engine are coal cars, fully loaded. That will take us a good four hundred miles. Car number four holds our weapons, which includes thirty and fifty caliber machine guns and 4.2 mortars."

"Holy shit," said Too Sack. "You start own war, Lally."

We continued on. "Car number five is loaded with only one item." We looked as the door slid open on the side away from the guards' views, and we were looking at an eighty millimeter field artillery piece.

"Damn, how in the hell did you get that thing in there?" asked Gordy.

"Don't ask. Let me tell you it was a major bitch," answered Lally.

Car numbers six and seven were loaded with food and water. "Everything we will need for a long trip," said Lally, grinning. "Hey, Shelburn, old Lally even got rolls of shit chaser, [toilet paper]. Car number eight had enough TNT and plastic explosives to blow up half of China.

"No wonder ole Chiang doesn't have anything to fight with. Old Lally maggot has it all," I commented.

The last car, number nine, was a caboose. Inside the back door, Lally had two fifty caliber machine guns mounted.

"Mercy, mercy, you have done well, old master," said Too Sack. "You do four point zero, very ding how."

Next, I questioned, "When do we make our move, Lally? Time is getting pretty damn close right now. Someone might start checking this train out soon. You know, Lally, you are not the only brain in Tsingtao.

"You're right, Shelburn, it's going to be real close. I figure the transport is about seven days out right now. The Reds can possibly break through in five to seven days. Let's wait for one more report. If we hear of any breakdown from the west, we got to haul ass. I'll wait until morning to pull off the guards. The next shift has been pulled off. I want all three of you on the train in the floor of the engine at 0400 hours. The guards go off duty then, so you watch. When they are out of sight, you get to the engine before first light. Got it, guys?"

"Yep, we got it loud and clear."

"I will join you no later than 0600 hours. I need to get one final report. It was reported last night, there was a pick up yesterday, further up the coast. A tanker loaded about five hundred Marines and some Nationals aboard, so that means they are not going to make it down here for us.

"If everything goes as planned, I think we can get going in the morning. If not, then we'll go the next morning. The train master comes on duty at 0800 hours; that will give us an hour down the track. No trains will follow us, so we don't have to worry about that."

"How can you be sure of that?" asked Gordy.

Lally grinned that shit eating grin and said, "Because, ole numb one, I think of everything. It seems all the engines in the yard have parts missing. Now, I wonder how that happened?"

At Headquarters in Tsingtao, 0500 hours, Lally had stayed up all night waiting for reports on the transport location and the Reds' movements during the night. He got what he needed. Sergeant Johnson said to Lally, "Look at this. The Reds have broken through Chin-Su; hell, that's only twenty-eight miles away." No sooner had this

212

message come through, when a report over the radio showed the transport was still three days out to sea.

Sergeant Johnson had orders to wake the General up if any new reports came over. After informing the General by phone, he put the radio system on full alert, ordering all personnel to destroy all records, and then get to the beach docking area as soon as possible. He set up a defensive perimeter around a one-mile zone with heavy-duty firepower and waited for the transport.

We later learned that US personnel were moved on up the coast to meet with another transport. Since we didn't show at the dock, we didn't know that. Lally doubted if they made it anyway. He thought the high-ranking Chinese officers would be able to leave if anyone did, and they would leave by chopper.

Just as Lally started to leave the Headquarters building, a bomb landed on the building next to the HQ. It killed everyone in it. There was no question now whether that damn transport would ever get here on time.

Code four operation Gung Ho was operational. It was now 0445 hours, Lally had to hurry. Widespread panic filled the area as more bombs were going off. Traffic was in turmoil as he raced to his jeep. He got out of the general area where the masses of people were and headed for the train yard.

As he arrived at the train, he yelled, "Let's moves this bucket of iron and wood, Shelburn, it's time to boogie."

"Hot shit, said Gordy, "we heard all the racket and got this engine fired and ready."

"The train is set; we must stop at the main line for a moment. I am going to blow this place up. I set explosives all over the place, just in case I decided to do it. This way, I know that no one will ever come down the south tracks for years.

We moved slowly gathering steam as Lally jumped off and ran to a little shack. He came running out counting off his watch for twenty-five seconds. Bam...bam...ka-bam...rip...snort! There was shit flying everywhere. "I

213

must have put too much charge in that one," he said. We all shook the dust and wood off us as we looked straight ahead. "Don't look back, it's bad luck."

"Fuck you, Lally," Gordy said as he looked back.

Too Sack said, "Me no look back; me wizard, and I know Lally's a Marine wizard." I didn't look back either. It was time to move forward, to whatever awaited us in the days ahead.

We knew we had to make it to Ti Po and then down to Shan-Hsin-Tai. Granting we made it that far, our next goal was getting through the big city of Soochow. Lally had orders cut from the Nationalist government, which gave us clearance on down the tracks all the way to Hong Kong. That is where we planned to cross over to freedom, but this had to be changed later on. It was his hope that by the time we took off, all communications to the south would be down, because of the Reds' invasion. If a call got through, we were goners for sure. Lally figured this would be Nationalist territory for at least a month, maybe more. Of course, all the papers were forged with the proper command signatures. Lally said he hated to sign Colonel Sing's name to everything, but there was no other way. We would have liked to take the Colonel with us, but we just couldn't take a chance.

We had moved about twenty miles down the line with no problems. Lally had a powerful radio on board so we could pick up any communications. Too Sack translated the following radio action after the Red attack. It was the first report that came through concerning our blowing up the rail center.

"Colonel Sing Wu, this is Major Turner. Sir, the Reds have blown the rail center."

"Great," yelled Gordy, "they think the Reds blew it!"

"Colonel, we have not accounted for the two Marines or Sergeant Lally, but they may be down at the beach. There is too much confusion right now; I'm afraid if they are not behind the blockade by now, they are dead."

214

"I understand," said Colonel Sing. "The choppers are arriving, and it's now or never, Major. Get your butt up here." The radio went dead.

Lally said, "I've got an idea. Too Sack, when we get out of Tsingtao's radio contact, I want you to send a radio message to the rail center located in Hong Kong and tell them we are on direct orders to escort a very important Chinese leader to Hong Kong, and we need their help on getting clearance."

"Holy shit," stated Too Sack, "I suppose we are carrying the Generalissimo himself."

"You got it, Too Sack. In fact, I've got an outfit, a black gown that the General wears. You are going to be the General, Too Sack."

"NO, crazy maggot Lally; they shoot ole Too Sack."

"Oh hell, Too Sack, they have never seen the General. Not any of them are going to get close enough anyway. We can't let that happen."

"Gordy, you know that Lally is a damn bonafide genius!" I exclaimed. "It's just crazy enough to work."

Lally interjected, "Of course I am, but there is a downside. When the word gets out around Soochow, there will be traitors and those against Chiang who will try to stop the train. But it's the best and only plan I have.

Hell, if they buy it down at Soochow, they will forward us and clear the rails on southward."

"Yes, Gordy, I see a little light at the end of the tunnel."

"Yeah, I know, but we both know it's a long shot."

Next I added, "So, it's been a long shot for us for many months."

"You're right, Shelburn. It good thing you got ole Chinese wizard and mi wa beeg wizard," replied Too Sack. "But, Shelburn, do we have to call Lally a wizard now?"

"No," I answered, "to us he is still ole Blue Balls. I was thinking, Too Sack," as I pushed Lally in the ribs, "what if we get to Soochow and the mayor comes out to

215

meet the great General with the great General's wife at his side?"

"No, no, me hears great leader in Canton. He no near Soochow; he probably is in Formosa by now. Me hear that's where he goes to set up new government."

"Oh well, it was just an idea."

Too Sack yelled, "Piss on maggot Shelburn's idea. Bo how!"

Lally seemed to have covered all the bases; the engine was one of the newer ones with the most power. All we had to do was shovel the coal to it. We all took our turns. Too Sack really liked to fire the coal to her, and sometimes he would take an extra turn. Since Gordy was a lazy ass, he more than welcomed Too Sack's extra duty. Lally finally got on Gordy about it. He asked Gordy, "Did you ever in your life work at a real job?"

"No," answered Gordy.

"Why did I know that?" he mumbled to himself.

We were now out of range. We could no longer hear the sounds of war. We were also getting out of radio range, which was good and bad. It was good because no one in this area could pick up anything out of Tsingtao; it was bad because we didn't know what was going on with Colonel Sing and our friends at Headquarters.

Lally said, "You know, Shelburn, they may all be dead right now."

"I wonder if we will ever know?"

"When we are old men, we will look back on this time as the most alive we have ever been," said Lally. "No one has ever done what we have done, or seen what we have seen."

"Yeah, and probably no one will ever even know this all happened," said Gordy. "They could take us out any second, the way we live."

"Bull shit, Gordy. Two wizards and one Gung Ho Marine will save Gordy's crazy Marine ass. We'll all live happy ever after. Right, Shelburn?"

"Right, Too Sack." Yeah, I guess I really believed we would make it out. It seemed damn impossible, but then again fate seemed to be on our side.

According to Lally's charts, there was a water tower about ten miles further down the track. That would be our first stop. So far we were running about twenty miles per hour. There were no big grades to climb, and it was all pretty smooth. Maybe it was too smooth. Several times Too Sack got on the train whistle to let small villages know we were coming through. Mostly they would just wave and look on.

As we rounded a big curve in the tracks, we could see the water tower, a tank that would probably hold five thousand gallons of water. Lally said we didn't have to worry about it being full, because the Nationalist government paid these villagers to keep them serviced. But then again, did they get their last check?

They must have gotten paid because we took on enough water to last us for at least another hundred miles. Lally said this had been a big worry of his. We won again. How long can it last? Lally said to me, "You make your own breaks, Shelburn. Nobody gives you any." Life was to teach me this was pretty close to the truth.

I noticed a Chinese Nationalist soldier standing near the engine with a woman and a child. I could see no threat, but still looked around for any sign of trouble. Too Sack moved from the water tower to the platform leading to the engine. The soldier started talking with Too Sack. We waited for the conversation to end, but the man continued on. Finally Lally said, "What does he want?"

"He want to ride down to Soochow with his family. She is from there and he say he on leave and family be safer there. If we won't take him to please take wife and kid."

Lally said, "Ask him for his papers."

Too Sack asked for his papers, and he said he had left them home in a big hurry. Lally said to me. "You don't get in that big of a hurry unless you are trying to make

217

it out of China. Too Sack, I think he is trying to do what we are doing. Beat the odds. What do you think?"

"Me think you right, Lally. Let me talk some more." After a ten-minute talk with Too Sack, he admitted he was trying to save his family. He was on leave when Mao's forces broke through at Tsingtao, and to return would mean certain death. He also said five of his men were nearby. They would like to join us, too. They were hiding.

"What make you think we not just shoot you?" questioned Too Sack.

The soldier answered, "It is rumored you have General Chiang aboard this train. I think not, because first, you would have already shot me, and me no see Chiang's Imperial guards."

Too Sack related his conversation to Lally. He had a good point for Lally. It would be hard to make this story stand up, without Chiang Imperial guards.

"Ask the major who he worked for in Tsingtao."

He answered, "Yes, for Colonel Sing Wu."

Sergeant Lally was silent for a moment. Then he asked the question that would determine if the major lived or died. "What is your last name, and where did you work? What building?"

As he talked, Lally looked at a Headquarters ledger.

Major Ti Da Wong said, "I worked at a quartermaster corps."

Lally looked at this roster of Chinese officers assigned to Tsingtao. It listed at the quartermaster compound a Major Wong. "Well, well, Major, it seems you are for real. Welcome aboard. We will brief you on the plans that are in motion and see if you still want to take a ride on the wild side.

He grinned really big at Too Sack and talked briefly with his wife. She smiled back at the major and us. After more conversation, it was decided that we would pick up the five men hiding near the water stop.

Major Wong gave a command and they came out. There were two lieutenants and three enlisted men. They were all very young. I doubted if even one of the enlisted men was more than sixteen.

Lally wasted no time letting these guys know who was in charge of the train. Too Sack and the Major talked about what was needed to make the men look like Imperial guards. The major said they would not pass for Imperial Guards unless they had a blue triangle-type patch on their right shoulder.

Too Sack said, "Lally, I get my ass chop-chopping to make those patches."

"How do you do that?" questioned Lally.

"Me a damn wizard, Blue Balls." Too Sack got busy cussing new Chinese words, intermixed with a few Lally faggots and blue balls. We got the drift.

Somehow Too Sack found some red and blue cloth. He wouldn't tell us where he found it, but Major Wong said the cloth would work, and Too Sack even had a little sewing kit. Hey, we're talking wizards here.

The major and his men, who were now are men, were a likeable lot. His wife was pretty, but very quiet. Her little boy was maybe two years old. For a child he did really well as we moved onward.

Twenty miles down the line; we passed a city called Cerci. We were making good time. Lally said we were on schedule. After we cleared the village area, we took the train off onto a spur for the night. There was no nighttime break for us; the Chinese could do all kinds of things to us in the dark.

A few coolies came out to see the train, which was a usual thing. They also came out to see if they could beg or steal anything. An old man about eighty years old came over and asked Too Sack if those were Imperial guards.

"Yes," answered Too Sack. "We have an important leader with us."

The old man wanted more information and said, "Rumor has it that you have the great General Chiang with you."

"No," said Too Sack, "we have an important General aboard, and we want to make sure of his safety to Canton. General Chiang gave us some of his guards to make the trip safer."

The old man shook his head in disappointment. He would have liked to meet the great Chiang. The old man wandered back to the small group of coolies to share the information he had learned with his people.

Then he returned and asked if we could spare some coal. Too Sack said, "We can't, because we will need it to get to Canton." The old man finally left.

Lally said to Too Sack, "Do you see any trouble from the old man?"

"No, he just old man who wanted to see the Generalissimo."

Gordy said, "You're something else, Too Sack. That old man was talking with the only general we have, Too Sack."

"Piss on you, crazy Gordy, me no look like general anyway," responded Too Sack.

"You will before we get to the next stop," I added. Lally had decided it was time to start the show. The word had been passed on down the line that General Chiang was with us. Lally thought that if he really was with us, no one would be able to get close anyway. The Imperial guards would shoot anyone that came close, and the Chinese coolies knew that, so we could show the general waving as we passed by. We didn't think it was dangerous at this point in time, because people from this area in south China had been followers of General Chiang. Lally reasoned that, even though they knew the Nationals were losing, the great General would come back and save them all from the Red cutthroats. We hoped his reasoning was good, really good.

The night went smoothly, and then at the break of dawn, we were fired and ready to roll. We planned to be at our next stop, Pakzinhu, by evening. This was a much bigger town and it could be a real test for us. The General had a battalion quartered here, with a Captain in charge. Lally had his name and all the information that would be needed. But the question each time we stopped was the same. Did a radio message get through before the Reds overran Tsingtao?

As we rolled across the dull countryside, my thoughts returned to Hollywood. I had a little brother who was starting junior high school, and I wondered how was he doing? I felt like I had deserted him. He needed me, because the family was so poor. I could have been the big brother I should have been, instead of running off to fight a war. I have always felt bad about that, and I always will. I don't think evolution had arrived within me, at that time. I was dumber than owl shit, thinking only of my adventures and myself. I was just another big dumb ass loose on the world.

"Lally, did you bring any shovels along?"

"Yes, Shelburn, but that blade on the front of the engine will do the job." We were really lucky; there was no snow for several days, but the weather was really cold.

As we moved closer to Pakurhan, Lally put the glasses on. "Oh boy," he said, "it looks like we got a big welcome committee. They have soldiers lined up at the rail yard."

"Are they lined up to shoot us?" I asked.

"No problem, it's an honor formation."

"Good," said Too Sack, "very ding how."

Gordy said, "Let's be ready for anything."

"Of course, we are always ready," said Lally. He gave a command to Major Wong in Chinese; he was getting very good with his Mandarin Chinese. He told the major to post his men and to shoot anyone who tried to get near Too Sack, our imposter for General Chiang. "Too Sack, get your robes on, and this time, and stay in the last car. Only when we get ready to move on will you come to the back door, stand, and wave to the people. And remember, the General always waves with his left hand first.

"How in the hell does he know that?" questioned Gordy.

"Hey, Gordo, he's a wizard, remember?"

"You got that, ole wizard?"

"Me got it, Lally maggot, me makes 4.0 General."

"Just remember what I told you. Now Major Wong will do all the talking. His wife will act like Madame Chiang. By staying behind the General, she can pass for Madame Chiang from a distance.

"OK, come to a stop about five hundred yards from the viewing platform and hold it, Gordy," Lally instructed Gordy who was acting as the engineer.

"Bring us up slowly now Gordy. About thirty yards from the platform and the troops, Major Wong will walk up to whomever is in charge, and we will hope for the best. Remember, if the area gets hot, Shelburn will throw open that door and fire an eighty-millimeter shot at them, as a warning. If there's a rush our way, fire into the crowd."

"I got it, Lally."

"Well, get your ass back there and be ready."

Major Wong walked up to an older Chinese man standing in front. With him was a Nationalist Captain. "I hope he don't know Wong," said Gordy.

"No matter, Gordy, they're covered.

As the Major stepped in front of the two men, the Captain saluted and said, "Major Wong, when did you get the honor of working with the Imperial guards?"

"Oh, yes," said the major, "I was working with K-2 when I met you."

"Right," said the captain. "Let me introduce you to the Mayor of Pakurhan." They bowed and shook hands. "It is my understanding, Major Wong, that the Great General Chiang is on board."

"Yes, it's true, Mayor, but I am sure you understand that no one will be able to get near him."

"Oh, yes, yes, we understand. We know the war is going badly, but can you tell us where the General is going? Yet, I'm sure you can't."

"True," said the Major, "but I can tell you, we can't trust anyone these days, especially since the word has already gotten out that he is on this train. But I will tell you this; the General is going to go by ship to Formosa. Then, he will travel to the United States to ask their Congress for more supplies to allow us to push the Communist Reds back in their holes."

The Major changed the conversation, "Major, we need to take on water at the spur south of town. Could you help us with security?"

"Certainly, Captain Sin Chi will be more than happy to hold the people back away from the train."

"Thank you, sir," added the Major. "I will see if the honorable General will step to the back platform and wave to the people."

"Very ding how, Major. The people of Pakurhan will remember this forever."

I thought, "Yeah, if they only knew."

As the Major started back to the train, Captain Sin Chi asked Major Wong one last question, "Major Wong, why do you have American Marines with you?"

"Without any hesitation Major Wong said, "They were assigned to the General's Imperial Guard as an act of support from the American government."

The captain saluted the Major and all was well.

Too Sack then came into view as we pulled away. He waved at the coolies, and they went crazy screaming, yelling, and waving. Then the Madame made a brief appearance behind Generalissimo Too Sack. This was an event these people would tell their grandchildren about. I hoped to tell mine about it, too, if I lived long enough.

About three miles out of town, we found a rail spur and a water tank. Lally said, "Just another day at the office."

In the early hours of morning, we were on the move again. We were all pretty proud of ourselves for pulling off our stunt, but we knew that all could end at any moment. We were playing a dangerous game.

Lally said, "You know, we could have our heads cut off by the Chinese, spend the rest of our life in federal prison, or we could go home heroes. Hell of a choice, right ole wizard?"

Too Sack said, "Me no have three choices, only one. I make it to Hong Kong or I die. Yes, and even if we make it to Hong Kong, it's almost impossible to cross the border. Many thousands have died trying."

"Yeah, but they never had two wizards either." We all laughed at that one. It was good to laugh again.

I went back to what we called our dining car. The major's wife and little boy were sitting and looking out the window. In broken English she asked me if I really thought it was possible to get to Hong Kong. In very bad Mandarin I answered that it was possible, but I didn't think we could take the train much further.

About then Too Sack came in and helped me explain. I think her name was Okach. That was close anyway. She asked, "How will we go without the train?"

"Well, lady, we have made it halfway across China already on foot, I guess another three hundred miles shouldn't be a problem," I continued.

"You just try to make Okach feel better." She countered.

Too Sack said, "Oh, no, old Shelburn believes we will make it."

"Are you really a wizard, Too Sack?"

"Yes, lady, Too Sack is really a wizard."

Then all things are possible," she said as she smiled and continued to gaze out the window.

It was getting dark again, and it was time to start looking for the town of Chung Chang. This time we were going straight through, and taking no chances. When we got about ten miles out from the city, Too Sack made contact with the rail center master, stating we carried orders from the Generalissimo himself to roll on through, because of security. The Yardmaster gave the clearance, and stated he understood the General was aboard, and would have troops guarding the tracks through the city proper. He also said we had clearance all the way to Nanchang, since he had radioed ahead. Too Sack thanked him calling himself General Ping Tai, one of the General's top staff.

Lally said, "Now that's a twist. Now you're the great leader and also a great general? Where in the hell did you get those stars?"

"You Marine wizard, you figure it out."

"Well, it sure was timely."

"Ole Lally not only wizard you know."

Lally said, "I'll tell you one thing, this is going too well. Let's don't go to sleep and stay focused." We didn't like to run at night, but Lally said we had to make up some time.

We ran all night, and by morning we had passed the town of Sha Ho, which Lally had said it was too good to be true. Too Sack had learned by radio with the rail master that we could take on water about fifteen miles out of the city.

It was just where it was supposed to be, and all went well.

We let the engine rest for a couple of hours, checked everything out, got off and walked down to a creek, took our first bath in days, changed clothes, and were ready to make our run to Nanchang, which was about seventy miles away.

The miles were flying by. We were making good time today because this area was really flat, and we were past the hills and steep grades. Braking these babies down was a hazard all of its own. We climbed on top of the cars, turned the wheels down, and brought them back up. With Gordy as the engineer, it was more hazardous since he always went faster than he was supposed to.

225

About twenty-five miles north of Nanchang, we passed a small town. We always slowed up, just in case. We always put the glasses on just to make sure someone didn't side rail us. Too Sack noticed it first, and then Major Wong. "Look at those signs!" Too Sack shouted to Major Wong.

"Well, Major, what do they say?" demanded Lally.

The Major said, "They say the Reds have broken through about seventy miles east of Canton." There was a series of signs set up in reading order. The next one said, "Must leave on spur at Nanchang and head for the sea. No way you can make it pass Nanchang and be safe. Good luck, great Chiang."

"Get the maps out," Lally said to Major Wong. They starting looking the railroad maps over.

Finally Major Wong said, "Right here, just north of Nanchang is a rail spur that leads to Foochow, a fishing village. It is on a small island. The only way in and out is a bridge with the tracks on it. The rails are only used in the summer. They are probably closed now, but we can open them."

"So what are you thinking, Major, try to get out by sea?"

"Yes, we can control this village, and all traffic as a National outpost. It would be the last area the communists would concern themselves with. It will give us time. I know that big fishing boats come in many times a year; the water is really deep here. We just have to catch one in time."

"How do we do that?" asked Gordy. "Do we become pirates?"

"Why not?" I added.

"What if they no want to give up ship?" questioned Too Sack.

"Now, Too Sack, that's a damn silly ass question. We shoot them," said Lally. "But first, we have to get there."

"It could be a trap, but I doubt it. Major Wong is excited. It will work, Lally, I am telling you, it will work."

"Yeah, if these maps we have are telling the truth, it says right here on this ocean depth chart that pick ups are made four times each summer and fall by this one company; the last trip in the fall by no later than October. So, we got one shot, maybe.

After another three hours of travel, we saw the rail spur leading off to the east; it was about 20 miles outside of Nanchang, so we figured this had to be it. We would have to travel slowly because we could see the rust on the tracks, meaning it had not been used for a while. We slowed down to about ten miles per hour. We were now moving toward the sea, but we had a mountain range to cross to get there. Major Wong said, "When we cross the river Min, it's only a few miles to Fu Chou and about twenty more to the village of Pa Tu."

"What about water, Lally?" I asked.

"No problem, Shelburn," said Lally, "we can make it all the way. We have enough coal and water."

"Well," Gordy said, "there must be something wrong, we have never gone this far without a firefight or something going wrong."

"Hey, Gordy, it's our turn to have some good luck, right ole wizard?"

Too Sack answered, "Wizard not depend on luck. Wizard depends on old Chinese teachings."

"Yeah, and I can fly backwards, too," I replied. There was a dialog of small talk that continued for the next few miles. We could see the mountains looming up ahead. "Let's hope our engine can handle it, right Lally?"

"Sure it can Shelburn, you worry too much."

From time to time, we had to hop from car to car to turn the wheels down or up depending on the grade. We were in the mountains all day. We stopped once to get off the train and look over the upcoming valley. It was very pretty, but a lonely part of the world. We could see for miles without seeing any signs of life. Once in awhile we did see some smoke though.

It was my turn to go back to the caboose. The major and his family were sitting in the rear seat watching the countryside go by. It was hard to talk to the Major. He knew some English and I knew some Chinese, but it made for a difficult conversation. The little boy smiled and came over and touched my face. Mostly he noticed my eyes. I wonder if he will remember this time and the white people around him, will he live to be a young man? These were questions that could not be answered.

Lally came back with news. He said that we were getting close to Nan Cheng, the only town of any size between the sea and us. "Major, I think we better stop here and wait until dark to go through. You might try and get through on the radio. See if they have a rail master, or anyone who will answer. That way we will know the tracks are OK. Also, let them know who we are and what we are doing. We will have to deal with this town as long as we are at Pa Tu."

"Yes," said the Major, " it's a good idea. I will explain if asked that the Great General has been airlifted to Formosa."

"Great!" said Lally, "that should cover us. Let's do it."

The Major got on the radio and contact was soon made with the Nan Cheng Police who had intercepted the call. They stated the rail center was too small for such a position, but that the rails were secure all the way to Pa Tu. He was also excited about news that the Great General was safe in Formosa. The Major told them that we were setting up a radio communication center, to contact ships in the area, and to direct a large shipment that would soon be coming from America, to help the defense of this area. The seed was planted.

We passed along the northern bank of Nan Cheng; alongside the tracks were the police and local officials.

They waved, and we smiled and waved back. Lally said, "Now this is the way we like it, right, Shelburn?"

"Right, Lally, just like we planned it."

The big test was about to come at Pa Tu. Everything had gone so smoothly. Lally was at the controls when we pulled into the small rail center at Pa Tu. He eased the throttle and we came to a halt. It was starting to get dark, but I could see that the streets were lined with Chinese Coolies.

Major Wong stepped off the train and saluted the mayor of Pa Tu. He gave the usual Chinese welcome, bowing all over the place.

The major conferred with the Mayor, whose name was Ni Wang; he was an older man about fifty-five, very short and skinny. Gordy said, "OK, Shelburn, what's this one's name?"

I studied the Mayor for a few moments and answered Gordy. "His new American name is Shike Poke." I named him after a little skinny guy back in Hollywood.

Pa Tu was a fishing village with about eight hundred people gives or takes a coolie. We saw no signs of troops, only the coolies, and no one was carrying weapons.

Major Wong was escorted to an area that was to be our headquarters. It was an old military post at one time and had been used in recent years as a sort of recreation center. It was walled in, and it had several one-story buildings in it. It overlooked the China Sea. We could see a hundred san pans docked nearby. There was a main street with a few stores. Lally said, "They sell to the ships docking nearby. I see several little shops that have Chinese silk items."

"Look, Shelburn, a push-push house," said Too Sack.

"That's a laundry house."

"Bull shit, old Shelburn, me know whore house when me see one. Who from China: me or you?"

229

"You are, old wizard," said Gordy. "But let's face it, if anyone in China knows a whorehouse, Lally would be the guy."

"You are right, ole Gordy. Lally Maggot, tell poor ole dumb coolie, Too Sack, is it a red light district or not?"

"Let me put it this way, Too Sack, did you ever see five girls standing in front of a laundry with their hands holding their twats?"

"Me no see hand on twat, you make that up ole Lally Blue Balls."

We got a good chuckle from that one. We were to find out later that if we wanted laid, with no questions asked, we went to the laundry building. Later, in the compound Gordy said, "Too Sack, ole Blue Balls can tell the difference between fish and twat, better than any human on the planet." Too Sack went away talking to himself in Chinese.

We arrived with our nine-car train, still loaded with enough firepower to start our own war. We posted guards and discussed what our options were.

Big problems waited to be solved, now that we had made it to the ocean. We had created several wizard-like moves to get there. Next we had to find a way to get across the Red Sea to Formosa. Should we wait for a trade ship and take a chance on Mao catching up with us? Or should we find another way?

"Of course, we find another way," said Lally.

Gordy said, "Just how in the hell are we going to do that? You heard the fishermen, trade ships are the only way."

"Maybe not, the Major was talking to one of the san panners, and he said there is a large sailboat docked down the coast about ten miles. They use it to run opium across to Formosa almost every two weeks."

"Now you're talking, Blue Balls," I added.

"Yeah, but it's controlled by the Green, and they have plenty of fire power." The Green was a gang of dope peddlers who were highly respected as killers and thugs.

"Shit, we took on old Mao and the Russians. Me thinks we can handle these assholes," added Too Sack. "What we do now, ole Blue Balls?"

"Mig wa bin, push-push wizard."

The Major let us know pretty quickly that we would have to behave and cause no problems with the village people. We needed their support to pull off the final chapter of our escape. Lally agreed, which was good. He had become more of a leader and less of a player as the months had rolled by.

For the first time in months, we realized we were limited by our size. Counting Major Wong and his five guards, we had a total of ten men, one woman and one child. However, our firepower was unequaled. We spent the next two weeks making fortifications. We planted explosives around our compound, to help with any attack from bandits, or from the Green, since they were nearby. We were just a few miles north of their port compound. We expected company at anytime. Major Wong was sure it would be a peaceful visit, at least the first time.

We lived in a two-story building: a brick and concrete construction. Lally wanted us back away from the stonewalls surrounding the compound, in case of any kind of an attack. We had running water and a shower house, which was new. Gordy said, "At least we have windows and can see for miles in most directions."

I said, "We can see the ocean."

"Yeah," Too Sack said, "and we can almost see Formosa."

Lally countered, "Sure, it's only four days by sea down the road."

Symbol of Opium Flower
The Green

The next day the Major, Lally, Too Sack, and a few of the trusted Nationals formed a plan. First, it was twenty-seven miles to the armed compound where the sailboat was.

231

The best information we had said it was between forty and fifty feet long. A crew of seven made the runs, but it would hold thirty and maybe more people. It was in a well-sheltered cove with armed guards all over the area.

We would have to send a scouting party down there to check it out. This had to be an all-Chinese party. Too Sack, the Major, and four Nationals would make the scouting trip. The weather had been bad, but it was clearing up. They decided the departure time would be at 0400 hours the next morning.

If they had not returned by 1800 hours, I was to come with all our major firepower, blow the hell out of the whole area, and make a run for it. I was also to drive halfway to the Cove, so we could make radio contact, since the radios were weak and would not get out more than ten miles.

As we headed down the coastline, we took two jeeps. They were mounted with thirties and one halftrack with a fifty caliber on board. At the halfway mark, I said goodbye and good hunting to the Major and Too Sack. I parked the jeep in the woods and waited for their return. I had one Nationalist soldier with me. It was a long wait with nothing to do. The National spoke only Mandarin, so we slept as we waited most of the day. At 1600 hours we heard the scouting party coming back. It was quite a relief.

Too Sack gave us a short run down before we started back, but I would have to wait until we made it back to the compound to get the complete skinny. Too Sack gave us the story when we got to the compound.

"So get to it, Too Sack," said Lally.

"OK, this is it. It looks possible, but it's very risky. The Major feels we will lose people on this one. We not only have the danger of taking the guards out, but they also have two gunboats at sea that will be looking for us, if and when we take over the ship. It's an old tub, but it had two five hundred horsepower engines to push it along. The Green must have made it one hell of a fishing, sailing, and gunboat. It's a large fifty feet vessel with a motor that

232

makes about twelve knots per hour. That means it will take us twenty to thirty hours at sea to reach Formosa."

"In good weather, but what about fuel?" I asked.

"We saw two extra tanks built in to make the trip. That's another problem. Maybe they refuel them at sea. Then again, we can also sail the son of a bitch," answered Lally. "We will see when we get more information."

"I don't think there is enough room to carry that much gas, anyway," offered Too Sack. "Another problem is timing, the weather must be calm, and it's too small a ship to make it through a large sea storm. Anyway, the Major feels we need to get a spy down there and see how they set up for these trips. Otherwise, the mission will fail."

"Has the Major any ideas on this?" asked Lally.

"Yes, he has a plan for this. It's damn good one, too," added Too Sack.

"The plan is this," continued the Major, "like I said we do some spying. Then we do some trading. The Green knows the ship and the sea. We trade them for a free trip to Formosa."

"What the hell have we got to trade?" said Gordy.

"A train with enough firepower for the Green to make deals with the Reds," said Lally.

"Very good, Sergeant Lally," added Major Wong.

"That is great plan! They trade or we blow their asses out of the water," I said.

"Right again," said Major Wong. "An exchange of information must take place. We will have to go there; they will have to check out what we have. It's a very dangerous business dealing with the Green, but they are going to be up a wall without help if they can't make a deal with the Reds. They may even be thinking of pulling out and heading for Formosa, but I think not, because Ole Chiang would run their asses off Formosa. The Green has made deals with Mao before. If we can watch out for the masters of trickery, we have found a way out of here."

"What do you think comrades?" I asked.

233

Lally looked around at us and we shook our heads in agreement. Lally said to the Major, "It's a go. Well done." Too Sack gave thumbs up. Our final plan had been formed and approved by the Joint Chiefs of Staff: Major Wong, Master Sergeant Lally, Sergeant Too Sack, Sergeant Gordy, and Gunny Peehole.

Major Wong decided a meeting should be set up with the Green. Instead of spying on them, he thought that we would get a good look at everything anyway if meetings were in order. The first thing we needed to do was get a body count of the Green. That, however, would be done by one of Wong's most trusted guards. Lieutenant Tie was to pretend he was a coolie, go to one of the clubs, and try to find out a little bit about the Greens. It was a very dangerous mission, but it had to be done. Lieutenant Tie was well trained in all the marshal arts, and he had been the champion of all Peiping two years before. The Greens were known for their marshal arts skills.

Within two days Tie was on his way to gather information. He was only to stay just a few hours. An escort would take him to the edge of town, and after four hours, he was to return. It wasn't that Tie couldn't be trusted, but if the Green captured him and made him talk, we would all die. Major Wong set Tie's return route from his mission so that Too Sack and Gordy would be in a position to see if he was followed. The jeep was moved to another location.

Too Sack recorded the next events. After three hours and twenty-two minutes, Too Sack heard a sound. From their position, he could see down the road and watch for a trap. Too Sack had made a sign and nailed it to the tree where the Jeep was before Tie left. He and Gordy watched. Too Sack was ready to come out from his hiding place as Tie entered the area, but he heard noise coming from another direction, so he stayed put. As they watched from their hiding spot, they could see the beating marks on Lieutenant Tie. More than twenty members of the Green came into view. They punched and kicked Tie some more saying he lied and must die. The commander said, "No, let's take him back. If what he told us is true, then we will do some trading on our own. So, if they have a train, we shall see it."

Too Sack also heard, after they had moved Tie out of hearing range, that they would try and trade Tie for a meeting. Too Sack said to himself, "Hell that's all we wanted in the first place."

Too Sack arrived at the compound and made his report to Major Wong and Lally. Too Sack made sure the Major knew that Lieutenant Tie was tortured and was in very poor condition at this time. The Major was very saddened, but simply said, "We now must wait for contact from the Green."

It didn't take long. A few days later, one of the Nationals came running up to Major Wong, saying that a san pan owned by the Green was docking at the pier. We all went down to the sea to take a look at our visitors. Gordy wanted to shoot them all. Lally said, "Damn it, Gordy, cool down. We have to wait this out."

There were three of them. They were all short and small with that sick grin on their faces, like three poisonous snakes waiting to strike. Major Wong addressed the leader. All the usual rolling horseshit took place, and then the three were escorted to our command building. After two hours Major Wong came out and the talks were over. The Green headed for their san pan and headed out to sea.

The Major conferred with Too Sack, and then we heard the demands of the Green. First, the Green decided we could indeed help each other. Next, they assured us that Lieutenant Tie was alive, and yes, he had been put through Chinese torture and was very brave. After that, they realized they could help us and we could help them. The Lieutenant had told the Green about our situation and our train. However, he hadn't told them what was actually in the cars.

"That's because he didn't know," I said.

"Right," said Too Sack and continues on, "so here is the plan they want us to consider."

The Green Plan

Number one--To make sure both sides abided by the joint plan, both sides would leave a hostage. Ours had to be one of the Marines. Theirs would be the Green Leader's son, Ta Ju Ping.

Number two--A limit of ten men would go on the first trip. It would take two trips to complete the plan.

Number three--The first trip would leave on October 15th. That gave us one week to get ready. The second trip would follow in approximately thirty days.

Number four--The Green would leave and set up operations in Formosa until the Communists gained complete control. In other words, Ping was saving his ass, by heading to Formosa.

"That's pretty much it," added Too Sack. "The Major will meet us in the morning with more details of the plan."

At this point, Major Wong entered into our conversation giving us more information. He said, "Between now and 0700 hours in the morning, we must decide which Marine will stay. Ping is sending his youngest son, which is a Chinese sign of faith, and expects us to leave the youngest Marine behind."

"You know what that means, Shelburn?"

"Yeah, am I going to die on Chinese soil?"

Lally said, "We can draw straws. Hell, they don't know who is the youngest."

"It's OK, Lally, fuck 'em I'll stay." I didn't want to stay at all. I had a bad feeling. One trip was shaky, and a second was pushing the old lucky charm. "Major, I got many concerns about this," I added. "I have no way to communicate with these assholes, and everyone is Chinese."

236

"No, that is wrong, old Ping's boy can speak English. He went to British schools."

"Nice try, Shelburn, me try that, too, if it gets me on first boat. I stay with ole Shelburn, Lally. We be OK."

"That would be fine, but they will only deal if everyone one is gone. They want no one left who can make trouble."

"No leadership," Gordy added, "yeah, they know Ole Shelburn is young and stupid."

"Piss on you, Gordy, I said, "they would never leave you behind, because you're so damn crazy. Poor ole Ping's youngest son would probably be hanging from a tree when they got back."

"Right on, Shelburn, Old Gordy, him crazy like goat," Too Sack added.

"OK...OK," said Lally, "turn it off. Let the Major finish."

The Major continued, "We will leave my five guards and Shelburn. They will leave five Greens and Ping's number three son. Everyone will stay at the Green's compound. It will be much safer. After the next meeting, if all goes well, we can make our final decisions.

We returned to our quarters. We had a lot to think over.

I asked Lally, "How long will the trip to Formosa take, Lally?"

Lally responded, "I think it takes about four days. It depends on the wind. After they get ashore, they may have problems, but I doubt it. The Formosans don't pay any attention to the far north. Those people don't have an Army up there, and each village takes care of its own area, sort of like a town Mayor with a council. Anyway, that's what Major Wong thinks. Plus, you got to remember they make trips over there all the time, so it's nothing new. Also, Chiang has not had time to get organized and take complete control. So, Shelburn, I feel that all will go well. We have been in much deeper shit."

Lally's words made me feel a little better, but I had heard about gunboats off the Formosan coast sinking opium ships before. During this night, I struggled with troubles in my dreams. I had some good ones, but most of them were bad. Before I went to sleep, my thoughts returned to "Hollywood" and those days that seemed so many years ago. My classmates were going to school, playing basketball, and dating the girls. I knew my childhood was gone; I had seen more than most people would ever see in their lifetime. All of a sudden, I was old before my time. If all went well, I would be spending my nineteenth birthday either on an opium ship in the China Sea or...?

ESCAPE BACK TO HOLLYWOOD

"My mind entered the days of "Hollywood" where Buster, Bugger, and I were at the show house watching Ken Maynard in a cowboy movie. My cousin, Shorty, was running the projector. We could tell because the film broke, and that meant one of us had to go next door and drag his ass out of Bob McCracken's Tavern. He always started the movie and then hauled ass for a snort or two. My little Peehole brain was thinking why didn't Oat Sebring who owned the show house get someone else? So one day we asked him. His answer was " Its hard to find anyone around ole Shelburn that has enough sense to run those 88mm projectors" I said Oat are you telling me Shorty is smart" his answer was Go home Peehole".

After the movie we stopped by the teen club. My cousin Bud Thompson and his crazy yes man Brooks were in a head to head with all four of the Davidson boys. All of a sudden, Pete Davidson landed a cheap shot on old Bill. Bud, in one quick shot, decked old Pete, and all hell broke loose. Bud and Bill always picked on us, but if anyone else chipped in they would help us. So we decided we'd better help or Bud would get us later. Ten minutes later, Jerry Davidson had one broken jaw, Bugger had his nose pointing the wrong way, and I had a lump on the head.

What a damn mess! After trying to regroup, we went on over to the pool hall, shot a few games, and decided that was enough for one day. I saw Lydia Hayes sitting on her porch. She called me over, and Bugger and Buster went on home. They knew I had been screwing Lydia and knew better than hang around. Lydia was a very pretty girl, but she was crazy about sex. No one wanted her for a girlfriend, because of the way she acted. There was always a girl like Lydia around. I for one was very happy about that fact.

BACK TO CHINA

More than one meeting took place in order to get the crew ready for the journey to Formosa. Actually things were going pretty well, considering we were dealing with a bunch of lowlife opium dealers.

The day finally came when the trip was set to go. We said our goodbyes and we all hoped for the best. As we made the final trip to the Marina, Lally said, "Shelburn, if something goes wrong, I'll be back. Whatever goes down, try and get to Chin Chow. Colonel Sing's parents are there, and they will hide you until I can get back. I will get back. If I am alive, I will be back." I knew he would if he could, and it was a special comfort for me at that moment.

As we pulled into the compound, Ping's number three son was waiting. He was standing with his five bodyguards. Major Wong's five guards were standing nearby. One of the guards could talk some American, so I didn't have to depend on the Green dragon's son, at least not completely. Standing close by was Lieutenant Tie. I knew he had been released, and Major Wong had talked with him. It seemed the Major was unhappy with him, but he also understood the cruel ways of the Green.

At that very moment, the Green had taken over our train and our compound. It was as Lally said it would be. They were sending Old Ping over for safekeeping, and his number one and number two sons would continue the opium trading with the Reds. Since they had been bedfellows before, they were sure they could strike up another bargain for control of China's opium trade.

I had an empty feeling watching the ship leaving the China Mainland, with all my comrades aboard. It was a sinking feeling, and it was all I could do to hold back the tears. With Ta Ju Ping looking on, there was no way he would spot what the Chinese called a weakness. I watched until the merchant ship became a speck against the sky. My last vision was of Lally, Gordy, and Too Sack waving. Finally, it was a part of history.

Ta Ju Ping was a small man, not much older than me, and he was sure of himself and his position within the Green. He was now the leader of all China's opium trade, just like his father. It was something he had been trained for since his birth.

He addressed me in English. His English was much better than mine. "Sergeant Shelburn, it is destined that we become comrades and friends. I know that our ways are different; our goals in life are far apart." He then continued to brief me on the hazards that awaited us during the next few weeks. Our schedule was filled with mostly busy work. We gathered supplies for the ship when it returned. I found, as the days went by, that Ta Ju was a very clever young man, much older than his years. Ta Ju's bodyguards were very loyal; they would attack any threat to his well-being. They would never leave me alone with him.

After three days, Ta Ju told his bodyguards to leave him alone. He wanted to talk to me without them. They at first refused. Ta Ju was really mad; he stood up and made the request one more time. "They have been told by my father, the great and honorable Ping, to never leave my side. I understand this, but there are things I must do on my own now," he told me. To make them feel at ease, he asked me for my weapons. He looked at me.

I said it was OK. I wasn't too damn happy about it. For years, my weapons were always with me.

We walked away from hearing distance... down toward the sea. Ta Ju spoke, "Sergeant Shelburn, we must consider plans, in case the ship is delayed or never returns. We must face this possibility." I agreed and he continued on, "As I stated to you, we are from different worlds. You think we are evil, and we think we are businessmen. Opium will be used, nothing can stop that, but it must be controlled. The amount of opium available must be limited, or the masses will become useless and drained of their senses. It could cause a total loss of the Chinese culture. Progress in this century will slow, and then we will be back to the Warlords and ancient times. The Green believed that the opium trade must be controlled. That is our mission in life." He was done talking and squatted down.

That meant it was time for me to talk. "Ta Ju, your words give me a better understanding of the Green and its mission in life." I wasn't buying into it all, but it was an interesting theory. "But why must the Green be so damn cruel? Tell me, do you believe in God and Jesus?"

"Yes," he answered. "I was taught in the British schools all about your God. Yes I do believe there is a super power in the sky, but I do not follow your rules, as in your God book. They sound good, but we must make our own rules in China. Concerning our cruel ways, it is necessary. Chinese only understand big punishment. A finger for a little crime, a hand for a bigger crime, and water torture for a crime against the Green."

He was finished. "Shelburn, we will talk about you. How can you survive if the ship fails to come back? Shelburn, there is only one-way, if I let you live; you must become a member of the Green. If it comes to this, I will help you, you can be sure of that, as I swear on my father's head, it will be done." With that statement made, Ta Ju walked away. The meeting was over.

I stayed on the beach looking out to sea for a long time. A time left with my thoughts. After a good hour, one of my guards brought my weapons back to me. Ta Ju had left some heavy stuff on me; it was too much and too quickly.

Meanwhile, the Green was stepping up activity. Many visitors, Chinese businessmen, were coming to the compound. I had no idea how big the Green operation was. One night I heard part of a conversation that led me to believe they had already make contact with the Reds, and it was going to be business as usual. I didn't feel this information was going to work in my favor. I could only hope that the ship returned, and if that failed, that Ta Ju would be good to his word. I also felt bad about Major Wong's Honor Guards, because even if my life was spared, I knew and they knew that they would be killed.

It had now been twelve days; they'd had plenty of time to make the trip, if everything had gone well. Ta Ju came to my quarters on the fifteenth night. I was to say the least, feeling very depressed. Ta Ju came right to the point, "It seems the ship is delayed for some reason. Do not panic, there are several reasons for this, the weather, delays in business transactions. Do not let this worry you so much, it will come, and if it doesn't I have told you, that life will go on for you, and in time you will be able to return to America. I too may someday go to America. I have read many books; I know all about your country. What state are you from? And what is your real name?"

I answered his questions, "I am from Indiana and my first name is Jesse."

"Oh, yes, that's Xien in Chinese. It's a famous name, yes--Jesse James, Jesse Owens, and Jesse of the God book, yes Jesse you will be fine. I like you, and I have heard of all your firefights and of your bravery. Very ding how."

He bowed and the talk was over.

It was day twenty-two, and my hope had faded into fear. I remembered General Patton's words, "When going into combat, never take counsel of your fears." It was Patton's words that had carried me into the unknown, so many times before.

242

On day twenty-three, Ta Ju told me that my guards would be executed the next morning, and if I told them, I would also be shot. He said, "This way I will know I can trust you. I am of the Green. We believe in these three things:

Bravery, honor, and trust. The trust is what I am looking for." The execution was to take place after the sun went down on the next day, the twenty-fourth day.

My plans were set. I told the Guards of the situation. They would be overpowered before dark. Instead, we would try to shoot our way out of this. I would never turn them over to the Green. Our plan was simple and a long shot. The odds on winning were like 50:6.

We met near the beach at 1400 hours, set up some explosives, and hid some ammo and weapons. I told them the words of Patton, "Don't go into battle to die for your country, let the other son of a bitch die for his." I also added, "Most fights are won by the guy who gets off the first punch."

The Green had their little teahouse session every afternoon at the same time. We had the building rigged to blow, and the plunger was in Private Chan's hand, waiting for my signal.

Most of the Green were in the building, but I had not seen Ta Ju. I felt very bad about Ta Ju , but he had to die. To let him live would mean that we all would die. I gave the signal and a huge explosion followed. No one could have lived through that. The Beach guards came running up and we took them all out. Only Ta Ju could not be accounted for. We checked the wreckage and identified every body. None fit Ta Ju or his two lieutenants. They had vanished in thin air.

Now, we were in deep shit. There would be so many Greens at the compound by morning; we would never make it out. I sat down by the sea. We were resting before we made out next move, and the guards were watching for any kind of movement.

Lally Returns with the Green's Ship to Take Us to Formosa and Freedom

Like a shining light, I looked into the horizon and saw the outline of a large San-Pan. As it got closer, I could see it was the Greens' San-Pan. I said a few prayers. As Lally came into view, I said to myself, "You cut it pretty close."

After the excitement, I realized we had another problem. The Green would still have control of the boat, and with Ta Ju not on the shore, anything could happen. As the ship got closer, I saw Lally and Too Sack. I put the glasses on them and could not see any of the Green on board. As the San-Pan docked, we ran over and I yelled at Lally, "Where are the Greens?"

He yelled back, "We shot the assholes, Shelburn! Where are your Greens?"

I yelled back, "We shot the assholes."

We had a lot to talk about, but loading up with supplies and getting out of the bay by daylight, was priority one. One hour before daybreak we were under way. I took a long last look at Mainland China, and turned my attention toward the future. I knew we were far from safe, but we were in a hell of a better position than we were just a few hours before.

I asked about Gordy and all the others. I asked many, many questions. Lally spent the first hour at sea updating me on all that had taken place. Lally went on to tell me about their journey to Formosa and their return.

"Shelburn, where in the hell do I start?" said Lally, as he asked himself. "Well, first of all, we had no trouble getting across the China Sea; we never even saw a ship. However, as we tried to dock in Northern Formosa, a San-Pan came out to meet us. It seems that somehow Old Ping had gotten the word out about our arrival. Ping had greeted them as they got close to our ship. Major Wong heard enough of the conversation to alert us that a return was not in the Greens' plans. They took Ping and his guards into shore first. Then, they returned to take us ashore, saying there was not enough room. But we knew that was bullshit, because we could see there would have been enough room. Major Wong was sure they would return, because the boat was loaded with opium. He was also sure they would come back loaded with plenty of firepower to take us out. Major Wong told me to take the two remaining Greens aboard ship to meet their ancestors when he gave me a signal. This was to be done by knife only. Gordy and I found two spear guns aboard and shot both Greens at the same time. We finished them off with K-Bars, dumped the bodies, pulled up the anchors, and left the area. That is why it took us so long. We had to travel down the coast until we could get to a major city or village. We ended up at Taipei, where we went ashore and contacted Nationalist Headquarters. Shelburn, I will never forget that call as long as I live."

"Well damn, go on, Lally," I yelled.

"OK, OK, well anyway, I get an operator at the Headquarters, and tell them who I am and what our situation is. In fact, I had to tell four different officers, before I got to the man who could help us. The operator then said I'll transfer your call to the Commanding General of the Formosan Army. Now we are getting somewhere, I thought.

Next I heard, "Sergeant Lally, do you know whom you are talking to?"

"Holy Shit, you made it, Colonel!"

"Yes, and I am so happy that you are alive, only now it's General Sing Wu."

"Shelburn, it was like talking to a ghost."

"That's unbelievable, Lally," I said. "How did he make it?"

"He got a chopper out. He knew nothing of our taking the train, or anything about what happened to us, so I told him about the deal we made with the Green. He set a time for us to meet him, and he sent troops to escort us to Headquarters."

"The ship was taken over by Nationalist guards, and we were taken to General Sing's quarters. He really was glad to see us. I told him about Ping's son and how you had to stay. After catching up on everything, a plan was formed to bring you out."

I asked, "Why didn't they just send a warship back."

"Well, you can't see them right now, but we have two escorts with us. So you see, Shelburn, life is really getting good again."

"Damn right," added Too Sack, "old maggot Lally is a Marine wizard."

Yeah, it was like old times again.

I asked Lally about Ping and what had happened to him. Lally told me, The Nationalist Government is looking for him. When he is found, he will go to prison for crimes against the government."

Symbol for Operation China Gold
Operation China Gold
January 1949

We spent a few weeks getting the skinny, or having no duty. We just saw the sights and had a good time. However, it was soon time to get back to work. Too Sack said, "You owe Formosa lots of money for the trip back to China's mainland, maybe as much as $50,000."

"Up yours, Too Sack, I already paid my dues."

We reported to headquarters the next morning.

Too Sack, Gordy, and I were given orders to report to an area called Hsingkao by the Formosans. The Nationals had taken over a five-square mile area and used the area as a training camp. There weren't many signs of life in this area, until we went behind a newly erected fence, a fence that seemed to go on for miles.

We could see ten rows of six-men tents set up, so this was going to be some kind of tough training. Too Sack said, "No poon-tang, no nightclubs for long time, old Shelburn."

246

"It will be ding how with me, Too Sack. I think it means we are going back to the mainland, old buddy."

It looked as if more than five hundred Nationals had been picked for this operation. We spent this balance of the evening getting our personal equipment set up and waiting for more information. Everyone already on hand had been arriving for the past week, and nobody knew anything.

However, the following morning, it all came to light. At 0900 hours, just after the morning meal and exercise, a face with General's stars attached, came walking to the platform, one General Sing Wu.

He spoke in Mandarin, "Comrades, General Chiang has developed a plan for our return to the mainland, for a mission of great importance. Your job is to set in motion the start of our return to the mainland." This was greeted by loud cheering. General Sing continued his speech for about forty-five minutes, most of which we had heard many times before. Finally, he assigned us to different units. Our unit was the demolition unit. Our commander was none other than Too Sack himself. We had a total of twenty men, and none were trained in demolitions. It seemed for the next three weeks we would be training them with explosives. From Too Sack, I tried to find out what we were up to. Too Sack repeated what General Sing had said, "At this point in time, it's best no one knows." This, of course, gave me an even bigger desire to know.

Lally had told me before I went on leave that Gordy and I would be assigned to General Chiang's Headquarters, and what he assigned us to they could care less. Our new Operations Commander was a member of Chiang's inner staff, a Lieutenant General named Ging Tung. He was a line soldier in Chiang's Sixth Army. Tung was an average-sized Chinese man. However, he was an odd looking guy. His ears were too big for his head, and as Too Sack surmised, his neck was too small for his body. Gordy said, "Well, Shelburn, you have named everyone in China, so what are you going to call this asshole?"

247

After a careful, full thirty seconds of thought I said, "His new name is Model T."

Too Sack replied, "What that mean, Model T?"

"Well, Too Sack, many years ago, back in the US Of A, someone built their first car. It was a Ford, and each car had a model name, so they called it a Model T. I have good reason for this name, Old Wizard, just listen up, and I'll give you the skinny. The Model T had a little body, big doors, and small tires. If you had one of these, when you got done driving, you would always open both doors and leave them open for a time. Every time you would go by a house with one of these cars parked in the driveway, you would always see the doors wide open. The doors were left open, because the fumes were a bitch. The Model T with its doors left open, looks just like General Tung."

Gordy said, "Yeah, with the doors open, that looks like Ole Tung's ears, right Shelburn?"

"Right," I answered Gordy. "Too Sack, do you see the logic now?"

"No see logic, it's a bullshit story, Shelburn. You put on ole Too Sack. Me want to see picture of Model T."

"By damn," said Gordy, "that's easy, I got a Life magazine that shows the damn thing." When we got back to the barracks, Gordy looked up the picture of the Ford, and Too Sack took a look.

"Holy Dung, you right, old Shelburn! That picture of Tung all right." We had a good time with that one.

Our training included the old "Tai-chi-Chuan", an ancient exercise they still do. Too Sack yelled something in Chinese. "Jen-ching-wei?" I asked. "What does that mean, old Wizard?"

Too Sack grinned and said, "It means 'Oh, the joy of being Chinese." Maybe, maybe, we never knew with Too Sack. He could have been saying kiss my ass for all we knew.

I broke Too Sack up as we finished our morning exercise. I said in perfect Chinese, "Confucius say man must tell truth before one dies."

Too Sack looked at me and answered, "Yes, oh Shelburn Faggot, you becoming number one Coolie, very ding how." He was very impressed, I could tell, because he continued to pat my back all the way to the head.

Great decisions are made sometimes at nature calls, like our conversation that continued on. Too Sack said, "Me no like Model T name, it's too long."

"Well then, old Wizard, I've been thinking about that, and you are right. I am hereby giving the order to call Colonel Tung 'Auto', which is short for Model T. What do you think?"

"Very ding how, it's a four point 0."

COVERT OPERATION

The plan or reason we were here was unclear. We thought it was to set up a staging area for some exposition on the mainland, but it didn't make sense. We didn't have the firepower for such a thing. Another interesting thing took place. Gordy and I had to go see a very interesting lady. We thought we were going to get laid. Instead, we were made over to look Chinese. We even had some needlework done to our eyes to make them pull some to look slanted. They also had some kind of dye that turned our skin to look more Chinese.

When we got back, Too Sack laughed his ass off and said we were two of the ugliest Chinese ever created. We even had our heads shaved and had a phony pigtail hanging off the back. Too Sack said we could pass for two opium dealers who were smoking up the profits. I think he was right.

For several days the Nationals got a big laugh. Then the new wore off and they finally got used to us. It was now a part of us.

Gordy said, "You know, Shelburn, Sing must be very high on the Generalissimo's pecking order to go to all this trouble to get us in on this operation. Hell, as far as the

249

Marine Corps knows, we are standing guard at Chiang's palace."

"You're right, Gordy, Sing Wu will someday be in charge of all China."

We had been back on Formosa now for about two months, a lot had happened in that time. It was now January 1,1949. Mao had control of most of China, but not everything. There was still fighting going on. We could not completely dismiss the idea of a mainland attack. Too Sack said he'd heard that our mission was not an invasion, but something more like a rescue. Hell we had just gotten out through shit house luck. Going back was a real kick in the ass. Anyway, they separated us from the training group and put us with a smaller group. I looked around, and I saw that all these guys were the General's most trusted men, all from Mainland China. We decided whatever it was, it was important.

All members of the command unit were Nationalist soldiers who had come across with the Generalissimo from the mainland. It seemed everyone on this mission was hand picked. Too Sack said, "Shelburn, we are on this mission to get somebody or something, not to do any attacking. Look at our crew. Everyone is dressed up like coolies not soldiers. The ship itself, a freighter, had no flag, which was not normal for any vessel on the seas. Me no see National flag on freighter before."

"I think you're right. Too Sack, maybe we will never know, but it sure as hell must be important."

The Reds had control of several areas within a hundred miles. So far, they didn't have control of Shanghai.

The water looked black as coal, as I looked into the wind. After five hours at sea, all of a sudden I saw China's mainland. Too Sack saw it at the same moment. Our eyes met and two young, but old warriors, sensed awareness of our situation and of this moment in time.

Our job was to get ashore and stand guard on that shore. A special unit was to go ashore, do its job, and return. No timetable was given to us, and we only got that information after we were almost ready to dock.

We soon learned that the Reds had not been in this area, and the people thought Chiang was still fighting in China. We arrived at daybreak. The special unit of about thirty Nationals dressed like coolies and heavily armed went ashore. All we could do was watch.

Gordy said, "You know, Shelburn, all that training we did for this mission was a cover. What we trained for has nothing to do with what's going on here. We arrived in a freighter, not a combat ship."

We could see a place Gordy and I knew really well, the Pearl Hotel. It started to make sense now. "Damn it, that ole Chiang is one smart coolie!" I exclaimed. "You know what's next door to the Peace Hotel?"

"I don't know, what?"

"The Bank of China, where all of China's gold is kept."

"Holy shit, we will be the most famous bank robbers of all time!"

"Yeah, well, I could be wrong, but we will soon know. Hey, I still got some diamonds, how about you, Too Sack? Where do you keep yours?"

"Me keep diamonds in my ass, me take them out when have to do dung trip, and then put them back."

"Not a bad idea. Gordy, maybe we can go home rich after all, mine are still back at the base."

We were docking off the Huangpu River as we were moored by the bund. This was across from the Hotel, so if it was the gold, depending on how much gold there was, it would take at least two or three trips. All we could do was guard the area near the freighter and wait. Within forty-five minutes, whatever was going to happen was about to happen. Several small craft were getting ready to go ashore, each had two coolies in it. After another wait of thirty minutes, they paddled back. Already a few coolies were onshore looking and watching.

251

I asked Too Sack, "What in the hell do they think is going on?"

Too Sack said, "The coolies on shore have been told what is going on and it is the gold. Soon you will see the prisoners. They think General Chiang has come back, and that he is taking Government property and traitors back to Formosa."

"Government papers your ass, Too Sack. They got the gold, man, they got the Gold." A total of five prisoners were taken on board and taken below. We never saw them again.

Too Sack said, "Wait a minute, Shelburn, me have to talk with you, now before we get back to the others." I could tell it was really important. I had never seen him act this way. It was like he was unsure of himself. "Shelburn, you do this for me?" he questioned.

"Hey, Too Sack, you name it. So what is it?"

"Me like to stay on mainland, old comrade." My eyes must have gotten very big, as Too Sack continued, "My family here. They not know what happened to me; the Reds not know me join the Nationals. Remember, me was in the Red army, when you find me? At Formosa me know I will never be able to return. I put up with Red bullshit until the great General returns."

"You know, Too Sack, that may never be possible."

"Yes, very true, Shelburn, but it gives Too Sack some hope. I one smart coolie. I can fool them, make them think I big time Mao buddy. You go home, Lally already go home, Gordy he go home soon, and ole Too Sack be all alone anyway. Me stay here, old Shelburn, where me born, you understand?"

"Yes, Too Sack," I understand. I was already crying inside.

Too Sack continued, "I always be with my comrades, in my mind forever. You are number one, always four point o. You tell Gordy and Lally, make them understand, OK?"

"OK, Too Sack," I answered.

252

Too Sack said, "I must go now, so no one see me. Tell them ole Too Sack got blown up by tank, OK?" He saluted me and gave me a hug. Then he walked briskly way, turning to look back one last time, as was the Chinese custom. He moved to the back of the freighter and I could see the outline of his small boat as he headed ashore.

Like it was ready on command, a wind picked up making the waves choppy and clouding my vision, or was it tears? Too Sack, too, was now a part of my past, but he stayed forever in my mind. I knew in that moment I would never see him again. The hair stood up on the back of my neck, just as it had when I said goodbye to Jack and Jill.

With all the coolies back on board ship, the Freighter headed out of the bund on the river Huangpu and headed for Formosa. I took my last final look at the China mainland. I knew this time it was for real. I would never return.

Gordy came up and said, "I can't find Too Sack." I had to tell him the story, Gordy was as sad as I was. We made a pact, while leaning over the railing on the Freighter, to never tell a living soul, other than Lally, about Too Sack being alive and staying in the mainline China. At headquarters in Formosa, we told that someone had tried to board the back of the ship. Too Sack attacked with his knife and both fell into the river. He was never found.

In a medals' presentation a few weeks later, Lieutenant Li Chin, our Too Sack, was given the Nationalist's Highest Order of Bravery, which was equal to our Congressional Medal Of Honor. General Sing Wu presented the award. Gordy said, "Is this medal for all the battles we fought or for bringing the gold over?"

"We will never know, Gordy. Let's think it was for fighting with the Great General."

We never found out about the prisoners who came back with us. It could have been a cover for taking the gold. We will never know. I do think, if it was the gold, Chiang had every right to take it to Formosa. Who in his

253

right mind would have left it to the Reds?   The Chinese people would never see a penny of it.

A few weeks later, Gordy and I were sent home. Gordy was due for discharge, and was sent to Great Lakes, Illinois. He was soon home. I was to be stationed at Camp Pendleton, until my time was up.

Gordy and I Go Home

I was in the office reading the morning mail. As the duty NCO, it was my job to read the morning report. Within this report was a casualty report on the MIA's and KIA's. Reading down the list, I came to the L's, and my heart just about stopped. Listed was my lifetime buddy and comrade Master Sergeant Lally as killed in action. Add Lally to the list from my past. What was going on? Were they going to take us all out? As I tried to keep my composure, I left a note for Captain Rollins, my superior. I told him about Sergeant Lally and that I wanted to put in for a three-day pass. Maybe a little R and R and some time to think would help.

I ended up in Los Angeles, and I went to see Marion. We talked of marriage, but not to the point of setting a date. Upon my return to camp, I received a letter from Gordy. He was living in Tennessee and working in a factory that made washing machines. He was married and had a kid. It seemed he was happy. At the bottom was a phone number. I called, and on the other end was my last link to China. I told him about Lally; it was a sad call to make. We were two old warriors talking about a time that seemed only yesterday, but was now a part of the past. It would be the last time I heard his voice, his last words were "Semper Fi, old Shelburn." Years later, I tried to find Gordy again, but my letters were returned, marked address unknown-return to sender.

I returned to my office and started going through my paperwork, trying to lose myself in my work. It's hard to explain, but it was like half of my family was wiped out.

We had fought the enemy and won, or did we win? Is this really winning? They say life goes on, but from this point in time, my life went downhill.

I started hanging out in the clubs; I never drank, but I was always ready for a good fight. The first major fight I got into, we cleaned out a bar in Los Angeles, and I got busted from Master Sergeant to Staff Sergeant. The next major brawl I got into, I was busted to Private and spent thirty days in the brig. I had tagged an officer.

My next assignment was in supply. I passed out clothing to recruits coming from boot camp to advanced training. One day, while doing my Mickey Mouse job, I looked up and an officer, a Lieutenant Colonel, was looking me in the eyes. "You are the former Sergeant J.L. Bedwell, better known as Ole Shelburn?" I showed interest. He introduced himself, and said he had just returned from Formosa. He was also a good friend of General Sing Wu.

"How is the General?" I asked.

"He is well," answered the Colonel. "I will be honest with you Private Bedwell, the General is concerned with your change of behavior, and he feels it has much to do with losing your friends in the China and Korean War. You must be wondering why, your request to go overseas to Korea, have been turned down? The answer to that is, the Marine Corps feels you have seen enough and have been through too much. It's that simple, and it's that final."

"What they want me to do is go through that psycho-testing bullshit to see if I am still zipped up, right?"

"Maybe so," said the Colonel, "never the less, I am here to try and help you regain yourself and your stripes. General Sing Wu has requested that you be transferred back to Formosa, and he will help you rebuild your life. Think about it a few days, Private Bedwell, and I will be back and talk with you again. I will return in four days."

I thanked the Colonel and decided I had some serious thinking to do. Returning to Formosa might make everything worse, yet how could they get much worse? It was my second hitch in the Corps, and I was a private; they don't have ranks any lower, of course my Master/Sgt. Rating was a temporary one. How worse could it get? What would they put on my stone when I'm out of here? Pvt. Bedwell? Sgt. Bedwell? Peehole? Shelburn?

I had just passed my twenty-first birthday as a private. I was a platoon sergeant at sixteen. Yeah, I would call that down hill.

Shelburn returns to Formosa from Pendleton to Complete His Time

Headquarters
Ops Building
Office Of General Sing Wu

Commanding General Sing Wu of the Formosan Armed Forces said, "Come in, ole Shelburn. It's good to see you again."

"Thank you, sir. I had no idea we would ever meet again."

"Life makes some strange moves. Sometimes, one never knows one's destiny," answered the General. "Of course you know why you're here, so let's see what we can do about things."

"First, Shelburn, do you want to move back up through the rank and file? Or do you feel you have had enough of the Corps?"

My answer was fast and to the point. "Sir, I have had all the thinking I need. If the Marine Corps would restore my permanent rank of Plt/ Sergeant, and give me an assignment here, I would like to finish my remaining enlistment time here with you. I know what I want now, but I don't think the Marine Corps will let me do it. In a short time my enlistment ends. In fact in just a few weeks, and at that time I would like to stay on your staff and do covert operations in and out of the mainland as a civilian. I would like to go to language school and learn to speak

256

Mandarin Chinese. Then, I would like to be assigned to your headquarters.

"Shelburn, I am now a General, granted I am not a Marine General, but General Chiang will soon be elected president of Free China, and the Americans will always have a force here. It is done."

Within a few days I was assigned to the special training called the

Language School. It was very hard for me. Of course, being in China and hearing the Mandarin sounds helped. I was in a class with mostly diplomats or dependents of diplomats. It was a struggle, but I had no other duties. This, of course, gave me extra time to study. It was unlike any other school I had ever been in. There was one subject only, and it was broken down into segments. The first segment was to see if you had the skills to go further. I completed the language course and looked forward to taking the second part later on. I was once again ready for a new assignment. The new course wouldn't start for another month. I was ready for re-assignment to General Sing's Command Headquarters.

I understood the language much better than I could speak it. I had come in dead last in the class, but I had passed.

I guess the Marine brass decided to discharge me, rather than extending my time. They gave me the final rank of platoon sergeant, which I think is now called Staff Sergeant.

My new assignment was as an honor guard to the Generalissimo himself; not as a Marine, but as a civilian. Sometimes I wondered if I would have been better off just going home. I had spent most of my service years, with the Chinese Nationals. The question about why an ex-Marine was part of the Great General's staff came up often. It was General Sing's job to handle that answer. I was a Marine, and I never forgot that for a moment.

General Sing summed it up for me when he told me, "Shelburn, the reason you were granted this assignment was not for your welfare. I must confess we had other motives. Don't get me wrong; your well being was part of our consideration. We also must face the fact that no one knows what to do with you. You're a National hero here in free China. You're also a pain in the ass at times. Yet, the Corps still regards you well. I think they were hoping to get you through this second enlistment, without any further backslides."

I answered, "I hope they make it."

General Sing continued, "What I am about to tell you must not leave this room."

"Sir, you know it won't, or you wouldn't be telling me."

He replied with a smile, "You know, Peehole, you can be a real pain in the ass."

"As you have been told, you will be on a mission soon. You were hand picked because of your work on the mainland and also your knowledge of demolitions. With this mission remember, things are not always what they seem to be. Accept it and go on." The general stood, and the meeting was over. "Nice to see you again, Shelburn."

I saluted and left the building. I was issued a uniform with an honor guard insignia. I looked myself over and decided it looked a lot better than the stripes you get in the brig. It wasn't really a Nationalist's uniform. It was more like what we gave to the war correspondents.

The next morning at 0900 hours, I was in the barracks getting ready to go to the beach and spend the day. I had a date with a very pretty girl named Okwa Cha. However, when the Lieutenant Colonel walked through the door with papers in his hand, I knew I just might be doing something else. It was Colonel Wang, a member of Sing's staff at headquarters.

"Gunny Bedwell, (well they still called me Gunny) you are requested to attend a staff meeting at 1400 hours this day at the command boardroom."

"Yes sir." I answered.

"The Colonel says it will be a happy meeting for you. General Wu tells me good things about you. He also says you get bored when things are peaceful. I am sure you won't get bored in the next few weeks." With that he left. I was full of questions and had no answers.

Operation Meiling

At 1400 hours, I was in the Headquarters building in the General's boardroom. Also in the room were General Sing, Colonel Wang, Lieutenant Chin, and four Nationalist officers. I had no idea why we were there.

The name of the mission was OPERATION MEILING. I soon found out it was named from a difficult route through the Nan Ling Mountains called Meiling Pass. I knew that General Sing was from that area. I wondered why this operation was not called Operation Pescador, because that was where we were going.

The General spoke, "Comrades, it has come to my attention that the Reds have plans to set up an outpost just off our shoreline in the Pescador Islands, just like they have done at Amoy and Quemoy. This cannot be allowed. This small gathering that you see before you is people who are specially trained for a mission such as this." It also contained those who were closest to the Great General Chiang.

Sing next went to the big war board, where a map appeared. It showed a close up map of the Island Group. "As you can see they are many islands, and each very small. Only three of them are large enough to use for any kind of facilities. It's like huge rocks or mountain peaks coming out of the sea all around each little island. It is not easy to land a boat in these waters; it can only be done between storms. The wind is another hazard, and it seemed to blow almost every day. The weather is one of the dangers, but there are others. The Reds may come across to check you out and to see what you are doing.

For the first week, you will be concerned with shipping supplies across the Strait. A few Formosans live on the main island of Taku as they call it. They are harmless fishermen. They number no more than forty. They will resent you being there, so try to make friends with them. We are sending with you some of the latest fishing gear to give to them as presents. I hope that will do the trick.

"After you have set up camp, which will be four man tents, spend the next few days checking out the Islands. You will be issued rubber, UDT type, and boats to get around the islands. They have small outboard motors on them, but never get more than 300 yards from shore. You might not get back. Most of the mining you will do will be within a hundred yards of the beaches, or I should say rocks. You will find more rock than you will sand.

The General was silent for a moment, and then he continued, "If you are faced with a force from the mainland intent on landing, fire on them, and call for air support. The Nationalist Flag will be flying from all directions. If you can get enough mines planted before they know what we are doing, you will not have to worry about an attack. Between the weather, and the mines, we doubt if the Reds will even try to land.

"Colonel Wong will be your commander. I will now turn you over to Colonel Wong."

Colonel Wong was an old friend from the Mainland days. He looked over at me and said, "Shelburn, again we find ourselves on another mission, one not so daring as our last."

"Yes, sir, I'm sure the Colonel is right."

"Colonel Wong continued, "If it were not for Sergeant Bedwell and his Marine buddies, I would not be standing here today. He saved my family and me from certain death. He is carried high in the Great General's watchful eye."

The Nationalist officers had heard all the stories about us, so there was no reaction to his statement. It was just accepted.

The Colonel continued, "This is not the complete group assigned to this mission. We will add at least twenty solders from the Army as guards around the islands. They are only trained to do work and serve as expert riflemen. Sergeant Yao will act as their commander. Sergeant Yun is our supply man, Sergeant Shih is our communications man, and Sergeant Major Tzu will be my second in command. Sergeant Bedwell, whom you may call Shelburn, will be assigned four members from our demolitions school. He will pick these men himself. I will perhaps add two more officers to work with us from the main island." (He meant from Formosa.)

"Three days from now be ready to board landing crafts and start the supply chain. Report to the docks at 0900 hours; this will be on Saturday. You will be given more instructions within the next three days. That is all."

As I walked out of the meeting, I looked back to say a word to Too Sack, and then I remembered I was alone. No Too Sack, no Lally, no Link, and no Gordy. I was alone.

The next morning I was given my list of Nationals who were trained in demolitions. None were from the mainland, and all were Formosans. It seemed that whatever Nationals were in the area were doing other projects or out of the military. Only one could speak broken English, so my Chinese lessons were going to be put to the test.

The men assigned to me were:

Private Han, whom I named Felix after the cartoon cat because he was quick.

Private Li, whom I named Popeye because he smoked a pipe and had big eyes.

Private Hsiung, whom I named Marvin after a science teacher I'd had.

Private Fei, whom I named Dipstick because he was slow, dumb and just plain stupid. It was beyond me how he had passed the demolition classes. Later, I found out that he had an uncle high up in the Formosan business community. That made it sound like the good old USA to me.

I let them know they would all have new names. I didn't tell them why. Hell, I didn't even know why. All I knew was old Buster and I named everything that was born in Hollywood, and it was too damn late to stop now.

One of the first things we did when we got to the islands was to build a dock, so we could unload supplies and dock the boats. We built a nice wide ramp that reached out into the water deep enough for us to get in and out. Taku was the only place we could find some shelter from the waves and the wind. It was located in between two huge rocks that jutted out of the sea.

Flex and Dipstick were unloading some of our equipment. We had presented Ed, the head coolie, or fisherman, with the new equipment, and he seemed to really like it. Dipstick had never gotten the word that we were going to let the fishermen use the dock. He had been told so, but then again that's why I named him Dipstick. He looked up and saw an incoming Sanpan and the fisherman was trying to dock the boat. Old Dipstick was giving him a load of shit. The fisherman refused to give in. He tied his boat up and gave Dipstick a Chinese finger. I could see this from about a hundred yards away. Flex was off a distance, and he was trying to get down there and tell Dipstick to leave the guy alone.

The next thing we saw was Dipstick with a stick of TNT in his hand breaking the fuse. He ran over to the San Pan and dropped it in. It blew the hell out of the Sanpan and the end of the dock.

I yelled at Flex to take the dumbass back to my office, which was a tent at that time, and I said I would deal with him later. If I had dealt with him then, the dumbass would have died. Next, here came the coolie fisherman, yelling in Mandarin so fast that even the Chinese wouldn't have understood him.

After an hour of trying to get the fisherman calmed down, we started to make headway.

Marvin told Dipstick he would have to pay for the San-Pan and his equipment. Marvin said to me, "Shelburn, the little prick wants to talk to his uncle."

I was so mad I couldn't see straight. "Tell the little bastard we are going to hang his sorry ass, if he even tries to call his uncle." Marvin relayed the message. As luck would have it, we had visitors for the first time. They were down at the dock trying to get their gunboat docked.

We kept Dipstick under guard and headed down to try and explain what had happened. The visitors were Colonel Chin and one of his officers. He looked up, saw me and said, "Remember, Shelburn, when he first took a look at Too Sack dressed like General Chiang?"

"Yes, sir," I answered.

"Well, do you remember what you said it looked like?"

"Yes, sir, I do remember."

"Well, as I remember it, you called it a cluster fuck. What would you call this, Shelburn?"

"Sir, a cluster fuck wouldn't do it justice."

Colonel Chin was just checking to see our progress. Most of the supplies were on the island, and we were getting ready to mine the area. Popeye and Felix were going out that afternoon to do some navigational charting on the east side of the island. Marvin and I were charting the east side.

Colonel Chin stayed for a couple hours and then returned to Formosa with Private Fei, Dipstick, in tow. It didn't take much to convince the colonel that ole Dipstick needed to be somewhere else.

After laying mines for several days, we ran out of explosives and had to wait for more to arrive from Taiwan so we could complete our job. In another week, we would have it all covered. No one could possibly land anything without a map. After one month the job was completed. We were to keep a few men on the island as spotters and security. We not only wanted to keep the Reds out, but we also wanted to keep stray fishermen from blowing themselves up.

Only one incident took place, and it happened four days before I was to return to Formosa. I got a call from the National on guard duty at 0300 hours. He informed us that we had what looked like a tanker off shore about thousand yards out. As I watched with my glasses, I radioed Colonel Chin at his home for instructions.

While I was talking to the colonel, I exclaimed, "Wait a minute, Colonel! They have a powerboat that looks to be about forty feet long, coming our way. It has a flag on it, but I can't make it out. In another two hundred yards, he is going to hit the mines."

"Let the son of a bitch hit them, Shelburn, maybe they will keep their asses out of here. Maybe there's a lesson to be learned." A moment later the boat hit one of the mines, and the explosion left nothing on the surface. The sea claimed it all as it always does. I never knew for sure whether it was the Reds or not. We did put up warning flares, which were easy to see from the ship or the boat. I never heard anything more about this mission off shore. A year went by, and there were no more missions of any consequence.

It was time to go home for good, yet what was home? Sometimes I thought it was Shelburn; sometimes I thought it was China. Marco Polo might have said, "Where is home?"

Everything changes. Nothing ever stays the same. My old granny, she was about ninety, once said, "Everything I know, everything I grew up with, and everyone I knew are all gone. I talk about things, and no one listens or cares. What's the sense of my even being here?" Hell, granny, I am only twenty-three, and I feel that way already.

As I complete this book, I read in the paper that the Chinese Reds were holding missile practice in this area. If you read about them setting off some mines that were set forty-five years ago, it was I. I demand the credit. As

264

Mongo once said at the Battle Of the Brotherhood Of Hell, "Yes, Shelburn, I fired, and I was honored."

Just when I was ready to go home, I was given one more mission. General Sing Wu gave me a solo mission.

Operation Hong Kong

After my return to Formosa, I was working with the Kuomintang government under General Sing Wu. I was assigned a solo mission. Never before had I been in this situation. I had always had my Marine buddies and Too Sack along.

After getting the skinny about the mission from the general, my first question was, "Why me?"

General Sing Wu looked me in the eye and said, "Shelburn, how many from the mainland days are still around me? Our comrades are all too old or dead. Who else understands the manufacture of diamonds? I can find men who are brave and willing. They're even capable, but none have your experience. Yes, Shelburn, you are the only man for this job." He grinned, "Now, if Too Sack was around, he would be my first choice, and if Master Sergeant Lally was still with us, he would be my next choice. You see, Shelburn, you are the only choice. Does that make you feel better or worse?"

I said, "Sir, you have made your point."

The Nationalist I was to meet was a diamond exporter; he was also an old friend of the Generalissimo. He had been using a dead man's identification and so far had pulled it off. However, Chiang was sure it would be just a matter of time before the Reds figured it out. It was time to get him out.

THE PLAN was simple; yet very dangerous. In his business all transactions had to be by courier from out of the country. Also, all his transactions were monitored. He could not even go to Hong Kong.

Something special had to be set up. Bribery had to take place. General Chiang still had a few high placed friends left on the mainland. How they set this up, I have no idea, but somehow the stage was set.

Fly to Hong Kong
February 3, 1950

I boarded a plane for Hong Kong on a very long and uneventful journey. All the information I had was very limited. I was to meet a Mr. Lee, a diamond importer. I was carrying twenty-five thousand dollars in American cash to exchange for diamonds. Actually it was all in worthless bank notes. Before leaving, I was well coached about the diamonds I would be buying and selling. As a courier, I wasn't supposed to know much about anything. I was just supposed to arrive at the hotel, meet the guy, and hand over a passport to Chiang's friend that would get him into Taiwan. I was given a five-year-old picture, so there would be no mistake or trap.

During the trip to Hong Kong, my seat was next to a middle-aged Taiwanese lady. Across the isle was a young Tourist couple. I could only find two who looked like agents, and they were also Taiwanese.

The trip was uneventful; just long and boring. I had seen more oceans during the past three years than anyone should ever see. I arrived in Hong Kong, which is a very big and beautiful city from the air. I got into a weird looking taxi and headed for the hotel. I was told that whatever room I was assigned to, I was to ask for a change after spending a few minutes in the room. I guess they figured if anyone was on to us, the room might be wired.

I was assigned to room 301, and I went directly to the room. After a few minutes, I called and asked for a change of room. I told them I wanted a room closer to the pool. They changed me to room 112.

When I walked in, I saw the light flashing on the phone. I picked up the phone, and a Taiwanese was on the other end. "Ole Shelburn, you did not think the general would leave you all alone would you?"

266

I answered, "You were one of the guys on the plane. There were two of you."

"Very ding how, you might make a spy yet. However, the middle-aged lady is also with us, but two out of three isn't bad. My code name is Gene Autry."

I answered, "And now I know why my code name is Champion."

Gene said that I was to be contacted the next day between 10:00 A.M. and 12:00 noon. He also stated that they were in room 124, but not to call or contact them unless a problem of any kind came up.

I slept for ten hours. Then, I got ready and went down to get something to eat. There were no CIA types at any of the tables. So, I went back to my room and waited.

At exactly 10:00 A.M., the phone rang. I picked it up, and the Chinese voice said, "The package will arrive tonight. Meet me at pier number twenty-three. I will be wearing a gray sweater and will have new blue shoes on. I am Chinese and forty-seven years old. Meet me in thirty minutes. When you find me, ask me for my code name; it is Fang Cu. If I fail to appear you must go to the embassy immediately." Then he hung up. At that moment I was ready to get my ass out of town. This spy shit was not my thing. Give me a machine gun and we will talk.

I was not sure if I should tell the guys from Taiwan that I got the call or not. I decided less conversation was needed, since they were in on everything. I arrived at pier number twenty-three five minutes early. I was glad to see plenty of light, and some people around. It was nothing like the things you see in the movies. I expected a car to drive by with guns blazing away at me. No such thing happened. I started walking down the leg of the pier that led directly to the ocean. I walked about seventy yards and then started back toward shore. It was then that I saw a man leaning over the bar looking into the water. As I got closer, I saw that he fit all the clues. The bright blue shoes stood out; it the only pair I ever saw in China on a man.

I walked past the man, not knowing whether he should speak first or I should. Deciding to let him make the first move I walked past him. No one else was within twenty yards at that moment. He was the first to speak, "Champion, it's good to see you are back in Hong Kong for a visit. Are you on your usual courier run?"

"It's good to see you, Fang Cu. You failed to buy the last time. Were my prices too high?"

He smiled and said, "Oh, your diamonds were of excellent quality. It was just that my cash flow was not in order for a large transaction at that time. Will you be stopping by my humble store before you leave?"

"Of course," I answered, "in fact, I'll be there in the morning."

"No." he replied, "I will be busy. Let's make it 1:00 P.M., if you can Mr. Champion, I would be most honored."

"OK, Fang Cu, you've got a deal. I'll see you then."

With that he turned and walked away. I had to adlib all that shit. No one had told me what to do or say to him. This spy business was for the birds.

Now it all was down to a few hours, at least that's what I thought at that time. The Chinese do everything on time, so I got down to Fang Cu's store on time. It was located in the old section of Hong Kong on the east side of the city. General Sing had given me the name of a place I had to go to. It was a place called Yangtze Traders.

I walked through a musty old building with 18th century German architecture. Inside the main room, I could see three people. One of them was Fang Cu, and the other two seemed to be customers. Of course, one can never be sure in this business. They were a man of European descent and a young Chinese woman. Fang Cu greeted me and waved me into a back room. I thought now the shooting and stabbings would start in the darkened rooms. My only defense if trouble came was my German P-38, at my back hooked into my belt.

268

Fang Cu spoke first, "Friend of General Chiang, there has been a problem, word came to us that the package was trying to be opened. The package was called into police headquarters in Peiping concerning his trip. It was feared, if he appeared, he would be detained. The package is now at a small airfield fifteen miles east of Hong Kong. I have no further information than ask that you return to your hotel and wait for orders. I wish for all of us this was over."

I said good-by to Fang Cu and headed for the hotel thinking its time for me to catch a plane for the USA. After returning to my room, the first thing I noticed was that the phone was blinking again. I picked it up and on the other end was Gene, "Champion, we have a change of plans. They are at the time are uncertain. How we can get to the package and get it out is an all-new operation. General Sing Wu feels you are the most capable to be in charge for this type of mission. He wants you to come up with two plans, and present them as soon as possible.

"We have looked for bugs in your room, so it's safe to talk.

This is what we know…"

At that point I said, "Why don't you just come to my room?"

He informed me it was safer this way-with less contact. "The information I give you is all we have, and probably that will be all we have.

The package is near an old unused airstrip once used by the Flying Tigers. Only a small plane can get in. He has his family with him, which makes it more dangerous. Whatever is done, no matter what it is, the only way into Hong Kong is the big bridge, or by way of the very dangerous swamps. We will meet at the dock near the big bridge at 8:00 P.M. tonight. I will be carrying a newspaper. My comrade will be out of sight, but nearby. I will find you. Good luck, Shelburn."

I thought to myself, "I will damn sure need it." Gene said one must cross the big bridge to get past the

269

checkpoint keyed my first thought. Really I knew of another way, if Sing could get me the equipment. It was called an aqualung.

My two bodyguards were the Taiwanese; they were code-named Gene and Silver. Two horses and one cowboy, oh well, it worked. I guess since I was an American, it made sense.

We met at the old German Club near downtown Hong Kong. We sat in a corner away from the other customers. No notes were to be taken.

Gene started the meeting, "Champion, tell us the reasons for your plan, and then we can get to the how of getting it done. Finally, tell us what we will need."

"OK, let's start with this. First of all, to get by the checkpoints is impossible. So we must do something these assholes know nothing about."

"What would that be?" asked Gene.

"We go underwater with aqua-lungs once we get the packages to the shoreline. But first, we have to get them to the shore. To do this with the information I have means the following. I read about a group coming from the mainland to a business meeting in Hong Kong. If they travel by rail, they will come within ten miles of our packages. However, if they come by car, they will come within twenty miles of our packages. That will make it much safer for us to intercept them. We need to find out how often this committee comes to Hong Kong, and whether it's the same group or always some others?"

"Excellent, Champion," said Gene, "very ding how. Go on, but I am pretty sure that the information I have says that several different groups of Reds come all the time. They have special permission from the British, so the British could help us. But I doubt if Sing would go for that since there are too many British working with the Reds now. However, we will find out for you."

"After you get this information, the orders, and the equipment, we'll be ready to act. This operation will be ready for the final step. First, I'll need four complete sets of underwater equipment. Next, I'll need time at the shore area to show them how to operate the equipment so they'll be able to breathe underwater. That will take about forty-five minutes or so. Also, I'll need to know the ages, sizes, and health of the packages. They do not have to be swimmers, but it will help if they are. The pick up after we get past the checkpoint must be planned with great detail. That is all I have at this moment, comrades."

I ended my conversation, but Gene and Silver had many questions about underwater diving. They were excited. The meeting ended. I would be contacted before the night was over. I returned to my hotel where I started thinking more about the plan, and then I, too, was excited.

Finally, everything was laid out. The plan had been approved, and the location was set. All the equipment and I would be loaded onto a British gunboat that made a regular run at midnight. This way the Reds wouldn't think anything was unusual. I had no idea how they got the British to agree. All I knew was when and how I left and what to do when I get there.

I would board the gunboat, with the underwater gear. This included a UDT rubber boat with all the equipment. I would arrive at the present location and paddle the boat ashore. There I would wait for my packages, which were supposed to arrive within the hour. I would wait no longer than three hours. By that time, it would be 1600 hours.

The next step was a quick course on how to breath underwater and use of the equipment. We had to don the gear and gut the rubber boat.

At this point I asked, "Why can't we just use the boat to take them back?" I found out that Red patrols cruised the waters until daybreak. That meant we had to cover three hundred yards to get to a thick swampy area near and bordering Hong Kong proper. The weather was always a factor, too. Storms came up quickly this time of year, and the sea could push us away from our landing point.

It was calm as I paddled the craft ashore. Again I was in Mainland China. Would it never end? I took all the gear off the boat and got ready to sink it. I sure as hell hated to do that. If all this shit went sour, or if they didn't show up, I could use the boat. I made up my mind to hide the boat. Then, I could use the same time frame and try to make it back. One lost ex-Marine would never be missed or even recorded by the Nationalists, the USA, or the Reds.

It was also the first time I ever changed an operation's plan. I figured it was time to do just that. After waiting about thirty minutes, I heard what I thought was a motor. Could it be the Reds, or was it my packages? My luck still held. A few minutes later, after the proper signals were given, all four were standing, grinning, and shaking my hand.

I wasted no time. I could speak some Chinese, and the man could speak some English, so it went pretty well. The kids held up really well. It must have been hell for them. They had been uprooted from their middle class living only to find out their daddy was a spy.

At 1530 hours, we were in the water and on our way. I tied everyone together. I had hooks connecting us so we could separate if things went bad. We could stay on top of the water as long as no lights or motors were heard. We had been in the water and on course about thirty minutes, when a light appeared off the shoreline of the mainland. I signaled the down sign. We stayed just below the surface. One of the kids was too buoyant, however, and I had to spend time keeping her down. We were losing time.

Later, we came up and the light was gone. We met a sea snake, one big son of a bitch. He circled us; he was just checking us out. But we were losing more time. As he got closer, I fired a spear at him and hit his tail end. He hauled ass, and we continued on.

It was time to get on top of the water again. Everyone was fine and in good shape. They gave me the ding how sign. In another hundred yards, we would be ashore. Only problem was, we were off course more than five hundred yards. I wondered if Gene was tracking us or had he lost us. I had a map of the swampy area, but many dangers were ahead. It wasn't danger from the Reds at this point, but it was danger from the creatures that lived in the swamps.

Finally, we made it out of the water and onto the shore. Everyone was too tired to move; we just huddled together and tried to get warm. However, we had to move about a hundred yards inland, and we were now half a mile from where we were supposed to be. With daylight coming we had to stay put. Going into the swamps was the last thing we would do.

At daybreak there were no signs of life, except for the patrol boats making a pass. We had no idea what they were looking for, or even if it was a British boat. About 10:00 A.M., I decided to go back to the shoreline to see if a patrol boat came by. If it was British, they could signal me with Morse code. Of course, I kept out of sight. An hour later a small private boat came close to the shoreline. Morse code signals told me they were the people we had been waiting for.

We stored our gear below, and we too stayed below. I heard a boat pass by. Later I learned it was a Red Patrol boat. I asked the same question again, "If you can come in daylight, why not pick us up off the mainland coast?" Again they gave the same answer. They couldn't take a chance of being seen on the other shore.

The packages were delivered from my hands, and that was the last I ever saw of Gene, Silver, and the packages. I never knew their names. They hugged me, thanked me, and that was it.

The next morning I took a plane back to Formosa and reported to General Sing Wu. My last China mission was over. There were no medals, just a thank you note from the great General Chiang, which I still have.

General Sing Wu was proud of us. He asked me to stay in Taiwan and work for the Kuomintang. But I was homesick, and it was time to go home. I loved the covert operations, but I had a gut feeling my luck would soon run out. As Too Sack once said "All things change and all things end."

I took one look as I boarded the plane that would take me back to the USA. I would have been better off if I had stayed in China.

Look and see what happened to me; I became an airman.

STOUT FIELD
INDIANAPOLIS, INDIANA 1951

Stout Field had been a fair sized base. Now it was just a shell of its former self. How could a Gung Ho Marine who bleeds green, ever become an AIRMAN? It's simple really: a girl, of course. It was about as military as a scout troop. I was bored out of my skull with the small town I grew up in. Also, if I went back into the military in the Air Force, I could retain my last rank. In the Marines, I would drop in rank. Remember an old song that says, "When a man loves a woman, or thinks he does, he would sleep out in the rain if it's what she thinks he should do." All this for a hot pants little girl. It was nuts!

I walked into Stout Field with a feeling of betrayal to the Corps. What in the hell was I doing? At one time, more than ten thousand airmen had been stationed there. At the time I arrived, they were in the process of closing it down. After two months, the only military presence was the five airmen who were left to guard the base. The base was loaded with airplanes and everything that airplanes needed to keep them running. All kinds of support units were still on the base. That means the equipment to support the entire base was still intact. A goodly amount of the planes and equipment had already made its way to other bases, however, we still had enough stuff on hand to start a good-sized war. (Actually, we thought about it a few times.)

274

The Staff Of the NEW Stout Field

Staff/Sergeant Orby Sellers, age twenty-seven, was in charge. He lived in Louisville, Kentucky. He was a short stocky guy, and he sort of looked like Edward G. Robinson. In fact, Orby thought he was Edward G. Robinson, an old actor who played in gangster movies. He even had an old black 1938 Road master Buick that he rode around in. He also carried a Thompson Sub-machine gun everywhere he went. Orby was nuts.

You already know about Staff Sergeant Jesse, Peehole/Shelburn, and Bedwell. Enough said.

Sergeant Randy Wilson, aged twenty-three, was second in charge.

He lived in Indianapolis. Randy was a real soldier of

fortune, but he just didn't know it yet. He reminded me of Lally: tall and a real ladies man. His mother ran a beauty shop in her home on North Illinois Street in Indianapolis.

Airman Posey Southern, eighteen years old, was just out of training at Lockland Air Force Base. He was the closest to a normal person there. He was a small guy about five feet seven inches tall who came from Cleveland, Tennessee.

Airman Terry Lindsey, nicknamed Jocko, was from Buffalo, New York.

He was eighteen years old. He was about five feet eleven inches, about an average sized guy. He was always in trouble with the law and with us. He was a pain in the ass, most of the time.

Duty at Stout Field

Life was simple. We five guys guarded the base. We rode around the fences in a jeep and ran off the damn weirdoes from Mars Hill, which was next to the base. It was just about as non-military as one could get. I knew the Air Force, except for the pilots, was more like a civilian job, but was this it??? They were a famous Westside Indianapolis bunch of mean sons of bitches. That's what they really were. Mars Hill was the first area to have gangs in Indianapolis.

I can't write everything that took place at Stout Field over the next eighteen months, because the book would end up being too long. But I will cover the more important details.

After about three weeks into this situation, we realized that we were really on our own. We went to Fort Harrison to get our pay, but other than that we never saw anyone or anything military. No one checked on us; I really think they forgot about us. After being in the Marine Corps, this was civilian life not military. It was about this time that things started to get crazy.

Trouble with Mars Hill

Orby liked to ride through Mars Hill. He would take someone as the driver, and he would sit in the back with his machine gun barrel propped out the window. It really pissed the Gang members off. Something else was making them mad, too. We had started having parties on base at the motor pool area, away from where the public could see us. We had most of the girls from the Westside of Indy coming to our parties. We had invited several guys from Fort Harrison, and so there were plenty of girls, plenty of booze, and good music. We had one hell of a set up. I never got laid so often before or since, it was something else.

Trouble started one night after we had a big party with fifty or so people there. We always had one gate open on the night of the party, so those who had to go home could leave. We still had one guy guarding the gate and two on patrol. On this night the gang set up a roadblock on both the North and Southside of the Gate. It was the only way out, and they attacked people leaving the party. The Mars Hill Gang busted up a couple of our guests and told them to never come back or else, it could get worse. We got a call from one of the girls when she got down to McCarty's Club. She told us what had taken place. We got on the radio and had Wilson, who was on patrol, report to the main gate. Orby had already left; this was not good news for anyone on either side. I was afraid it would make the papers, and our little playpen would be overcrowded.

Airman Southern and I got to the gate, and we could see a few cars lined up about two hundred yards down the road in both directions. I figured the gang's hero and leader, a kid by the name of Kelso, would be on the North end, where most of the action seemed to have taken place. It was an easy guess because, the south road led back to Mars Hill, and no one would be dumb enough to take that route.

I was right. Standing in the road with his thugs all around him was Kelso. I got out of the Jeep. I was armed with a forty-five on my hip and a thirty-caliber carbine cradled in my arms. I thought, "If this asshole only knew what he was facing, he would go home and land in mommy's arms."

"What's going down here, boss man?" I asked.

"Which one are you?" he asked. "Are you Orby?"

"Oh no," I answered, "Orby would have already shot you."

"So why this action?" He shifted his feet, grinned, and looked around at his yes boys.

"I am Sergeant Jesse Bedwell. Now that we know each other on a first name basis, let's get down to the problem at hand. Do you want a private talk, or do you prefer right here and now?"

"Yeah," he said, "right here and now."

I looked at the odds. Our odds were not good if there was a bottle or a pipe fight, since they had about twenty gang members on hand, and I assumed more on the way. "Your beef, Mr. Kelso?"

"Well, first of all we don't like Airrrrr Men. Second, we want you to keep your asses off our turf, which means this side of town. We want you to do all your business toward the North side of town. Third, we want you to leave our women alone. Now that's just for starters."

I wanted to tell this asshole that I had blown away more people than he could ever dream of, but I held my tongue. First of all chief I don't care too much for AIRRRRmen myself, since I am a former combat Marine, however "Mr. Kelso, You can shove your number one, two, three rules up you and your gang's candy Asses." Before he could respond or react, I locked and loaded the carbine and stuck it in his face. "Mr. Kelso, if anyone makes any kind of move, I'll blow your head off. You got that, shit bird?" Kelso turned white. "Now, get this rolling shit wagon down the road, before Orby gets here with his machine gun, and kills us all."

Kelso gave the signal for them to leave and yelled back, "You won't always have that weapon with you Sergeant. You're mine, Airrrrmannnn."

I almost shot the bastard, calling me a damn Airman. We got them out just in time. Orbie and Wilson arrived, and Orby was pissed that he had missed the action, but the rest of us were real glad. I was only trying to scare Kelso until he called me an Airrrmann. Orbie would have filled him full of holes; he reminded me a lot of a kid named Gordy, whom I'd known a long time ago.

The war was on. A week later, Sergeant Orby answered a call from one of the merchants in Mars Hill who said we had better come fast because two rival gangs were squaring off, and there were more than seventy kids on hand with more on the way. I loaded up my Jeep with Wilson and a couple carbines and headed toward Mars Hill. Orbie was in his Buick with Southern.

Our plan was to have Wilson and I step between the two groups, while Orbie sat in the back of his Buick with the submachine gun on his lap. Wilson walked between the two groups who were ready to do battle with long neck oil bottles backed up with pipes and ball bats. I saw Kelso standing in front of his gang, but I didn't know the other gang's leader.

"This is none of your concern, Bedwell, just back off, and you won't get hurt."

The other gang's leader yelled at Kelso, "So, Kelso, you got to have the military protect you?"

I asked, "What's your name, and what in the hell are you doing in Mars Hill? It seems a little stupid to me, but did you come to Mars Hill looking for trouble?"

Kelso added, "His name's Rocky Keller. His gang is from the South side, and they are trying to move the boundary lines, but like I said, we handle our own problems."

"Well, I'm sure you do," I answered. At that moment, a bottle sailed over my head, coming from the South side. All of a sudden, it all broke loose with Wilson and I right between both groups. Before they laid a hand on us, though, it stopped as fast as it started. Sergeant Orby Sellers was at his finest. He fired a burst from his Thompson over their heads, and then pointed the Machine Gun right at eye level. We could've now heard a mouse fart; silence was golden.

About that same time, the State Police arrived, and everyone ran. The County Mounties had squad cars blocking most of the area. After everything cooled down, a Lieutenant Baker, from the State Police, asked me what caused the problem, and did I know who the leaders were. Kelso was still standing within hearing distance, and he had his eyes on me.

"No, Lieutenant, I don't know. We just heard all the noise, and someone called us, so we came to see what we could do."

"I heard automatic weapon fire, Sergeant, who fired that?"

"We did, sir, from the Jeep. It was over their heads, of course."

Lieutenant Baker was weighing how to handle this, and he finally said, "Well, Sergeant, it looks like it's over. But try and keep that machine gun on the base."

"Ok, you got it, Lieutenant," I answered.

As we started to leave, I looked over at Kelso and said, "We also take care of our own." If Kelso or any of us had handled it in any other way, we would've all been in trouble with the civil police. Neither of us wanted that.

Things settled down between the Mars Hill gang and us after that. No one gave us any trouble, and we didn't give them any trouble either. In fact, Kelso and some of his gang came to some of our parties. We never became friends, but we never had any words after that night. I don't think he was afraid of Wilson or me, but Orby was another story.

After we had been on base for about three months, we became crazier. With no direction, we did some of the damnedest things one could ever dream up. One night we got a call from the Chief of Police down in Evansville Indiana, more than two hundred miles away. The chief got me on the phone since I was the only one on duty. The call came in about 11:00 P.M.

"Sergeant, we got something down here that we think belongs to you."

I answered, "And what might that be Chief?"

"Well, Sarg, we have one Sergeant Wilson, a blond female, and a full size truck from your motor pool."

"Well, Chief, I would tell you that Wilson is on a secret mission, but I don't think that will fly."

The Chief said, "No, it probably won't. He hasn't caused any problems, and he is sober,"

"I'll send a couple of MP's down to pick him up, and a driver for the truck first thing in the morning. They should arrive by noon. Is that OK, Chief?"

"Yeah, that's fine. It's just that you don't see an army truck with a blonde sitting up front, with her feet on the dash and her skirt pulled up over her head, driving down the main drag."

"Yeah, sounds like Wilson all right."

He laughed, and I hung up. We were about to save Wilson's horny ass one more time.

In walked Sellers, "What was that call, Shelburn? One of your bimbos?"

"No, Orbie, it was from the Chief of Police down in Evansville. He says he has something of ours."

"What in the hell has he got?" asked Orby.

"Well, he's got Wilson, Orbie. Seems ole Wilson took his girlfriend for a ride down south."

"Was he drunk?"

"No."

"Well then, why in the hell was he arrested?"

"Well, Orbie, now don't go ape-shit. I got it all took care of. To make a long story short, he drove Maxine down to Evansville in one of our trucks."

"He what!" screamed Orbie. "The silly son of a bitch is going to get us all busted. This is the same guy who thinks he's Edward G. Robinson. "So what in the hell are we supposed to do about it, Shelburn?"

"I told the Chief I would send two MP's down in the morning to pick him up."

"We ain't got no damn MP's, Shelburn!" screamed Orby.

"Well, I figured me and ole Southern could be MP's, or Apes, or A&P's for a day. I saw some of those bands in the NCOs office."

Orbie was rubbed his balding head, "You know, Shelburn, I don't know one damn thing about this, and you assholes are on your own." He had had his say and off he went, talking to himself and rubbing his head.

Airman Southern and I arrived at the jail at about 12:30 P.M. The Chief was waiting on us. He greeted us with a big grin, "Boy, your Wilson is quite a feller, ain't he, Sarg."

"Yeah, Wilson is a piece of work all right," I answered.

The chief continued, "That little filly he has with him is quite a looker. Two of my men about had a fight over who was going to bring her over from the women's lock up."

"Yeah," I answered, "Maxine is quite a hand full."

"Yeah," said the Chief, "she sure has a set of tits on her for an eighteen year old."

I thought, "Boy, I got news for you, Chief, Maxine wasn't a day over fifteen." Maxine was the first to arrive; she gave us a little wave and grinned at us. About then, here came ole Wilson. He looked like shit warmed over. He was glad to see us.

We put the handcuffs on him; signed some papers, and then we were on our way. After we drove off Wilson said, "Where in the hell did you get those MP bands?"

"Oh, they were in the NCOs desk. How do we look?"

"Good, good," said Wilson, "the best looking MP's I ever seen."

We all laughed. Maxine said, "Can we stop somewhere after we get out of town? I am HUNGRY."

"So am I," said Wilson.

Maxine continued, "It took us ten hours to get down here. Wilson had to pull over and screw me every twenty minutes." Southern about fainted on that one. It didn't bother me any, I had screwed Maxine a few times myself, but never every twenty minutes. She was a looker and loved to do it often, no lie about that.

At the first truck stop, we took the cuffs off Wilson and had some breakfast. We had come down in a blue Ford 4-door. Wilson and Southern were in the back, and both were asleep in five minutes. Maxine lay down with her head on my lap. She drew her knees up, and I could see she had on no panties or bra. It was tough on the ole ex-Marine, but being an Airrrrmannnn now, I could handle it. There were no every twenty minute stops for me. No way, well, maybe one stop would be OK. About half way back to Indy, she woke up and said she had to go to the rest

282

room, and I said so did I. I asked if I could go in her restroom with her. "Sure," she said, I'm ready if you are."

"Yes, darling, I'm ready." I think of Maxine from time to time.

A few days later we had another major problem. It was two weeks before payday, and none of us had a dime left. Orbie had a plan. Only his little beetle mind could come up with something like this. We were up in the Tower, as we usually were, and we could see the entire base from there. "Do you know how many flag poles we have on this base, Shelburn?"

"No," I answered, "and I don't give a shit."

"Well, I have counted them, and there are forty-one of them."

"So what's the plan, Orby, cut them down, sell the iron, and go to Leavenworth?"

"No, you know what they used to hold the poles up?"

"No, but are you going to tell me?"

"Lead, big heavy globs of lead."

No shit! Now he had our attention. "We can bury them with cement and make a hell of a profit. So what do you think, boys?"

"Well," said Wilson, "we already sold everything around here that's not on an inventory, so our ass is only good for twenty years. How much can we get for the lead Orbie?"

"I checked on the prices, and I figure we got about 10 tons of lead, based on the one I dug up."

"You dug one up?" I questioned.

"Yeah, I dug one up, asshole, how else would I know they were buried in lead. Anyway, I figured out the price of lead, and I think we could get around a thousand dollars. So, you ready to vote?" We all voted yes, because when you are hungry and broke, that kind of money looked very big.

It took about three days to get them dug up. We dug up the ones that the public couldn't see at night. One

283

problem was telling the junk dealer where we got the lead, so we showed up in an army truck to deliver it. Our plan was to use an old pick up truck that was military. We just painted the bastard, bird shit yellow, and later we would paint it back to Bird shit blue, the Air Force colors.

Orbie and I made the first delivery. All the rest were too candy assed to go. Orbie did the talking, "I got some lead here I want to sell. In fact I got several truck loads of it."

The guy looked over the pile of lead, "Looks like it was used to hold something up."

"I have no idea. Some guy had it at the back of his property and told me, if I moved it, I could have it. He was an ole coot and didn't know or care that it was worth good money. But we know what it's worth, we checked."

"Yeah, I wonder what that came from?" said the weasel looking shit bird.

Orby, being short-tempered and nuts, said, "Do you want its fucking life history, or do you wants to buy it?"

The old boy was a hillbilly for sure. He had a weed in his mouth; he was scratching his head, trying to get his 50 cents' worth. "How much you say you got?"

"Oh, about three or four loads I guess."

"I'll give you fifty cents a pound for all you got." We tried to get more but the little runt wouldn't come down. After making four trips we got paid. It came to $874.32. We about shit; we were rich.

The next day we went about restoring the flagpoles. We buried them in concrete. The task was over, everything was real fine, one hell of a plan, I thought that old Too Sack and I could not have done better.

I slept in the tower that night. When I woke up, I went to the big flight deck window and looked across the compound. My eyes must have been as big as Vera Dean's pussy. Every flagpole in sight was leaning toward hessey.

I got on the radio and woke the guys up. We spent all week reworking the poles. Southern said, "That's what we get for selling government property."

"Southern how would you like your ass hung upside down on one of those poles?"

He shut up, and the "dog days" of the flagpole caper were never mentioned again, by any of us. I did, however, salute and smile when we raised the flag each day.

Another decision was made concerning leave time. Since we made our own leave time, we had three on and three off. That was OK, but we wanted to have more days off at a time, so we could go to our hometowns. Orbie said, "Let's keep four guys here at all times. That means two on, two off, and the other two guys on leave. The leave time will be two weeks at time. How does that sound fellows?"

We all agreed it sounded real good. "However, we got to make sure whoever is on leave can come back in one damn hurry," I added.

"Yeah, you're right," said Orbie, "and since you and Wilson are the assholes who are always missing, it's odd you came up with that, Shelburn."

"You have to watch those ex-Marines all the time," countered Wilson. I gave Wilson the usual finger and it was a done deal.

Of course, that created a real problem for me, because I was in love head over heals as they say. It was hard to drag me back from Hollywood. On my second round of leaves, I stayed three weeks and pissed everybody off. And of course, the first visitor we ever had came while I was in Hollywood.

The Lieutenant from Fort Harrison wanted to talk to us about some changes in our pay schedule. He said he would come back in about four hours. One of the dumb asses said that I was on leave. Fast thinking Orbie said that meant I was across town, and that we called that leave. Then the Lieutenant said to make sure I was back by 1300 hours.

Orbie got me on the phone. I was at my girlfriend's house, of course. He told me to hustle my ass back. I told Orbie my car was broke down, which it was. Orbie asked me how long it took to get down there? I answered, "About two hours."

"Shit," he said, "a Jeep or one of the trucks would cut it too close."

I countered, "Take one of the ambulances, put the damn sirens on, keep it on, and come and get me."

"Good idea, Shelburn, we will have your ass back here with time to spare. You owe me maggot."

I answered, you got it, ole master baiter."

At 1130 hours, a military ambulance arrived in Shelburn. Two dumb-asses came out with a board and told me to lie on it. Just then a State Police car rolled up. Wilson explained that they had to take me to the base hospital. It was nuts. I loved it.

My time at Stout Air Force base was cut short one Saturday night, while I was on the town in Indy. Two guys jumped me from the side of an alley, knocked me out, and left me lying on the ground. The next thing I knew I was in a hospital. I remembered a police officer asking me questions as I moved in and out of consciousness. When I awoke the next morning, I knew I was in a hospital, and I knew my name was Shelburn. When they brought me in, I must have been wearing civilian clothes, because that was what was in the closet

My mind was a mess. It told me that I was in the Marines on leave, and that I had to get back to Camp Pendleton. After that I told them I had to get back to Formosa. I remembered everything about being in China, but nothing before China. It was Sunday, no one was around, and I got dressed and left without being checked out. I went to the Highway and hitchhiked a ride; I was on my way back to Oceanside. After four days I arrived at the base. I got my last ride with another Marine. It was 4:00 A.M., the guard asked no questions and in we went. I remembered Barracks 15 somehow from the past. I reported to casualty barracks, and waited for headquarters to open up.

Before it opened, a Sergeant asked me who I was and what the hell was I doing there? Then, the MP's came. I was not taken to the brig, but another temporary holding area, and told to wait. A Personnel Officer called me into his office and asked me many questions.

I told him I must be AWOL because I came home on leave from Formosa, got knocked in the head, and could not remember anything that happened from the moment I went on leave. After two days in the hospitals holding area at Pendleton, the Personnel Officer and a psychologist returned to talk to me. They told me my real name was Jesse Bedwell. I had been discharged from the Marines several months before. There were no warrants out on me, neither civil nor military. I had just had a memory lapse, or amnesia. They felt my full memory would be restored in a few days or weeks.

They had obtained a voucher of money for travel funds back home from the Red Cross. My family would be waiting for me at the Indianapolis, Indiana, bus station. The Personnel Officer said, "You do have an outstanding combat record, Marine. I would seek consultation with your family doctor once you're back home."

They had no idea I was still in the Air Force. I was escorted to the bus station in Los Angeles. I was on my own. My mind was still trying to sort things out; I was still confused at times. I decided I was going back in the Corps, and I was not going home. I wrote a postcard to my family saying that I was going back in the Marines. I also told them what had been going on.

Four blocks from the bus station was a Marine Recruiting Office. In twenty minutes, I was back in the Corps as a Staff Sergeant. I had no idea that people at Stout Field were looking for me. The paper work must have burned the wires on this one, yet at this time only a few days had passed. Hell, I was in both services at the same time! Oh hell, oh hell!

As a re-enlistment bonus, I was given two weeks before I had to report for duty. My new duty station was

Camp Jejune, North Carolina. I had time to stop by home on the way.

I was a very surprised Marine when I got off the bus in Indianapolis. I was picked up by the Air Police and taken to the Indy city lock up. I still had no idea what in the hell was going on.

The next morning in came two Airmen from Stout Field to pick me up and take me to Fort Benjamin Harrison. It was Orbie and Wilson, and as soon as I saw them I knew them. But, I still couldn't connect them to my recent past.

They must have been told I was a nut case, because they didn't talk to me. Later, I asked Orby what in the hell they were doing in Air Force uniforms? I remember someone saying, "We're sorry, Shelburn, we hope you get better."

I spent some time at Ft. Ben Harrison, and then I was transferred to Mt. Clemens and Selfridge Air Force Base. I was in a locked ward, awaiting something. After several weeks, the AWOL and the second enlistment were canceled. I continued to see doctors for the next several months. One day I could remember everything. I just woke up one morning, and it was all clear. Since then, I have had a few bad dreams, but the amnesia was over.

I stayed on at Mt. Clemens, finished my enlistment, and went home for good. I will always remember what an Air Force General told me. He said, "Son, when you got knocked in the head, if you had just wandered off, and it hadn't gotten on the police blotter, you would have had a general court marshal. Many thought you made it all up, but the records from the police and doctors made it quite clear. Someone knocked your brain loose for a while. Good luck, Marine. I call you that because, even though you are wearing an Air Force uniform, you were and will always be a Marine."

I returned to civilian life for good. I was told to stay to hell away from recruiting offices.

Epilogue

Lally, our leader, checked out in Korea along with what is referred to as "the forgotten few" at Ko San Reservoir. Never in my lifetime have I ever seen a more capable combat leader. He was fearless, but not foolish. He was strong, but not uncaring. He was Master Sergeant Lally.

Too Sack, our Chinese wizard, has not been heard from again. I tried to find out about what happened to him while I was in Formosa, but I never could come up with anything. The only thing I did come across was after the Korean War. One of my buddies got hold of the one of the Chinese Division rosters of those who fought the Marines in Korea. It listed one Captain Li Ping, not his real name that is known only to me.

The dates of their combat in Korea, connects to the same time Lally lost his life at the Ko San Reservoir. The mind plays funny tricks on you sometimes. In my mind and in my dreams, I see Too Sack and Lally coming together in combat. Could it be? No, I suppose not, but I will never know.

When I said goodbye to Too Sack, after we had taken the gold out of China, he stayed on the mainland to be with his relatives. He was a member of Mao's Communist army when we found him. He had had his uniform blown half off his body. He was sitting by the road in a small village. He asked to stay with us and was with us for the next two years. We fought side by side in numerous battles against the Red Army. I have pictures of Too Sack guarding communist prisoners.

It is my belief that Too Sack is one of the top leaders in today's Mainland China.

I can prove it beyond the shadow of a doubt. If I released this information, it could cause many problems/

So, at this time, I am seventy some years old. I don't give a shit what anyone thinks. I laid my life on the line for good old Uncle Sam .

Gordy, my a little bit crazy point man and lifelong buddy, where are you? I have put my address in the Leatherneck magazine, several times with no response.

Link, killed in action during Operation Snow White, I finally contacted his family and told them of Link's days in China. I told them of his bravery, which was unequaled in combat.

Sometimes, one war brings together people from the next war, like the lady in Hoopster, Illinois to whom I send a card each year. She lost her son in Vietnam, along with one of Link's cousins. It's a small world sometimes.

General Sing Wu was one of General Chiang's greatest soldiers. He was fearless in battle, believing in an eye for an eye. He was good to us; without the General, none of us would have ever made it past Port Darien.

If I had to rate the Generals I have read about, or seen in person, or that I have served under, I would rate them, as follows: (Combat Field Generals) and the grunts you would want with you in combat.

No. 1   George S. Patton, Army. He captured more prisoners, and more territory than anyone in history, including Alexander The Great.

No. 2   Douglas Macarthur, 5 Star Army General. Twice he was awarded the Congressional Medal Of Honor. As far as I know, no one ever has ever had that honor.

No. 3   Chesty Puller. USMC. He was awarded the Silver Star several times. But because he pissed off Congress, he never got the Medal of Honor, but he should have.

No. 4   General Sing Wu, Nationalist Army. He was Chiang Kai Shek's closest   friend. A master warrior.

No. 5 General Howling Mad Smith, USMC. He was one tough guy; one of the meanest Sob's the

290

Corps has known. He was an outstanding combat leader.

The Soldiers

No. 1   Too Sack, Nationalist Chinese Army. He is my hero forever; I have a thousand reasons for saying so.
No. 2 Audie Murphy, Army.-The most decorated solder in World War Two.
No. 3 Top Gun Lally, USMC. He was a wizard, just like Too Sack. He was one of the Corps finest, a master of women and leader of men. If only I'd had his skills.
No. 4 Link, USMC. He was the quiet one, who looked harmless. Yet, he was deadly in combat. He was my friend; he helped me when the hard times came. He died in combat fighting in China and is buried there. Semper Fi ole comrade.
No. 5 Gordy, USMC. He was a sadistic little bastard. In wartime you want Gordy by your side. In peacetime leave the little bastard in the barracks.

A few years later, while visiting my cousin Bob Hauger in Indianapolis, we were watching Castro's famous tank ride into downtown Havana.

Riding in the lead tank with Castro was the former Stout Field Airman Top Sergeant Jocko Wilson. He had been missing for some time; he was AWOL from the Air Force. It was rumored he had become a Soldier of Fortune. I went to see if his mother was still on North Illinois Street, but was told she had died the past year and there were no other family members they knew of. Jocko was never heard from again.

I told you that most of this book contained truth, mixed with fiction. All my characters were real and stories about them have more truth than fiction. Those that are still alive I have changed the names, and it's time they all were left to history. Too Sack was always writing down old Chinese sayings, sometimes from Confucius.

Too Sack had his own philosophy:

"We travel many roads, some good some bad. We meet many good people and many bad; we have good times, as well as bad times. We find love, and we also manage to find hate. We hang onto our good memories, and forget the bad.

We must bury all of our bad memories in the sand."

Too Sack, Somewhere in Manchuria 1946

It is time now to say goodbye one last time to my comrades. May you rest in peace and those that remain, I say to you:

"Here is to us, those like us, damn few left. Gung Ho and Semper Fi, Mac."

Too Sack.... Lally.... Gordy.... Link...Mae Ling....Sergeant York.... Captain Chin...Major Wong Mongo...General Sing Wu...General Chiang Kai Shek.... James Wu.... Jack and Jill.... Jocko.... Smiling Jack.... the Sisters from Canton.... The Ancient One.... Lieutenant Williams.... Bugger.... Buster.... Peehole.... Shelburn.

The Ancient One told me, many years ago. You will spend your final years in China; also you will live a long life like me. He told Lally he would die fighting a war, not in China but in a country nearby. He told Too Sack he also would become a powerful leader. With Link, he said his visions were not clear. The Chinese have great visions and most come true. Only time and God know the final chapter. I may yet return to Formosa for my final days, as the Ancient said so many years ago. I came close to doing just that a few years ago.

He also stated I would die in a fiery death in the year 2004. At that time, in 1947, it sounded like a good

292

projection. However, since it's now 2003, it has gotten my attention. He did counter this with a final statement on the subject. He said, "Unless the God in the sky decides to keep one Peehole on the earth for a longer time."

I am not sure how much longer I can work on the book. It's starting to get to me. I have dreams that bring every thing back like it was yesterday. Sometimes, I find myself crying for the dead. I can't talk about the one thing that would make it a best seller, Too Sack's real name.

I believe the day is near when China will attack Formosa. If we help, we will be in a war with China. Or perhaps China will find an excuse to attack us. Maybe it will be over the Panama Canal. I don't think the present US government has the guts to stand up to China's takeover of the canal. Oh yes, they will try to control it. We have already let them in. We can take out a drug dealer to keep the Canal open, but not the Communists of China.

We have treated the Nationalist Government of Free China like shit ever since World War Two. They are the ones who helped us take Japan out by giving us attack bases. They are also one of the few who paid us back their war debts by providing us landing fields for our aircraft in WW II.

Fifty years ago we fought the Red Chinese grandfathers who were young and outnumbered us a hundred to one. Four Marines and four hundred Nationalist soldiers of Chang Kai Shek outsmarted and out fought them a hundred times over. As a seventy four year old, I would still answer the call to fight.

I have learned that the person that I am sure was Major Lai Kun, was shot in 1999 for spying for Formosa. The years are on line. His first name was Liu; his last name was the same. Things have started to add up. I knew him quite well. Once I can confirm this, I will let it all hang out.

Those who know me know these aren't just words. I am old. What have I got to lose? I have lived my life. I hang around so that maybe I will be able to help my son. I

293

only have a few years left, and I would go to help out Formosa (as long as the Nationalist are in control).

Some of today's rationale for letting Formosa come under the control of Red China goes like this, "Well, it's just an island where General Chiang Kai Shek took his troops after he lost the civil war. They lost, why support them?"

Well, how do you think they lost? I covered that in the book so no sense going over it again. However I would like to.

"Soon I predict the people of Taiwan will turn against the great General Chiang. They will give him hell for routing out the Japanese and turning the country into a major player in the world of business."

Sound crazy? Not really, they never wanted the Nationalists there in the first place. It makes no difference; they were not born in Formosa.

What will they do with all the offspring of the Nationalists? Ship them out too? Next will they tear down all the monuments of the great general?

I think of China as a time in history, as a primitive culture. I have no regrets. I am proud and grateful to have been a part of history and the China Civil War.

Most of what I know or have seen has changed or is gone, including those who were part of my life.

"All things change, and all things end."
Jesse Bedwell

If one can return after life's journey is over, I will find a way. For all of my life, when I get knocked down, the fight has just begun. Some may say I am cocky, but those who have passed my way know the merit to these words. The masters taught me: Lally, Too Sack, Gordy, Link, and General Sing Wu.

"My last thoughts in my final moments of life will be of - my son, my son, my son.

294